MW00893597

THE LITTLE RED BARN

AN OLYMPIC ROMANCE

DOROTHY RICE BENNETT

Copyright © 2019 by Dorothy Rice Bennett

ISBN: 9781088706886

All rights reserved including the right to reproduce this book or portions thereof in any form whatsoever.

For information: dorothyricebennett@yahoo.com

Cover design and website by Barbara Gottlieb
www.gottgraphix.com

Published in conjunction with
Ronni Sanlo Consulting
www.ronnisanlocom

Printed in the United State of America

ALSO BY
DOROTHY RICE BENNETT

NORTH COAST: A Contemporary Love Story

GIRLS ON THE RUN

THE ARTEMIS ADVENTURE

INNOCENT SPUR-OF-THE-MOMENT DECISIONS CAN CHANGE YOUR LIFE

1

The cutter-rigged sloop heeled sharply to starboard as the *Lavender Loafer* rounded the northwestern tip of the continental United States and entered the Strait of Juan de Fuca. With Kate at the helm, Steve loosened the main sail as the yacht lessened its tilt then adjusted the twin jib sheets to support the boat's new direction.

An early morning sun sparkled on the water before them, and the two sailors smiled at each other with satisfaction. They had left Hawaii nearly eight weeks earlier, planning for Seattle in early summer, and had meandered their way around the Pacific, sometimes supported by good winds, sometimes stalled in the doldrums.

Now, with great relief, they were finally sailing north of Washington and south of Vancouver Island, B.C., headed through the Strait and into Puget Sound to Seattle. As they made way, Kate could see rugged mountains rising to starboard.

"Olympics, right?" she called out to Steve.

Slender, sinewy, Steve nodded. "Yep. They're not the tallest mountains in the world, but majestic just the same. A wild, untamed range."

Kate's blonde curls flipped about her head in the light morning breeze. Tall, muscular, and deeply tanned, she gave Steve a warm smile as he came back to the cockpit of his boat. Her blue eyes twinkled. "This is one place I never expected to see. Thanks for bringing me here."

"You're welcome, m'dear," he said, giving her a lopsided grin.

***

They had met that spring at a touristy bar in Honolulu. Kate skipped the hula dancers performing for the crowd and went to the bar, settling a couple of seats from an attractive, casually-dressed man. Noting each other's choice of a local brew, they saluted in acknowledgment. He was clean shaven and graying, appearing in his fifties. She was somewhere in her thirties, a tall natural blonde clad in faded jeans and a blouse tied at her midriff; with broad shoulders, small breasts and slim hips—a swimmer's body. Her total look was self-assured, uncaring of opinion. They immediately recognized something comfortable and familiar about each other.

Shortly, the two moved their beers to a table and began talking in earnest. Steve Gutierrez, an American live-aboard sailor for the past thirty years, clearly could afford the life style. Katherine Marguerite Brighton had been a world wanderer for the past five years, hopping freighters and sailing vessels wherever they were headed, particularly around the South Seas. She made a welcome addition to any vessel or crew.

"Where are you headed now?" she had asked Steve.

"Seattle, I think," he said.

"Why Seattle?"

"Well, I've been out of the loop a long time. I have relatives, or I think I still have some, in Seattle. A brother, his wife and children. For whatever reason, I'm feeling a need to reconnect, and I decided to spend part of the summer there. When fall comes, I'll head back to warmer climes."

"Sounds interesting. I've never been to Seattle."

"Want to come along?"

Kate thought for a moment. "Well, I'd be happy to crew for you, to earn my keep. Just as long as the deal doesn't include 'benefits.'"

Steve broke into a hearty laugh. "I don't think we'd climb out of bed on the same side," he observed. "I'm gay as a goose. That's why I'm out here on the ocean, instead of San Francisco pursuing a career. I left in my twenties to escape AIDS. I could have been a rich man and died young; I decided to be less rich and live longer."

Kate's eyes twinkled. "In that case, I guess I can admit that we might climb out of the same side of the bed, just different beds."

He smiled. "So, you also fly the rainbow flag. I wouldn't have guessed it immediately. Now that you say so, I can recognize that in you. I suspect we'll do just fine on my boat."

Preparing the sloop, they had stowed supplies for six weeks. "Shouldn't be that long, but we'll take extra just in case," Steve had said.

"Just in case" turned out to be unexpected doldrums when the boat lay motionless for days on a glassy sea. Steve and Kate stretched out on the deck, using as little energy as possible and eating almost nothing. With the sun bearing down on them, the cabin below was sweltering, and they remained topside. Kate asked about using the engine to move them closer to Seattle. Steve checked the weather and said the air was flat all the way to the coast. They couldn't make it that far on the fuel they had. So, they sat. And began to worry. What if the wind didn't come up again? What if they ran out of food and water? It was a grim prospect. Kate had written in her personal logbook words that were now perhaps prophetic: "Innocent spur-of-the moment decisions can change your life." Maybe she had made a huge mistake in deciding to crew for Steve on this adventure to Seattle.

After more than two weeks of drifting helplessly on motionless water, they felt the hint of a breeze. Within hours, that hint had morphed into a real wind, and they were on their way again, short of supplies and physically drained, but with hope.

***

Now under both sail and engine, they moved through the Strait toward Port Angeles. "We have several hours to Sequim," Steve explained, "where I'm thinking of spending the night. I'd like a quiet sleep and to gas up before tackling the Seattle harbor."

Slightly after noon, Port Angeles's sprawling waterfront appeared to the south. With excitement Kate watched the harbor and its long spit slip by. The former logging town was sitting on hills overlooking the Strait with the Olympic Mountains rising behind it. Kate was enthralled with the view.

Amusement clearly showing on his now-bearded face, Steve watched her. "You should be here in the winter when there's snow on the mountains. Then it's *really* gorgeous."

"I can imagine." Kate took a bite out of the sandwich he had brought up from the galley. Their pantry was nearly empty, but to Kate, at this moment, a peanut butter and jelly sandwich was just as good as steak. Her stomach was talking to her and food, even with very stale bread, was welcomed. She washed down everything with a soft drink, thinking how glad she was that the doldrums were behind them.

"Tell me again, where are we stopping?" Kate asked.

"Sequim."

"Never heard of it."

"I'm not surprised. It's a small town, by comparison to Port Angeles and Port Townsend. There's a long spit and a lighthouse. The first English explorers landed there. Behind the spit is a broad prairie. The town grew up behind the prairie and at the foot of these same mountains. It's very pretty. Between the town and the prairie, I think there are about thirty thousand inhabitants."

"Spell the name," Kate requested.

"S-e-q-u-i-m," replied Steve. "You drop the 'e' and pronounce it like 'squirrel' or 'squirm,' instead of like 'sequins.'"

"Any idea what it means?" Kate questioned. After nearly two months at sea, she was hungry for details about the land before them.

"I read someplace that it's a Native American word meaning peaceful. Originally a farming community, the town has become a popular spot for retirees."

"And it has a marina."

He nodded. "Named for the actor, John Wayne. He used to keep his big remodeled WWII boat up here. The marina is now controlled by local government but his family still owns an RV park nearby."

Kate shrugged and shook her head. "Sequim. That name seems familiar to me for some reason, but I can't place it."

***

Later that afternoon, they passed the long New Dungeness Spit and its white lighthouse. Then Steve sailed into Sequim Bay, headed for the John Wayne Marina. As they glided up to the guest dock, Kate jumped from the boat and tied off the lines while Steve went to check in with the harbormaster.

"There's a nice restaurant here," Steve called to her on his way down the dock. "Why don't we have a real dinner before we crash?"

Anticipating a satisfying meal, Kate was only too happy to comply.

***

Sated from a grilled salmon plate, Kate sat in her berth in the bow of Steve's sloop and tried to figure out why the name "Sequim" seemed so familiar. Checking her MacBook contact list, she discovered an entry for Marianne Summers, address and phone in Sequim, Washington. Surprised and delighted, Kate called the number. There was no answer, so she left a message saying she would try again in the morning.

Drifting off to sleep wasn't as easy as Kate had expected. Marianne was now a mysterious presence in her mind. Kate mentally retraced her years at Cornell University and her encounters with Marianne, who had been a graduate student. As she recalled, Marianne was working on an MBA while Kate was in liberal arts, coupled with participation on the swim team. Kate's swimming coach thought she had excellent potential to qualify for the Olympic team. Before her death from cancer, Kate's mother had been a big supporter of Kate's swimming ambitions. Marianne, several years older than Kate, also enjoyed the sport and came to college meets and occasionally practices. With this interest in common, Kate and Marianne had gradually become friends. After Kate's graduation, they had kept in touch through letters and emails, but Kate hadn't actually seen Marianne in years.

As she mused about how much fun it would be to reconnect with her college chum, Kate finally dozed off.

***

Steve was up early, moving around the deck overhead. When Kate emerged topside, he announced, "I was planning on sailing to Seattle today, but I've decided to stay a day or two and do some exploring. If you need to be there right away, I can point you toward downtown where there's a bus that goes into the city."

Kate considered that idea for a moment. "Actually, I have some friends who live here. I'd like to look them up. Maybe I'll have a reason to stay, too."

Since she was not sure whether she'd remain on the boat or move to a motel, Kate gathered up her things and stowed them in her duffle bag. She didn't have a lot to pack, hadn't needed much since wanderlust had taken command of her life. Besides her laptop and her cell phone that doubled as a camera, she owned only a few items of clothing, along with a swimsuit, jacket, minimal cosmetics, ballcap, sunglasses, and sport shoes that she wore everywhere. *What else did she need?*

After organizing her pack, Kate stood in the cockpit to check the skies. The morning was sunny and growing warm. She could see a few white clouds around the horizon; overhead it was clear blue. Seemed like a good omen for a nice day.

Her phone buzzed, startling her. When she pulled her cell from a pocket, Kate saw that Marianne was returning her call.

"Hey, Kate." The voice was warm and mature. "Where are you calling from? Here in Sequim by any chance?"

Kate responded. "Yes, Marianne, I'm at the marina."

"Well, if you have time, come and see us. 356 North Seventh Avenue. Truck in the driveway. White house. Flowers around it. We're home today."

"Got a couple of things to do first, but I could be there later this morning."

"Okay, looking forward to seeing you. If you find yourself hopelessly lost, just call."

"My cell has GPS—I'll find you, I'm sure."

***

Steve was busy with some minor maintenance at the bow of the sloop. Kate told him what she was doing. He nodded. They hugged. "Let's keep in touch," he suggested. "That way we'll know whether we're going on to Seattle together or not."

Kate nodded and gave him a goodbye wave as she strolled up the dock. Once in the marina parking lot, she searched her phone's GPS for a Sequim map. It appeared there were a couple of ways to walk into town. She decided to take the Olympic Discovery Trail. *Sounded interesting since it was designed for hikers and cyclists.*

With her duffle over her shoulder, her aviator glasses and ballcap in place, Kate marched up a fairly steep incline along a connecting road toward the trail. After two months on a constantly moving deck, her gait was at first a bit rocky. However, she gradually regained her land legs, and breathing in the fresh morning air, she topped the hill, located a trail sign, and turned onto the paved surface headed west toward Sequim. After crossing a beautifully curved former railroad trestle nestled in evergreens and spanning a creek, she continued to walk along the trail that paralleled Highway 101, sometimes visible through tall pines and cedars.

Washington Street soon appeared, and the trail followed that route. Kate smiled at the rustic landscape with the Olympic Mountains rising ahead to her left, lots of green trees and bushes everywhere. She was amused when she saw a sign posted to protect a local elk herd from highway traffic.

***

Less than a mile later, just as Kate was developing beads of sweat and tiring from hauling her duffle, businesses appeared around her. Among them, she noticed a small red barn with cars parked around it. It obviously wasn't a working barn, in the farming sense of the word, but as she approached, she saw a sign: "The Little Red Barn, Coffeehouse and Deli."

Perfect! Kate thought. She had skipped breakfast. Maybe coffee and a breakfast sandwich would suit her well. Kate strolled in. The interior was dark and cool, with pictures of old farmhouses and barns decorating its plank walls. Several customers were seated at round wooden tables. No one looked up at Kate; they all seemed focused on their laptops and phones.

Approaching the counter, Kate faced an attractive young barista dressed in a low-cut country blouse, a short black skirt and a white apron. The outfit amused Kate, but it certainly fit the general décor. The barista's nametag read "Angie."

Kate smiled. "Hi, Angie. I'd like a tall coffee straight and some kind of sandwich."

Angie smiled back and winked. "Sure. What would you like on your sandwich? Bacon, ham, sausage? Egg or egg whites? Havarti, gouda, or Swiss cheese?" Her voice was deep and melodic.

While contemplating her choices, Kate had time to observe that Angie had dark brown eyes and shining long auburn hair worked into a single braid down the middle of her back. She was shorter than Kate and well endowed.

"Wow, let's see," Kate mused. "How about bacon, regular egg, and Havarti?"

"Perfect! Coming up."

Kate paid with a credit card.

"Have a seat. I'll bring your food to you."

Kate nodded and sat down at a table. A sign announced free Wi-Fi, and she pulled her laptop from her duffle, signing onto the Internet. Having been off the grid at sea, she hadn't touched her email since departing Honolulu. There was, as she expected, a long string of messages awaiting her attention.

Smiling broadly, Angie soon arrived with Kate's order, which she carefully placed on the table. "Coffee straight and sandwich. Anything else?"

Kate looked at the food and then up at Angie. "No thanks, I'm good."

Angie nodded. "If you need anything else, just holler."

She turned away and Kate watched her walk back to the counter. Nice buns under that soft revealing black skirt. *Actually, nice figure altogether. Big brown eyes, cute face. Hmmm.*

Telling herself to forget Angie and return to her task, Kate opened one email after another. Some she quickly scrapped. For a few she typed out brief responses. Others she left for later. As she worked, she chuckled a couple of times. Some of her old friends had a good sense of humor She returned the repartee. While her attention was mostly on the emails, she suddenly sensed she was being watched.

Kate glanced up and saw Angie standing behind the counter studying her. A tickle ran up and down her spine. *Maybe the barista is a lesbian? That could be interesting.*

She finished her task, heaved a sigh, and slapped the computer closed. Looking up, she saw that new customers had entered the coffeehouse. Angie was busy serving them. *Not much chance to check her out. Save that for later, too.* Kate experienced a little shiver of pleasure.

Pushing her plate aside, she left a tip on the counter with the little cash she had, picked up her duffle, and headed out, noting the café's posted hours.

Angie, she committed to memory. A little voice inside said, *Innocent spur-of-the-moment decisions can change your life.* Kate laughed to herself. *Life is an adventure, isn't it?*

***

Within half an hour, during which she tried to keep her mind off the delightful barista, Kate had passed through the center of Sequim. It wasn't a fancy town, but there were motels, restaurants, coffeehouses, gift shops, and even a lumberyard—all of which appeared to be thriving concerns. A rather old grain elevator stood just off the main street and seemed to recall the area's past connection to farming and railroading. *Probably not so much today.*

When Kate reached Seventh Avenue and turned north, she expected—having known Marianne at Cornell—to find a trendy neighborhood, something elegant and expensive. Not so. After passing small businesses, she came to a group of manufactured houses—not run down, not fancy either. Kate was taken aback. She had always expected that Marianne would be very successful.

Arriving at 356, Kate walked up the driveway. A curving path led to the front door. She observed that the side entrance was equipped with a ramp and wondered why. The front door had the more common couple of steps up to a small porch. Ringing the doorbell, she waited.

***

After a moment, the door opened. Someone Kate didn't know peeped out at her. A tall lanky woman with buzz-cut brown hair and hazel eyes was clad in a flannel shirt, cargo pants, and work boots. She smiled at Kate. "You must be Kate Brighton. I'm Jake Summers. Marianne's on the phone. She'll be a minute. Come on in."

Kate stepped into a comfortable living room—homey with sofa, recliners, chairs, a fireplace along one wall, and opening onto a dining area with a kitchen off to the side. Nice paintings on the walls. Looked like originals. A walker stood in the corner. Kate frowned.

"Have a seat. Would you like something to drink?" Jake asked. Her voice was deep and husky.

"Water, please," Kate replied from her position at the end of the sofa. "I walked in from the marina. Then stopped for coffee, but I'm still a little thirsty. It sure is heating up out there."

"Yes, August. We would gladly have picked you up. You didn't need to walk all this way."

"I wanted to stretch my legs. Been on a rocking sailboat for the last eight weeks and needed a land adjustment." Kate grinned and Jake smiled back at her.

"Okay, water it is. Sounds like fun, being on a boat," Jake called as she went into the kitchen and returned with a bottle of water. "Hope you don't mind bottled. The local water is quite safe, although we just don't care for the taste."

Kate nodded. "This is fine. Cold and wet."

Just as Kate took her first sip, she saw someone enter the room. Someone in a motorized wheelchair. That took her by surprise. Marianne. Kate was shocked to see her friend confined to a chair. Sweet face, now a little rounder than in her youth, and settled, mature body, surrounded by the metal and leather of her wheeled conveyance. Marianne wore a short-sleeve blouse and dark-colored slacks. Kate noticed that her brown hair was turning gray, and her blue eyes were circled by dark-rimmed glasses.

Marianne smiled as she rolled forward. "Hello, Kate, glad you could come and see us." She positioned herself where she could look at Kate and be close to Jake, who had dropped casually into a recliner.

"It's great to see you again, too," Kate said. She was so unsettled by Marianne that she was almost speechless. Normally they would have hugged, but Kate felt awkward and remained seated.

Clearly observing her discomfort, Marianne opened the conversation. "Well, well, well. The infamous Kate Brighton, here in our living room."

Kate blushed.

"I kept track of you after Cornell for several years when you were in New York. Then you disappeared. I wondered what happened, but I didn't have a clue how to find you."

A shiver ran down Kate's spine; she had always felt uncomfortable under Marianne's perusal. "Yeah, I left the advertising business and went walkabout. I've been all over the world—well, mostly the South Pacific. This spring I was in Honolulu and had a chance to crew on a sloop coming to Seattle. The owner stopped at the Sequim marina yesterday, so I decided to take a little time and explore the area. Realizing that you were here, I knew this place had to be special."

Jake grinned. "Well, you *are* in for a treat. People come up here, take in the scenery, and become hooked. They either return later or just never leave. It's become kind of a coastal mecca, especially for retirees, including lesbians."

Kate shrugged. "The town looks nice. I mean, nothing really special, on the surface, as I walked through it. But clean air, water, beautiful scenery, peace and quiet—yeah, I can see it for seniors." Then Kate shook her head. "Yet for lesbians? I don't quite get that."

Jake and Marianne both laughed. "You will if you hang around long enough. There are probably more lesbians here per capita than anywhere outside of New York City."

Kate sat up straight. "Really?" *That was hard to believe.*

Marianne smiled. "Maybe not actuarially. However, there are many lesbians living here and lots of social activities."

"I've always thought of gay folks as largely city people. Concerts, opera, movies, theatre, good restaurants. How can you satisfy that in a rural area?"

Jake smiled this time. "You're really in for a surprise if you choose to stick around. More culture here than you would guess."

"Hmmm."

Marianne looked at her questioningly. "So, what *is* your plan?"

"Not sure. Steve, my sailor friend, is here for a day or two then going on to Seattle. He has family there he wants to see. I'm going to visit with you and then decide whether to stay here or go on to Seattle. After that, I have no plan."

Jake and Marianne looked at each other. "Why don't you stay with us?" They both spoke in unison and then laughed.

Feeling a bit unsure and at the same time pleased, Kate replied, "I wouldn't want to put you out."

"Well, we don't have an extra bedroom, but this sofa makes out into a large bed. I doubt if it's any less comfortable than sleeping on a boat," Marianne said with a bit of a grin. "Or in a motel."

Kate nodded. "Okay, if you're sure it's no trouble."

"None at all," Jake replied.

"Well, then, I'll stay." Kate smiled, beginning to relax.

***

Marianne started to roll away. "If you'll excuse me, I'm on the clock. I have to return to work. Jake will show you around." Without waiting for a reply, she sent herself back in the direction she had come.

Confused, Kate looked after her.

"She works from home for IBM," Jake explained. "Lots of folks here do something similar. That way they can have a pristine environment for their families and still make a decent living. Many big companies let their trusted employees work online. Of course, Marianne's hours are different because her job's on eastern time. She starts early in the morning and wraps it up by mid-afternoon."

Taken by surprise, Kate nodded. "Wow."

Jake grinned. "How about a tour of our mansion?"

"Sure."

Jake walked her into the kitchen, pointed to the closed door of Marianne's office then showed her Marianne's specially equipped bedroom and bath. Jake had the second bedroom, smaller and filled with all sorts of books on carefully preserved antique wooden bookshelves. Kate guessed Jake loved to read.

They exited the side door, and Kate realized there were two vehicles parked in the driveway. One was a truck that probably belonged to Jake. The other was a van that Kate immediately guessed was equipped for Marianne. At the back of the driveway was a detached garage. Jake took her toward that building and used a remote to open the door. Inside were workbenches, stacks of wood, cabinets and tools, and on one wall various pieces of hiking and skiing gear.

"I'm a carpenter," Jake explained. "I build furniture for a living. For fun, I turn driftwood pieces into art." She showed Kate some of her handiwork. Kate was impressed. "I also hike and ski, as you might guess."

Kate had a million questions about Marianne and Jake and their obviously unique relationship, but she figured she could ask later. This whole world was unlike anything she had ever known except maybe when she would visit New England in her youth.

***

An hour later, Kate and Jake continued their conversation over lunch in a local burger café. Because of her different work hours, Marianne had not come with them. Jake had run some errands and shown Kate a bit of the town. While munching fries, Jake explained, "Marianne and I have a nice dinner together each evening—the rest of the day we're pretty much on our own."

As Kate finished her burger, she dared to ask, "What happened to Marianne to put her in the chair?"

Jake sighed. "Got hit one day out on the 101 while headed to Port Angeles. She survived the crash, but her back was really torn up. Three surgeries. It's doubtful she'll ever walk again."

Kate considered that. “It must have been a real challenge to your relationship.”

Jake looked pained. “Yeah, we came up here for the wilderness. The chance to do things together, like camping, kayaking, hiking, exploring. We bought an RV and were planning to travel during her vacation periods. My work comes and goes but I make a pretty good living. It’s just not regular like hers. All our plans went up in smoke with the car crash. The RV is in storage. She’s in the chair, and if I want to hike or kayak, I have to do it by myself or with other people. Not the same, I assure you.”

“How does she feel about being so limited? Is she in a lot of pain?”

“Pain, so-so. Limited, yes, and she doesn’t like that a bit. However, you know Marianne. She’s a trooper. She bounces pretty well with what happens in life. Now and then she becomes a bit down, and she can be touchy and critical sometimes. Waste bothers her. Since she’s lost many opportunities, she hasn’t much patience with anything or anyone being abused or tossed away.”

Kate frowned. *Something about Jake’s observation made her uneasy. She wasn’t sure what it was and at the moment she was uncomfortable asking.*

***

After their lunch, Jake stopped briefly at the local Home Depot and the Walmart then drove Kate around the Dungeness Prairie, formed by the open land between Sequim and the Strait of Juan de Fuca. “This prairie once housed nearly a hundred dairies,” Jake told her. “Today there are only a couple. Some farms, a few with decent acreage. Mostly lots for houses, many separate and sitting on perhaps five acres, not crowded together like in town. The view of the Olympics is incredible. The downside is weather exposure—the prairie can become very windy, since it’s largely unprotected and in the path of northwest prevailing winds.”

Jake stopped the truck at one point to show Kate how the Olympic Mountains rose to the south behind Sequim. From this location, they had a good view of numerous jagged peaks. Kate agreed that the mountains were spectacular and she decided to return and look around more.

By the time they arrived back at the house, Kate was beginning to understand why people came here in such large numbers—including lesbians. She had also decided she was going to stay longer than she first expected. Her curiosity had been aroused, and she didn't want to leave without having it satisfied. *And there was that barista.*

2

Angie opened the squeaky door of her tan '85 Ford sedan and climbed inside. The hot sun had made it warm and sticky. Praying that the car would start so she could get some cooling from the A/C, she turned the key and listened as the engine grumbled, hiccupped, and finally turned over. The A/C rattled and stirred up dust but it ran, and she settled back into her seat with a sigh of relief.

Now that her workday had finally ended, she needed to pick up the kids from the Boys & Girls Club then stop at the Safeway. Her tip earnings today would be enough to buy a package of hot dogs, buns, a bag of chips, and a bottle of milk.

Angie uttered a heavy sigh. *How was she ever going to keep this up?*

Taking several deep breaths as the air inside the car began to cool, she told herself that things would improve. *Just survive one day at a time and somehow money will show up. There had to be something good out there, someplace. This was just a rough bump in the road. Had to be.*

Whenever she started worrying about money, her mind would flip to Zack and their ill-fated marriage, his departure from her life, and her family's subsequent shunning. Thinking about that was inevitably a downward slide into the throws of depression, so she forced herself to stop the thoughts. Instead, Angie mused about the woman who had come into the coffeehouse that morning. Attractive in a rugged athletic sort of way, and with an incredibly deep tan. *Where would someone get a tan like that up here?* And her eyes were penetrating. Angie liked her casual manner. *She'd sure like to see that woman again sometime.*

***

When Angie entered the children's play area at the Club, Mark and Sarina were looking for her. Mark, eight years old and good-natured most of the time, waved. He was dark like Angie with brown eyes and wavy hair so shiny and beautiful that she hated to cut it. However, she forced herself to whack it off every few weeks for him to fit in with the other boys. *The long hair would come later, when he reached an adolescent rebellion stage.* Mark was slender and hadn't started to gain height yet, but Angie thought he would eventually be tall like his father, or she hoped so. Sarina was wearing a frown. Now seven and a little bit stocky, she had a determined streak. *Mimicking her mother, perhaps?* Blonde with blue eyes that came from Angie's mother, Sarina could be emotionally volatile—happy one minute and down the next. She was harder to manage than Mark, who tried his best to roll with the punches and be agreeable.

Hungry for her attention, the two children were all over Angie. She gave them both big hugs and asked what they had been doing all day. Sarina bubbled about a game they had been playing. Mark waited to put a word in. "What's for dinner?" he finally asked. "I'm hungry."

Angie ruffled his hair. "How about hot dogs, chips, and a glass of milk?"

Mark started to say something then stopped himself. "That's fine, Mom." Just a hint of disappointment slipped into his voice.

Angie gave him an extra hug.

***

When they were buckled in, Angie drove to the nearby Safeway. Waltzing into the store, they shivered in the suddenly cold air. As they passed the meat counter, Mark stared at the steaks but kept quiet as Angie continued walking and picked up a package of hot dogs on the deli isle.

Sarina was still talking about the project at the Club. They had cut out clothing for Barbie dolls, glued the pieces together and dressed the dolls. Then they had a little contest to see whose outfit was the best. "I came in second," Sarina trilled a trifle loudly. Angie patted her and suggested she keep her voice down, all the while telling her how proud she was.

At the checkout counter, Angie's tip money lacked a few cents to cover the bill. "Oh." She pondered what to do, as the clerk stared at her, not unkindly. Angie was a regular.

"I got it," Mark said, pulling some coins from his pocket.

Angie was surprised. "Thanks, Mark, for saving our butts. Where did you find the money?"

Mark flushed. "From Grandpa. I helped him out in the barn, and he paid me." He looked down at the floor, clearly embarrassed.

Noticing the color in his cheeks, Angie put an arm around his shoulder. "That's all right, Mark. I'm glad you could help Grandpa. You're such a big boy now."

The bill was paid and they returned to the car.

***

Home for Angie and her children was an apartment building just north of the 101 Highway, a three-story structure that accepted government-subsidized residents. They had a two-bedroom unit on the second floor. Outside stairs, no elevator. Otherwise, a decent place for them to live. The complex had a large swimming pool, and Mark and Sarina often spent time there during the summer months.

With groceries under one arm, Angie guided the kids ahead of her and climbed the stairway to their apartment, where she used her keys to open the door. It was hot inside. "Go turn the air on," she instructed Mark, who quickly headed for the thermostat.

"Why is it so hot?" Sarina queried, as if she hadn't been told many times before.

"Because it's summer," Angie said patiently. "Because I can't afford to keep the A/C on when we aren't here. It will cool down in a few minutes. If you are too hot, you and Mark can go down to the pool until dinnertime. Remember, only go in the water if there's an adult around. Mrs. Johnson is probably down there with her kids. Tell her that your mama asked if she could keep an eye on you, okay?"

Mark and Sarina hurried into the bedroom they shared. Sarina took her one-piece swimsuit into the bathroom to change privately, while Mark pulled on his swim trunks by his bed.

When Sarina emerged, a towel over her shoulder, the two headed downstairs to the apartment pool.

"It's 4:30 right now. I'll give you thirty minutes," Angie called to them.

"Okay, Mom," Mark yelled back. "I'll tell Mrs. Johnson. She always wears a watch."

***

Angie slumped into a well-used chair in the dining alcove. She sat for a moment, forcing herself to breathe deeply and attempting to relax. This was her first real pause of the entire day.

Her routine—drop off kids, work, pick up kids, get groceries, fix dinner—was followed five days a week. The other two days, she was home, trying to keep both Mark and Sarina busy, the apartment cleaned up, and some kind of food on the table without spending a dime. It was difficult, some days virtually impossible, and very exhausting.

If only Zack hadn't walked out. They had been married for nine years and created two beautiful children. It hadn't been the best of marriages, although most of the time they got along reasonably well. Or, so she thought. Suddenly, one evening, he accused her of being sexually unresponsive. She hadn't understood where he was coming from. He had been her first and only sexual partner, from fifteen years old and marriage at sixteen. *What did he mean?* She soon learned that he had found another woman who was sexually aggressive and wanted a divorce. His parents had been angry with him because they liked Angie and loved the kids. When he announced he thought Angie was a lesbian, everything changed. Shocked and offended, they wanted nothing to do with her.

Angie had been devastated. Forced out of the house they shared, left alone with the kids and no real financial support coming from Zack or his family, she had taken a job as a barista and located this low-rent apartment. She felt she was letting the kids down, but she had barely finished high school and was doing the best she could. Confused by his accusation, she read up on lesbians on the Internet and allowed herself to be seduced by one lesbian woman who often came into the coffeehouse. It wasn't a lasting relationship; however, she found that she *did* like sex with a woman a whole lot better than with Zack. *Maybe he had been right.* That didn't excuse the way he had shed her and the children without providing any plan or passage into a future without him. Living in a small town, even though she had been born here, did not offer many options, and seemingly everyone in town "knew" her secret whether she wanted them to or not.

A year had passed, Angie had accepted Zack's label and started to identify as lesbian. She began seeking women as occasional partners when she could find them. Not easy with two kids and no money. *And who in their right mind would take her on?* After Zack, she was wary. People promised things then changed. Hard as it was to keep going, Angie still felt bitter over the divorce and wasn't sure she could trust herself or her children to anyone.

Angie sighed. Ruminating on the past always made her feel sad, so she stood up and started to fix dinner. She boiled the dogs on the stove and warmed up the buns in the microwave. She found a single can of baked beans in an almost empty cupboard and opened it. The kids would probably just want to eat the beans cold, since the apartment was still rather warm. She opened the potato chips and poured Mark and Sarina a glass of milk. Everything went on the table. She almost gagged at the thought of this dinner—just like so many other nights in the past year—but conversation with the kids would help. And they'd watch TV later. When they went to bed, she would read. She had a new romance novel from the library. *At least there was happiness and escape in lesbian fiction.*

Angie was ready to go down to the pool in search of the kids when she heard them climbing the stairs. Just in time. They were both wet from head to toe and wrapped in beach towels.

"Come on in," she said, forcing a smile. "It's time to eat. Just sit on your towels. Your wet suits will keep you cooler. Food's on the table. I'll be right back."

While they hungrily consumed their dogs—Mark had poured ketchup on his while Sarina preferred mustard—Angie went to the bathroom. After relieving herself, she straightened her uniform. She would change after dinner. Looking in the mirror, she studied herself. Her tiredness was obvious. She pasted a smile on her face. For a second her eyes sparkled. Like in the old days, or when she had a nice customer at work. *Like this morning, in fact. That woman was hot!* Angie frowned. *She was probably a tourist and would never return.*

***

Later that evening, after Angie had read to the kids, tucked them in bed, and turned out their light, she went into her own bedroom, stretched out on her queen-sized bed and picked up a novel that was lying open on her lamp table. *Gambling on Love* by Susan Swiffert. She had finished the third chapter but hadn't yet encountered a second major character—who would eventually, of course, become a lover for the heroine. Angie began reading, suddenly flashing on these words:

She strode into the café, tall, blonde, and tomboy. Her blue eyes matched her blue denim shirt and she gazed over aviator glasses. Her jeans were skin tight, revealing luscious curves, and her boot heels clicked on the hardwood floor. The stranger approached the service counter and smiled languidly at the young server stationed there.

Angie laughed to herself. *That was certainly overkill.* Maybe this book was a comedy. Suddenly, her mind flipped back again to that morning, to the tall, deeply tanned blonde who had come into The Little Red Barn. Angie remembered the tingle that had run up and down her spine when she first saw the woman, who was very attractive in a somewhat masculine way. When she sat at the table engrossed in her computer and chuckled to herself, she had a delightful, charming laugh that was a touch alto. The woman exuded so much magnetic energy that Angie had found herself trying to connect with her—knowing all the while how futile it was. Angie wondered then, and again now, if this woman were a lesbian. She looked like one, yet Angie had learned that looks didn't mean anything. In fact, since Zack had abandoned her, she had found that looks could be quite deceiving, especially in a farm town where women often dressed and acted like tomboys. It didn't mean a thing about their sexuality.

Angie sighed. *Oh, well.* The woman hadn't paid much attention to her, just paid her bill and moved on. She seemed older, in her late thirties probably. *Maybe it was best that nothing had happened between them.*

Angie returned to her novel, realizing that the plot was about to thicken and the book would be much more interesting.

3

The following morning, Kate walked briskly across town to The Little Red Barn. She wanted some good coffee and she wanted to see if that barista Angie was around today. She also needed the exercise and wanted to think about things a bit, away from Jake and Marianne.

Dinner the evening before, which Jake had assembled quickly, and which had been quite tasty, was a real revelation to Kate. The two lesbians seemed very different from each other—especially now that Marianne was handicapped—but they were different to begin with. Marianne was urbane, sophisticated, well-educated with a BA and MBA from Cornell, and working for a giant corporation. Jake was outdoorsy, backwoods, and didn't appear to have diplomas on her wall. She hailed, Kate had learned, from Kansas. It just seemed unlikely that two such different women would do well as a couple. *What drew them together?* Kate had spent dinner trying to find out.

"Where did you two meet?" she had asked.

They looked at each other and grinned. "On the Appalachian Trail," Marianne admitted.

"What?" Kate exploded, screwing up her face in disbelief.

"For reasons totally different, each of us had decided to walk the Trail that summer. I was starting from the north end, and Jake was starting from the south," Marianne recalled. "We met at an encampment somewhere in the middle. After we talked for a while, there was an attraction, and neither one of us wanted to leave."

Jake, quiet until now, spoke up. "It became clear that in order to continue sharing with each other, one of us was going to have to go backward. It was easy for me to kind of give it up, so I turned around and accompanied Marianne all the way back to Georgia."

"I lived in the Northeast," Marianne explained further, "and Jake was living in the South, We spent a year commuting when we could find the time. The next summer we met each other

at that same encampment and walked from there to the north end of the Trail—that way Jake could do the whole thing, too."

Marianne smiled. "By the time we had completed the entire Trail, we really knew that we were meant for each other."

"I bought an RV," Jake added. "We spent summer vacations traveling the country. When we reached the Pacific Northwest, we decided we were home. I knew I could make a living here, and Marianne arranged for her job to become mobile. She'd been doing that in bits and pieces when we traveled. When we moved here permanently, she arranged for it to be full time."

Marianne smiled wistfully. "We were having such a great time with our life together until the accident. Since then things have changed a lot. I feel as bad for Jake as I do for myself. She's lost her hiking partner, probably forever."

Jake looked at her gently. "You know, Marianne, no matter what, I love you."

Marianne sighed. "I love you, too! And I think you are a saint."

***

Kate shook her head as she walked along Washington Street. She wished she loved someone like that, for life, regardless. Thus far, that kind of devotion had eluded her. She had met any number of very attractive women, some with whom she had built friendships, some she had bedded. However, no one had gotten under her skin enough to make a permanent commitment. Now pushing forty, she was still looking.

Her self-examination was interrupted by the realization that she had arrived at the coffeehouse. She looked at the place. The Little Red Barn. Kind of silly. She chuckled. She supposed that it fit the area. *Certainly, lots of barns around here.*

Kate entered the now familiar establishment. One person sat at a table. A group was closeted in a private conference room off to the side. Kate was glad that the coffee bar was quiet. She wanted a chance to talk to Angie, if she were there.

A barista stood with her back to Kate, assembling something at the counter. Her long dark braid seemed like

Angie's from the day before, but Kate wasn't absolutely sure until she turned around. *Angie.*

Feeling more confident, Kate strode to the counter.

"You came to see us again." Angie smiled at her warmly. "What can I do for you today?"

"I just walked across town, and I'm kind of warm," Kate said casually. "I think I'd like some sort of iced latte today. Cool me off."

Angie grinned. "Sure thing. Anything else?"

"What about one of those croissants, that chocolate one. I'm a sucker for chocolate."

Angie nodded. "Got it. Sit down wherever you like, and I'll bring everything to you."

"Don't I have to pay first?"

Angie shrugged. "You can, or I can run a tab, and you can pay when you leave."

"That's friendly."

"We try to be." Angie turned to start making the latte.

Kate backed away slowly, glancing around the room to decide where she'd like to sit. She also noted, again, how cute Angie was. Nice buns. Nice boobs. Beautiful hair. Although she had paid attention to Angie yesterday, Kate was even more impressed the second time around. Angie's eyes had a delightful sparkle, and Kate could imagine unbraiding those long, beautiful locks and running her fingers through them. *Mmmmm.*

Forcing herself back to reality, Kate picked a seat and opened her computer to check her email. There was a message from Steve that he was going to move on to Seattle and that if she wanted to go along, she needed to be at the dock by noon.

After just a moment's hesitation, Kate sent a reply. "Met some friends, want to stay in Sequim a while. Give me details on how to find you in Seattle. I'm sure I'll be over there in a few days. Don't want to lose touch. Thanks for everything."

As Kate hit the send button, she mused to herself about how important those few keystrokes might turn out to be. Sequim had never been on her agenda. She had never even heard of it. *Strange place with a strange name.* Now some inner voice was telling her to stay. No question about it. Steve would pull away from the dock, she wouldn't be there, and that would be that. She shrugged as she felt a tingle run down her spine. *It was a decision, and decisions had consequences.*

Angie brought her iced latte and chocolate croissant and set them on the table, along with a napkin and a straw.

Kate nodded, “Thanks! Looks good.”

Angie teased with a big smile. “You’re welcome.” She started to turn away and then stopped. “I don’t remember seeing you around town. New here?”

Kate grinned. “Yep. Came in two days ago on a sailboat from Hawaii. Have some friends here on the west side of town, and I decided to check the place out.”

Angie nodded. “Well, it’s interesting, I guess. However, Hawaii sounds like a lot more fun to a girl who’s hardly ever been out of Sequim.” She winked and Kate gave her a big grin.

Just then an older man entered the coffeehouse. Angie turned her attention to this regular customer. “Hi, Joe,” she said while walking back to the counter. Since Carly, the other barista, was handling orders from the drive-thru, Angie focused on taking Joe’s order.

Kate watched out of the corner of her eye then went back to her email. As she opened different messages and decided whether to delete or answer, she kept thinking of Angie. She’d sure like a chance to know her better. *How could she do that?*

***

During the next few minutes, Angie filled orders for two more coffees, an iced tea, a couple of sandwiches, and a glass of fresh lemonade. It was nearly lunchtime. There was now a steady stream of customers in and out the front door. Carly went to the back room on break, and Angie had to cover both the drive-thru and the counter.

As she bustled about and greeted each new person, Angie had a sensation that eyes were watching her. *It must be that woman off the sailboat*, she thought to herself. Then she wondered why that woman was so focused on her. She didn’t really have time to think about it, but the question was there. *Hawaii. Wow!*

When Carly came back to the counter, Angie bustled over to Kate's table, where she was still engrossed with her computer. She had finished her food, and Angie picked up the plate. "Is there anything else? A refill on the iced latte?"

Kate looked up and smiled. "Oh, yeah. I could use another one. Thanks!"

Angie nodded and went to fix the drink. When she brought it back to the table, she said, "I'm going on my lunch break now. If you're ready to leave before I return, just settle up with Carly, okay?"

Kate nodded. "Oh, sure." She started to look at her computer and then suddenly asked, "Do you go out to lunch or eat here?"

Angie looked at her with a raised eyebrow. "We have a back room and a short break. Why do you ask?"

Kate blushed. "Sorry. I didn't mean to be rude. I was just hoping for a chance to talk with you for a moment, and you seem really busy. I thought maybe a break or after work—"

Angie shook her head. "Not here. And I don't have a lot of free time anyway. I have to pick up my kids after I leave work."

Kate looked surprised. "You have kids?"

Angie nodded. "A boy and a girl, seven and eight."

"Oh, okay." Kate seemed to be searching for words. "You look really young. I never thought about you having kids."

"I was young when I got married." Angie frowned. "Well, I've got to go on break. Thanks for coming in. See ya around."

***

Kate watched her walk away. She would have sworn that her gaydar was picking up a signal. *Married with kids. That put the odds on the other side of the fence.* She sighed. *Too bad. Very attractive looking.*

Returning to her computer and feeling a little deflated, Kate finished up her email for the day. She paid her bill with Carly and walked out of the coffeehouse.

Now what? *Maybe she should have left with Steve.* Whatever she had been thinking of, it was now gone. Just walking around town had its limitations, and sleeping on the sofa at Marianne's and Jake's house wasn't terrific either.

If she planned to stay and explore, Kate would have to find some wheels and a place to bed down. Considering that, she remembered passing a couple of small motels, very basic and probably not expensive. Local independents. There was also an auto repair center that had cars with for rent signs on them. *Maybe she should invest in a week here and then go on to Seattle.*

Kate marched herself back toward downtown. She stopped at the first small motel she saw and arranged for a room for a few nights. When she left Sequim Elkwood Motel, she hunted up the auto repair center. Although the rental offerings weren't great, she signed up for a gray 2003 Chevy sedan. Her father would turn over in his grave, but then cars were *his* passion. She hadn't owned one while living in New York City. While sailing around the Pacific, her land transportation had been varied and quite simple. So, the sedan would do as long as it ran and had A/C, which thankfully it did. *At least*, she mused, *she'd kept her driver's license current.*

Once she had wheels, Kate used her cell's GPS to explore Sequim and the Prairie. She didn't know where she was going most of the time and just wandered generally north until she came to a road that ran along the Strait of Juan de Fuca. It was different to look at the Strait from the landside instead of Steve's sailboat. She could see islands and what must be Canada to the north. When she glanced back to the south, the Olympic Mountains were stunning. She had enjoyed the ride with Jake the day before but, out here by herself, she felt more focused. She snapped a few photos with her cell and was really beginning to grasp why people liked it here—water on one side and mountains on the other. Not every place had both. And the sky today was still a beautiful blue with a few puffy white clouds around the horizon. She stood by the sedan, breathed deeply, and for the first time took notice of just how clear the air was.

By midafternoon, Kate was back on Sequim's east side. Although she would return to Marianne and Jake's for dinner, she didn't want to interfere with their carefully ordered life by hanging out at their house. *Maybe when she went back, she should take a dessert or some fruit as an offering for the meal.*

With that thought in mind, she stopped at a local grocery, one near the coffeehouse. It was mercifully cool inside. Kate walked up and down the aisles, trying to decide what to pick up for dinner, plus a couple of snacks to put in her motel room. She was headed for the checkout stand when she saw Angie enter the store with her two children in tow. They nearly bumped into each other.

"Oh, hi," Kate said, stumbling around her words, and trying to deal with Angie's incredible attractiveness and the reality of her two kids at the same time.

"Well, hi to you," Angie replied. "This is Mark and Sarina." She put her arm around Sarina and nodded at Mark. "I'm afraid I don't know your name."

"Kate. Kate Brighton." She gave them all a big smile.

Mark put out a hand for a formal shake. "Hello. We're on our way home, as soon as we buy some food for dinner."

Sarina grinned. "We're going swimming."

Angie suddenly brightened. "Do you have a pool where you're staying?"

Kate shook her head. "No, I didn't see one. It's just a little motel down the street."

"Well, you wanted to talk to me. If you still do, why don't you come up to the apartment building and join us poolside? I have to watch the kids, but I can talk then. It's Elkland Apartments, up on the hill just by the highway. There's marked visitor parking. The pool's nearby. I'd say in a half hour, maybe an hour at the most, we'll be there."

Kate thought quickly about making an excuse yet, despite her hesitation, she agreed. "Okay, I'll see you there. Complete with swimsuit. An hour."

They waved, and Angie and her little family turned to their shopping, while Kate checked out.

***

Kate had just enough time to cross through town to Marianne's and Jake's home. She parked in front and saw Jake working in the garage. Kate strolled up to her.

"Hi," Jake greeted. "I was wondering where you had disappeared to."

"Well," Kate explained with a smile, "I rented a car and a room in a little motel. I think I'll stay here a few days and look around."

Jake's face fell a little. "You were welcome to stay with us, and we'd have loaned you the SUV or the truck."

Kate put a hand on Jake's shoulder. "I know you would have, but I don't want to make a lot of extra work for you. I'll be around, and I hope we can go hiking one day soon."

Jake smiled at the word "hiking."

"I'm still coming to dinner. What time will you be eating tonight?"

"Probably about six. That okay?"

"Sure. I'll be back by then. I brought some dessert for you." She held out the package from the grocery.

"Oh, thanks." Jake smiled warmly.

"I'm going to grab my stuff out of your living room and put it in the motel, okay?"

"Sure," Jake shrugged and a little frown crossed her face. "I hope we didn't do anything to put you off."

"No way. I just kind of need to explore, feel the town out on my own. However, you've mentioned all kinds of things I'd like to do with you. I'm not gone, believe me."

Kate offered Jake a big grin, allowing her to visibly relax. The two walked up the ramp to the back door and stepped inside. Kate grabbed her duffle bag and then loaded it into the rental car. Jake chuckled at the sedan.

"Not much, I know, but I don't need a lot right now. Just wheels."

***

Kate hustled back to the motel, opened her duffle on the bed and pulled out her swimsuit. She borrowed a small and threadbare motel towel—it was what they had and would have to do. She donned the swimsuit and pulled her clothes on over it, noticing that she was nervous. She also grabbed her Dopp kit, since her hair might be wet if she swam and she might need to comb it out. She made sure she had sunscreen and sunglasses. *Overkill—a sign of anxiety.*

Locking her motel door, Kate jumped into the sedan and drove east again, looking for the Elkland Apartments. She finally saw a sign with an arrow and remembered Elkland was a big complex on the side of a hill. She turned off Washington and drove up to it, putting the sedan as directed into a visitor's space. Before she climbed out of the car, she paused a moment to ask herself what was she doing, chasing after a woman with two kids? It made no sense to her, and yet she was dedicated to following her unexplainable attraction. *Probably a big mistake. Innocent off-the-cuff decisions. . .*

The swimming pool wasn't hard to find because Kate heard children yelling and laughing somewhere nearby. She followed the sounds to the large kidney-shaped pool that was surrounded by ground-floor patios and apartments on three sides. There were chairs, a few tables, and some sunning benches. Half a dozen kids were in the water, and a couple of mothers were seated nearby keeping an eye on them.

At first she didn't see Angie. Then her eyes adjusted to the surroundings, and she recognized her, perched alone on a bench. She was wearing a swimsuit covered by a short-sleeve blouse. Even seated with her legs crossed and flip-flops on her feet, Angie was beautiful. Kate couldn't miss that, for sure. *Soft curves, gorgeous skin. That marvelous long dark braid down her back.*

Kate approached, as Angie yelled at the children frolicking in the water. A game was in progress with an inflated ball. Angie monitored the action and alternately gave instructions on game play and politeness to Mark and Sarina.

When Kate stood beside her, creating a shadow in the afternoon sun, Angie glanced up. Her face lit up with a broad smile. "Oh, you're here."

"Yep. Looks like a nice place," Kate said awkwardly, looking around at the apartment building.

"Yeah," Angie agreed. "It's hard to become used to not having a house and yard, but this is pretty nice, as apartments go. I'm just lucky they accept Section 8."

Kate wasn't sure what that meant. She assumed it was some kind of government subsidy—that thought left her with even more questions about Angie than she had had before.

"Sit down." Angie patted the bench. "The kids are in the midst of a game. I'm so happy seeing them having fun that I just like to sit here and watch."

Kate dropped down beside her and studied the pool, the kids, and the game for a moment. She was soon able to separate Sarina and Mark from the other children. Sarina had a swim cap on. Mark's dark head and his slim body popped up as he jumped to receive or send off the ball.

"If you want to swim, it's okay," Angie said. "We're allowed to have guests."

"I'll just watch for a minute before I jump in," Kate replied. "How come you had to give up your house, if it's not too rude to ask?"

Angie's jaw tightened. "My ex-husband Zack decided I wasn't a good enough wife and found a replacement. He filed for divorce, not much came my way in the form of a settlement, and he hasn't been paying child support. He kept the house and now has another wife and a child on the way."

Kate grimaced. That was really ugly. Even not knowing Angie well, she felt instant sympathy for her. "So, you are the principal breadwinner."

"Yep, and I have only a high school education, barely that. My options are a bit limited. I do what I can for the kids. A roof over their head and food on the table. That's about it."

Kate let those details settle over her. "That's rough."

Angie looked at her for a moment. "I have to live day to day and hope the next one is better. As long as I don't think about the big picture, I do all right."

"No family around to help?"

Angie shook her head. "My parents are Mennonite. They wrote me off when I got involved with Zack at fifteen. It was stupid of me, but I was fifteen, what the hey. Zack's parents are here, too, and they speak to me sort of. Although they don't approve of me, they love their grandkids, and they help me a bit with them, like occasional care or transportation."

Kate was very curious. "You seem to be a very nice person. What's not to like about you?"

Angie gave her a somewhat sarcastic look. "Well," she said quietly, paying attention that no one was watching, "Zack divorced me because he said I was a lesbian. Based on finding a girlfriend who was more responsive to him sexually. I hadn't a clue what he was talking about at the time. I had never known anyone else intimately."

Kate's heart skipped a beat. *Was this the opening she was looking for?* "That's a strong statement to make about someone you have vowed to love for a lifetime. Have you come to understand why he said that? Just as an excuse to end the marriage?"

Angie shook her head and took a moment to yell at the kids. "No, I figured out later, after study and some life experience, that he was right."

Kate held her breath. "You now identify as lesbian?"

Angie nodded and added a bit sarcastically, "Not that it does me much good." She stood up and went over to the pool to say something to Sarina. Kate sat marveling at how beautiful Angie was and how relieved *she* was to find that her own gaydar had been correct after all. *Despite the circumstances.*

***

When Angie returned to the bench, Kate wasn't there. Surprised, she looked around to see where Kate had gone. At first, she saw nothing then felt relieved when she found Kate's clothing lying on the end of the bench.

Angie took another visual survey and discovered Kate poised to dive at the deep end of the pool. She held the pose while two children moved out of her path and then executed a perfect competition dive, surfaced and stroked her way freestyle back to Angie's side of the pool.

Angie's mouth had dropped open at the vision of Kate posed to dive, tall, broad shouldered, slim hipped, with small breasts under her tank suit, wind-blown blonde curly hair.

Obviously, a swimmer. Angie hadn't noticed that in her jeans, shirt and sport shoes, but now it was very clear. *And incredibly beautiful to watch.*

Kate completed a few lengths of the pool as kids quickly moved out of her way. Sarina stopped playing ball and looked at Kate. Her mouth made a big "O" and she looked up at Angie. "Mama, look" she called, pointing to Kate.

Angie nodded, thrilled to be watching a skilled swimmer in action. *Swimming*, she thought, *was one of the most beautiful sports ever created.*

"Mama, it's like watching Esther Williams!" Sarina yelled across the pool.

Angie grinned. *Kids. Where would a seven-year old come up with that?* She shrugged. *TV, obviously some old movie on TV.*

After a few laps, Kate pulled herself out of the water and immediately was surrounded by Angie, Sarina, and even Mark.

"That felt really good," Kate said with a grin. "Haven't been able to swim for a while."

"What are you, an Olympian or something?" Angie managed.

"Well, almost. But not."

Sarina tugged at the towel Kate was using to dry off. "You're like a movie star," she enthused.

Kate laughed. "You mean like Esther Williams?"

"Yeah, that's the one."

Kate leaned over and picked up Sarina in her strong arms. "Well, young lady, that's an awfully nice compliment. Esther was a pretty good swimmer."

"And beautiful, too," Angie interjected.

Kate looked at her mischievously. "Who, Esther or me?"

Angie blushed. "Both."

Kate put Sarina back down and tousled Mark's dark hair. "Sarina likes swimmers. What do you like?"

Mark grinned broadly. "I like swimming okay, but I want to be a ballplayer."

"Baseball?"

"Yeah. Right now, Little League." He looked at Angie. "When Mom gets the money."

A frown crossed Angie's face. She was never going to be able to meet all of Sarina's and Mark's needs. And at this moment, she felt like her inadequacies as a parent were right out there in front of the whole world, especially this attractive woman beside her. *Everything, even the simplest thing, took money she didn't have. What must Kate think?*

***

Kate suddenly remembered something. "I need to put sunscreen on," she said to the kids, "because I jumped into the pool without it." *Too much ogling Angie*, Kate mused to herself.

Thankfully, she had remembered to put a small tube in her jeans pocket, and she smothered her face, shoulders, neck and arms with the cream, as Sarina and Mark watched her every move. "You have such clear air up here that the sun is beating down full force with UV rays. Got to protect myself."

"We're used to it," Mark commented. "We're in the sun all the time and we get really brown. Mom makes sure we don't do too much time outside until we're tanned."

Kate nodded. "Smart mom." She stopped just a second. "However, I'm older and have to take extra care of my skin. Don't want skin cancer."

Sarina studied Kate a moment. "You're really brown already. You still need sunscreen?"

"Yes, cutie, just because I'm brown doesn't mean my skin couldn't absorb UV rays. Better safe than sorry."

The kids nodded. Their eyes drifted back to the pool.

Angie sighed. "Well, I need to go up and start dinner."

She turned to a neighbor and asked if the woman would watch Sarina and Mark for a few minutes.

Then Angie looked back at Kate. "If you don't have plans, you are welcome to stay—"

Kate grinned. "I would love to, but I promised friends that I'd be there for dinner. I'll hang out here for a few minutes, if you don't mind, maybe do a few more laps, and then I'll dress and move on."

As Kate started to turn away, Angie reached out for her arm. "Kate, I have to ask you something. You asked about me, and I admitted that I'm a lesbian. What about you? What does my being a lesbian mean to you?"

Kate gave her a warm smile, reached out, and hugged her briefly. "I'm a lifelong, card-carrying member of the clan. And proud of it."

For a second, they both smiled at each other, and then Kate stepped away. "This was fun," she said. "Maybe we can do it again another day."

Angie looked hopeful. "I'd like that."

4

Dinner with Marianne and Jake that evening proved entertaining and informative for Kate. She also had an opportunity to share with them the details of her day.

Jake hovered over a fragrant casserole dish filled with chicken, potatoes, cheese, broccoli, and a delicious sauce that she had prepared that afternoon. Kate watched Jake set the dish at the center of the table and felt her mouth literally watering. Remembering how she and Steve, during their two weeks in the Pacific doldrums, had lived on soda crackers and peanuts, Kate was very much looking forward to these tasty home cooked meals.

While she was watching Jake fill the plates, Marianne rolled up to the table and focused on Kate. "I hope we didn't inadvertently push you out of the house," she commented, looking concerned.

"Oh, no," Kate assured her. "I just don't know how long I'm going to stay in Sequim or even this peninsula, and I felt that, sooner or later, I'd be out using your car when you needed it, or I'd be in the way with all my stuff here in the living room. It was just easier to dump everything at a motel and arrange for a rental. I didn't want to overstay my welcome."

Jake studied her a moment. "I do hope you'll still go with me up in the mountains," she mentioned. "I'd really like to show you Hurricane Ridge."

"No problem. We'll do that, and probably some other things as well." Kate gave her an easy grin, trying to lessen her apparent uneasiness.

Marianne was clearly very curious about Kate. "What were you up to today? Were you able to see anything?" she asked with an intent look.

Kate suddenly felt something maternal coming from Marianne. She *was* a few years older and had probably been maternal toward Kate during their college days. At the time, Kate had been so focused on her mother during swimming practices that she hadn't been aware of Marianne's big sister caring.

"Oh, yeah. I drove out on the prairie—that's what you called it, I think—all the way to the water and looked out on the Strait toward Canada. Really cool. Then I photographed the mountains from there. You are quite right, Jake, the Olympics are much more impressive from that angle."

Jake nodded. "Glad you got to do that."

"So, what else did you see?" Marianne pursued, "besides checking into a motel and renting a car?"

Jake and Marianne both watched expectantly as Kate took a bite of the casserole, savoring the mingling of flavors. After she had momentarily enjoyed being the center of their rapt attention, she began her story. "Well, you know that coffeehouse on the east side, The Little Red Barn?"

They both nodded. "I'm not especially fond of the name but their coffee is excellent," Marianne commented.

"Well, I've been dropping in there for my morning brew. You were telling me there are lots of lesbians up here, right? Well, that was hard for me to believe. However, I've met one already. A young barista."

Jake chuckled to herself and covered her mouth with a napkin to hide a grin. Marianne took on an even more maternal look.

"And?"

"Well, we talked a bit, and she invited me up to her apartment complex to go swimming with her and her kids."

Marianne looked over her glasses at Kate. "Her kids?"

Kate scooted around in her seat, feeling awkward with Marianne's questioning look and furrowed brow.

"Her name is Angie. She was married really young and has a son and a daughter. She's divorced now, because her husband labeled her a lesbian, after bedding someone else more to his taste. Angie was upset initially but after doing some exploring she's decided she likes women better."

Jake nodded and then asked, "She a local then?"

"Yeah, her family goes way back. She said something about them being Mennonite."

Marianne nodded. "Several pioneer families who settled in the 1850s in Oregon and Washington were Mennonites. We see their descendants around town now and then. They are usually farming families. The women all have long hair and wear traditional dresses, down almost to their ankles, and don't use makeup."

"Are they like Amish?" Kate asked.

"Similar in traditional dress and strong family values," Marianne explained. "Mennonites do drive cars and live generally modern lives, where, as you've probably heard, the Amish live quite differently from most of us, 'off the grid' as they say."

Kate looked thoughtful. "Well, Angie does have a long braid down her back. I've only seen her in her uniform at work and by her pool in a swimsuit with a shirt over it. I don't know if she's *that* traditional. The hair, maybe."

"So," Marianne noted with an amused smile, "you've been swimming already in her pool. You don't waste time."

Kate chuckled. "She wasn't in the pool. Just her kids. I dived in and did a few laps for fun. I didn't know it would cause a stir, but her little girl called me 'Esther Williams.'"

Marianne laughed. "Hardly."

Kate bristled. "Why not? I thought it was cute."

"Well, my dear, Esther was tall with broad shoulders and slim hips, like you. However, unlike you, she was very well endowed above the waist and very feminine."

Kate couldn't stifle a laugh. "I know, no boobs and no hips. A little masculine. In other words, a dyke."

They all laughed. Then Marianne advised, "Well, have fun with her. Just be careful—a single parent with kids, she might not have a dime to her name, and you'd make a good catch. Unless, maybe, you *want* to settle down in a small town and raise children."

Kate was quiet for a minute, running that idea around in her head. "Certainly not something I've ever thought about," she finally admitted. "Small town living or taking care of kids."

***

Angie and Carly grabbed a few minutes between customers to talk. Carly, whose curly carrot-topped head and freckles seemed to suit her, was curious about this new thing going on with Angie. "What happened with you and that blonde who came in?"

Angie leaned against the counter and grinned. "You wouldn't believe it. I ran into her in the grocery store. She had said she wanted to talk, and I invited her to come to the apartment building where the kids would be swimming. I didn't think she really would do it, but she came. Swam in the pool with the kids, and Sarina thinks she's another Esther Williams."

Carly laughed. "That swimmer in those old MGM musicals?"

Angie nodded. "Yep."

"Well, I don't quite see it, but if you say so."

"Carly, she made a dive off the end of the pool that was to die for. At some time, she's been a competitive swimmer and has all the strength and grace that go with that. She played with the kids, and they really liked her. I get chills just thinking about it."

Carly frowned. "Well, Angie, she's not from here, and I'd be willing to bet she'll be moving on. Don't let your heart be broken."

Angie nodded. "I know. I don't want Sarina and Mark hurt, either. We've had enough pain for a lifetime."

Angie's cell rang, and she pulled it from her pocket. It was the shop's owner on the line. She motioned to Carly, who nodded and went back to the drive-thru window to serve a customer who had just pulled up.

***

Kate had considered avoiding the coffeehouse for a day to be less obvious in her attentions to Angie. She finally muttered, "What the heck," and went anyway. Kate thought about what Marianne had said, but she didn't feel there was much danger of getting trapped. After all, she would be leaving soon and she might as well enjoy getting to know Angie a little while she had the free time. *Angie was* so *cute, despite the complication of her two kids*.

When Kate stepped inside, the eating area was fairly quiet. However, behind the counter, there was a discussion going on in lowered tones between Angie and Carly. Angie glanced up at Kate but immediately returned her focus to Carly. Then Angie pulled out a cell phone and tapped in a number. Apparently, no one answered because she put the phone back in her pocket and returned to the conversation. "They aren't home," Kate overheard her say.

Not wanting to intrude, Kate paused a moment, studying the paintings by local artists that were hung on the walls. Mostly landscapes and local barns, some of them impressionistic. Not bad work, she thought.

Finally the chatter broke up, the other barista returned to the drive-thru window, and Angie stepped back up to the service counter. Kate approached to place her order.

Angie was friendly yet seemed a bit stressed. She told Kate she would bring her food. Kate went to sit down at a table and opened her computer.

A couple of minutes later, Kate looked up to see Angie standing there, latte and breakfast sandwich in hand, and a questioning look on her face.

She put the food down, Kate thanked her and then observed, "You look troubled. What's up?"

Angie hesitated a moment. "I might have to ask you a favor."

Kate nodded. "Okay. What favor?"

"Well, one of the afternoon workers had an emergency and can't come in. It doesn't happen very often, and they know I have to pick up Mark and Sarina after work. The manager can't find anyone to work and is insisting that I stay until closing today. I've called my in-laws, who sometimes help with the kids, but they aren't answering their phone. They may have gone to Silverdale for the day."

Kate pursed her lips. "So, you need someone to pick up Mark and Sarina, take them home, and watch them until you arrive, right?"

Angie sighed. "Yes, that's about it. I don't feel I know you well enough to be asking something like this. I just don't know what else to do."

"It's okay. I don't mind. I'm only hanging out anyway. Might as well be useful."

Angie pulled a key ring from her pocket and took off a key. "Here's the key to the apartment. Mark and Sarina will recognize you if you just go in the front door to the Boys & Girls Club. It's on Fir Street just before Fifth. They're always ready and waiting when I come. You can do something with them in the apartment or take them swimming. They can find suits and towels themselves. I'll be there a few minutes after six."

Kate nodded. "Sure. No problem. Don't worry. Just keep your manager happy, and I'll see that the kids are safe."

Angie smiled with relief. "Thanks." She pointed at the latte. "You'd better drink that before it gets cold."

***

While Angie served the next few customers entering the coffeehouse, Kate spent the time on her computer. Little by little she was catching up on that pile of email that had accumulated since she left Honolulu. She was always surprised by how many friends she still had. Maybe the pictures she occasionally sent from foreign places kept them interested. Whatever the reason, it was nice to have friends.

When Kate had had enough of the email, she closed the computer. Angie was serving a customer, but Kate caught her eye and waved a "thumbs up" to let her know everything was okay. She left the coffeehouse, trying to decide what she wanted to do until 3 p.m.

***

Thanks to her phone's GPS, Kate easily found the Boys & Girls Club. Shortly before the appointed time, she strolled into the building and looked around. Children of all ages were engaged in activities throughout the clubhouse—sports in one large court, arts and crafts in one room, a reading session in another, and a cooking project in the kitchen. If kids needed somewhere to hang out in the summer or after school, it looked to Kate like this was a pretty good place.

Before Kate could develop a case of nerves because Mark and Sarina didn't appear to be anywhere around, she noticed Mark in the reading group. He was looking up at a clock on the wall. He politely excused himself and came out of the room. He went next door and pulled Sarina out of her arts project. She started to object. Kate could see Mark mouthing the words "it's time to go." Sarina sighed, picked up her things and put them away.

The two children were walking toward the front door when they simultaneously recognized Kate standing there.

"Hi," Mark said hesitantly, "where did *you* come from?"

"Where's Mama?" asked Sarina.

Kate leaned down closer to their level. "Your mom had to work longer today. She asked me to pick you up and stay with you until she gets home. Is that all right?"

"Sure," Mark said.

"Why didn't Grandma and Grandpa come?" Sarina asked plaintively.

"Your mom couldn't reach them on the phone."

Mark nodded. "Probably in Silverdale."

"That's what your mom said. Is it okay for us to go now?"

The two kids agreed and followed Kate to the Chevy where she put them in the back seat of the sedan, helped them fasten their seat belts, and climbed in the driver's seat.

Mark spoke up, "Sarina's supposed to have a child's seat, but we're only going home, so I guess it's okay."

Kate hid her discomfort and smiled. "That's very responsible of you, Mark. I'll drive very carefully. It's only a few blocks." *She was* so *unprepared for this.*

***

Kate surveyed the apartment. Mark and Sarina marched to their bedroom to drop off their things. What furniture there was in the living room was worn—a beige sofa and a couple of overstuffed chairs. An older style TV in the corner. A simple table and four plastic chairs filled the breakfast nook.

She stepped into the small kitchen and opened a cupboard, more shocked than surprised to find it nearly empty.

Mark came in behind her. Kate turned to him. "I was thinking I could help your mom by getting something together for dinner. However, there's not much here."

"Yeah, Mom buys most of our food every day after work. She takes her tips and gets us something to eat."

Not wanting to show Mark how much that image turned her stomach, Kate looked away. She checked the other cabinets then looked in the refrigerator and the freezer. Almost nothing beyond a few condiments anywhere. Kate felt really uneasy. She made a quick decision.

"Okay, how about we go shopping instead of swimming today? We'll surprise your mom."

Mark grinned. Kate could see wheels turning in his head. Sarina seemed excited just by the idea of going to the store.

***

After they climbed into the sedan again, Kate asked Mark where the best grocery was. He gave his opinion and Kate asked him to tell her how to find it. She had a pretty good idea but she wanted to allow Mark to show off his knowledge. He explained clearly how to reach the Safeway, and she let him know that she was impressed.

When they entered the store, Kate had each child take a smaller cart, and together they went through the aisles. Fresh meat, frozen food, canned goods, vegetables and fruit, ice cream, and finally Kleenex, toilet paper, and soap. In each section, Kate asked Mark and Sarina which products their mother used. They never failed to come up with an answer and seemed like responsible kids. She trusted what they said and put the items in the carts.

She helped them push the heavy loads to the checkout counter. Sarina was a little distracted by some of the goodies offered near the checkout stand, and Kate let her pick out a package of sugar free gum. Mark shook his head and said "No, thank you," when she offered him something. His eyes grew very large when he saw the total on the register as Kate paid with a credit card.

Kate looked at both of them. "We're doing this to help your mom. It's kind of our secret, okay?"

Mark looked at her. "You mean don't tell her how much it cost?"

Kate smiled at him. "Kind of like that."

***

Kate drove back to the apartment building. She had some concerns about what she had just done and about asking Mark and Sarina not to mention the cost to Angie, but what did she know about handling kids? She was just winging it and trying to be nice.

The trio made several trips up and down the stairs with the bags of groceries. Kate let them unload the sacks into the refrigerator, freezer and cabinets—and toiletries into the hall closet and bathroom. Both children seemed to know where everything belonged and they were excited about the fun of putting it away. Kate was proud of them, and she felt that despite the unfortunate things that had already occurred in their lives, they seemed like basically good kids.

When everything was put away, Kate looked at her watch. "We did that in record time. There is still time for a swim before I make a surprise dinner for your mom. Would you like that?"

Enthusiastically, the two children changed quickly into their swimsuits. When Kate, too, was ready, they went down to the pool area. Kate swam a few laps because swimming always took away her stress. Still having some concerns about how Angie would accept what she had done, she hoped the effort to be helpful wouldn't blow up in her face. As her body began to relax, she was able to focus on the children. Mark was already tossing a beach ball with other kids. Sarina, who was clearly a beginning swimmer, was awkwardly crossing the shallow end of the pool in a kind of dog paddle.

Kate approached her, and when Sarina reached the wall and stood up, Kate commented, "Sarina, you're doing really well. Do you like to swim?"

Sarina grinned. “Uh-huh, but I can’t do it like you do.” She frowned.

“Would you like me to show you some tricks?”

Sarina’s eyes opened wide. “Uh-huh.”

Kate decided to start with the backstroke because breathing wouldn’t be an issue. She helped Sarina flip over onto her back and float for a few minutes. Then she encouraged her to kick her legs, showing her how. Kate let her kick in a circle while holding her arms. When Sarina’s kicking looked good, Kate showed her how, one arm at a time, to reach down into the water and make a circular stroke over her head, back and down, then up again. Sarina giggled with pleasure. She clearly was having fun.

In just a few minutes, Kate’s efforts produced a Sarina who was independently crossing the pool on her back, touching the wall, then standing up. “That’s good, Sarina,” Kate observed. “You’re really getting the idea. You keep practicing that. Later I’ll teach you how to make a turn. Then you can cross the pool both ways, like they do in swim meets.”

Sarina was bubbling. “Oh, thank you. I love it. It’s lots of fun.”

Kate kept an eye on her while moving over to Mark and his group. She watched the kids toss the ball around and then decided to show them a few refinements. As she deftly handled the beach ball, they all watched her arm and hand movements, and then each one tried to do the same thing. Mark seemed to be the most intense about it and she thought he mastered the moves well.

By the time they returned to the apartment to prepare dinner, both kids were happy and seemed to have a sense of achievement.

“You can help me or watch TV while I put together the dinner,” Kate told them, after they were all toweled off and dressed.

Kate was a little surprised when Mark wanted to help and Sarina chose to watch TV. Although she didn’t care, she had expected it would be the other way around. However, Mark was a little older and seemed to understand how hard his mother worked to make a life for them. She wondered, underneath, how much he still must be dealing with loss.

Mark helped Kate find sufficient cooking utensils to pan fry a large steak for all of them to share. Meanwhile, they used the microwave to bake potatoes. Mark helped cut up the vegetables as Kate made a fresh salad. Watching him, she wondered if there was a potential chef in the making.

Shortly after six, Angie came through the door. "What's cooking? I smell something good!" she commented, as she noticed Sarina on the floor before the television set and Mark and Kate both working in the kitchen. The table was set for four people.

"We went to the grocery this afternoon," Kate admitted, "and picked up a few things so you wouldn't have to cook."

Angie's eyes filled and she wiped away a tear that slid down her cheek. "That's nice of you. What are we having?"

"Let's see, fresh salad, baked potatoes, and steak," Kate said. "Ice cream for dessert."

"Wow!"

Mark gave his mother a hug, holding his hands out carefully. He didn't want to smear food all over her clothes. "Kate helped Michael, Cooper, and me handle the beach ball better so we can have more fun playing in the pool," Mark told Angie.

Sarina called from the living room. "She helped me swim the backstroke."

Kate smiled to herself. *The little one had ears, anyway.*

***

Kate had kept the dinner "age appropriate," and they all sat down to a good meal. The surprise held until Angie went to the freezer to put away the ice cream and saw all the food. Then she opened the refrigerator, closed it sharply, and went to the cabinets. Everywhere she looked there was food.

A storm broke over her face. "Where did all this come from?" she asked a bit harshly.

"We got it for you at the store," Mark said.

Angie turned to Kate. "You did this? You surely know I can't afford all this."

"Of course, I know. That's why I bought it for you."

"You shouldn't have done that," Angie sputtered.

"Sorry. I've been living in the South Pacific for the past five years. People there believe that sometimes good things show up unbidden. You just have to accept them as manna from Heaven and let it go. No harm done."

Angie huffed and tried to settle down. She took a few deep breaths. "Okay, I shouldn't have jumped all over you. Thank you for what you've done for us. But please don't do it again."

Angie's angry voice had cut through Kate, leaving her frustrated and upset. She shrugged and said bitterly. "I can't promise that if I see a need, I won't try to fill it. Since you say so, I'll try not to do it again."

***

Kate picked up her things and without a goodbye left the apartment. Angie gathered her children, both appearing stricken, and sat down with them on the sofa. She pulled them close, as she cried openly. Mark looked at her worriedly. "She was just trying to be nice, Mom."

"I know, Mark, I know."

"She was going to teach me how to do a turn at the wall," Sarina complained with disappointment.

"I'm really very sorry, Sarina," Angie sniffed, now feeling real regret. *Her defensiveness could really be in the way sometimes. Now what?*

5

From the overlook at the Hurricane Ridge Visitor's Center, the mountain peaks of the Olympic Range appeared before Kate's eyes in their magnificent splendor. Awed by the view, she uttered the only word that came to mind: "Wow."

She and Jake had driven the lengthy winding road from Port Angeles for a close-up look at the heart of the Olympic National Park. Visually surveying the peaks before them, Jake commented enthusiastically, "They aren't the tallest peaks in the Continental United States, but the Olympics form a dense ring of wild and untamed mountains—and the only large mountainous range contained within one state in the entire country. That's what I've heard, anyway."

Standing beside Kate in front of a protective concrete wall, Jake added, "The Olympics are gorgeous in the summer, but you should see the mountains topped with snow in the winter. We're a mile above sea level here, and when it rains below, lots of new snow piles up at this elevation. The parking lot will have six to eight feet of snow for months. Sometimes it doesn't melt completely until summer."

Kate shivered. She was visibly impressed. She could have stood there all day looking at those jagged peaks, the fluffy white clouds that hung out above the mountains, the green meadow around the visitor's center, and the several deer that wandered through the meadow totally unfazed by hundreds of tourists.

After a few moments, Jake asked, "Did you want to have lunch here before we begin our hike?"

"Sure," Kate agreed. "I'm famished."

They strolled into the deli, ordered sandwiches, sodas and chips then took the food back outside to one of the picnic tables scattered around the viewing deck.

"Thanks for bringing me up here," Kate mouthed between bites. "This is really special, and I would never have known about it."

"You're welcome. This is always the first place I bring guests. I think it's pretty amazing," Jake replied.

"I'm *really* beginning to understand why people move here," Kate admitted. "Having *this* in your back yard is incredible!"

***

After they finished eating, they strolled around the parking lot while Jake pointed out various walks on which park visitors could hike back into the mountains.

"These look good," Kate mentioned, "but wasn't there a path along the side of the road as we were coming up, kind of by a spring, that was more rustic than these paved walkways?"

Jake grinned. "Yeah, I know that one. Okay, we'll go back down the road a bit, park as close as we can and take that path. It's a long trail, but we don't have to do it all."

Half an hour later, they were on a rough trail that began with a steep uphill climb. Jake had worn thick work boots strong enough for the job. Kate was a bit underdressed in her regular sport shoes, and she knew her feet would complain tomorrow, along with every other muscle she hadn't recently used. However, she was anxious to keep going. The landscape was incredibly beautiful and covered with many varieties of trees, plants, and wild flowers.

After the intense uphill climb, the two women found a stopping place and paused briefly to look around and chat. Kate had been following Jake on the way up, and looking up at Jake's movements, she had noticed how much Jake physically resembled a man. Kate hadn't been aware of that around the house or in town, but on this hillside, it was apparent. The effect was enhanced by Jake's Wrangler khaki cargo shorts and her loose-fitting brown T-shirt. Kate had worn jeans, for protection, and a tank top covered by a nylon jacket that she soon repositioned around her waist. She did remember to slather herself with sunscreen, really needed at a mile-high altitude. Both she and Jake wore sunglasses and ballcaps.

Thinking about how different Jake was from other lesbians Kate had known, she eventually decided to ask her about it. *Hopefully, Jake wouldn't be offended.*

At their next rest stop, during a water break, Kate took a long pull from her bottle and then smiled at Jake. "You're very powerfully built, aren't you?"

Jake grinned. "You noticed?"

"Hard to miss, walking behind you."

"Yeah. When I was a kid, I was definitely a tomboy. I did most everything with guys while I was growing up," Jake recalled. An amused look crossed her face.

"Was that ever a problem for you? Any identity issues?" Kate hinted.

Jake shrugged. "There were times I thought I was more boy than girl. And sometimes I thought my life would have been easier if I had been born a boy. Of course, for a variety of reasons, a lot of women think that."

"Did you ever consider doing anything to change your sex?"

Jake thought for a moment before replying. "Well, yes, I did, very briefly. Physically, I felt closer to being male, and I did question it. Especially when my name, Janelle, always turned into Jake. Nobody ever called me Jan. It was almost as if the woman in me was invisible."

She turned and started up the path and, for the moment, the subject was closed. Kate followed and they went another mile or two. When they hit a flat place with a fallen tree by the side of the trail, Jake sat down. Kate joined her.

"To continue my saga," Jake continued, "I read what I could about sex change. It's a big thing now but was relatively rare when I was of the age to be concerned about it. But there *were* articles out there. I read them and thought about it a lot. I thought life might be more fun for me as a man, yet when considering the testosterone and the other hormones you have to take to bring out the male parts, I started to worry about the psychological changes that would occur. I wasn't sure I wanted that," Jake explained.

Kate looked at her questioningly. "I'm not sure I understand what you mean, exactly."

"Well," Jake offered with a little smile, "to speak very broadly, testosterone plays a role in making men aggressive and competitive. Women, whose chemistry centers on estrogen, tend to be nurturers and compromisers. Now I'm really generalizing, I know. After I read up on it, I decided I'm more comfortable with my womanly insides, even though outwardly I might appear more like a man. I concluded I wasn't really transsexual and let it go."

Kate nodded.

"Meeting Marianne really made the decision for me," Jake added. "She saw through my masculine exterior and connected with the psychological woman inside. She spoke to and loved that woman, and I came to appreciate that part of me more. She wouldn't have wanted me as a man, because she doesn't tune into that. I saw that she loved me enough not to try to change me, or feminize me. She left me enough space to exert the masculine part of myself. After her accident, I've had to be both caring woman and physically caretaking man. Now I'm being needed and wanted all the way around. I suspect I'm as happy as I've ever been or ever expect to be, despite the issues that have been brought on by Marianne's physical limitations. In short, I'm happy being me, as I am."

"Wow," Kate sighed. "That's impressive. Thanks for allowing me into that part of your life. I'll see you with new eyes now."

Jake patted Kate's thigh. "Thanks for letting me talk about it. I don't often have a chance to share anything about the deeper, more complicated me, except with Marianne, of course."

They continued upward and then across a valley, going another couple of miles, until Kate's feet started complaining and their water supply began to run short. They agreed that it was time to turn around. On the way, at resting places, Kate used her cell phone to snap pictures of the mountains. She took a couple shots of Jake, and Jake returned the favor.

By the time they returned to the truck, Kate was feeling quite satisfied by the exercise, the beautiful scenery, and the talk. During the last few years, she had been having fun and living at a superficial level. Somehow, this visit to Sequim was changing her focus. Life was richer, people were more complex, and maybe *she* was more complex than she had been allowing herself to be.

***

Kate awoke in her motel room. *What to do with the day?* She wanted to go back to the coffeehouse and see if Angie was still angry with her. Maybe it had been overhanded, trying to help and spending that much money on food and supplies. Perhaps she shouldn't have done it, yet there was a need, and she felt for the kids, living on hot dogs and baked beans. And she felt for Angie, who had been dumped and wasn't prepared to raise two kids by herself. *However, that didn't make it right, buying everything just because she had the money to do it. Maybe just dinner would have been more appropriate.* Kate had gotten carried away, and Angie's pride had been hurt, since it drew attention to how little she had and how much Kate had by comparison. She hadn't really considered Angie's feelings, and, if she were honest with herself, she didn't know Angie well enough yet to spend that kind of money on her. *Maybe if she apologized, Angie would let it pass.*

If Angie didn't forgive and forget, there was nothing else for Kate to pursue in Sequim. It was probably time to move on to Seattle. *More her world, anyway.* At least, it would have been more her world before she took off on her five-year exploration of the South Seas. *Maybe it was time to go back to that world. She was almost forty. While she was playing in the sunshine, lots of life was passing her by.*

***

After taking a shower, donning the last of her clean clothes and running the rest of her skimpy wardrobe through a coin-operated machine provided by the motel, Kate decided she was hungry. Time for a coffeehouse, somewhere. *Okay, time for The Little Red Barn.*

Worry dogged Kate's steps during the five blocks to the coffee bar. *Was Angie working today? Heck, what was her schedule? Did she work weekdays or part of the weekend too? Would she speak to Kate, if she were there? Should Kate tell her she was moving on to Seattle, leave a phone number with her, in case? It wasn't that far away, she could come back to visit, if—*

Kate pulled up short. Angie's aging sedan was in the parking lot. She *was* there. Kate took a deep breath and let it out. *Oh, my, here goes....*

Compared to the hot sunlight outdoors, the coffeehouse's interior felt delightfully cool. Kate pulled off her ballcap and sunglasses and hunted a table to claim. Then she looked up and saw Carly at the register. *No Angie.*

Kate heard someone behind her and turned. Angie stood there, dirty dishes in her hands, and smiled broadly at Kate. "Sit down. I'll bring your order. Tall latte and a breakfast sandwich, egg, bacon, and Havarti, or something different today?"

Kate was dazzled by the unexpected smile. Words failed her. "Uh, yeah, okay, tall latte and that breakfast sandwich. The one you said. Perfect."

"Coming up." Angie winked at her and passed closely by on her way to the counter. Her gorgeous hips swayed, well, perfectly.

Kate sighed. She had really learned to appreciate hips in the tropics. In the islands, women moved so nicely, so sweetly, so beautifully. Works of art. Now she had found one who had the moves, right here in the good old USA. Kate sat down—rather, she tumbled into a chair. *Whatever she had expected, it certainly wasn't this, this Angie.* Kate fumbled open her computer and stared at her email but her eyes didn't focus on a thing.

Momentarily, Angie brought Kate's latte and her sandwich and set them down on the table. Before Kate could say a word, she leaned over and whispered, "Sorry I overreacted. The kids were devastated. You had made them happy, and then I ruined it by getting upset."

Kate shook her head. "It was my fault. I should have bought something for dinner and let it go at that. I got carried away, trying to impress you. I just shouldn't have done it."

"Well, whatever." Angie straightened up. "We're all grateful, and we want you to come back and help us eat up some of that food."

Kate grinned, relieved. "Sure, anytime. Well, anytime in the next few days."

Angie's eyebrows shot up. "You're leaving?"

"Well, I stopped off here on my way to Seattle. I only planned to stay a day, and I've been here nearly a week."

Angie looked deflated. "Oh."

Kate put a hand on her arm. "Nothing's set in concrete. I'd love to do dinner with you and the kids and have a chance to know all of you better."

Angie looked a bit dubious yet said, "Okay, me, too."

Angie glanced at Carly, who was giving her signs that she should complete her tasks.

"When do you want me to come?"

"How about tonight?" Angie asked as she backed away.

"Tonight's good."

"Six o'clock?"

"I'll be there."

Angie nodded and returned to work. Kate could see Carly saying something privately to her, but Angie waved her off and then became busy with other customers.

Now, Kate wondered to herself, *what could she do until 6 p.m.?*

6

The following day, Kate joined Jake and Marianne for the evening meal. After consuming a plate piled high with homemade fish and chips, the three women tackled slices of watermelon. Kate loved the fresh flavor of ripe fruit, and the melon was more heaven to her than a fancy, calorie-rich dessert.

Dining with the couple was becoming a comfortable habit for Kate. She found Jake's complexity fascinating, and she had known Marianne for so long that there was an ease between them allowing for interesting, even confrontational discussion.

While they were eating, Marianne seemed to be studying Kate, and Kate guessed that there was something on her mind. After downing the last bite of her melon, Marianne put aside her fork and began to speak. "Since you showed up last week I've been remembering things about our shared past," she offered, giving Kate a warm smile.

Kate grinned. "I suspect so. There's nothing like a surprise visit to stir up old memories."

Marianne nodded. "I've been mentally trying to put a timeline together. I graduated from the MBA program about the time you'd have been starting your junior year, right?"

Kate glanced upward for a moment and then grinned. "Yeah, that's about right."

"So, when I moved away, you were heavy into the swimming program and being groomed for the Olympics. I don't remember your major now—"

"Econ. I took tons of arts and music, but my major was econ. It came easily to me because of my dad's businesses. I'd listened to conversations about buying, selling and investments from the cradle. Although I think I would have enjoyed psychology or even English lit, the econ came easily for me. It was better to pick that, with my long hours in the pool, instead of opting for a subject I knew less about and would have to research more," Kate explained.

Marianne considered her words then nodded. "Makes practical sense, I guess. Then your mother became ill at the beginning of your junior year, and passed?

A frown crossed Kate's face. It was still hard to talk about that year. "Yes," she said, her voice suddenly strained. "Cancer. It took her fast and hard. She was gone almost before we had a diagnosis."

Marianne uttered a deep sigh. "Sometimes our lives can change in an instant."

Nodding, Kate wondered if Marianne was referring to her auto accident.

"So, then you dropped swimming and went into marketing?" Marianne's voice lifted into a question mark.

Kate paused a moment, swallowing a big lump that had suddenly formed in her throat. She could feel Jake and Marianne both looking at her intently. "Mom had always been at the pool."

"I remember her there," Marianne recalled. "Sometimes, I used to sit beside her and we'd talk."

Kate sighed and nodded. "When she was gone, I went into shock. I couldn't access my feelings or my memories of her. All I could feel was her absence, a big hole in my life. And my drive to swim just disappeared. I'd look up into the stands, where she always had sat, and she wouldn't be there. I would hurt so terribly that my timing was off, my stroke was off, my desire disappeared. The coach and I talked and agreed that I should take time off to grieve. We both hoped I would come back, but it never happened. I couldn't shake the connection. Not knowing what to do, I listened to a counselor who suggested that I still major in econ, add other subjects that would strengthen my business focus, and take fewer liberal arts classes. While I still took another psych class or two, most of my junior and senior year were filled with business courses."

"Did that help?" Marianne asked kindly.

"Yes, and no. Remember, as an only child, I was the apple of both of my parents' eyes. Mom couldn't give birth again, and my dad didn't get his dreamed-of son. I always wanted not only to be smart but also strong and athletic to please him. Then Mom responded to my swimming, and I was pleasing her as well. When I didn't have Mom any longer, I tried to please Dad. His whole life revolved around business deals, hence the move to New York City and ten years in marketing and promotions."

"And how did you end up leaving there and going to the South Pacific?"

Kate took a couple of deep breaths. "Well, one day my father suddenly dropped dead of a massive heart attack."

Marianne gasped. "How awful."

Kate blanched. "I struggled terribly with my mom's death, and I found it even harder to lose Dad. To lose them both. Most people I know have a least one of their parents a lot longer than I did."

Jake nodded. "That's quite a loss."

Marianne raised an eyebrow. "And your dad's death sent you halfway around the world?"

Kate frowned. "Being totally alone was hard. Worse was the reality that I had no one else to please. Problem was, now I missed both my parents, and everything reminded me of them. I needed a new goal, one for myself, only I didn't know what. I couldn't stand going home to an empty estate, so I sold the property. I inherited a huge trust fund, and I didn't *need* to work for a living. To be productive, I needed to have a reason to work. I couldn't find one. With Dad gone, I admitted to myself that I didn't really like the career I was pursuing and couldn't see devoting the rest of my life to it."

Jake spoke up. "So, you left the country to find someplace away from everything to figure out what you wanted for yourself?"

Kate nodded. "Pretty much that's it. I thought I'd find something that had meaning, something that I could devote myself to. Thus far, it hasn't happened. I tried Australia and New Zealand and then moved on to smaller locales, tropical islands especially. I've had some girlfriends, casual and sweet romances. I've lived on the beach, in a hammock, in bamboo houses. I thought if I made life simple, got out of the rat race, I could see things more clearly. All that happened was that I found I could do absolutely nothing. I could live cheaply, like many of the natives. I swam in the surf. I lay in the sun on the beach and tanned and read books. Since I didn't need money, I just had fun."

A frown crossed Marianne's face and she looked at Kate questioningly. "And that was enough for you?"

Kate shrugged a bit uncomfortably. "Maybe yes, maybe no. I just know that I finally experienced a yen to come back to the US. I wasn't even conscious of wanting that until I landed almost by accident in Honolulu where I met Steve Gutierrez, and he was sailing to Seattle. Suddenly, I wanted to go along with him. I don't know what it all means yet, but here I am."

Jake grinned. "And you've already found a girlfriend."

Kate studied her for a moment. "Maybe. I don't know. We'll see how it goes."

"Complicated, huh?"

"Yep, that's for sure."

Jake stood up. "I don't want to be a spoilsport, but the Mariners have a game starting. They're at home and tied for first place, and I'd like to see it, if you don't mind."

Marianne looked at Kate. "You like baseball?"

"It's okay. Having been away from the sports hubbub, it's not really high on my priority list," Kate admitted.

"How about coming out back with me then, while Jake watches her show."

"Shouldn't we clean up the dishes? I can help."

"Never mind. Jake will do it later. Just follow me, and bring our drinks."

Marianne wheeled herself to the side door, which opened easily with a push of her hand, and glided down the ramp to the driveway. Kate followed, carrying two glasses of ice tea and admiring the competent way Marianne maneuvered herself around.

In the back yard, there was a glider swing with an awning over it and small side tables at both ends. Marianne motioned Kate to sit in the swing. As soon as Kate was seated and had put their drinks on a table, Marianne positioned her chair across from her.

"Jake sometimes picks me up and we sit in the swing together," Marianne said, a bit of blush in her cheeks, "but I'm fine this way. We can talk, and there's a breeze that keeps it from being too hot—a real advantage, being this close to the Strait and with only a prairie between here and the water. We also have a little bug protector that keeps the mosquitoes away. We don't see a lot of them, just during the evenings in August."

Kate studied a canister hanging from a pole and nodded.

"Actually, Kate," Marianne said, after taking a sip of tea and setting the glass back down, "I've been wanting a chance to speak with you alone ever since you arrived. There's something I want to say to you, and I'll only say it once. If I start to nag too much, I'll drive you away, and I don't want that. Having seen you as a dedicated, committed college student with a great future ahead, I find it hard to see you now as a kind of lost, almost forty-year old woman who is wandering the face of the earth."

Kate colored slightly with embarrassment. "It must be a little bit of a shock," she allowed.

"I might not feel it as strongly if I hadn't had my own freedom abruptly taken away from me. There is much I miss and wish I hadn't lost. Not having the ability to walk—and realizing how iffy my future is—makes it very important to me to do what I can with every day that I have. Seeing you rudderless, while healthy, bright, and sitting on a fortune, does makes me a little uncomfortable."

"I don't need the money, at least not now."

"I'm not saying you should go back to New York, or live in a fancy house, drive a foreign luxury car or have your own airplane. I don't care if you ever have those material things. Jake and I could have those too, but we chose not. At the same time, when there are many needs in the world, to just sit on money is irresponsible."

Kate laughed. "I tried to buy Angie some groceries, and she practically threw me out of her apartment."

Marianne chuckled. "Well, maybe you need to learn some finesse about your charitable acts. That's something Americans have been accused of lacking for many, many years. We either pretend a need isn't there, or we throw money at it. You studied psychology. It takes a little understanding to know when and where and how to gift money and make the gesture appropriate to what the receiver really needs and can handle."

Kate nodded. "Yeah. I just saw that her cupboards were empty, and the kids were living on mostly junk food. I bought all these supplies so they could eat healthy. I guess she felt that I was calling attention to her difficulty in providing for her children. That didn't make her feel good, and she got defensive and angry with me."

Marianne nodded and continued, "Anyway, to return to my point, life is passing you by, Kate. Forgive me for lecturing you, but it's time to grow up. It's time to recognize a bigger reality beyond just what you feel at the moment. Do you understand what I mean?"

"Yeah, I think so. My last five years have been a little self-indulgent. I realize that. I just lost my rudder when my dad died and I've been drifting ever since."

Marianne smiled. "Welcome back, kiddo."

Kate grinned. "Thanks. It'll take some time, but I'll figure out something meaningful to do, worth doing. And I'll do it."

Marianne shifted in her wheelchair and raised an eyebrow. "Just don't wait until it's too late."

7

Jake maneuvered her Toyota truck around twists and turns in the road while Kate focused on all the evergreens, the white clouds dotting a sun-drenched blue sky, scattered houses on both sides of the road—some fancy, some simple—and brief glimpses of Sequim Bay to her left. At one point she caught sight of sailboat masts in the marina on the opposite shore.

Kate tried to focus her mind on why they were here on East Sequim Bay Road. Jake had told her about The Colony, a private RV-park owned, operated, and inhabited by lesbians. Although a large group of lesbians living together was a strange concept to Kate, she nevertheless looked forward to checking it out. When Jake offered to show The Colony to her, she jumped at the chance for a guided tour.

***

The name had come up at dinner the night before, and Jake had given some history. "A couple of lesbians visited Sequim maybe twenty years ago because one of them, Marilyn Bothell, had inherited from her late grandfather considerable acreage overlooking Sequim Bay. She wasn't decided about what to do with the property, and she brought her partner along so they could both take a look."

After getting a nod of understanding from Kate, Jake continued her story. "At the time, there was quite a bit of undeveloped land on east shore of the bay that is some distance from Sequim. When they saw the acreage, Marilyn quickly envisioned the possibilities. Her partner agreed and they incorporated. They had lots and streets laid out, named the place The Colony, or TC, as it is often called, and invited lesbians they both knew to visit. Before long, the place began growing. A large group of lesbians had developed land in Arizona as a winter watering-hole, but Arizona was too hot for most of them in the summer, and TC proved a perfect place to escape the heat. There is water access, just inside the protective spit that separates Sequim Bay from the Strait. There are gorgeous views from the land that slopes downward toward the water, including the mountains to the south and the New Dungeness lighthouse to the north. Now, several years later, TC is almost fully developed."

***

At the end of the winding road, Jake pulled the dark green Toyota in front of a gate and entered a code into a box. The gate swung open. As they entered, Kate noticed a stone and brick wall snaking around the perimeter that made TC appear very private.

Kate's first reaction was that the property had a hodge-podge look. Some structures provided permanent housing, what Jake termed "park models." Others were basically trailers settled permanently by added skirting and porches. Some were RVs, trailers, and fifth-wheel campers, just sitting on the lots with trucks and SUVs stationed nearby. A few lots were empty.

As they drove slowly up and down the narrow gravel streets, Kate began to realize that the purpose was flexibility. Some residents lived there permanently while some drove back and forth from the Olympic Peninsula to Arizona or other wintering places. Some were summer renters or short-term visitors. TC, while private, was open to a variety of women with differing interests.

Jake stopped in front of an empty lot on the last street near the shoreline. Kate noticed a dock at the end of the property and figured that some of the women must have kayaks, dinghies, sailboats or other watercraft that they could launch from the dock and the ramp beside it.

"This is our lot," Jake explained. "We rent it out to short-term visitors now. We used to stay here ourselves in our own fifth wheel, before Marianne's accident. Now we come out occasionally, but she's much more comfortable in the house, which we've arranged for her needs. We put the camper in storage, trying to decide whether to sell it or what. Now that you are here, I'd be glad to bring it out and set it up for you on the lot. It offers dining for four people, decent lounging in the living room, a small but functional kitchen and bath, and a queen-sized bed that's quite comfortable. The sofa opens into a bed that will sleep another two people. What I'm thinking, Kate, is that you can feel free to stay out here for as long as you want. This location will be a lot more cozy than a motel room, and you can bring Angie and the kids here for dinner or to spend the night. It will allow you to host her, or them, and have a chance to get acquainted. You'll also have an opportunity to meet some of the local lesbians and get a better idea of what brought them here. I know this world is very different from Ithaca, where you grew up, or New York City, or even the South Pacific."

Kate nodded and looked around thoughtfully. She had no idea how long she would stay. TC was a drive from Sequim—maybe twenty minutes or so—which would have consequences in terms of Angie and the kids. On the other hand, it had some advantages, as Jake had suggested.

"What do you want for rent?"

Jake grinned. "A lot less than a motel room," she quipped. "Actually, there are monthly fees on the lot that cover water, septic, electricity, and communications like TV and Wi-Fi. If you'd cover that while you're here and keep the unit cleaned up, I wouldn't ask for any more."

Kate considered the idea for a moment then nodded. "Okay, I think I would like to experience this lifestyle. I don't know how long I'll be here, but it would be a treat to try this, if you'll show me how to care for your fifth wheel."

Jake smiled. "No problem. I'll set it up and write down for you everything that needs to be done. It's not much as long as it's parked and connected to electricity and a water/sewer system. Is tomorrow okay?"

"Sure. As soon as I can move in, I'll check out of the motel."

Before they left, a woman accompanied by a small terrier walked up. In addition to large sunglasses, she was sporting colorful flowered Bermuda shorts, a print-design tank top, sandals, and a wide-brimmed floppy hat. Her gray hair sticking out from under the hat was wiry and very butch. "Hi," she said to Kate, "I don't mean to intrude, but are you moving in here?"

Kate responded, "Sort of," as Jake chuckled.

"Hi, Sid," Jake said and leaned down to fondle the ears of the terrier. "Hello, Fluffy. Is your mama treating you good?"

Jake looked up at Sid. "We're putting our RV in here tomorrow to allow our friend here, Kate Brighton, to stay for a little while. Maybe you'll help her meet some of the women?"

Sid grinned. "Oh, sure, I'll introduce you all around. There's a picnic this Sunday. If you're here, you can meet a lot of us all at once."

"That sounds like fun," Kate responded with a friendly smile. *She had no idea if she would really want to do that, yet it was good to be pleasant.*

"Great. See you tomorrow."

After Sid and her dog moved away, Jake turned to Kate and said quietly. "She's the biggest gossip in TC. Anything you do or say will be all over the park in minutes. She's not a bad soul, doesn't mean any harm, she just needs to have something to share. New people provide that for her."

Kate smiled. "Thanks for the info, and maybe the warning. I'll try to be careful what I give her to talk about."

Jake laughed. "She's also on the social committee. She'll tell you about everything that's going on."

Kate frowned. "So, this is kind of a retirement lifestyle?"

Jake smirked. "Look who's talking. Isn't that what you've been doing the last five years?"

Kate broke into a grin. "Okay, okay, point well taken. Maybe this will be a wake-up call for me. Do I want to live like I am forty or seventy?"

Jake shrugged. "Your choice."

***

Back in Sequim, Kate said goodbye and thanked Jake for all she and Marianne were doing for her. *This rural experience was providing a whole new wrinkle to her life.* Kate climbed into the Chevy and drove across town straight to The Little Red Barn, being anxious to see Angie. It had been a couple of days since she was in the coffeehouse.

Angie lit up like a Christmas tree when Kate walked through the doorway. She pointed at an empty table and leaned in close as Kate slid into a seat. "I was afraid you had decided to leave. I'm really glad to see you."

Kate smiled. "I wouldn't go without telling you first and saying goodbye. Right now, I'm hungry."

"The regular?"

"Sure. You've got me down, haven't you?"

Angie smiled. "Well, in most things no. In breakfast preferences, I think I have it."

Kate watched her hips sway as Angie moved to the counter, and she studied her long auburn braid. *Wouldn't it be great to undo all of that shining hair and just run her fingers through it?* She imagined all those gorgeous locks blowing freely in the breeze and realized that it reminded her of some of her favorite women in the South Pacific. She heaved a big sigh, shivered with anticipatory delight, and then opened her computer.

When Angie brought her food, Kate asked directly, "When can we talk for a bit?"

Angie sighed. "Not a good day."

Kate looked disappointed but quickly recovered. "Okay, tomorrow I'm moving into a trailer out at TC. Do you know what that is?"

"Sure, who doesn't? That's the lesbian compound out on East Sequim Bay Road."

"Some friends of mine staked me to a place there, and that's going to extend my stay here. After I'm settled, would you like to bring the kids out there to look around and have dinner?"

Angie grinned. "Cool. I've never been. Although it's rumored to be a bunch of crusty old women in trailers, I'd prefer to decide for myself. And if you're cooking, I'd sure like to come. Maybe then we'll have a chance to talk a bit."

***

Kate stood watching attentively as Jake maneuvered the fifth wheel into position, disconnected the truck, lowered levelers, and tied onto electricity, water, and waste. Kate didn't expect ever to own such a large movable living space, but she did want to understand how it all worked. If she was going to stay at TC for any length of time, who knew what might happen and whether Jake would be around to fix things that might go wrong.

As Kate observed Jake's every move, a voice, high pitched and musical, unexpectedly said, "Hello, there! You're back again."

Turning, Kate nearly bumped into Sid and her terrier. "Sorry," she apologized.

"No problem." Sid gave her a big smile. "We've all been waiting for your arrival."

Kate lifted an eyebrow and glanced around at the surrounding RVs and park models, expecting to see faces at every window looking her over. "Oh," she said, not knowing what else to add.

"I'm out walking my dog. I don't want to bother you. Just wanted to say hello."

Sid waved and moved on up the street as Kate turned her attention back to Jake, who had finished the connections and was opening up the RV to check that everything was working. Kate followed her inside as she started explaining things. Electrical switches, the cable for the TV, the Wi-Fi codes for her computer.

The fifth wheel was modern and very well appointed. Kate was impressed. Leather, real wood instead of plastic trim, stainless steel kitchen appliances. At first, the unit seemed to be narrow. After Jake opened the slide-outs, it became much more spacious.

Jake grinned at her look of amazement. "If you don't need a lot of square footage, you really can live in one of these things. We just traveled for short periods, but lots of folks use them full time."

Kate grinned. "All I've got is one duffle bag to my name. And a computer. I can hang out just about anywhere. This is a real luxury for me." Having mentioned her gear, Kate climbed down the steps and retrieved her duffle bag and computer from Jake's truck. She returned and quipped, "Now I'm moved in."

Jake gave her a hug. "Welcome to TC."

"Thanks. I hope I'm not overwhelmed by all these women, like that Sid."

Jake smiled. "Well, it's just the same as any neighborhood. There are happy couples here, unhappy couples, happy and unhappy singles, depressives, drinkers, recluses, social types, troublemakers. More than one hundred lots, with as many living situations. You'll figure it out."

"Are most of them retirees? Older women?"

Jake thought a minute. "It's summer, meaning there are several short-time visitors renting spaces. They are often younger, still employed, and on vacation. Once the summer is over, most of those will disappear, and you'll have the year-round gals, made up of a small group of retirees, and the summer owners, mostly retired, who pick up by the first of November and head to Arizona or elsewhere, returning around the first of May the following year. They are of all ages, yet mostly older women."

Kate sighed. "I don't know why I'm asking you all of this. I don't expect to be here long, and I'm really wanting to get to know Angie, not all these older women."

Jake touched her shoulder. "They can't make you do or be anything you don't want to be. Just say you're busy. There might be one or two that will bug you a bit, but you don't have to entertain their fantasies. You're like new meat, you know, and tasty looking."

Kate laughed. "Okay, I'll ride back to town with you and pick up my car. I have the code for the gate, and I should be okay on my own. Groceries, I guess, will be first on the list."

During the ride back into Sequim, Kate was thoughtful. She hoped that Marianne and Jake's generosity in letting her use their vacation home was really in her own best interest. Each time she went to town, it would be at least a twenty-minute drive. At the motel, she had been right around the corner from everything. And all those lesbian women? She didn't know if that would work for her but, she reminded herself, she was only going to be here a short time. The RV would be less expensive by far and a better place to bring Angie and the kids. Although money wasn't an issue for her, the motel wasn't good for entertaining, and she assumed that short-term rentals would not be easy to find. So, she was lucky. She'd give this a try.

8

Mark reached up to knock on the door and then returned his hand to the safety of Angie's grip. In the other hand, he carefully held a bottle of red wine tucked against his chest. Sarina's hand grasped her mother's as well. Knowing that Kate was inside, Angie's eyes were focused on the door, and her heart was pounding. Mark glanced around, as did Sarina. A couple of folding camp chairs had been placed before an outdoor barbeque from which emanated enticing smells of grilling meat. Sarina's eyes opened wide, and she looked at Mark. He smiled at her and smacked his lips.

Kate pulled the door wide open. "Hello! Come on in." She motioned them to enter the RV. "Just watch your step as you come up. Can be tricky."

When the three guests were inside the air-conditioned space, Mark presented the wine to Kate.

"Oh, thanks, but you didn't need to do this."

"Mom says we can't go to dinner without bringing something. She thought you might like this."

"Pinot noir," Kate read from the label. "Oh, that's a great one."

"It's from a local winery," Angie added. "Thought we could support them and have you sample some of Washington's finest. That is, if you drink wine?"

"Sure, I do." Kate chuckled. "Well, sit down and make yourselves at home."

The kids plopped down on the edge of the sofa, as their wide eyes wandered everywhere, taking in a strange world they had never experienced. Angie glanced around the room for a second, too. "This is pretty fancy. I thought you were renting some old RV."

Kate grinned at her sarcasm. "Surprising, huh? It belongs to friends, and they are letting me use it," she explained. "Feel free to look around, all of you. I just about have dinner ready."

"Are you sure I can't help?"

"Nope. Got it. Just make yourself comfortable."

Angie peeped into the small yet complete bathroom and examined the tightly packed bedroom with its queen-sized bed, built in closets, and additional storage under the bed. As she looked, she heard music from a stereo system. A shiver went down her spine, not just from the air conditioning but also from a sense of excitement as she grasped that people *really* owned RVs like this.

***

Angie and the kids were seated at the small table, as Kate passed plates to them, each with a sizzling steak and a hot baked potato. She then sat down with her own plate and a big salad bowl. "I put butter, salad dressing, salt and pepper on the table. If there's anything else you need, hopefully I have it. I just stocked up a little at the grocery. I might not have gotten everything." She laughed.

Mark and Sarina looked as if their mouths were watering. "Go ahead, eat," Kate suggested. The two kids dug into their food as if they had never had a meal before.

Angie watched them and Kate, who had opened the wine and poured a glass for Angie and herself. The kids had been given a cola.

"This is delicious," Angie said, as she tasted her first bite of steak. "You found a tender cut of beef."

"Porterhouse, I think," Kate shrugged. "I looked at the filets but decided maybe to save those for some special occasion." She winked at Angie.

Dessert included sliced fresh peaches and whipped cream with a chocolate chip cookie on the side. The kids were delighted.

***

When they had finished eating and put everything away, Kate turned on the large television and seated Mark and Sarina before the Disney Channel. The flat-screen TV held their attention, and they were happy. "Your mom and I are going outside to talk a little," Kate told them, and they both nodded, already hooked on an animated movie.

Kate led Angie outside, while carrying the rest of the wine and two glasses, and they sat before the dying heat of the grill. A refreshing evening breeze wafted toward them from Sequim Bay. The sun was just about to dip behind evergreens and the Olympics to the west.

"This is very nice," Angie said. "For all of us. A lovely meal, a beautiful spot outdoors in nature—something we don't have a chance to experience very often. You could easily spoil Mark and Sarina, and me, too."

Kate smiled. "It's very hard to find an opportunity to talk with you. I'd do anything to create a safe place where we can get to know each other. This isn't much, but it's heaven for me right now."

Angie blushed.

Kate took a sip of wine and watched Angie for a moment. "You're beautiful, you know. I can't take my eyes off you."

Angie's cheeks reddened further. "I'm not accustomed to having attention like this," she admitted. "And, you're an eyeful yourself."

"Oh, shoot. I'm almost forty, and I'm way too old for you. Yet I can't help myself. I'd give anything to spend time with you, alone."

"Kate, wait a minute. If I thought you were too old, I wouldn't be sitting here with you. I may seem desperate and, financially, I'm strapped, but I have too many responsibilities to play games. Age is not just chronology. I'm younger than you by several years, but I would guess that I'm older than you in providing for children and having them to consider as well as myself. I don't think you've experienced that, right?"

Kate frowned. "Not that, no, not in the way you mean it. Yet losing both my parents early aged me in another way. You've lost your parents, too, just not by death. And maybe being shunned is even worse. Aside from that, you're right that my life is very easy compared to yours. I can do and buy what I want when I want. I'm spoiled that way. I can't deny it."

Angie looked at her squarely. “Well, understand this from the beginning. I won’t be pushed around. My husband and two families have rejected me. If I want to be involved, I will. If I don’t, I won’t. Don’t think, just because you have money, that I’m a little girl you can manipulate. I’m here this evening because I find you fascinating—and not just because you’re rich. That’s nice. It’s just not everything.”

Kate sipped her wine and visibly relaxed. “I’m glad you said that. It’s a relief. I wouldn’t want to push you around, yet I’m afraid of doing just that. I’m happy that you can stand up for yourself.”

Angie, too, settled back into her chair. “Well, let’s leave money and age and all that stuff out of this. Of course, we can’t ignore Mark and Sarina. Otherwise, let’s just be two interesting women trying to learn whether or not we have something to offer each other.”

Kate watched Angie in the glow of the setting sun. “I want to kiss you. Maybe lots more than that.”

Angie smiled. “That’s a lovely thought. Just not here, not now. We’ll have to plan for that.”

***

Kate lay in bed that night. Sleep eluded her. She was excited, more excited than she had been for a long time. The evening had been wonderful. Having Angie here was very sweet and enticing. And the kids, she really liked them. She also knew that there would be no Angie without them as well; at the same time, she had to separate Angie out from them in order to have intimate moments with her. She just couldn’t jump her bones, lovely bones though they were, on impulse. It would take patience, organization and a support system—something that at the moment she didn’t have.

***

Kate had stewed most of the night about how to find the needed support so that she and Angie could be alone. Angie had so many problems to solve on a daily basis that Kate felt she should find someone to care for Mark and Sarina for an overnight, or even better, a weekend. She didn't know Angie's neighbors or the women at TC. The only place she had to go was to Jake and Marianne. She hated to bother them with this problem, but she needed to talk to someone.

She found Jake out in the garage, putting away tools. "Hey," Jake said when Kate walked up. "You have good timing. I fixed some really delicious soup for lunch, and it's just about time to eat. Marianne has a noon break today. Will you join us?"

Kate smiled. *Good food always relaxed the nerves.*

Inside the house, Jake spooned up three bowls of soup. "I make this rich soup with lots of fresh vegetables plus tortilla chips and seasonings thrown in. It's my own, with no recipe. Marianne likes it, and it's good for her digestive system, with the chair and all."

Kate nodded, although she could only guess at all the things Marianne had to endure. The soup smelled delicious. This morning was cooler than it had been since her arrival. Soup was perfect. She commented on that.

"Yep, officially, right now is our hot time, and yet as Labor Day approaches and school begins, we start to have touches of fall. By the middle of September, we could be into the rainy season. It might become chilly."

Jake motioned Kate to sit and she slipped into a seat. Just as she did so, Marianne wheeled herself out of the office. "Hey, good to see you. How are you surviving out at TC?"

"Great," Kate said. "I love the RV. It's comfortable, and the bed sure beats a V-berth on a sailboat! I stocked up on food, and I've already had Angie and the kids out for dinner. They all loved it. The kids really got into the big TV, and Angie and I sat outside and talked."

Marianne smiled. "That will get the gossips going."

Kate frowned. "What do you mean?"

"You mean the women haven't crawled all over you yet? With all due respect, if you put a group of women together, they find lots to talk about. If you sat outside with Angie, there must have been a dozen eyes watching you from behind curtains and blinds."

Kate grinned. “Well, one woman, Sid, has been around a several times, with her little dog, but I haven’t been out much to meet many people. Sid’s okay, just lonely I suspect, and curious.”

“I’m glad they didn’t bother you and Angie. Just remember that the average age out there is somewhere between sixty and eighty-five, and many of the women no longer have partners. Anyone new in the resort makes good conversation while they are playing poker or dominoes.”

“Well, I’m not building my life around TC. It was just kind of you to let me use your trailer. Much more comfortable than a motel room. And it worked very well to entertain Angie and her kids.”

There was a moment of silence as they all lifted spoons and downed their bowls of soup. Jake had put some crackers on the table along with glasses of ice tea, and for a little while they quietly focused on eating.

Finally, Marianne asked, “So, how is it going with Angie?”

Kate took a deep breath. “I find her really fascinating. She’s beautiful, feisty and determined. She’s young yet old for her age, maybe because of the responsibility of two kids as a single parent.”

Jake asked, “You like the kids?”

Kate nodded. “Very much. They are both sweet and undemanding. If you give them a treat—even just watching a special TV channel—they are very happy, and they don’t complain about not having all the things they could want. Yet they do have goals and ambitions, like Mark wanting to be on a baseball team, and Sarina dreaming of become a great swimmer.”

Marianne asked, “Can Angie give them the things they want?”

Kate shook her head. “I’m afraid she’s going to need a lot more help and support than she’s getting right now. Her parents have basically written her off.”

Marianne studied Kate. “So, what are *you* needing?”

"A chance to have a weekend with Angie. Maybe go on a drive to the ocean, have some fun, talk and get to know each other."

Marianne's eyebrows shot up. "Maybe some sack time, huh?"

Kate's face colored. "Well, we're both attracted to each other. We've admitted it. But when she isn't working, she's with the kids, and I know that's not a good way to start anything. We need a little privacy."

Marianne and Jake looked at each other. Jake gave a slight shrug.

"Well," Marianne said, after taking a deep breath, "I don't know for sure what we can do to help you. It's clear you need someone to take the kids for a weekend, and that could become a big job on a repeated basis, for a while anyway. I don't know if we can take that on or not. What we should do, I think, is have them here for dinner. It's not the only way, but it's what we can do, with me in this chair. Jake's a good cook, as you know, and she can whip up something the kids will like. We can all spend an evening talking and getting to know one another. After that, if we feel comfortable—all of us with each other—then maybe we could suggest that the kids come and stay with us for a couple of days. Angie would never leave them, I'm sure, if she didn't feel she knew us and that they were safe and would be well cared for. Then you could have your weekend of fun and, well, more fun."

She winked at Kate. Jake put a hand to her face and chuckled behind it.

Kate felt a wave of relief. "That would be incredible," she said to Marianne. "I was really stuck for how to create space for us."

"Well, no promises beyond dinner. We'll see how it goes."

"Understood."

9

Kate had come to The Little Red Barn to have breakfast and see Angie.

When Angie brought her order to the table, Kate tried to slip in some enticing information. “I may have some help for us in having time together. I have friends here. That’s why I stopped in Sequim in the first place. Marianne and Jake. They live on Seventh Avenue, up from the Safeway. They’re nice people.”

“Lesbians?”

Kate couldn’t help but grin. “Angie, I’m a lesbian. Who do you expect my friends would be?”

“Okay, I know. Just understand that I haven’t spent a lot of time in that world, and when I have, it’s been very secret. The Colony is one thing. It’s out there somewhere. However, Seventh Avenue is neighborhood, near the school and their club. I have to digest all of this.”

Noticing that the coffeehouse was rather quiet, Kate grabbed the opportunity to explain. “I met Marianne in college. She was a graduate student when I was an undergrad. She watched swimming practices along with my mom. I haven’t seen her in a long time. I didn’t know she had had an auto accident and is confined to a wheelchair. Her partner, Jake, is a good and sensitive woman who has built her life around caring for Marianne. She’s sweet and very dedicated.”

Angie sighed. “Okay, I’m probably over-reacting. They do sound interesting. How do they play into this private-time scenario of yours?”

“They want us to come to dinner and spend an evening. Because of Marianne’s limitations, that’s the easiest way for them to entertain us. If we get along okay, then they may offer to take the kids for a weekend, and we can go to the coast or do something fun with each other.”

Angie studied Kate’s face for a moment. “I’ve got to get back to work. When are we supposed to do this?”

“You set the date that works for you, and I’ll propose that to them. I’m sure they’ll work it out.”

Angie shrugged. "When I get home tonight, I'll look at the calendar for the kids, the Boys & Girls Club, signing up for school, etc., etc. Then I'll pick an evening I think will work. Okay?"

Kate smiled, relieved. "Yes, perfect."

***

Jake decided that Mark and Sarina might be more comfortable with an informal dinner. She heated up the backyard grill, pulled up some chairs by the swing, added a folding table that they could all sit around, and used paper plates and utensils. Spills wouldn't hurt, and nothing could get broken.

Marianne had wheeled herself around to show Angie and the kids the house. None of them had spent time inside a manufactured home, but Angie allowed that it was a nice place. The kids' eyes opened wide at all the medical aids in Marianne's bedroom.

At first, both Mark and Sarina seemed a little hesitant around Marianne. She took a moment to explain her wheelchair and how it worked. Then she allowed each one to sit on her lap while she drove them around the living room. Soon they were laughing and giggling, and Marianne had two new friends. Angie looked pleased with Marianne's comfort level around her children.

They all talked their way through a dinner of sizzling hamburgers, French fries, chips, and a choice of cookies or fresh strawberries for dessert. Sarina and Mark both chose milk when Jake offered it or colas. Angie smiled gratefully, both at Jake for the offer and to the kids for making the better choice.

When the meal was done, they continued to sit outside as the daytime heat melted away. Sconces kept the mosquitos from destroying their fun.

Jake asked some questions of the kids. To Sarina, "I hear from Kate that you are a budding swimmer."

Sarina blushed. "She's been helping me. I'm not very good yet, but I want to learn."

Kate grinned and winked at Jake. “Sarina’s been watching some old Esther Williams movies on TV. I think that’s her inspiration.”

Sarina frowned. “She was. I like watching Kate swim even better. She’s a good diver, too.”

Marianne winked at Kate. “Too bad you gave up competitive swimming. Look at all the fans you could have.”

Kate blushed. “Well, I’m putting my skills to good use with Sarina, so it’s not a waste.”

Jake focused on Mark. “Now we know what Sarina loves. What about you?”

“I want to be a ballplayer. Kate’s been helping me, too.”

Jake thought for a moment. “When do they sign up for Little League? Maybe you could join that and have a chance to play on a team.”

Angie started to say something, but Kate cut her off. “Great idea, Jake. I’ll check it out for Angie and see what needs to be done to get Mark enrolled.”

***

When they had returned to Angie’s apartment, while Mark and Sarina were getting ready for bed, Angie pulled Kate aside. “I wish you wouldn’t hold out so many hopes for them. I can’t afford uniforms and equipment. Swimming is one thing because we have a pool here, and she has access. Little League is expensive. Mark has to live within the limits of my income.”

“Angie, I know this is hard for you, and it feels complicated. Let me step in and do a few little things that Zack would have provided if he hadn’t walked out on you. The kids shouldn’t have to suffer because of his failures as a father.”

“When you say these things, you’re talking about commitment. Are you saying that you plan on staying here permanently?”

Kate shrugged. “I haven’t thought that far ahead. Can’t you just let go and see how things play out?”

Angie pulled up to her full height. “I’ve learned to live with disappointment. But you can’t promise things to kids and then let them down.”

"Who's let them down, besides Zack and your family?"
"You speak double-talk, you know that?"

***

Despite her fears and misgivings, Angie looked forward to a weekend with Kate. Marianne and Jake had offered to keep the kids, and she felt confident that Sarina and Mark would have a good time with them.

She had not been alone with Kate since they met. It was scary to think of two whole days and one night with her. In her heart of hearts, she knew that if things didn't go well, she could, and would, call it off, regardless. Kate was a big turn-on for Angie, and she tingled every time she allowed herself to think about being with her alone and touching each other. She was also very scared. They were very different in every way. This could be a big mistake, allowing herself to feel emotionally drawn to someone like Kate. The physical attraction she couldn't control. *Desire was or it wasn't, and in this case, it definitely was.*

***

Sarina and Mark were delighted about staying with Marianne and Jake. Each carried a backpack with needed personal items, and they excitedly greeted both the women at their front door. Angie hugged the kids tightly, as Kate stood behind smiling to herself and giving a wink to Jake. Then the two climbed into Kate's rental Chevy, waved goodbye to the foursome on the front steps, and pulled away from the curb.

Although Kate had no problem finding her way to the entrance of Highway 101 headed west, as soon as she was on the roadway, she said to Angie, "I kind of know where I'm going, but I'm counting on you to point out the sites since you've always lived here."

Angie laughed. "I'm really good at Sequim and the Dungeness Valley. Everything else, well, it's been years since I've seen any of it. And my memories are covered over by a veil of tears."

Kate grinned. "You'll remember. I'm sure you will."

***

Traffic was heavy, with numerous RVs and trailered boats traveling west and more of the same returning east. Kate was a little surprised, and Angie explained. “This is the last weekend of August. Kids around here start to school next week or just after Labor Day. This is about the last weekend for family vacations, and the Olympic Peninsula is a popular place for camping and hiking. Did you know that the Olympic National Park is the second most visited national park in the US?”

Kate chuckled. “I *knew* that you’d be the perfect tour guide.”

Angie wiggled her eyebrows, and they both laughed.

Angie then added, “You realize that the 101 is the only highway on the Peninsula, circling around from east to north to west to south, passing around the mountains and the park. That’s another reason for the traffic.”

Kate nodded and tried to figure out how to safely pass a slowly moving vehicle pulling a trailer.

***

After working their way through downtown Port Angeles, they continued on the two-lane road westward. In half an hour, they had reached Lake Crescent, and Angie suggested they pull off at the exit for the Lake Crescent Lodge. The lake, extremely blue, extremely deep, and surrounded by small mountains, was a favorite attraction of the national park. Kate pulled into a parking slot in front of the lodge, and she and Angie walked down to the dock.

Kate clicked some pictures with her smart phone. “This is incredibly beautiful. I had no idea.”

She asked Angie to stand by the railing while she took a few shots of her backed by placid water and green mountains. “You are one gorgeous lady,” she admitted with a little sigh.

Angie blushed. “Now you.” She took Kate’s phone and told her where to stand, snapping some photos. “Too bad there isn’t someone around to take both of us.”

Kate, being Kate, quickly rounded up a willing tourist and the two of them stood shoulder to shoulder holding hands for a picture. Kate thanked the gentleman, who smiled and moved on.

"That was fun," Angie whispered. "It's the first time we've held hands. It felt really good." *She didn't acknowledge the waves of electricity that were running throughout her body.*

Kate smiled at her gently. "Felt good to me, too. We'll have to do that more often."

***

Back in the car, they resumed the westward trek, turning off on a state route that wound through hilly countryside and eventually connected with a similar road headed for coastal communities Clallam Bay, Sekiu, and Neah Bay, all bordering the Strait and facing Canada's Vancouver Island to the north.

"Neah Bay is the most northwestern community in the continental US," Angie explained as Kate focused on handling the many turns in the road. "It's the home of a Native American tribe, the Makah, historically a fishing tribe, and one of the most remote in the west. Many tribes are near major highways, like the Jamestown Tribe in Sequim, and have casinos to support their people. This tribe is located too far away from any population center for that, but somehow they found money for a lovely museum. We should stop there so you can better understand their history."

Kate grinned to herself. She'd much rather find a motel and take Angie to bed than tour a museum—she also realized that even if Angie were feeling some of what she was feeling, it wouldn't do to pressure her. *They needed time together, doing just what they were doing.*

When they reached Clallam Bay, the roadway turned west and ran along the waterfront for several miles to Neah Bay. The day was sunny, and Canada's Vancouver Island was clearly visible to the north. Mileage markers showed that they were nearing their destination, but the route was narrow and slow going. Kate tried to be patient. She was *really* anxious to be free of the car and sharing a more active experience with Angie.

***

Finally, they arrived in sprawling Neah Bay and pulled into the parking lot of the Makah museum, a large and impressive structure. Kate took Angie's hand as they walked to the front entrance.

A reception center and gift shop opened onto the main museum comprised of several large rooms under a high ceiling. Whaling and fishing canoes hung in the expanse along with the skeleton of a whale. Various rooms told the history of the Makah tribe, including how hundreds of years ago its coastal village by Ozette Lake was submerged by a Pacific storm and the tribe forced to relocate to Neah Bay. Examples of native art and clothing were shown, along with tools used in fishing. A longhouse replica depicted family life.

Kate was particularly impressed by several lifelike, gorgeously painted murals on the walls showing the meeting of sky, sea, and land. She pulled Angie close and risked putting her arms around her as they both studied the breathtakingly real images. *Kate's heart beat fast as she reveled in Angie's warmth, her natural fragrance, her beautiful dark hair, subtle touch of perfume, and her softness.* Angie remained quietly in Kate's embrace, seemingly comfortable with the intimate touch.

Once back in the Chevy, Kate spied a small roadside café where they obtained fresh fish sandwiches and sodas. They sat at an outdoor picnic table, during which Kate felt Angie's eyes on her. *The look was of a hunger not satisfied by sandwiches, and Kate knew she was broadcasting the same yearning.* Nevertheless, they both sighed and consumed their tasty lunch before proceeding to the afternoon's main event, the famous Cape Flattery Trail.

10

The popular trail began in a paved parking lot and wound downward through a rainforest to a bluff overlooking the Pacific Ocean and the isolated Tatoosh Island, home of the historic Cape Flattery Lighthouse. Located on Makah land and maintained by the tribe, the three quarters of a mile downward trail was gradual, but it changed from gravel, to mud, to wooden planks, to tree ring ovals, to steps up and steps down, to side trails leading to lookouts, and finally to a platform on which to stand and look out at the ocean. The coast at this most extreme point included a high bluff, punctuated by rough rocks and dark caverns into which ocean water swelled then drained back out again.

As they walked carefully along the trail, Kate and Angie saw numerous birds—flying, sitting on branches, plucking among leaves, and squawking in bird-speak. Wind blew through the dense thicket of trees, giving a magical quality to everything. *This is like a Disney setting*, Kate thought.

With that idea in mind, Kate grinned and silently slipped behind a large tree trunk.

Turning and not seeing her, Angie called out with some anxiety, "Kate, where did you go?"

Then suspecting that Kate had hidden for fun, Angie also circled the tree. Kate stood smiling, reaching for her, and Angie slipped into her arms. Kate kissed her. Angie kissed her back—at first gently and then with deepening passion.

Hearing voices on the trail, Kate released her and whispered, "That's a hint. More to come later."

Angie looked up at her shyly and with deep longing. Her eyes sparkled.

They moved along the rugged trail, both watching their steps carefully. Several times Kate put out a hand to steady Angie's footing. She was always rewarded with a warm and grateful smile.

The trail was crowded with visitors who seemed to speak a variety of languages from many parts of the world. Sometimes Kate and Angie had to step aside to let older or more vulnerable hikers pass by. A few times others made way for them.

***

When they finally arrived at the lookout spot, Kate took pictures of the historic lighthouse and Angie with the lighthouse behind her, then passed her phone to Angie, who repeated the same for her. A young Asian man offered to take a picture of them both. With gratitude they posed, holding each other close. Kate whispered in her ear, “This is our first day together alone. Never to be forgotten.”

Realizing their time was flying by, Kate felt an increasing sense of urgency, as she guided Angie back up the trail. Once in the parking lot, Kate asked innocently and with a broad smile, “What do we do now?”

Angie grinned. “Well, we go back the way we came, almost. We’ll stay on the state Highway 112 this time and go through the town of Joyce where there is a little cafe that I love. It serves everything made with blackberries, and in late summer, the Peninsula is covered with blackberries. I think you’ll like it.”

Although Kate had been dreaming of a motel somewhere, a private place where she could have this beautiful angel all to herself, she acquiesced. She didn’t want to push Angie any faster than she could go.

***

The cafe in Joyce proved worthy of Angie’s predictions. They shared tasty hamburgers with blackberry milkshakes and then took slices of blackberry pie in containers for later. Since Joyce was only a few minutes west of Port Angeles, they rejoined the 101 to head back to Sequim.

As they approached the Sequim Avenue exit, Kate finally risked asking, “Are we taking our little party to your place or TC?”

Angie grinned. “Does it make a difference?”

Kate shook her head. “Not to me. If it does to you, then you make the choice.”

“Well,” Angie said with a wink, “I think TC might be more fun and maybe safer.”

“Safer?”

“Understanding neighbors, at least.”

Kate chuckled. “Okay, TC it is.”

***

They passed through the security gate at the RV resort just as the sun slipped behind the Olympics. There was an incoming tide, and with Kate’s window rolled down, they could hear gentle waves from the Strait rolling up onto the spit.

Kate parked on the gravel next to the RV, and they both climbed out, each of them suddenly looking a bit nervous as they approached the darkened coach—equally scared and excited about what would surely come soon.

Kate opened the door and flipped on a light switch. Angie followed her inside. They stood for a moment looking at each other, seeming at a loss for the next move.

Kate cleared her throat. “I guess I didn’t plan everything. I’ve been out of the loop for so long that I don’t know how to behave. I should have had an iced bottle of champagne and a couple of flute glasses ready, and maybe some roses,” she admitted.

Angie’s face broke into a broad smile. “I wouldn’t have known how to react to all that. I’ve never been treated to such fine things. Let’s just be ourselves, okay?”

Kate’s shoulders dropped. “I do have a bottle of red wine, if you like.”

Angie nodded. “Red is perfect.”

Kate rummaged in the kitchen until she had everything she needed. “It would help if I really knew my way around this RV,” she quipped.

Once the wine had been poured, they sat down close to each other on the sofa. Kate reached out to clink glasses, and they both sipped.

Then, glancing around a bit awkwardly, Kate noticed a wall lamp, stood up to turn it on, then flipped off the overhead light. "That's better, don't you think?" she asked. The light was softer now, more intimate.

Angie nodded, suppressing a little giggle.

Kate checked to see that all the blinds had been pulled—something she *had* thought about before picking Angie up that morning—and then settled back on the sofa.

"Relax, Kate. You don't need to impress me. If I didn't like you a lot and find you very attractive, I wouldn't be here. And if you didn't feel the same way, you wouldn't have gone to all this trouble to set up a weekend for us."

Kate sighed. "I guess I'm nervous."

Angie put a hand on her arm. "Why? You have surely had a lot more experience with women than I have. You must have dated these past years?"

Kate took a sip of wine and nodded. "Yes, I did. Maybe it didn't mean as much to me."

Angie leaned closer and kissed Kate on the cheek. "You want to tell me about it or save that for later?"

"Later." Kate set down her glass and turned to kiss Angie, at first gently, and then, as Angie responded, much more intensely. She pulled Angie close and could feel Angie's heart beating as rapidly as her own. *This was what she wanted, what she had dreamed about.*

***

Moments later, they had abandoned the wine and the sofa for the infinitely more comfortable queen-sized bed in the back of the RV. Angie stretched out invitingly, and Kate moved closely beside her, eager to touch Angie's beautiful curvaceous body. Their kisses became more earnest, and their fingers began exploring. Clothing was quickly tossed to the floor, as they sought skin contact. Angie's hands grasped Kate's strong, broad shoulders, her powerful hips and thighs, her small firm breasts. Kate cupped Angie's soft and rounded breasts, stroked her shoulders and hips. The kissing moved onward, everywhere skin was available. They groaned to each other as they allowed their intense attraction, suppressed until now, to bubble up. Their kisses became hungrier, more demanding, as desire overrode all rational thought and feeling. Kate sucked Angie's nipples desperately and nipped at them until they stood tall and Angie stiffened, groaning with desire.

Then Angie pushed Kate down onto the bed and put her mouth over Kate's very sensitive breasts, tonguing her taut nipples until Kate breathed heavily and shivered with excitement. Kate regained the top position, gently touching Angie's face, teasingly fingering her neck, and gradually moving downward, grasping her shoulders, circling her breasts, massaging her waist and belly, and with increasingly passionate gasps stroking the soft mound between her legs, where Angie was wet and waiting.

Then Kate stopped. Angie looked for a second startled. *What next?* Kate pushed herself aggressively against Angie, bringing tingles to both of them from head to toe. Angie's brown eyes grew dark and she grasped Kate hungrily, giving back in kind everything that had been given to her. Highly excited, she too pulled back for an instant. They stared at each other and then kissed with still increasing passion. Fingers and tongues explored, heightening desire as they moved almost in unison toward that well lubricated mound. Kate pushed fingers into Angie's core, and Angie responded in kind. Hearts pounding, faces flushed with heat, eyes dark and dilated, they stroked again and again, until suddenly they both climaxed, holding each other tightly as they crashed in release. Sated and exhausted, they fell back on the bed, hands intertwined.

There was a long silence, the room still except for their heavy breathing.

"I can't believe it," Kate finally whispered. "That was fantastic. What you do to me."

"I could say the same," Angie returned, resting her head in the crook of Kate's neck. "It's never been that good for me."

They lay quiet for a while, tired, happy, fulfilled. Needing nothing except each other lying close, touching.

***

Snuggled close under a sheet, they drifted off to sleep. Sometime later, Kate shifted and awakened. Angie immediately woke up as well and tossed off the cover.

"Bathroom," she whispered.

"Just around the corner. It's small, but it does the job."

After the sound of a flushing toilet, Angie was back. Now they were both wide awake.

Kate put her arms around Angie, noting that the room felt cool. Dawning light was peeping through the closed blind slats. Kate pulled a comforter over both of them.

"Thanks," Angie mumbled. Then her eyes flew open, and she studied Kate. "When I came into the room, in the light, I could see you lying there. I had first noticed your tan that day at our swimming pool. Now I realize that you are tan all over. How did you get that way?"

Kate laughed. "Lying nude on a beach, swimming nude in the ocean."

"Really?"

"Well, I lived briefly in Sydney, Australia, and then in Christ Church, New Zealand, but after a while I moved on to smaller islands. Bali, Moorea, Raiatea. Some places were very primitive; some had very relaxed social standards. At a few spots, I would have sworn I was the only one there."

"Why did you leave Australia and New Zealand?"

"Remember, at the time, I was running away—from everything. I was still grieving and I was sad for a long time. When you are an only child, there's something deeply cutting about losing both parents, especially the last one. I felt totally alone and disconnected from everything. I woke up having nightmares and anxiety attacks." Kate sighed as she remembered those times.

"Australia and New Zealand," she continued, "the cities at least, were not that different from America. Hustle and bustle. That reminded me that I was not working. I looked at billboards and advertising ideas came in my head. I didn't want to think about that.

"So, I moved on to smaller locales where society was a lot more basic. I could be cut off, with no computer, phone, or email, for long periods of time. I craved the feeling. I thought that if I could survive with nothing, then I'd be okay. I wanted to keep everything simple. I swam, sunbathed, read novels, found people to adopt me for a few days, here and there made a girlfriend, for a little while, and then moved on."

"Meaning there are lesbians in the South Pacific?"

Kate laughed. "There are lesbians everywhere. Some of the places I stayed, they wouldn't have used the word. Sexual expression was just rather fluid. A young woman could have a baby on her hip, a man in her life, and still be ready to play with me. No commitment, no responsibility, just physical enjoyment. A woman plus woman sexual relationship has few side effects. You pleasure each other then walk away. No problems left behind and no guilt, either."

Angie sighed. "I can't imagine that, but then my responsibilities started at sixteen, so I'll never be in that place."

Kate reached up and stroked Angie's hair. "You wear that mantle well. If I hadn't met your kids, I'd never have realized you could be twenty-six. You look so young to me."

"I feel twenty-six and more on some days."

Kate smiled. "Your hair is very soft and such a beautiful auburn color. Every time I look at you, I want to run my fingers through it, but that would mean undoing that braid."

Angie kissed her. "I'd love for you to do that."

They both sat up, Kate leaning back against pillows with her legs encircling Angie. First, she undid the clasp that held the braid. Then she unraveled the strands, cross by cross, until Angie's hair flowed freely in waves down her back. Kate took the hair, more than waist length, and held it in her fingers, raising it to her lips and sniffing. "So beautiful," she whispered.

Angie shivered. "That feels funny. Good funny, I mean. It makes me tingle all over."

Angie turned to face Kate, and they kissed, first brushing lips lightly, then beginning to explore. They slid under the sheets, Angie's hair flowing over them both, and began to make love.

***

Kate fixed breakfast. Bacon, scrambled eggs, toast, orange juice, and strong coffee. "I should have had mimosas," she quipped, and Angie laughed.

They both exclaimed about the quaking muscles they had in their thighs. "You'd think," Angie noted, "after being on my feet all day, nearly every day, a little sex wouldn't do that to me. But it did."

"What about me? I'm a swimmer, and still I'm shaky this morning."

After they both laughed, Angie asked, "What do you want to do today?"

Kate gazed into Angie's eyes. "I'd love to stay in bed with you. However, I suspect maybe we should come back to earth gradually, before we pick up the kids."

Angie sighed. "You're right, I guess. I must admit bed really sounds nice."

"I know, but let's shower and dress and take a walk somewhere pretty."

Resigned to the inevitable, Angie agreed.

***

An hour later, freshly dressed and with Angie's hair pulled back into its customary braid, they left the RV and headed through TC down toward the water and the spit that separated Sequim Bay from the Strait. The tide was low. They walked hand in hand for a while along the spit, enjoying the light morning breeze and the sunshine. Only a few fluffy white clouds floated in Sequim's vast blue sky.

As they returned to the RV, they passed a few Colony residents who looked at them questioningly. While walking her dog, Sid waved. She seemed to sense their intimate closeness and didn't intrude.

***

The two spent the rest of their time together quietly walking hand in hand at various Sequim sites that offered cool shade, like Sequim Bay State Park, covered with tall evergreens, and the Dungeness Refuge out on the Prairie overlooking the Strait. Kate told her some of the things she had shared with Marianne in the beginning, about her mother's death, her need to please her father, and how her career in marketing had consumed her, leaving no time for a dedicated relationship.

***

Standing next to a fence by the bluff looking toward Port Angeles in the distance, Angie spoke up. "This weekend has been incredibly wonderful. I hope there will be more—and that this isn't a dream."

Kate smiled. "There definitely will be more. I love your kids and I enjoy being around them. I also need time with you to build our relationship. Whatever it takes to arrange for that, we will be together like this again soon."

Angie rubbed a hand along the railing. "You don't think you'll move on again? You said you moved a lot in the past five years. You stopped here by accident and you were going to Seattle. Maybe you'll wake up one morning and be ready to go there, or somewhere else?"

Kate pulled her into a hug. "Being with you this weekend has answered a lot of questions for me. I'm not going anywhere, Angie, unless you want me gone. From my perspective, if I were headed to Seattle, it would be to visit, and you'd be coming with me, and likely the kids as well. Now that I've met you, I have no plans to be anywhere else other than here."

"That's a big commitment, coming from you."

"I know. It's because I love you."

Tears spilled out of Angie's eyes. "I feel like I'm falling in love with you, too, and it scares me to death."

Kate pulled her even tighter. "I know, I know. It scares me, too. But I'm here and I'm here for good."

***

When they pulled up to the Seventh Avenue house and climbed out of the Chevy, Sarina and Mark came running from the garage, followed by Jake. The two children enfolded themselves in Angie's arms, and she gave them both big hugs.

"Look what I made," Mark said, revealing a carved wooden figurine of Darth Vader.

"Look at mine," Sarina exclaimed, holding up a carved doll.

Watching from behind, Jake laughed. "They got excited about my work projects, so we found some spare pieces of wood, and I showed them how to carve."

Angie looked at Jake with one raised eyebrow.

"Not to worry. I was with them all the time, and I showed them how to handle the tools in a way they wouldn't get hurt. They've been involved in this project most of the weekend."

"I wanted to do a storm trooper. This one was a bit easier to complete," Mark confessed.

Kate stepped forward and looked carefully at each piece. "I think they're great! You two are amazing!"

"We watched a movie and played some card games, too," Sarina offered.

"And we camped out in the living room last night," Mark added.

Angie looked surprised. "My, you certainly kept busy."

Jake guided everyone into the house where they sat down in the living room. Jake explained the unusual set-up of a tent on the carpet. "Since we don't really have a spare bedroom, and the sofa would be tight for two, I thought setting up a tent was a good activity. We laid out two bedrolls for them. It was pretend camping, but I think they enjoyed it. Right?" She looked at Sarina and Mark, and they both nodded enthusiastically.

Marianne came whizzing into the room from her office. "Did you two have a good time?" she asked, looking back and forth between Angie and Kate.

Angie grinned. "I took Kate out to Neah Bay, and we walked the Cape Flattery Trail. We also stopped at Lake Crescent on the way out and dinner in Joyce at the blackberry place on the way back."

Marianne smiled. "That's a fun place to eat."

Kate added, "Today we did some trails here in Sequim. There is a lot to see, just around town."

Jake nodded. "This is a great time of the year to do it."

Marianne grinned at Angie. "Well, your two young ones were fine, I think. They were helpful and courteous, and I must say you've done a good job with them. They're welcome here anytime. We've all had fun this weekend, right kids?" Marianne winked at Sarina and Mark, who both nodded at her and smiled broadly.

Angie sighed. "I'm really glad. It's hard not to worry."

Kate glanced at her watch. "It's late, I know, and I'm sure you two would like to have some quiet time. We need to take Sarina and Mark home and get them ready for bed. I don't know how to thank you for all you did for them and for us this weekend."

Jake grinned. "Our pleasure. We had a good time, too."

There were hugs all around, then Kate and Angie put arms around the kids and led them to the car.

11

Angie sailed through work the next day, physically tired yet mentally exhilarated. She had never dreamed she could have such a good time as she had with Kate during the weekend. It wasn't only the incredible lovemaking, which still made her shiver, but the whole package—how much she enjoyed being with Kate, talking with her, sharing a beautiful outdoor experience. Being funny, affectionate, appreciating things like the museum and the Cape Flattery Trail, and sharing a blackberry shake at the little cafe. How everything fell together for Mark and Sarina—it all made for an amazing weekend.

It felt almost too good to be true. However, Angie tried not to let fears cast a negative shadow. Kate had called her during the morning and expressed her gratitude for their wonderful time together. Angie was happy about the call though she explained to Kate that she needed to spend time with the kids this evening, so maybe they should wait a day or two before trying to get together again. She could hear the disappointment in Kate's voice, yet Kate seemed to understand and accept her decision.

Early in the afternoon, Kate unexpectedly showed up at the coffeehouse. Angie was totally surprised. Before she could say anything, Kate took the lead. "I don't want to bother you, but could I have your car keys for a few moments?"

Angie scrunched up her pert nose. "What for?"

"I found a car wash downtown, and I cleaned my car. I thought maybe yours could use a wash, too, and I know you're busy. I just thought I'd do it for you."

Angie frowned. "How much does it cost?" She reached into her skirt pocket.

Kate laughed. "For you, nothing. Just let me say thank you for the weekend by getting your car washed. It's not too much to ask, is it?"

Angie giggled. "When you put it that way, okay, here's the key. You'll be back by the time I get off, right?"

"Sure, no problem."

Kate headed for the door. "See you later," she called.

Angie turned to Carly. “I don’t know about her.” She smiled and heaved a big sigh.

“It’s clear she really likes you,” Carly replied.

Angie sighed. “It’s mutual, I’m afraid.”

***

Since Kate was not eating with Angie and the kids that evening, she dropped in on Marianne and Jake. Jake grinned and Marianne rolled her eyes. “Okay, now we’re going to get the lowdown?”

Kate looked deflated and started to turn away.

Jake grabbed her arm. “Come on. I made a tuna dish for dinner, and there’s plenty to share.”

Over the meal and a glass of wine, Kate told them in more detail about her weekend with Angie and how wonderful it was.

“I’m glad for you,” Marianne said. “Now that I’ve met Angie personally and had her kids around here for a couple of days, I feel that you’ve had a stroke of good luck in meeting a *very* nice woman and mother of two delightful children. I still have a little unease about it, though.”

Kate raised an eyebrow. “About what?”

“You.”

Kate shrugged. “Why?”

“Well, you’re involved with a woman who is one step away from homelessness. She has very little support, if any, from her family and lots of responsibilities. She’s doing a good job, by the skin of her teeth, no less, and you come along with your background, the good and the bad of it, and your money, and I’m just not quite sure how this will all play out.”

Kate looked affronted. “Now she has me, and I can give her all the support she needs.”

“In a way, yes, because you have tons of money. How much I don’t know and don’t particularly care to know.”

“I don’t know either. I leave that to my accountant. I just know I can do whatever I want.” Kate stuck her chin out defiantly.

Marianne sighed. “That’s exactly what I mean. You can do and you can overdo because you have it. Angie struggles to get through a day, keep the rent paid and food on the table. Every day she succeeds, she gets just a little stronger and the stark reality of her situation becomes a little less daunting. You can just look at her and see that she has pride, and she needs that pride. She also needs to be able to figure out what she wants on her own. You bring the potential of a tidal wave of excess into her life—because you have it and you think you care about her.”

“I *do* care about her.”

“I know you feel attracted to her, and right now you think you love her, am I right?”

“I do love her. I’m sure of it.”

“For how long?”

“Well, it has to play out. Maybe we’re right for each other and maybe not. I can’t make that decision without spending time with her and seeing how we do.” Kate felt on the spot. She didn’t want to admit to Marianne that she had assured Angie she was staying for good.

“Then maybe one day, it doesn’t seem right, and off you go?”

“What if I do?” Kate felt cornered and looked testy.

Marianne took a deep breath. “Kate, I care about you. You know that. At the same time, your track record stinks.”

“Those things were set off by my mother and father dying. I don’t have any more parents to lose.”

“It’s how you handled those losses that concerns me.”

“I don’t get what you’re saying.”

Jake broke in to the conversation.

“Kate, you’ve been here barely a month. You don’t know Sequim or if you like this area enough to stay here. I think Marianne is suggesting that you need to be patient with things and with yourself before you get overly involved—for yourself and for Angie.”

Kate studied Jake for a moment. “Well, if I don’t like it here, I can always move.”

“And Angie?” Jake asked.

“Well, she could go, too.”

“Would she want to?”

"I don't know. I haven't asked her." Kate looked frustrated. "All this is theoretical. We're just trying to get to know each other and build a relationship. You're predicting catastrophe before we begin."

Marianne reached out and touched Kate's arm.

"Dear Kate, neither of us is trying to be fatalistic. However, for an almost forty-year old woman, you are a little bit like a teenager. Not quite dry around the ears."

Kate took a deep breath and let it out. "Sometimes I *feel* like a teenager."

Marianne nodded. "Well, in that sense, Angie is more mature than you. She's gone through the pain of childbirth and given life to two beautiful children. Her world revolves around giving them a chance—perhaps making sure that the same things don't happen to them that have happened to her. Neither you nor I have given birth. It's hard to understand exactly what her world feels like, that kind of mother-child bond."

Kate sighed and her shoulders relaxed. "Yeah, I've thought about that. I wouldn't want to do anything that would hurt her or the children."

Marianne nodded. "Well, for the time being, just try not to overdo it. Don't give too much. Don't promise too much. Little things are okay. Drop in with a pizza for dinner. Take her and the kids to a movie."

"I washed her car today," Kate offered with a hopeful grin.

"Just as long as you didn't *buy* her a car."

"She needs one."

Marianne sighed. "Kate, listen to me. Spend time with her when she can, give her space when she needs it, respect her pride and her privacy, and don't buy her things she can't afford and which will make her dependent on you."

Kate shrugged. "Okay, I hear you."

"No cars and houses, right?"

"A house. I hadn't thought of that."

"Kate!"

"She needs a better place to live. The kids are sharing one bedroom."

"It won't kill them."

"Well, not now, but when they start to mature sexually."

"That's a few years from now. Give them a chance. They're fine."

Kate sighed. "Okay, okay. It's just hard not to help."

Jake put in. "Marianne and I both understand how difficult that's going to be. Doing and buying things come easy for you. Maybe this time you will have to focus on developing other relationship skills."

Kate nodded. "Could I have another glass of wine?"

***

On Wednesday evening, Kate showed up with a pizza, fresh salad, cokes, chips, and watermelon, and Angie glowed when Kate stepped into the apartment.

School had started the day before, and Sarina and Mark were already involved in projects on the living room floor. Angie called them for dinner. They came to the table bursting with excitement.

"See what I drew?" Sarina asked, pushing a paper in front of Kate. The picture was recognizable as flowers, very colorful ones, in a vase.

"Oh, that's really pretty," Kate replied. "You are quite the artist." Turning to Angie, who was setting the table, she asked, "They have homework already?"

Angie shook her head. "Very little actual homework at their level of school. However, they did art projects during the day. Both Sarina and Mark were so excited that they brought their papers home then sat on the floor to draw images similar to what they'd done in class."

Kate grinned. "I bet they also bring home good report cards."

"Yep." Angie nodded with maternal pride.

Mark walked up with his drawing, predictably boy-like, of a truck on a road in the woods. "Very good, Mark," Kate said, roughing up his hair.

"What was the assignment?" she asked him.

"An object in a setting."

Kate raised her eyebrows. "Okay, Sarina did flowers IN a vase, and you did a truck IN the woods, right?"

They both nodded happily.

"Sit down. Dinner's on."

***

While they ate enthusiastically, Kate asked the kids questions and winked now and then at Angie, who eventually blushed and reached over to give a little thump to Kate's arm. Kate laughed.

When they were finished, Kate suggested to Sarina and Mark, "While your mom's cleaning up and I'm helping her, why don't you two make another picture? Try to think of an object that you like and put it into a setting, just like you did before."

"That's easy!" Sarina called out, as she and Mark moved back into the living room and sat down on the carpet with their papers and crayons.

Since the kids were out of sight around the corner, Kate risked hugging Angie from behind as she stood at the sink. "Mmmm," Angie murmured, turning her head to receive a light kiss.

Kate remained at her side, as if they had done it for years, while Angie rinsed off the dishes and utensils they had used for dinner and Kate arranged them in the dishwasher.

"Did they have dishwashers in the South Pacific?"

"Better yet, did they have dishes?"

"Well—"

"Some places yes, but mostly no, at least where I was hanging out."

When the water was turned off and the dishwasher door closed, Kate reached out to Angie and spirited her away from view into the corner of the kitchen.

She pulled Angie into a hug and then a deep kiss, which Angie returned. "I want you so very much," she whispered in Angie's ear.

"Me, too. But not tonight. Maybe by the weekend we can work out dinner and an evening together."

Kate sighed. "That's what I was afraid of."

Kate moved in for another kiss, a long one, and they separated just as Mark emerged from the living room and looked up at them quizzically.

"What's up?" Kate asked Mark, covering as Angie, blushing, moved to clean something on the counter.

"I finished my picture. I wanted to show it to you."

"Great!" Kate took the paper and looked at a stick figure boy holding a bat at home plate and a ball flying through the air toward him. "Perfect," she said, showing the picture to Angie.

"Why am I not surprised that you drew a baseball picture?" Angie grinned and pinched his cheek teasingly.

In a moment Sarina, who also wanted to show off her work, joined them. She had drawn a diver standing at the tip of a diving board above a blue swimming pool.

Angie grinned at Kate. "Wonder what brought that on?"

Kate shrugged and blushed. "Don't know."

Sarina scrunched her nose. "You do, too. That's you getting ready to dive."

Kate smiled. She didn't say anything yet noticed that although younger, Sarina had a little more drawing ability than Mark. Both showed their interest in sports by the choices they made.

"Well," Kate said, "now that dinner is over, would anyone like to watch a movie?"

The two kids both chimed in enthusiastically, "Oh, yes. What movie?"

Angie raised an eyebrow then relaxed when Kate pulled a DVD out of a pack she had carried with her. It was Disney's *Finding Dory*.

They all settled in the living room, the kids stretched out on the floor, and Kate and Angie seated side by side on the sofa.

When the movie had started and Sarina and Mark were enthralled with the animated story, Kate slid even closer to Angie and put a hand on her thigh and started rubbing her leg. Angie pushed her hand away and whispered, "not now" but also winked at her.

Kate sighed and watched the movie.

12

Kate struggled to fill her time until the weekend. It wouldn't do to hang around the coffeehouse and bug Angie. *She could be a dolt sometimes, but she did understand that much.*

At TC, and with a cup of home-brewed coffee cooling beside her, she pulled out her laptop. Thanks to Jake's thoughtfulness in getting her connected to the Internet, she began exploring. She realized she wanted more real information about this place.

First, she spent a couple of hours learning about Sequim: its history, politics, school system, neighborhoods, relationship to the mountains, the Strait, and the Olympic Peninsula. Except for Port Townsend, she had sampled some of the local area, yet there was much more that she wanted to see and understand. When she had digested enough demographics for the day, Kate turned to websites for the Boys & Girls Club, YMCA, and Little League, organizations that might be useful for Mark and Sarina. Each site revealed considerable new data.

For example, Little League was a spring sport. Never having participated in it, Kate had no idea. That meant Mark had to wait until the first of next year to register and try out for the team. She made a note to ask if he had a bat, glove, and ball.

Putting that aside, she checked out the Sequim YMCA. It had an indoor pool. Since the apartment pool was outdoors, and Sarina—if she really wanted to swim—needed to do it year-round, Kate had to find the right spot for her that was available continuously. The Y pool appeared to have three lanes marked for lap swimming. That wasn't a lot, Kate thought. Sarina really needed an indoor lap pool.

The Boys & Girls Club was an eye opener for Kate. Fees and registration were modest for after-school programs. In the summer, however, the offerings were expanded to keep kids busy and provide daycare for working parents. Mornings were called "camp" and there was a hefty registration fee for those hours. *No wonder Angie was struggling, even with her government subsidy housing. Maybe the grandparents, who normally dropped the kids off in the morning, were helping?*

Kate sighed, closed her computer and sat in thought. *The computer could only go so far. Some details would have to come from Angie, and for that Kate would have to wait. The Little League was a dead issue for now, but she could pursue more information regarding Sarina's swimming.*

Having nothing else pressing to do, Kate jumped into the Chevy, waving to Sid and another lady out walking their dogs. She left TC, drove into Sequim and turned north on Fifth Avenue, where the Y was located. The parking lot was nearly full. Inside, she noticed fitness rooms where several people were working out—most of them "Q-tips," *Kate's private term for seniors*. Behind a glass partition, she saw a big swimming pool complete with diving boards at the deep end.

Asking at the counter if she could take a closer look, Kate received a go-ahead and entered the pool area. A water aerobics class was in session and took up most of the pool, including part of the designated swimming lanes. That bothered Kate, because it appeared that lap swimming wasn't given a fair shake. She checked the schedule and found that, yes, water exercise classes consumed more time and space than anything else. She did see a notation that after Labor Day, the high school swim team would be using the lap lanes for a one-hour block of time weekdays. That confirmed for Kate that the high school didn't have its own swimming pool. "Hmmm," she said to herself.

Back at the front counter, she asked about the lap lanes and found that she had pretty much been right. "Is there any other indoor pool with marked lap lanes around here?" she asked.

The clerk, a friendly, gray-haired older man, nodded. "Port Angeles has a public pool at Lincoln and Fifth that has several designated lap lanes. They also have a swim team, I think. That might be your best bet."

Kate jumped in the sedan and headed for Port Angeles. As she drove along, listening to music on Sequim's FM radio station, she realized that she was getting a bit tired of this Chevy. She wanted something more in a car, and the longer she stayed here, the longer it looked like she was going to be staying. The car rental had only been intended as a brief convenience.

Now she started studying the cars zipping by, looking at their design and features and what people were driving. It didn't take long for her to realize that SUVs were the thing, and the winners were the Honda CR-V and Subaru Forester. She kept seeing one or the other of them pass her as she remained in the slow lane. In every color in the rainbow. She had to laugh to herself. On the islands, she had seldom driven any kind of vehicle, and the pace had been quite slow. "I've been more retired than the retirees," she kidded herself aloud.

At the edge of Port Angeles, she passed a Honda dealer and then a Subaru dealer. She quickly noted their locations and returned her focus to the street ahead.

The public pool proved easy to find. Kate was impressed that this facility was largely salt-water, even though some chlorine was used around the pool area, and there were six marked lanes. Clocks at both ends and pool swimming records posted on the walls made it clear to her that competitive swimming was significant. That's exactly the environment she wanted.

At the front desk, she asked the staff questions about fees and swim training. Kate explained that she'd been a competitive swimmer in college, and although she wasn't a certified trainer, she had a little girl, the daughter of a close friend, who wanted to learn to swim and compete. She asked if there was a time, half an hour to an hour after school, evenings, or weekends that she could bring the child and work with her in a lap lane.

The young clerk was helpful, suggesting that there were times when the pool was quieter and therefore more likely to have a free lane. She explained the fees for students outside the Port Angeles school district. Kate made notations and thanked her.

On the way back to Sequim, Kate saw the Subaru dealer coming up. Impulsively, she pulled into the lot. A salesman approached her before she could even step out of the Chevy.

"I think I'm looking for a Forester," Kate said to the paunchy balding man. "Top of the line with all the extras."

The salesman smiled and, without looking at his inventory sheets, said, "Sure, we have one that's perfect."

"Wait," Kate explained. "I want a low-mileage, used SUV, a model back. Still top of the line, just not as flashy as brand new."

The salesman, whose nametag read "Nathan," thought for a moment and then commented, "I think I can still accommodate you. We have a blue one, last design. It's got everything, leather, moon roof, GPS, fog lights, rack, alloy wheels, etc. You want to see it?"

"Sure." Kate couldn't believe her luck. She followed the man into the used car lot. The blue Forester sat in a prominent place. To Kate it looked like new, not a mark on it. "How do you happen to have one like this?"

"Oh, we have a long-time customer who always wants the newest car. Loves Foresters. He buys one, drives it for twenty-to-thirty thousand miles, and then trades it in. He was just here last week and bought a bright red model, leaving us this blue one to sell. It's in excellent condition, with only 29K on the odometer."

"Sounds like it's my lucky day. How did it last a week on the lot?" She was joking, but the salesman took her seriously.

"Well, we sell a lot of white, black, beige, and gray vehicles. When people want color, they seem to go to red or green. This blue isn't as bright, and they just don't sell quite as much, at least on this lot, or maybe I should say, for me."

"Well, I love blue, the color of water, so for me it's perfect."

Kate totally forgot about the CR-V and didn't bother to comparison shop. She wanted the blue Forester. She paid with a credit card which just about blew Nathan away since she had no trade in and didn't try to talk him down in price. When the card cleared easily, he appeared most relieved and happy.

"Now," Kate said, "I'm driving a rental. I have to turn this car in and then ask a friend to bring me to pick up the SUV. Is that okay?"

Nathan shrugged. "No problem. It'll be sitting right here with your name on it when you return."

Feeling good, Kate jumped into the Chevy. Now, no matter what she decided to do, she had wheels. She chuckled to herself because she had never bought a car and she thought she had bluffed her way pretty well through the process. She drove back to Sequim and went looking for Jake. Lucky for Kate, Jake was in her shop and said, “No problem. I’ll tell Marianne that I have to run into PA for a few minutes. Then we’ll drop off your Chevy and go get your new wheels.”

***

Two hours later, Kate, followed by Jake in her truck, pulled out of the dealership in her Forester and turned onto the 101 headed for Sequim. She told Jake before they left that she was going to stop at Big 5 Sporting Goods. When they reached that point, they waved at each other, as Kate pulled off and Jake flashed by.

***

In the Big 5 store, Kate went straight to the baseball section. She examined baseballs, bats, and gloves sized for youthful players. She tried to remember which hand Mark used for throwing and catching. She guessed him to be right handed. After examining the merchandise, she picked out a basic right-handed fielder’s glove, a youth bat, a ball for Mark, and an adult fielder’s glove for herself. She also picked up a youth swim cap and goggles for Sarina.

At the counter, Kate pointed to the baseball equipment and told the clerk, “This is mostly for an eight-year old boy that I’m going to help learn the sport. I’m not sure whether he’s right- or left-handed. I assume that if I’m wrong, I can exchange this glove.” The clerk nodded.

Kate paid for the merchandise and climbed back into the car. She was already enjoying the Forester. It certainly beat the rental, although she would have to actually read the owner’s manual. *Way too many technical things to figure out!*

***

Jake had invited Kate to dinner that evening, and when she showed up in the Forester, Marianne quipped, “It’s looking more and more as if you’re staying here.”

Kate laughed. “I probably am, or I think I am. Should I later decide to leave, I can use the Forester anywhere in the US, or I can sell it or turn it over to Angie. I’m not really tied up into having things.”

“Or—at least thus far—people?” Jake raised an eyebrow yet grinned at her.

Kate’s jaw tightened for a second, and then she relaxed and smiled. “That’s a low blow, my dear friend, even if technically true. I’m going to ignore it, because my life’s changing.”

They sat down to one of Jake’s creative dinners, and Kate brought them up to date about the swimming venue and the baseball equipment. “I’m not sure about anything, but I just bought the stuff. If I’m wrong, I can take it back.”

“I’m sure Angie will be grateful,” Jake said.

Marianne had looked out the window at the Forester in the driveway. “Nice wheels. I hope you got a good deal on it.”

“Deal?” asked Kate. “The guy told me what they wanted for it, and I handed him a credit card. What kind of deal?”

Marianne grinned. “You have a lot to learn about shopping, Kate. Making a deal is all the fun when it comes to buying cars.”

***

Late Friday afternoon, Kate showed up at Angie’s apartment building. The kids were in the pool. Kate brought her suit and while ogling Angie now and then, she swam with Sarina and played beach ball with Mark. She was relieved to see him tossing the ball with his right hand.

After dinner, there was a show on TV the kids wanted to watch, and Angie gave them permission to leave the table. When they had disappeared into the living room, Kate gave her a silly grin.

“I sure would like to jump your bones,” Kate kidded softly.

"Patience, my dear." Angie chuckled behind a covering hand.

Kate winked. "There's something I need to talk with you about."

Angie raised an eyebrow. "Such as?"

"Well, this week I've done research for activities for the kids. I found out that Little League isn't until the spring, with registration after the holidays."

Angie frowned. "Didn't I tell you before that I can't afford the fees for that?"

Kate put her hands up, asking for a moment. "Let me explain it all first, okay?"

Angie sighed. "Okay."

"I know you can't do it all, and as *I* said before, I want to help with the kids. One thing for each child. Mark loves baseball, and this fall I want to work with him on hitting, fielding, catching. When registration comes, he'll be ready for the tryouts and comfortable and confident. I have the time and the skills. He has the need. I can pay for the registration and whatever the uniform will cost. I'll just do what Zack should have, could have done—had he been a gentleman instead of a rat."

Angie couldn't help but smile. "Okay, I get it."

"Now, Sarina wants to swim. Although it may be a passing phase, it's what she wants right now. I can help her with that. Even if she drops it later, she'll learn skills from structured practice that will help her physically and in school. It isn't a waste. I've checked out all the local facilities, and the best place for her is the Port Angeles public pool where there are several lanes marked for lap swimming and times set aside for workouts. Later, if she's interested, I can also teach her to dive properly and safely at that facility."

"We've got a pool right here," Angie protested.

"Yes, but it's a play pool with that kidney shape. It wasn't designed for serious swimming. You can only make a stroke or two before you run into someone or the wall. That's not productive. And it's an outdoor pool, meaning that before long it'll be uncomfortable to swim in, if they even keep the pool filled and heated during the winter."

Angie looked at her thoughtfully. "Going to PA is more than an hour travel time, plus swim time, and showers and changing. At least two hours each time you go. That's a lot for you to dedicate and maybe a lot for her to do. She's only seven, remember?"

"I know. I thought twice a week. One evening during the week and once on the weekend. I'll kid and joke with her and make it fun."

Angie pouted. "I thought we were going to spend time together on the weekends."

Kate laughed. "Are you jealous?" Kate risked a little peck on Angie's cheek. "Yes, we're going to do things on the weekend, sometimes all of us and sometimes you and me. You've told me that everybody has to be considered. We'll have to plan ahead, that's all. If we take a whole weekend, for a trip or something, then I'll switch the swim practice just for that weekend."

"Sounds like you have us all scheduled for the next year. You talk like you are a permanent member of this family." Angie looked at Kate with an amused smile.

Kate laughed. "Look, I've got nothing to do around this town, and you have way too much work. I just want to relieve you a little and add some fun and learning for the kids. I'll fill my time and enjoy it, and you'll have support."

Angie raised an eyebrow. "What happened to your visit to Seattle? You said originally that you came here to see your friends and then you were moving on. You are sounding less and less like a visitor and more like a permanent resident."

Kate whispered into Angie's ear, "You want me to leave?"

Angie grabbed Kate's arm. "No, of course not. It's just that we've only had one weekend together. I can't believe that you're making these commitments to me as well as to Sarina and Mark. I wondered about it all week. You could do much better. Find a professional woman with money, and the two of you could go on cruises, tour the country, set up a business, whatever, without kids to take up your time and energy." She lowered her voice. "You could make love whenever you want without having to be careful of little eyes and ears and young minds that question everything."

Kate scrunched up her face. "Too easy. No challenge. I like it better this way."

Angie sighed. "I hope so, because if you change your mind, you'll leave three broken hearts behind. Hearts that have already been hurt more than once."

Kate put her arms around Angie's shoulders. "I promise not to break your heart."

***

As Kate drove back to TC that night, she could feel Angie's touch all over her skin and smell her delicate perfume and hairspray. Kate was tingling and happy. There was one nagging concern. Her own heart was vulnerable, too. She hoped that she wasn't being a super saleslady, selling more than she really had to offer. *Promising things was easy to do. Fulfilling those promises would be harder, and her track record was iffy.* She'd left a lot of sweethearts behind in the South Pacific. She didn't want to do that again. However, commitment was scary.

13

Sarina swam the length of her lane as Kate walked along the pool edge, watching her stroke. The little girl improved each time they worked together and Kate was pleased that Sarina was taking swimming seriously.

Kate wore a tank suit, so she could enter the water occasionally, stand beside Sarina, and show her some modifications to her stroke and kick that would make swimming the lane's twenty-five meters easier and faster for her. They focused on backstroke and freestyle. Sarina liked backstroke because she didn't have to worry about breathing. Kate acknowledged her preference but mixed up the workout. That way, Sarina could make progress in both strokes.

During the ride to Port Angeles and back, they chattered. Sarina was still a bit star-struck and seemed to consider Kate her personal Esther Williams, yet as they talked together, Kate could sense that she was becoming more real to Sarina and less a celebrity.

***

While driving to Port Angeles, Kate was also acquiring an education about fall on the Olympic Peninsula. Sequim was definitely experiencing a weather change. The days not only became cloudy and shorter, rain showed up often and "sun breaks" appeared rarely.

One evening, as they drove home with headlights on and windshield wipers making a little rocking noise, Sarina commented, "I'm glad you found an inside pool. Sequim can be really cold. Sometimes it snows. I couldn't swim if we didn't go to this pool. I just hope the roads stay open for us." She giggled.

Kate smiled. "Not to worry, Sarina. Whatever the weather, we'll figure it out. I'm happy you like swimming so much that you want to swim even in the winter."

"It's fun. You make it fun. I feel good when I swim."

"I'm glad. One of these days, we'll have to take Mark and your mom along. Then they can see how well you're doing."

Sarina frowned. "Okay, just not yet."

"You feel a little shy?"

Sarina nodded. "A little. When I get really good, then they can come."

Kate touched Sarina's shoulder. "You're already good, especially for your age. When's your birthday?"

"Soon, I think. November 7. I'll be eight."

"That's in a few days! We'll have to think of something special to celebrate your name day."

"I really like you, Kate. You're nice."

"And I like you, too, Sarina."

***

When they arrived at the apartment, Mark was working on a project at the dining room table, and Angie was engrossed in a book in the living room.

Sarina gave Kate a big hug and trotted off to the bathroom to shower and put on her night clothes. Kate had worked with her to make sure the child kept healthy and went to bed clean after swimming. Sarina had already learned to wash out her own swimsuit, and Angie had reported to Kate that she was being conscientious about it.

Angie put down her book and looked up at Kate. She smiled warmly and her eyes sparkled.

"Good workout?" she asked.

Kate nodded. "Yes, very good. She's doing quite well and seems dedicated. I had to chuckle because she's already worried about driving to the pool when it's snowing."

Angie laughed. "Well, there's a point to that. Some winters we have almost no snow, and sometimes we are shut down for days. Even at her age, she has seen enough snow to understand that it can prevent us from doing our favorite things."

Kate smiled. "Maybe, for her sake, this will be a mild winter."

"Hopefully."

"And she told me she has a birthday in a few days. Keep me updated on that, will you?"

"Sure."

Kate looked over at Mark. "What are you doing, my young friend?"

"I'm looking up things. They showed us how animals grow. I liked the butterfly, how it's a caterpillar and then has a cocoon before it becomes a butterfly. I wanted to know more, so Mom showed me how to find it on her computer."

Kate looked at Angie in amazement. "It's fantastic. Kids today are able to do things way beyond what I could do at their age. Of course, we didn't have laptops, but I just can't believe it."

"Yep, they can be rather precocious. This one," she nodded at Mark, "is very smart."

"He'll be nine?"

"After the holidays. He was born in late January."

Mark called them over to see the pictures of butterflies he had found on the Internet. They were impressed, and Kate felt proud that Angie had such amazing kids despite what had happened with Zack.

Shortly, Sarina was out of the shower. Angie told Mark he was next. He nodded, closed the computer and headed for the bathroom.

With no young eyes in sight, Kate and Angie risked a close hug and some deep kissing—always ready to pull apart as needed.

Angie led Kate over to the sofa.

"I've got an idea," she said, holding Kate's hand. "Sarina's birthday will be Sunday. I want to do something nice for her, but I don't want it to be all about presents. I've been trying to think of something we could do that would please her."

"You mean like an activity?"

Angie nodded. "It's supposed to be nice this weekend. We don't have many sunny days in the fall, but if the forecast is correct, it would be a great time for a day trip with the kids. Someplace on the coast, like Rialto Beach, where we don't go very often. I'm not sure they've ever been there. It's beautiful and we need to go, if we are, before the coast becomes too windy, wet, and cold until next summer."

Kate smiled. "That's great and the trip will honor her day. We can load up the Subaru with anything you need to take.

Have a picnic, whatever you want. I'd love to see this Rialto Beach. I've never even heard of it."

***

Sunday morning fulfilled its promise with sunny skies and expected high temperatures in the low 60s. "Enjoy this while it lasts," Angie quipped as she and Kate loaded the SUV cargo space with bags of snacks, a cooler with drinks and sandwiches, blankets, sweaters, everything they could think of that they might need.

Sarina and Mark bounced down the stairs from the apartment filled with excitement about the excursion. Both were dressed in T-shirts, jeans, and hoodies, and carried sun glasses.

Angie examined them and then asked, "Sunscreen? Did I pack sunscreen?"

Kate nodded. "I saw you put a tube in the bag with the snacks."

"You're sure?"

Kate grinned with amusement. "Yes, I'm sure."

Angie sighed. "Okay, then I think we're ready."

***

Highway 101 gave them little grief. Relieved, Angie explained to Kate, "Last year or the year before, there was a big construction project on the 101 that tied everyone up for months. Forks, the last community before the coast, is about ninety minutes from Sequim, but it took much longer to get there while the road was torn up. Glad that's behind us."

"So, we're going to Forks?"

"Almost. We turn off just before. By the way, Forks' biggest claim to fame was that series of books and movies called *Twilight*."

Kate nodded. "I remember that."

As they drove along, Angie checked on the kids in the back seat. Both were buckled in and entertaining themselves quietly. "How's my birthday girl?" Angie asked.

Sarina gave her a big grin. "I don't have to be in a special seat anymore! I'm big now."

They sailed through Port Angeles. As they passed Race Street, Angie pointed out the sign to Hurricane Ridge. "In the winter, they try to keep the road open at least on weekends. It's fun to go up there when there's snow."

"I can imagine. I went there with Jake one day, and we hiked on a trail. I thought it was incredibly beautiful in summer. I suspect it is equally lovely in winter."

"Maybe we can take the kids up and play in the snow."

Kate swallowed. *Of course, they could do that, but hearing Angie say it pointed out how involved Kate had become, sliding into this relationship without really thinking about all the ramifications.* Day by day, even week-by-week, it was easy to live it. Now Angie was talking about winter, and Kate was committed to helping Mark after the holidays with the baseball program. *Staying one night at the marina and walking into a coffeehouse were maybe going to change the rest of her life. Innocent spur-of-the-moment decisions . . .*

***

Kate pulled into the Rialto Beach parking lot. Before they had even opened the Subaru's doors, she exclaimed, "My goodness, this looks like another planet!"

Angie laughed. "That's what I said. I call it a lunar landscape."

Sarina unhooked her seat belt and climbed out of the SUV. "Look, Mama. The trees are white!"

Jumping out as well, Mark exclaimed, "Wow, those are amazing!"

With everyone excited, Kate figured lunch could wait. Her stomach was rumbling, but she could hang on a bit. The four of them walked quickly up a rugged path, stepped over fallen tree trunks, and worked their way out onto the rocky beach. An incoming tide created thundering wave action along the shore. Giant trees, those still standing and those with their fallen trunks stretched out along the beach, were all bleached white, making them look ethereal and otherworldly.

"I've never seen anything like this," Kate admitted.

Angie tried to explain a little. "It's something to do with the angle of the beach and the wind direction during winter storms. Less than half a mile away, there's another beach that's oriented to the south, and the tree trunks on that beach are brown, normal old brown. Nothing like this chalky look."

Kate and Angie walked while the kids ran and climbed. Mark responded to Angie's warning to be careful that Sarina didn't take a fall.

"They are such responsible kids," Kate observed.

"Yes, they are. They were always good, but after Zack walked out, I was afraid for them. Luckily, they came through. Both of them seem to be understanding, and they've remained adorable children despite everything."

"You know I'm no expert on kids. They seem older than their actual ages. Am I right in sensing that?"

"Yes. Zack was a good father; I'll give him that. He taught them a lot of important things. We had acreage, though not officially a working farm, and we had some chickens. He showed them early about caring for and protecting vulnerable creatures. We both read books to them at night, and they were reading themselves before they started school."

"Is sitting in a regular classroom boring for them?"

"Possibly. We've talked about it. I don't want to push them too hard. I want them to have as normal a childhood as possible. At the same time, I've discussed with their teachers their reading skills and that they may need a little extra work to keep from getting bored. So far it seems okay. I've not heard many complaints from either of them. And they get along with the other students. Their sadness, and they have some, is about losing their father and about me working all the time and being strapped financially. I haven't always been able to hide my tension and anxiety from them."

Kate put an arm around her shoulder. "We're going to change that."

Angie smiled but didn't say anything.

***

At a picnic table, they enjoyed a happy lunch, with kidding and joking all around. One of their packages held chocolate brownies as a treat. Angie stuck a candle in the brownie she gave to Sarina. The little girl's face lit up with delight. Kate produced a match, lighted the candle carefully, and Sarina blew it out before the ocean breeze could do it for her. They all sang "Happy Birthday" and gave Sarina big hugs.

When they had stowed their gear back in the Forester, Mark approached Kate. "Kate, I'd like to walk on the beach."

"Me, too," Sarina chimed in.

"Okay, we'll do that, all of us, huh, Angie?"

Angie nodded.

"We're also going to take some pictures to remember today. Be prepared to smile."

Mark laughed. "That won't be hard." He posted a wide grin.

The kids ran ahead. A couple of times Kate and Angie briefly risked holding hands. Angie smiled at Kate who returned a loving look.

At one point, Kate stopped before a fallen tree that had a nearly round hole at its base. It resembled a picture frame. She asked Angie to stand in the hole, and Kate took her picture in several poses. Then Angie asked Kate to do the same while she snapped Kate's picture.

They heard Mark's voice behind them. "Now you both get inside. I'll take your picture."

"Do you know how to take a picture on a smart phone?" Amused, Kate asked the question lightly.

"Do I look like a dummy?" Mark challenged.

"Okay, let's see what you can do."

Angie and Kate both sat inside the frame, snuggling close together. Mark held up Kate's phone and grabbed a shot.

"See?" Mark showed the picture to Kate.

"Hey, that's good. You can be a photographer someday!"

Sarina was now standing behind Mark. "Let me try."

Mark handed her the camera, and Angie and Kate posed again.

"Hold still!" Sarina ordered. Then she took a picture and showed it to Kate.

"Yours is good, too! Wow, what talent in this family." Kate pumped a fist.

Sarina grinned, as if she had a mission. "Would you stand close together and put your arms around each other?"

Angie's eyes popped open, and Kate suppressed a smile. They did as Sarina requested.

"Okay, now hug for real."

Both blushing, they hugged.

"Now kiss each other."

Kate turned to Angie and gave her a gentle kiss.

As they separated, Angie whispered, "I think we've been outed."

"Thank you! I got it," Sarina reported enthusiastically.

Mark came up to look.

"My turn," he said. "Birthday girl, move into the picture with them."

Sarina happily posed in front of the two women.

"Now sit down on the tree with Sarina between you."

After all of that, Sarina exchanged with Mark, and she took photos of him with Angie and Kate.

"Too bad we can't get all four of us," Sarina sighed.

Sarina's comment was overheard by another beach visitor, a plump middle-aged woman who walked up to her. "Honey, I'll take a picture of all of you. I have a phone just like this. Now you go stand with them, all right?"

Sarina went into the group, standing close to Kate. The portly graying woman took a few shots of all of them.

"Thanks," Kate said to her, taking her phone back.

"You have a nice family," the woman commented, giving Kate a wink then moving on up the beach.

Totally surprised, they stood for a moment just staring after the woman. Then they happily looked at the pictures.

***

Sarina and Mark wanted to hunt for unusual rocks. The two children spent another half an hour just walking on the beach looking for anything worth taking home as a souvenir. Kate and Angie walked along by themselves. Kate snapped more pictures. Angie just looked at the scenery, Kate, and her kids. A gentle, soft expression on her face suggested that she was feeling a happiness that she hadn't experienced in a long time.

"Should we go somewhere and buy them souvenirs? Something special for Sarina?" Kate asked.

"Well, there are places in Forks, and La Push is an interesting Native American community. But you have to drive back up the road several miles, cross a bridge, then come down again on another road to reach La Push, although it's maybe a block away from here on the other side of the Quillayute River. You just can't get to it directly unless you are a strong swimmer!" They both laughed.

Angie thought for a moment. "You know, they're having a very good time. Sarina's been acknowledged. But they'll be tired, and tomorrow is work for me and school for them. I think their rocks, the photos, and the memories are enough for today, don't you? We can do the rest another time, maybe next spring."

Kate nodded in agreement. She could see the tiredness in Angie's eyes. Young as she was, she often looked worn.

"And," Angie suddenly added, "We need to do Lake Crescent on the way home."

***

Lake Crescent, where Angie and Kate had stopped briefly on their weekend outing to Neah Bay, was a welcome pause in managing the 101's curves. This time they spent a few minutes in the historic Lake Crescent Lodge. Rustic and beautiful, the facility had a lovely dining room overlooking the lake. They checked out the gift shop. Kate got Angie's approval to buy the kids souvenir pins to put on their backpacks. "As long as it's something little," she reminded Kate.

They strolled out on the pier, and Kate took dozens of photographs of the deep-blue lake reflecting late afternoon shadows. She took pictures of the kids and Angie against a railing with the water behind them. The kids took photos of her and Angie. Another stranger, a man, this time, stopped to capture all of them together.

"We have this phenomenal luck with photographs," Angie quipped to Kate.

Finally, they headed back to Sequim. Along the way, Kate asked Angie if she wanted to have dinner somewhere. Angie sighed. "I suppose we should, but let's keep it simple, maybe a pizza."

Kate chose to pass through Port Angeles, saving further exploration for another time, and continued on to Sequim, where they went to her favorite pizza parlor. She ordered a big pizza, salads, and drinks, to eat in, and they all slumped at a table, happy and exhausted. Mark and Sarina still managed to blow the papers off their straws, demonstrating that kids were always kids.

After the pizza, they seemed a bit revived. Kate pulled a present for Sarina out of her folded jacket. It was a new bright blue swimsuit, and Sarina was ecstatic. Angie was a little surprised, but she nodded at Kate approvingly. While it was a gift, it was appropriate.

When they arrived home, Mark and Sarina helped drag the remains of their picnic back up the stairs. Then Mark announced, "I'm going to take my shower, Mom."

"Okay." Angie looked at Sarina. "You're next."

When the two were out of sight, Kate held Angie in her arms. "They obviously know about us," Kate whispered, "and it's clear they don't care. They want a family, and we're it."

Angie's eyes were closed as she leaned against Kate's chest. "Yes, I know. I told you they're smart."

Kate encircled Angie with her strong arms. "Well, as much as I'd love to talk you into going to bed with me, I know you're tired, and I need to go home myself and clean up. By the time I make that drive, I'll be ready to collapse too. I can feel it coming on. I *do* want a rain check on bed—maybe in that lodge out there by the lake that we saw today. Okay?"

"That would be lovely," Angie murmured.

They kissed, and Kate asked Angie to tell the kids goodnight for her.

14

Alone in her bed in the fifth wheel, Kate thought sleep would come easily. It didn't. She kept running the day through her head. How much fun it was, even though very simple. *Low key, yet truly beautiful.*

Before turning out her light, she studied the photos on her cell. How incredible Rialto Beach was, how gorgeous Lake Crescent. Each one unique—radically different shorelines and expanses of water. Rialto Beach was a wild, rocky, and rustic survivor of vicious winter storms; Lake Crescent was deep blue and placid, surrounded by low green mountains and a sandy beach dotted with rental kayaks, rowboats, and fire rings.

Kate became tearful. She hadn't expected Angie and her two children to touch her so deeply. But they grew on her every moment she was with them. They were good people, all of them, despite the rough time they'd had. The children had been caught between two parents not suited to each other. Now they had a mother who was killing herself to keep food on the table. A mother who was bright, capable, and should be doing more with her life, for much better pay, than serving up coffee at The Little Red Barn.

Realizing just how much she was beginning to care, Kate experienced a wave of pure panic. For years, she had tried not to become involved with anyone. In college, she was into swimming, then into surviving her grief. In New York she was a marketing expert every waking moment. And in the South Pacific, she played, romanced, then moved on. In her heart of hearts, she had known that places like Bali, Moorea, and Raiatea were not her destiny. Eventually, she would go home.

Now, every day, she felt more and more that she *was* home. That the Olympic Peninsula was her destination. *And that thought absolutely scared her to death.*

***

In her bedroom, Angie also was awake. She longed for sleep, yet she couldn't forget the day. She too kept reliving every moment. How much fun she had had showing Kate some of her favorite places, beautiful spots she had known since childhood. And seeing in Kate's face that she was impressed, that the beauty was touching her.

Angie knew that Kate had walls, and Kate had shared some of the reasons why. Angie didn't know all of it, but what she knew was enough.

Admittedly, she was crazy about Kate. Angie tried not to make a big deal of it. She *did* think about it, trying to make sure it wasn't the money, or what the money could buy. Kate was a decent person. Angie could see that. Kate wanted to help, she was interested in all of them, recognized their problems and tried to find solutions. She was willing to give from what she had, rather than hoard her nest egg as some wealthy people might do.

As attractive as Kate was—and Angie didn't care about the age difference—she was also a problem in a way. *A problem for Angie's pride.* Having been totally rejected, tossed away as if she were nothing, Angie needed to achieve something on her own, to prove to herself that she was worth more than what her family or Zack thought about her. *She needed to take care of herself, not just be taken care of.* She was a lesbian. She knew she couldn't help it, and to her, being a lesbian wasn't bad or wrong. She still wanted to become a nurse, had always wanted to do that. If Zack had been more concerned, she could have gone to school while she was married. But he had such a traditional view of life, the woman at home with the kids. She understood, and in some ways, he was right, because Mark and Sarina were probably better off for the time and attention they'd received in those early years. However, when they started school, she could have begun college, at least part time, and worked toward achieving her own dream. He wouldn't hear of it. So, there was stress between them even before the dreaded lesbian issue came to light.

That thought reminded Angie that he must have been unfaithful to her. *How else would he have known she was a lesbian? Or else he had had partners before her, maybe that, too.* And maybe because she quickly became pregnant, twice, with all the attendant physical and emotional upsets, he hadn't realized that she was different until after the children were born, when she *should* have become the responsive sexual partner he wanted.

Oh, well, there was nothing Angie could do. To relive her life would bring the same result. She was born a lesbian. She needed to live as one and be as happy as possible. And Kate made her happy.

Whether their relationship would last or not, she had no way of knowing. It was a big unanswered question. At least Angie had learned she could be happy with a female sexual partner, and now she was actually falling in love with a woman.

***

When Kate wasn't spending time with Angie or with the kids, she continued exploring. She drove around Sequim proper, then the hills going south toward the mountains and the prairie going north toward the Strait. She looked at neighborhoods, at homes dotting the prairie. She saw all kinds of houses, from very old ones going back to pioneer times, to very trendy recent construction. From manufactured homes, to trailers on lots, to expensive mansions with acreage. While growth in the area had not been structured or orderly, there was something for everyone and every budget.

At first Kate felt most comfortable with the mansions. Some were really beautiful, and she was drawn to them. Although the landscape was different from Upstate New York, the houses had a feel to them that was familiar. After her first reaction, and after looking at several large homes, she realized that what had been fitting in her childhood wasn't necessarily where she was now as an adult after five years in the South Seas living on and needing almost nothing. Personally, she wasn't sure that she even wanted a house of her own. Upkeep, lots of upkeep. Time, energy, and money. She had all of those things, but she'd rather be with Angie, or taking Sarina swimming, or playing with Mark. *Why do all that work when you could have fun?*

Still, properties interested her. She gradually shifted to smaller, more practical houses with less land. And neighborhoods. Although she didn't talk to Angie about it, she started thinking about them. *What kind of home would be good for them? What kind of neighborhood?* Of course, Angie by herself couldn't afford better than her current government-subsidized rental housing. But Kate *could* afford it. She'd do anything to move Angie out of that stuffy little apartment and into a house with space and privacy for all of them. *Did she just include herself in that "all"?* Kate found herself musing over that thought for some time.

In her wanderings, while driving one morning east toward the John Wayne Marina, Kate discovered Wetlands Acres. She thought it a strange name for a housing development but out of curiosity she drove through the front gates and around the community. In several places, she found stands of trees and plants just off the main street, and at each there was a sign indicating wetlands areas and not to trespass.

The houses in Wetlands Acres were varied in size, color, design features, and floor plans. In general, Kate would have described it as a nice working-class neighborhood. Most homes were in good condition and the yards, fairly small, were kept up. She didn't see any for sale signs, which suggested that people resided there for a while. A good indicator, she felt.

As Kate drove around, she saw a young woman pushing a baby stroller followed by a small dog on a leash. Kate slowed down and waved. When the woman smiled and waved back, Kate stopped.

"You live in here?" she asked.

The woman nodded. "Yes. Can I help you with something?"

"Well, hi, I'm Kate Brighton, kind of new here."

"I'm Janie Hanson, and this is my little girl, Catherine, CC for short, and Rocky, my doxie mix."

"Have you lived here long?"

"Three or four years, I think. Although my husband works over in PA, we like living here in Sequim. I'm currently busy taking care of CC and we're expecting again the first of the year." She blushed.

Kate smiled. "That's great. So, you like Sequim. How is this neighborhood?"

"I'm happy here. It's kind of divided between retirees and young working people. We all get along pretty well, and if you need something, there's always somebody around here to help. It's pretty safe for pets. It seems like everyone has at least one dog, or a cat, anyway."

"Any of the houses have swimming pools?"

Janie grinned. "I don't think so. We're in the county and on septic. Yards are small. I don't think a pool would fit in here terribly well. The swimming season is short, anyway, and you'd pay a fortune to heat a pool. You want to swim, you go to the Y, I would suspect."

"Well, thanks, and have a nice day. Bye, and bye, CC and Rocky!"

Kate drove out of the neighborhood and on to the marina where she sat on a bench and watched the gentle tide coming into Sequim Bay. While surveying the scene, she continued thinking. *It was hard to know what would be good for Angie and the kids.* She tried to envision them in a variety of settings, from the places she had seen. Her conversation in Wetlands Acres had given her the impression that swimming pools in backyards would be hard to find, and maybe that made sense, given the climate, and the fact that much of the local housing, especially newer housing, was outside city limits and therefore dependent on well water and septic systems.

The easiest thing for her to do would be to ask Angie where she would like to live. But Kate hadn't yet learned to heed the warnings from Marianne and Jake. She just assumed that Angie would say the expected, that she was fine where she was. That didn't create space for Kate in the scenario.

So, instead of talking with Angie, Kate called a realtor and began looking seriously at houses.

15

After riding with a realtor through the Sequim-Dungeness Valley, inspecting several homes and not finding any that felt just right, Kate returned on her own to Wetlands Acres. The neighborhood had an appeal to her that she couldn't quite explain, and she wanted to know more about the community. She also wondered how long it would be before any properties came up for sale.

While driving through the streets, she encountered an older man, definitely a senior, who was pulling weeds in his front yard. She stopped and asked him a few questions about the development. He gave her a little background, and then she asked if he knew of any available property.

The man adjusted a ballcap on his graying head. "I only know of one," he said, "just down the street, a for sale by owner. 540 Friendship. You might check on that."

Kate thanked him and drove around until she found a house with a small "For Sale" sign by the walkway that she hadn't noticed earlier. *Not an attention-getting realtor's sign, for sure.*

Climbing out of her SUV, Kate walked to the front door. The house seemed to be bigger than most in the neighborhood and in good condition. She knocked.

A withered gray-haired woman pushing a walker opened the door and looked up at Kate from a face saddened with grief.

Kate felt uncomfortable. "I don't mean to trouble you," she began, almost apologetically. "I saw the sign, and I thought I'd ask some questions about the house."

The woman sighed. "My husband of sixty-four years died three weeks ago, and I have to sell our house. It's too much for me to take care of."

Kate blanched. She knew all too much about grief and was tempted to leave. "I'm sorry for your loss. If this is a bad time, I can come back later," she blurted out.

The woman closed her reddened eyes for a second and then shook her head. "I've got to do this. Now is as good a time as any, if you don't mind the way I look."

"You look fine. I'm Kate Brighton. I'd just like to look at your house, and it doesn't have to be perfectly cleaned up. That's not important."

"Okay, Norma Jackson here. Well, come on in."

Despite her sadness, her unkempt look, and her messy home, Norma did a good job of showing Kate around and pointing out the features of the house. There were two bedrooms, one of them quite large and with its own bath, and the second one smaller. They were toward one end of the house behind a large two-car garage. There was an open floor plan for the living room, dining area, and kitchen and a vaulted ceiling over this great room.

Beside the front door, on each side of the entryway, were two generous rooms. As they stopped there, Norma gave Kate the one smile she had offered. "They call these 'bonus rooms.' You see, you can't have more than two bedrooms in here—rooms with closets—and two bathrooms. It's 'cause of the septic system. You *can* have rooms without closets and baths. Most of the houses have one extra room that people use as an office or TV room. The second one, built into maybe half a dozen houses, usually ends up being full of storage."

The elderly lady pushed her walker toward the back of the house where she showed Kate an enclosed sun porch and a fenced back yard. Behind that were tall trees, mostly cedar and cottonwood, that formed part of the wetlands.

"Well," Norma said with a sigh. "That's it. I'll be moving to an assisted care facility in a few days. I don't have family to care for me, and I can't manage a place this large."

"I understand," Kate said. And then she thoughtfully added, "Do you have an idea of how much money you want or need to get for the house?"

Norma sighed. "Charlie had a friend here in real estate, or real estate law, one of his old cronies, anyway. He told me that if I could find a buyer, he'd draw up the papers for $1,000, which is a lot less expensive for me and the buyer, than if we had to use a realtor."

Kate nodded. "That sounds about right. I haven't bought a lot of houses in my life, but I think a direct sale for cash would benefit everyone."

"Under those conditions, I'd take $200,000 for it, as is, no inspection. With a realtor, it'd be worth several thousand more, yet there would also be those extra expenses and things that would have to be fixed."

In her marketing days, Kate would never have let a good deal escape. She knew instinctively that the house was worth more than Norma's figure. At the same time, she could see that Norma wasn't up to doing battle for that additional money and needed to be someplace more appropriate to her needs.

"If I offered you $220, 000 cash for the house as is, would we have a deal?"

Tears flowed from Norma's eyes and down her cheeks. "Yes, there is no way I could turn down that offer. Are you in a position to do that?"

Kate smiled and gave Norma a warm hug. "Yes, Norma, I am. If you call your friend who'll draw up the papers and tell him you have a buyer, I'll call my accountant in New York and have the funds transferred here to my bank account. I know it will take several days for filing of forms and paperwork, but I can assure you that you'll have your money and can move where you'll be safe and cared for."

***

On Saturday morning, a couple of weeks later, Kate showed up a little unexpectedly at Angie's apartment. Angie was surprised yet pleased to see her. Kate stepped inside, gave her a hug and a kiss, said hello to the kids, and then asked, "Angie, I know I didn't give you any warning, but is there any way I can take you for about an hour and show you something? It's special and kind of important."

Angie looked at her quizzically. "What are you up to now?"

"Just tell me, can you come?"

Angie sighed. "If you don't want the kids along, I'll have to find somewhere for them to stay. Maybe Vicki, next door. I'll go see what she's doing."

Angie disappeared into Vicki's apartment, as Kate sat down in the living room. Mark and Sarina were stretched out on the floor watching an old movie on TV.

Shortly, Angie came back. "Vicki and Bob are just going out to do some shopping. They have room for the kids in their van, and she said they could go along then stay in their apartment until I get back. So, I guess I can go, whatever it is you have in mind."

Angie turned off the TV, despite protests, and herded the kids next door. They shrugged and adjusted to the new situation. Vicki's daughter, Susan, was only a couple of years older than Mark, and they got along pretty well.

After the apartment was locked, and Kate and Angie were in the Forester, Angie fastened her seatbelt and asked pointedly, "What have you got up your ass this time?"

Kate had learned not to take Angie's sarcasm too seriously. While she wanted to be respectful of her, she also had learned that Angie could be stubborn even when something good was proposed to her. Since Kate could be that way too, she certainly understood. And, to be fair, Angie—having been stung more than once—was always skeptical of any new idea.

***

Kate drove out of the main part of town, turned down the road that went by the marina, and then at the top of a small hill, turned into Wetlands Acres. Angie rolled her eyes but kept her mouth shut.

Kate made a couple of turns and stopped before a large blue house with white trim.

"Somebody lives here, or are you getting into real estate now?" Angie quipped.

"I just want your opinion about something."

"Okay, show the way." Angie sighed as she climbed out of the Subaru.

Kate pulled a key out of her pocket, causing Angie to raise an eyebrow, and opened the front door of the house. Although there were a few boxes sitting on the floor here and there, the house was mostly empty.

Kate gave Angie the tour, starting with the bonus rooms, then the kitchen and the open dining and living area.

"Kitchen's nice. Needs updating, but it's a decent kitchen. Plenty of cabinet space." She surveyed the great room. "Big. I like the vaulted ceiling."

Down the hall, she said the guest bathroom was okay but needed work. The master suite was "huge" and could hold a king-sized bed, and she "liked" the bathroom except for the handicapped adaptations. She wasn't old enough to think those were necessary or attractive. The last bedroom was okay—smallish, still okay.

The sun porch pleased her, and she liked the fenced back yard, until Kate mentioned "nice for a dog." At that point, she gave Kate a dirty look.

And then Kate explained about the wetlands, as much as she knew about them.

Angie listened to all of Kate's discussion, then thought for a moment and looked around the house. "So, what, is this all about? Are you going to rent this place or something?"

"No, I bought it."

"You bought it?"

"Yes, I bought it for you."

"For ME? Without even asking me if I want it? Or want to live out here in the country? Where my kids could stand in the rain and cold to wait for a school bus? In a house that needs to be fixed up and painted before anybody would want to live in it?"

Kate paled. "I thought you'd be pleased. At least, I hoped you'd be pleased."

Angie threw her hands up in the air. "You and your money. Your goddamned money! You can just buy anything you want. Well, you can't buy me and the kids. Take me home."

Angie stormed out of the house, climbed into the Forester, and slammed the door. She sat there fuming as Kate rather humbly locked the front door, settled into the SUV and started the engine. Kate opened her mouth to say something. When she saw Angie's firm jaw, she kept quiet.

When they reached the apartment building, Angie climbed out of the Subaru without saying goodbye and walked up the stairs to her apartment.

Stunned, Kate sat for a moment and then drove away.

***

Jake grilled fish outside that evening and, along with a salad, baked potato, and fresh cookies for dessert, served up a very nice meal. When she brought everything inside to the table, she commented, "We're lucky to be having some warm days this fall. Usually, by this time, it's gray and rainy. I thought it would be fun to grill while I still can."

Kate had brought a tub of chocolate ice cream for their dinner, and Marianne announced it was her favorite. During dinner, Kate was very quiet, and Marianne had taken notice. However, she waited until the meal was well underway to speak.

"Okay, spill. Something's going on," Marianne began.

Kate finished her bite of food. "I bought a house." Her voice sounded subdued instead of excited.

"You bought a house?" Marianne looked stunned.

Kate nodded miserably.

"You need a house?"

"Well, I bought it for us."

Kate nodded agin, looking forlorn.

"For us? You mean you, Angie, and the kids?"

"You've decided to move in together already? It's only been a few months."

Kate shook her head. "We've talked about me staying here most likely, and about feeling love for each other. But not about moving in together."

"What possessed you to buy a house?"

"Stupidity, I guess. I wanted her to have a decent place to live, instead of that little apartment where the kids have to share a bedroom."

"Kids have shared bedrooms for eternity and I don't know that it's harmed their development, at least in most cases," Marianne observed.

"But there's a boy and a girl and they have no privacy."

"Spoken by an only child who grew up with all the privacy in the world, right?"

Kate shrugged, embarrassed.

Jake quickly interjected, “Marianne, I think Kate’s pretty miserable already. She’s clearly made a mistake of some kind, and I think she feels bad enough. Let’s not dump on her some more.”

Marianne smiled. “You’re right, Jake. I do become a little harsh once in a while. I hate to see anything wasted, whether it’s people, relationships or property.”

“I think Kate was trying to do a good thing, and it just misfired on her.”

Kate gave a wan smile to Jake.

Marianne studied Kate for a moment and then spoke up again. “Without trying to beat you down further, Kate, I do want to pass on one word of advice. I did say this before. You need to learn to communicate. Angie may be younger than you, less educated than you, not a world traveler, and so on, but she has had valuable life experience, and she’s an adult in her own right. She needs to be respected.

“When you want to please her, help her, support her, there is nothing wrong in that, as long as you don’t go out halfcocked and do it without consulting her. This house, whatever it is, might have been perfect if she had had a chance to see it, think about it, process it, without having it dumped in her lap as a done deal. I won’t say any more.”

Kate nodded. “You’re right, absolutely right. She got very angry when I took her to see the house, and she found everything wrong with it, and now she doesn’t want to speak to me. I don’t know what to do.”

“Probably nothing,” Jake suggested kindly. “Be patient. I know that’s hard for you. After she has time to think about it, she may see that you were trying to help, not hurt, and she’ll want to talk about it.”

“I hope so.”

Marianne put a hand on Kate’s arm. “Leaving Angie out of the discussion for a moment, I want to know all about this house. I’m sure Jake does, too. And how did you find it?”

So, Kate told them about her journeys around town looking at subdivisions and neighborhoods and the prairie. And about her attraction to Wetlands Acres and her return a second time looking for a house.

"Despite the funky name, that's a pretty good subdivision," Jake commented. "It has a good reputation as a safe family neighborhood. In the beginning, there were some questions about building within a wetlands area, and they've had a few problems with water seeping into places where they didn't want it. But the development has been there more than twenty years and is pretty much built out. It's a nice basic place, it's pretty, and the residents seem friendly."

"That's what I thought," Kate said.

She told them about Norma and her needing to sell the house because her husband had died, what she wanted and what Kate offered.

Jake looked at Kate thoughtfully. "I think houses in that area are selling for $260K and a few for even more than that. You got a steal. However, your Norma couldn't have gotten that much without doing the remodeling and upgrading, and it sounds like she wasn't in a position to do it. You more than met her asking price. She'll never be sorry she sold to you, given the circumstances."

"So," Marianne asked, "are you going to move out of TC and into that house now?"

"I thought I was, but if Angie doesn't want to live there, I may just rent it out or fix it up and turn it over. It's more house than I need by myself."

"Well," Jake suggested, "don't do anything rash."

***

A few days later, Kate was stretched out on her bed in TC, trying to decide whether to attend a potluck dinner being held up in the clubhouse or go into town to eat or maybe try out the local casino. Nothing seemed to appeal. Since her awkward scene with Angie, she had no taste for anything.

The phone rang. In her doldrums, Kate just picked up the cell without looking and tapped the button to answer.

"Hi, Kate, it's Angie."

Kate sat bolt upright. "Yes, hi, Angie. How are you?" She swallowed hard and her heart pounded.

"I'm fine. How are you?"

"Oh, I'm okay." Although she wanted to add "missing you," she thought better about complaining.

"Look," Angie said abruptly. "I've thought a lot about that house. I still think you were wrong to buy it, but I may have overreacted. At this point, I think I'm ready to talk about it without blowing up. I had to cool down a bit, to be honest."

Kate made a fist with her hand. "Yeah, I know how that is."

"How about we have dinner, maybe tomorrow evening, someplace private, and discuss the house?"

"You want to go to a restaurant, come here, eat at your place, or what?"

"A restaurant, I think, where we can talk. Vicki will take the kids for dinner and keep them until I get back. She said it was no problem."

***

Angie and Kate met the next evening at a small restaurant downtown that had been a house then remodeled into a decent eatery. They found a quiet table in a corner where they could talk.

"I'm going to have steak." Angie smiled. "I seldom have a chance for steak. I have an empty spot for steak."

Kate relaxed into a grin. "I seldom eat steak either, except that night at TC." She stopped, feeling embarrassed, remembering that special evening and not knowing yet where what Angie was thinking. "I'll join you. Some wine to go with?"

Angie nodded without adding anything to the conversation.

"Any preference?" Kate asked, nervously.

"I like the reds myself. I know you are supposed to have certain wines with certain foods, but I usually choose a red, anyway."

Kate placed an order for a glass of her own favorite, a sweet Riesling, and for Angie a Merlot that she had selected from the menu.

Once their food orders had been placed, Angie picked up her wine glass and held it out to clink with Kate's glass. "Peace?" she asked with a shy smile.

"Peace," Kate responded with relief.

Angie took a sip of her wine, savored it, and then set the glass down. "Let's talk about the house."

Kate swallowed again. "I'm so sorry."

Angie shook her head and raised a hand. "Enough. Let's both accept that you blew it and move on. Let's see what we can salvage."

Not quite sure what Angie meant, Kate looked at her questioningly.

"When this happened, I was ready to tell you to scram. After thinking about it, I decided to try to turn a negative into a positive."

"And that is?" Kate queried hesitantly.

"Well, a house is walls, floor, roof, foundation, windows, heating and cooling, water services and electricity and so on."

"Yeah?"

"That's the house. But a house isn't a home. It's what you put into the house that makes it a home. Decorations, furniture, etc. Those are things that make it comfortable and for people to want to be there."

"Okay, I get that."

"So, I decided that I can forgive you for buying a house that I would never have chosen, if you can allow me to do the decorating and make it a place I where can feel at home."

Kate smiled. "That's perfect. I'm not good at that anyway."

Angie added, "It means carte blanche. I decide and you pay."

"No problem."

Angie fingered her wine glass. "That house needs a lot of things done to it. Some immediately. Some could wait. The walls inside need painting. The floor, tile and carpeting need to be fixed or replaced. Those need to be done now."

Kate agreed. "Okay, no problem with that."

"If those are set to be fixed, then we could order furniture, my pick, and we could move in soon. Although eventually the bathrooms and kitchen need upgrading, I can live with them as they are for now. As long as everything functions."

Kate looked at her lovingly. "I don't see any issue with any of that. You have the right to make your choices, and I'll accept whatever they are. I might have some opinions about the room that I hope to make my office, but everything else would be yours totally. Upgrades and all, appliances, color choices, everything."

Angie gave Kate a peck on the cheek. "I can live with that. My only other demand is that you talk to me before you do anything else major that ultimately will involve both of us. And for the future, you don't buy a house for a family without first asking the woman to live with you."

"I know," Kate admitted. "I have a lot to learn about building a relationship. Marianne has reamed me out over that, more than once."

Angie grinned. "Marianne is a wise woman."

***

After dinner, they hugged and kissed goodbye. Before walking away, Angie informed Kate that she had found Mark and Sarina a sitter for Saturday evening, and if Kate wanted, she could come out to TC to spend the night "working on our relationship."

Kate happily agreed as a tingle went up and down her spine.

16

The house's interior had been painted a pale mint green. Dark hardwood floors throughout gleamed with a new-floor shine. In the apartment, Angie and Kate were engaged in packing up the bedroom for the move, with Mark and Sarina busy corralling their own belongings.

Kate's cell suddenly jingled. Noting the caller, she stepped into the hallway. "Yeah, Steve," she said into the phone, "great to hear from you. What's up? You sound stressed."

Kate listened for a moment. "My goodness. That's terrible. So, you are in Newport Harbor. Okay, let me see what I can do. I'll get back to you as soon as I can."

Scratching her head, Kate returned to the bedroom. She sighed as she looked at all the boxes and considered everything they had to do this weekend. "Steve, the guy I came here with on his boat?"

Angie nodded, her body visibly stiffening, expecting something bad.

"Well, he's had an accident at sea. He's in Newport Harbor in Oregon, and he needs me to help sail his boat to San Francisco."

Angie frowned. "Now?"

"Yes, now, ASAP. Apparently he hurt himself pretty badly."

"Can't he stay there until he gets well?" Angie asked plaintively, as she surveyed the box she was filling.

"I don't know all the details, but I guess not. He wouldn't have asked if he didn't need me to come."

"So, what do we do about this?" Her hand swept the room.

"I don't know. Let me call Jake."

Angie sighed deeply, shrugged, and went back to her packing.

***

On the living room sofa, Kate sat on the one empty spot she could find and called Jake and Marianne. She sighed with relief when Jake answered.

"Hi, Jake. I have a question for you. What's the fastest way to go from here to Newport, Oregon?"

"Hmm," Jake responded, "plane, I guess. Maybe a couple of hours. However, I doubt that there's any commercial service from the Olympic Peninsula. You'd have to round up a private pilot with time to take you."

"What's your advice about that?"

"Well, Sequim's airport is pretty small. I think you'd do better finding a pilot in Port Angeles."

Kate heard Jake speaking to Marianne in the background. "Wait, Kate, we know a woman who lives out at Diamond Point. There's a private field there, and she has a plane. Marianne's looking for her number. If she's around, she could fly you there sometime today, I would think."

Kate let out a deep puff of air. "Okay. I'll hang on."

After a brief pause, Jake read off some numbers that Kate wrote down.

"Woman's a lesbian, by the way. Member of our lunch group."

"Lunch group?" Kate asked.

"I'll tell you later."

"Okay."

Kate tapped in the digits and waited through several rings. Just as she was about to give up, a voice came on the line.

"Holly Sanders here."

"Hi, I'm Kate Brighton. Jake Summers gave me your number because she said you are a friend and a pilot."

"Yes, I know Jake. Do you need something?"

"Yes, I have a friend who urgently needs my help in Newport, Oregon, and I have to get there the quickest way possible. Jake suggested you might be able to help."

"Let me check the weather. I think it's supposed to be okay along the coast. Hang on a second." She disappeared and then returned. "It's clear from here to Newport right now. I'm not a commercially licensed pilot, but I can take you if you cover the gas and any expenses. I'll have to top off the tank before we leave here and pick up some fuel in Newport for my return flight. It's a little over two hours each way."

"The money's no problem."

Holly gave Kate the directions to her home in Diamond Point.

Kate called Jake then reported to Angie. "Jake's going to take me to a pilot who can fly me directly to Newport."

Angie nodded. "And what about the move?" Her tone was a touch sarcastic.

Kate sighed. "I'll remind Jake that we were moving this weekend and see what she can do. She was already picking up the U-Haul, and maybe she can just devote the day to helping you load here and unload at the other end. I can't imagine that she wouldn't, under the circumstances."

Kate hugged them all goodbye. Angie's face clearly expressed her apprehension about Kate's departure. Sarina and Mark stood quietly, looking sad.

***

Holly Sanders met Kate and Jake at her front door. She was dressed for flying, and when Kate first saw her, with short cropped light brown hair, blue eyes, and a slender yet strong build, she thought she was looking at a clone of Amelia Earhart.

Before Kate could open her mouth, Holly said, "I know, Amelia Earhart. Sorry about that. You look like you've seen a ghost. Not to worry, I'm real and have lots of air miles under my belt. You'll be safe with me."

Kate sucked in her breath. *Had she really looked that shocked?*

Jake shook Holly's hand. Kate was amused. To her, that was sort of a guy thing.

"Okay," said Holly, "let's head for the plane and get ready. Coming, Jake?"

Jake followed the two other women around the house to a large garage that served as an airplane hangar. She glanced at Holly's single-engine aircraft sitting before the building, took in the airstrip just a few feet away and gave a raised eyebrow to other houses along the tarmac that had similar garages.

"Well," Holly said to Kate, "I'm gassed up and I've done my prelim check. So, if you'll haul yourself into the passenger seat, I'll climb in here and we'll be off."

Jake stepped back and watched quietly as Holly started the engine and maneuvered the plane onto the asphalt runway. She waved goodbye as, after revving the engine briefly, Holly and Kate took off and lifted quickly into a blue Sequim sky.

***

Jake sighed and returned to her truck. She now had to pick up the U-Haul then drive to Angie's apartment for the moving job.

When Jake arrived at Elkland, Angie and the kids were all over her.

"It's okay," Jake soothed. "Kate's in the air with a good pilot. In a couple of hours, she'll be calling from Oregon to tell us she's arrived safely. Meanwhile, we have a lot of packing to do, right?"

Jake started with the kids' bedroom, helping them assemble boxes, showing them how to put soft things around the outside to absorb shock and place their delicate treasures to the inside where they would be protected. Sarina and Mark were quick learners and in the next hour had their room almost completely packed.

Angie's bedroom also surrendered to quick organizing, then she and Jake headed to the kitchen, the room requiring the most work from everyone. For once, Angie thought, it was a good thing she didn't have lots of belongings.

***

After skirting the Olympic Mountain range, Holly hugged the Washington coast so Kate could watch the waves crashing on beaches.

"You really lucked out on this trip," Holly mentioned. "It's nice today, but tonight the wind is expected to pick up, and a storm is coming in, first to the north and then moving southward along the coast all the way into California. Tomorrow I might have been hesitant to make this run."

Kate grinned. She was becoming accustomed to the engine noise and the up and down motions of the aircraft. Not terribly different from a sailboat.

"What is this trip all about, and what's the urgency, if you don't mind my asking?"

Kate sighed. "Steve Gutierrez, a sailor I met in Honolulu, took me on as crew in June for a run to Seattle on his sloop. Supposed to take three to four weeks. We floated around the North Pacific for weeks in doldrums until we finally latched onto a wind that blew us right into the Strait. We became good friends on the trip, which lasted nearly two months. I remained in Sequim to see Marianne, who's an old friend."

Holly nodded.

"Steve went on to Seattle to visit friends, and I don't know what he has done since. This morning he called me from Newport saying he's had an accident and needs help to sail his boat to San Francisco. At this point, I don't know any more than that. On the phone, I could hear stress or pain in his voice. I assumed he wouldn't have asked this if there weren't a good reason." She shrugged. "Unfortunately, I was in the midst of helping my girlfriend and her two children move from an apartment into a house I bought."

"That must have been hard to walk out on."

Kate nodded and sighed. "Luckily Jake has become a really good friend in just the few months I've been in Sequim. She not only connected me with you but will spend the rest of the weekend getting Angie and the kids moved. And if I'm not back right away, she'll be the one helping them set up things and seeing that the utilities are taken care of as well. My girlfriend works full-time at The Little Red Barn. Do you know it?"

"Of course. My favorite coffeehouse, when I am in town."

Gradually feeling more comfortable, Kate glanced around the plane, checking out the back seats, the instrument panel, thinking about the low-wing. "What is this, anyway?" she finally asked.

"Piper Cherokee."

"What's that mean?"

"Well, it's the model name for a popular aircraft first built in the early 1960s, I think. It was designed to be an inexpensive, entry-level, single-engine aircraft. It's proved reliable and is now a classic still popular with many pilots. Although I could afford a newer, fancier plane, I'm happy with this one."

Holly looked to be about fifty, an attractive fifty, with a touch of gray in her hair. "How long have you been flying?" Kate asked.

"Since I was a teenager. Once you get the bug, it never goes away."

"You have a partner? Jake suggested you were 'one of the family.'"

Holly laughed warmly. "Oh, Jake, you've outed me again. Yes, I have a partner, and, no, she isn't a pilot, although she occasionally flies with me. Susan's a veterinarian and works at one of the animal clinics in Sequim."

"Are you from here?"

"No, Orange County, California."

"Why did you come up here?"

"Think about it. The Peninsula has beautiful scenery, gorgeous skies, changeable weather, but nothing too extreme, and it's not crowded yet. It's reasonably safe to fly, as long as you don't challenge a major storm—like flying in the mountains when there's thunder and lightning. I take friends along who do photography, and together we capture some really great pictures of this amazing landscape. I think I have the best possible view!"

***

They soon passed over the mouth of the Columbia River, and Kate noticed changes in wind currents as they crossed into Oregon.

"See those sandy islands down there in the river, at the mouth?"

Kate nodded.

"That's the Columbia Bar. It's one of the most dangerous spots for boaters anywhere, when they are trying to enter the Columbia from the ocean. There have been lots of Coast Guard rescues along the bar—and also rescuers who have died in the attempt."

Kate looked at the big bridge crossing the Columbia from Washington to Oregon and asked what the city was. She didn't remember.

"That's Astoria. A Victorian town with lots of beautiful buildings, marine museum, and a monumental column on a hill. Even at this height, if you look down, you might be able to find the column. Wait, I'll tip my wing." Holly lowered the wing on Kate's side of the plane, and indeed, Kate glimpsed a tall, white tower on an oval field.

They continued flying along the Oregon coastline and past coastal towns that Holly identified for Kate. Taking a deep breath, Kate admitted there was a lot she hadn't seen of the Pacific Northwest.

While watching the landscape below, Kate remembered something she wanted to ask. "Jake said you were part of a lunch bunch. What did she mean?"

Holly laughed. "Outed again. She's talking about a group of professional lesbians who meet for lunch about once a month, mostly at TC, or sometimes in private homes. These women want a place to socialize with friends without their personal lives being compromised. The group's been around for several years. There must be about forty women who participate when they are in town. Some are still working but most are retired. They live well and travel a lot."

Kate nodded. "No wonder I haven't heard of it. It's restricted to couples, right?"

Holly nodded. "Pretty much. Most of these women have been with their partners for many years. Although it's a social group, it's not aimed at singles wanting to date."

Mulling that over, Kate looked out the window. *No wonder Marianne and Jake hadn't mentioned this group to her, since in no way was she qualified to attend. Maybe someday.*

***

After Lincoln City, Holly began gradually to descend for a landing in Newport. The airfield was just south of the main part of the city and located on a bluff overlooking the ocean.

"As long as visibility is good, this is an easy airport to use," Holly said. "When it's stormy or foggy, I wouldn't be landing here."

They settled onto the runway for a gentle landing. Kate was really grateful to Holly for dropping everything and making this emergency flight to Newport. She voiced her thankfulness.

"Not to worry. This was fun for me, and we're on a mission of mercy." She grinned at Kate.

They stepped into the flight office to report Holly's plane, now parked off the tarmac, and to file a flight plan for her return trip later in the day. "Anybody heading into town anytime soon?" she asked an employee behind the counter.

"Let me check." The older man had a slight stoop to his shoulders and a receding hairline. He reached for a phone to make a call. He asked a question, nodded, and put the receiver down.

"Go around the building and look for a green 2500. A guy named Bob ought to be there someplace. He's driving into town in a couple of minutes."

"Thanks! I appreciate it!"

Kate wondered what they were looking for until she saw a big wide-bodied truck sitting in the gravel. It was painted green and tall enough to have running boards.

A man stood by the truck talking on his cell, evidently Bob. He ended the conversation and turned to them. "You the gals wantin' a ride to town?"

"Yes, that's us." Holly gave him a grin.

"Well, climb on up. One o' you's in the front an' one behind."

"Holly, you take the front."

Holly and Kate pulled themselves up into the cab, and Bob climbed aboard. "Where you's headin'?"

"Just downtown," Holly said. "You can drop us off by the street that goes to the marina."

Bob nodded. They gave him first names, and he replied in kind. He asked where they had come from and commented that he thought "Sequim" was a funny name for a town. By that time, they had completed the distance into central Newport. When Bob stopped, he pointed out where they needed to go.

Holly thanked him and offered him money. He declined. She shook his hand then she and Kate climbed down from the truck. He waved and drove off.

"Now," Holly said, "I'm going to sit down to a nice lunch before I go back to my plane and return to Sequim. The weather should be good at least until dinnertime, and I'll be home by then. So, I'm going to treat myself."

Although she was worried about Steve, Kate also was hungry. "I'll go with you, maybe take something for Steve. And it's my treat, after all you've done for me."

Holly identified a good fish house a few doors away. They entered and settled down with menus and soft drinks. When the server came, Holly ordered a shrimp salad and Kate chose halibut and chips with a second order to go.

They didn't talk much, focusing on their food. "I'm a bit afraid of what I'm going to find when I reach Steve's boat," Kate admitted. She explained a little of Steve's background and why he was living on a boat.

Holly seemed empathetic. "Well, then, I'm going with you. In case your plans change, I don't want to leave you stranded. So, I'll face this Steve thing with you, and then we'll take it from there."

Armed with the carryout meal, the two women left the restaurant and entered the marina.

"Do you see his sloop?" Holly asked.

Kate glanced down the line and saw something familiar. "I think so, about six boats down on the left."

When they got to the *Lavender Loafer*, Kate could see damage, although fairly minor, to the topside. The mast seemed solid. Maybe it would be safe to sail the sloop.

"Steve," Kate called out as the two women gingerly stepped on board.

"Down here." His voice sounded muffled.

Kate peeped into the open hatch. Steve was stretched out on a bench in the main cabin, a pillow behind his head. Followed by Holly, Kate climbed down the companionway steps. She nearly gasped when she looked at Steve. His face and head had cuts that were crudely bandaged. His left leg was definitely broken, stabilized with a home made splint. His right arm hung in a sling, looking as if he had injured his arm or shoulder. Looking around, she realized that everything in the cabin had been tossed.

From a hesitant three feet away, Kate said, "Steve, this is Holly, a pilot from Sequim who flew me down here."

Steve nodded and offered a pain-filled smile. "Sorry not to be more presentable. I had a little accident."

Kate was appalled. "Did you trip and fall down the steps?"

"No, the boat was hit by a rogue wave. I don't know where it came from. There had been some wind and a bit of wave action, but I had no idea. I was down here, and suddenly the boat rolled, and I went flying around the cabin. When everything stopped rocking and rolling, I dragged myself up to take a look and saw there was still a mast and a mainsail. Although both jib sheets are gone, I have backup sheets and lines in storage down here. I was so shocked that it took me a while to realize I was bleeding and my leg was splintered. I turned on the engine and thankfully had enough gas to make it into Newport Harbor early this morning."

Kate went up to the V-berth in the bow and pulled out two canvas-covered sails from a locker. "I'll take care of this," she said to Steve and then hauled the bags up to the deck where she began work on replacing the missing jib sheets.

As Kate moved around above, Holly remained below deck with Steve and told him, "We brought you some lunch."

"Oh, thanks. I don't remember when I've had anything to eat. I've just been lying here swallowing aspirin and booze."

Holly helped him with the meal, holding it steady while he picked up the fish and chips with his one good hand.

"You need to be in the hospital immediately," she said to him, kindly yet firmly.

"I know, I know. But I can't. This boat is my home. I have a slip in the Bay Area where I stay for the winter. The weather here is turning. That wave was my warning to sail home. If I go to a hospital here, I'll be tied up for weeks. The boat will sit here until it's too late to take it on the ocean until next spring. It snows here and won't be a good place for me to be living then."

Holly sighed regretfully. "I get it. Just so you realize that you're taking a lot of health risks to sail in this condition. You are what, about five days out of San Francisco under the best of conditions? By the time you and Kate arrive there, you could have infection, and treating your leg will be much more complicated."

"I know, but I can't stay here. Kaiser will take complete care of me there."

Holly studied him. "What first aid supplies do you have on the boat?"

"Rubbing alcohol, aspirin, some bandages, maybe even some ibuprofen, if I could just find it."

"Where would it likely be?"

"There might be something under the sink here in the galley, or in the bathroom, or a storage bin in the V-berth, or even these side pockets here in the main cabin."

"I'll see what I can find." Holly rummaged around the boat and returned a few minutes later with bottles and bandages. She began to work on Steve's wounds, swabbing them with alcohol and cotton balls and applying fresh coverings.

"Thank you, I can't tell you how grateful I am." His voice was stressed with pain.

When Kate returned from topside, Holly talked with both of them. "I understand the situation. However, you can't leave here headed south until at least tomorrow morning, possibly noon. The storm coming in this evening should be a quick one, and it's headed south. It will run ahead of you after the front passes. It'll be rocky out there on the ocean, yet doable, I think.

"I would suggest you have a good dinner, stock up on supplies for the trip, clean up down here as best you can, and try for as much rest tonight as possible before you even think about taking off. You have a lot of sailing ahead of you." She looked at Kate and added, "And one person doing it."

Steve shook his head. "I'll try to spell her at the helm, and she can rest, maybe in the daytime, when I can see better."

"I don't know how you will be able to stand at the wheel," Kate observed.

"I have a step stool that I can sit on. Even though I'll have to sit, I'll do what I have to, to help us get there."

Holly nodded at him. "Guess you have a plan." She stood, making ready to leave.

"Thank you, Holly, for your help," Kate said. "You've gone way beyond."

"No problem. I had some first aid training while becoming a pilot, so it's not hard for me to handle things like this."

Holly climbed the steps up to the deck. Kate followed. "Thanks so much," Kate said quietly, pulling out some $100 bills and passing three of them over to Holly. "If this doesn't cover your expenses, I'll give you more money later."

Holly shook her head. "This is more than enough. Before I leave, I'm going to walk to the nearest drugstore and pick up better cleansing and disinfecting supplies for you to change Steve's bandages. I'll also find out where the nearest grocery is, because you're going to have to stock up before the rain comes tonight, enough for five days if not six. He doesn't have much down there to feed two people."

Kate grinned. "Holly, you're a marvel."

"Well, I'll be back in a few minutes, and then I'll go to the airport and hightail it out of here. Home safe by dinner!"

***

Kate cleaned up the cabin, talked with Steve, and made a grocery list while she awaited Holly's return. A few minutes later, the pilot climbed back onto the sloop. "Here's the stuff. A market is a couple of blocks to the north. And I've found a ride to the airport. I'm off."

Kate hugged her warmly. "Thanks again. I'll see you back in Sequim."

Kate followed Holly to the deck and then watched her stride down the dock. *What a good woman.*

After Holly was out of sight, Kate looked around the cabin as she went back down the companionway. *So much to do!*

She had to call Angie, clean and organize the boat, find some dinner for them, go to the grocery—and she needed to learn more about Steve and what had happened to him since they were last together. She also had to tell him about Angie and the kids. *Boy, was he going to be surprised!*

17

Jake and Angie were loading the U-Haul when Angie's phone chimed.

She put down a box she was carrying and tapped the phone. She nearly cheered out loud when she saw that the call was from Kate. "Oh, I am *so* glad to hear your voice. Jake's been here and we've been packing all morning. Marianne showed up at noon with pizzas, salads, and cold drinks. We were exhausted and very grateful when she arrived. She stayed to eat with us and then packed several boxes of kitchen things, sitting down of course. She just left. We're now loading the truck."

"Good to hear that," Kate replied over the phone. "Holly Sanders, my pilot, landed in Newport by noon. It's very pretty here, by the way. We both went to the boat, and everything's a mess. Steve has a broken leg, I'm sure, head cuts, a bad shoulder, and who knows the condition of his ribs. The boat itself came out well, considering."

"What happened?"

"Rogue wave. He was below deck and got thrown around."

"Sounds like he needs to be in the hospital."

"Right. I agree. Only cold weather is about to arrive. He lives on his boat and needs to sail back to San Francisco. He's scared to be caught here, with little insulation onboard for keeping warm in snow, wind, rain, cold—everything that will hit this coast during winter. He already has a slip reserved down south and has friends there who can help him. He's a Kaiser Permanente patient and he's fully covered medically in the City."

"Wow. It's a crazy solution, but I understand. What a mess! I know you have to respect his wishes, yet are you going to be handling the boat alone?"

"Pretty much. We leave tomorrow. Have to wait out a storm coming through tonight; it'll move on south tomorrow morning. You may not see much of it up there in Sequim. I'm more than two-hundred miles south. We'll follow that storm. It might be a little rocky, but I think we can make it. I looked it up on the chart. It's 459 nautical miles from Newport to San Francisco."

"You'll see the Golden Gate Bridge!"

"Yes, sail right under it. About five days from tomorrow."

Angie sighed. "That's a long time. I don't mean to complain, but the timing is terrible."

"I'm very sorry, Angie. I do hope you understand. Jake will help, and Marianne, too. Things will be taken care of. And when I'm back, I'll pick up the slack to do whatever hasn't been finished."

"I know. I just miss you. I feel really safe when you're around."

"I'm missing you, too. Just think of me thinking of you, and we'll stay connected."

"Okay, I'll try."

"Just remember that I can't call you while at sea. No coverage. If we land somewhere for supplies, I'll try to give you a call. Otherwise, I'll have to wait until I reach San Francisco and Steve is safely in the hospital."

"All right. I guess, then, that this is goodbye."

"Yes." Kate laughed. "Yes, baby, this is goodbye—for now."

***

Angie returned to her task. Jake nodded as she came up the ramp with a loaded dolly. "Kate arrived in Newport?"

"Yeah, she's sailing tomorrow for San Francisco with this guy, Steve, on his boat. At least five days on the water with no connections, and this Steve person is badly injured. It's scary."

"She'll be fine. Kate's very capable."

Angie sighed. "I know."

***

When the U-Haul was loaded, Jake drove the rental truck with Mark in the passenger seat. Angie and Sarina followed in the Ford sedan.

Angie was quiet for a few moments as she remained a safe distance behind the truck. Then Sarina looked up at her. "Mama, I'm excited to be going to a house, but I'm scared, too. I won't know anybody there."

Angie nodded. "I feel the same way, especially since Kate isn't here. This was all her idea, and now she's not here to help."

"Jake's here. And Marianne, too."

"I know. It's just that there's a lot to do."

"We'll do it, right, Mama?"

Angie sighed. *She was leaning on her daughter. She was supposed to be the brave one and make it safe for the kids*. "Yes, we'll do it, Sarina."

After a couple of turns and a mile of uphill roadway, they entered Wetlands Acres.

Friendship Boulevard circled the neighborhood. Loyalty Way, Love Lane, and Hospitality Drive cut through the center. Angie rolled her eyes. She just hoped the place would turn out to be hospitable because she could use some friends right now.

Jake backed into the driveway of the house, and Angie parked in the street. Having been there twice, Angie realized that her reactions kept changing. She had grown up on farming land, and Zack had owned a house and some acreage at the edge of Sequim. She had moved there when they married. This living close together, side-by-side, was something she had never really experienced. *Well, people were also very close to each other in apartment buildings. Angie and the kids had survived that. However, apartments seemed temporary, and this might turn out to be their permanent home*. "Think positive," she whispered to herself.

With a sigh, Angie climbed out of the car, pulled a house key from her pocket, and prepared for battle.

***

Angie and Jake—followed closely by a somewhat subdued Mark and Sarina—walked through the house.

"Thank goodness we've had the keys for several days," Angie remarked to Jake, "to have the walls painted, the carpeting removed, and the wood floors sanded and refinished. Kate had the electricity turned on, set up a cable account, and was here when the beds were delivered. Now, with her gone, we won't have any other furniture until she gets back."

Jake nodded. "It may not seem like it now, but still, you're lucky you had a furnished apartment because we didn't have an awful lot to bring over."

Angie nodded. "I know." She glanced around. "Well," she sighed, "best get to it."

When she brought in the first load from the truck, Jake commented, "I think this is mostly for the kitchen. Do you want me to stack these in any certain place?"

"I want to clean thoroughly before I put everything away. Just make a pile in the middle of the floor. As soon as I find the box with the cleaning supplies, I'll start with the refrigerator, then I'll do the cabinets. I think we'll have most of the stuff put away by this evening."

Jake reached out and pulled Angie into her strong arms. "Try to relax, Angie. You look very tense. This will be all right."

Angie hung onto her new friend for a moment. "I know. It's just such a big adjustment."

Jake nodded and released her. "Which rooms are which, so things end up where they belong?"

Sarina and Mark were busy exploring, going from room to room and in and out the back door to see the patio and the yard and then opening up the garage. They were already laughing with the fun of their adventure.

Shrugging at the kids and their antics, Angie walked with Jake to the front door. She pointed to the large "bonus" rooms on either side. "This one on my right will be Kate's room. Like her study or something. I have to make sure there's a cable and Internet outlet in there for her. I have no idea what wall it goes on."

"We'll figure it out."

"On the other side is Mark's room. He can play man of the house." She grinned at Jake then reached down and felt the mattress of the new twin bed that had been delivered. "Mark will like this, I think."

Jake laughed. "His own room? He'd better!"

They walked down a hallway, past the guest bathroom and then into a smaller bedroom, which would be Sarina's. "Thankfully, it has a good-sized closet because Sarina loves clothes."

At the other end of the hallway was the master bedroom and *en suite* bath. The room was empty except for the king-sized bed that sat nakedly in the middle. "Kate insisted on this, even though I'm supposed to decorate the whole house. I've never slept on a king. I suppose if sometime down the road all four of us end up sleeping together, a big bed would make sense."

"And maybe a dog or two, or a cat?"

Angie scrunched up her nose. "Don't even think about it!"

Jake laughed.

***

When dinnertime approached, all the boxes were in the house and some had already been emptied. The refrigerator was filled and several stacks of dishes were sitting on the counters. The pantry was yet to be done. The kids were playing on the floor in Mark's room with a few of his toys. Angie could hear their laughter and was glad they were having fun. She felt totally overwhelmed and exhausted.

Jake came in from the garage. "I just got a call from Marianne. Dinner is ready at the house. Let's take a break and go there for some nourishment and a few minutes rest."

Angie closed her eyes. "Sounds heavenly."

"After dinner, we can drop off the U-Haul. The place will be closed, but they told me where to leave the truck and keys."

"Did you have to pay for this?"

Jake put a hand on Angie's arm. "Not to worry. It wasn't much, and I know Kate will pay me back when she gets home. It's no biggie, believe me."

"I hope not."

***

Angie drove her car and followed Jake back into town. They turned onto Seventh Avenue and were soon parked before Marianne's and Jake's home. Angie uttered a sigh of relief, not only because she was feeling empty and tired, but also because being in their home felt familiar. They were becoming like family.

Marianne was rolling around the kitchen and good smells came from the oven. The dining-room table was set. They dropped into their usual seats. The only one absent was Kate.

Marianne wheeled herself up to Jake with the last dish in her lap. She handed that to Jake and then pulled up to her position at the head of the table. She had them all hold hands as she said grace. Then she started passing a large bowl. "Since it's getting cooler, I made a stew. There's plenty of good meat chunks, vegetables and potatoes, everything we need to keep warm and filled up."

"Mmmm good," Mark piped up.

"I love stew," added Sarina.

Angie closed her eyes, grateful in this moment. She enjoyed Marianne's and Jack's one-dish meals. Stew also brought good memories of fall family times before Zack's defection.

After they were served, Marianne asked gently, "Any word from Kate?"

Angie nodded. "Early this afternoon. She arrived there about noon and said that a storm is passing through tonight. She thought they could set sail sometime tomorrow. It's about five days or so to San Francisco. Steve, the boat owner, is in pretty bad shape. Kate will be doing most of the sailing."

Marianne nodded. "Kate's very resourceful. She'll figure out what needs to be done. They'll arrive safely, I'm sure."

Angie was proud that the kids remembered to tell Marianne how much they liked the stew. They even told her which veggies were their favorites. Both devoured the beef chunks because they seldom had eaten real beef in the past year although, admittedly, food choices had improved since Kate's arrival on the scene.

Marianne rolled into the kitchen and returned with a plate of fresh-baked cookies for dessert. "Oh, chocolate chip!" Sarina was ecstatic.

Marianne smiled. "Glad you like them. I'm a bit of a chocoholic myself."

When they were done clearing the table and the dishes were in the dishwasher, Marianne inquired, "Are you going to do more work tonight?"

"I hate to think of it, but we *have* to make the beds before we can go to sleep. The sheets for my bed are still in the packages. They should be washed first."

Jake stood up from her chair. "Oh, I can help you there." She went to a closet and came back with a set of blue cotton sheets that she handed to Angie. "These were from our bed before Marianne had the accident. They're clean and in good condition. I just hadn't gotten around to giving them away. You can put them on tonight and leave the washing until later when you have more energy. Use these afterward as a spare set."

Angie sighed, tears stinging her eyes. "That's perfect. Thank you *so* much, Jake."

"Anything I can do?" Marianne asked.

"Not tonight, I don't think. But tomorrow, if you can come over for a while, you could hand me things from boxes and I can place them on the shelves. And you could help organize the lower part of the pantry if you like."

Marianne nodded. "That sounds great."

***

Angie and the kids followed Jake to drop off the U-Haul, then Jake climbed into Angie's car for the ride back to town.

"Everything seems terribly far away," Angie sighed as they crossed Sequim.

"It's less than two miles from where you lived before. I think it's because it's all so new to you. You'll adjust."

"I hope so."

Once they arrived at the house, Jake assisted Angie in locating the sheets and blankets for Mark and Sarina's beds and helped her get them made. Then they tackled the new king-sized bed. Queen-sized blankets and comforter would have to serve until she could buy new ones.

The evening air was cooling down, and Sarina complained of being cold. Jake located the thermostat, showing Angie how to set the furnace for the night.

"If there's anything else you need, I'll stay. Otherwise, call us in the morning when you're ready, and Marianne and I will help you finish putting things away."

"Okay, that's great. Right now, I'm just dreaming of bed."

"I can imagine. I'm pretty bushed, too. Do you have food for breakfast, or should we bring something?"

Angie shook her head. "Breakfast I can handle. Sandwiches for lunch would be great. I have to go to the store eventually, but I'm not looking forward to that."

Jake hugged her. "You're here. The worst is over. Everything will be better day-by-day, as the bugs are worked out. Just remember that as long as Kate is away, I'm her backup. I'll do whatever you need, and Marianne will want me to do that."

"Oh, thank you, Jake."

After their friend left, Angie took one glance into the laundry room then turned off the light. She couldn't start laundry now. Mark and Sarina were in Mark's room. She heard their voices and went there. With hardwood floors throughout, the house seemed to carry noise, which she found a little strange. But she did like the floors better than that cheap, not very clean carpeting in the apartment.

Mark looked up at her a little sheepishly. "It's going to be weird to sleep out here alone. I'm used to being with Sarina."

"Well, you're a big boy now and it's time for you to have a room of your own."

He looked a bit crestfallen. "Okay, Mom."

"Both of you need to prepare for bed. Did you find your toothbrushes?"

"Yes, Mama," Sarina said proudly. "We put everything in the hall bathroom."

"I'll help you figure out how the shower works. I want you both to take a shower, brush your teeth, and jump into bed. After I've cleaned up, I'll say goodnight. We're all tired and need to sleep."

A few minutes later, Angie came to Mark's room. He was sitting on the side of his bed, looking uncomfortable.

"Come on, hop in. I'll pull the covers up and kiss you goodnight," Angie said. "I know it's hard until we have some furniture in here."

When she had him settled, she turned off the ceiling light. "Do you want the door open or closed?"

"Open."

"Okay."

Angie moved down the hallway and replayed this same scene in Sarina's room.

"It feels strange, Mama, without Mark here."

"I know. You'll get used to it. When you have all your things put away, you'll feel better."

After kissing her goodnight and tucking her in, Angie turned out the ceiling light.

Going back to the master bedroom, Angie looked at the big bed. It, too, seemed foreign. There was no place for an alarm clock except on the floor. The room felt huge, with not a single piece of furniture in it except the bed.

Angie turned off the hall light and fell tiredly into bed. She felt so exhausted that she was sure she would sleep no matter what. She stretched out, closed her eyes, and then tossed and turned, her mind refusing to shut off. She thought of each thing that needed to be done. The list was overwhelming. *Shoot. She needed to sleep. Why couldn't she forget all this stuff, just for a few hours?*

Suddenly, she felt a presence beside her. Two little bodies.

"Mama," said Sarina.

"Mom." It was Mark.

"Mama, can we just sleep with you for tonight? I'm scared, and I know Mark is scared, too. We want to be with you."

Angie sighed. *They were right.*

"Okay, jump in here. I'll scoot over to make room for you."

Angie ended up on the left side of the bed, not her usual spot, with Sarina to her right and Mark next to his sister, both their heads on one pillow.

She pulled them close. Safe together, all three slipped into a deep sleep.

***

The next morning, they awoke still tired. Nevertheless, there was work to do. Angie pushed herself, and the kids responded politely to whatever she asked of them. Breakfast was a hassle, because half the items they needed were still in boxes somewhere on the floor. They opened a few and found the right utensils or acceptable substitutes and made it through the meal, standing by the counter. They had no table or chairs. It was especially hard for the kids, but they tried to be careful and not make a mess.

Shortly after breakfast, Angie assigned tasks to Mark and Sarina: finding the linens to go into the hallway closet, separating empty boxes from ones with things still in them, and starting one laundry load in the washer after she located her cleaning supplies. Just as she was doing this, Marianne's van pulled up in the driveway. The house didn't have steps, but there was a threshold and Jake had to help push Marianne's wheelchair over it. "I'll have to build a little ramp for this," Jake commented to her partner, and she nodded.

Marianne had brought sandwiches, chips and drinks for lunch, and these were stowed away in the kitchen for later. Jake brought a card table and four chairs. "I know it will be a few days, at least, before you have dining-room furniture, and since we don't need these on a regular basis, you can use them until you have something of your own."

Angie sighed. "What would I do without you two?"

"We're just glad we can assist," Jake commented and Marianne nodded.

With everyone's help, by the end of the morning almost everything had a home. Jake then broke down the empty boxes and piled them for recycling at one side of the garage. When she returned from the garage, Marianne and Angie were setting out lunch.

Marianne had made both egg salad and ham and cheese sandwiches, more than they could use for lunch. "Just keep them in the refrigerator to help out, tonight or tomorrow," she said.

Angie leaned over and gave her a kiss on the cheek.

***

After lunch, Marianne was ready to rest. "I'm not used to this much work," she quipped. "I need a nap." She wheeled herself to the front door. Jake helped her over the threshold. "See you later," Marianne called as she directed herself to the van.

When Marianne was gone, Jake offered to go to the grocery with Angie, provided Angie could drop her off on the way back. "If you really don't mind, that's a great idea. Two heads are better than one. We need quite a few supplies, I'm afraid."

Angie made a grocery list, knowing it was the first of many, and then she and Jake took off to go shopping, Mark and Sarina buckled in the back seat of her sedan. At the store, she, Jake and the kids worked together. Angie read off things that were needed, and each one took off to look for them, bringing back items to put in the basket as Angie checked them off. *Moving*, she sighed, *no fun at all. Exhausting.*

At the checkout counter, Angie's eyes widened and she swallowed when she saw the total bill. Jake noticed and offered, "Look, let me get this, for today. You have so many other things to deal with, and I don't mind. You can always pay me back later, or Kate can take care of it."

When they were in the car, Angie looked over at Jake. "That's why you said you'd come, to pay the bill," she said gently.

Jake shrugged. “I didn’t know, for sure, but the thought did occur to me that you might need more than you could afford. I didn’t hear you say that Kate had given you any money when she left.”

Angie sighed. “No, she didn’t. She was in such a hurry, she didn’t think, I’m sure.”

Jake smiled at her. “I’m sure, too. And I’m not worried about getting repaid.”

When they stopped at Jake’s house and she hopped out, her last comment was, “You’re going to be short of furniture for a while. We have several folding captain’s chairs that you could use in your living room. And they aren’t too heavy to move wherever you need them. If there’s room in your trunk now, we can stick them in, or I can bring them by later in the truck.”

They managed to shove all the chairs into the car, and Jake waved them off.

For better or worse, and without Kate, Angie and her children had moved into Wetlands Acres.

18

The next day, being Monday, brought a new set of problems. School. Angie had not met anyone in this new neighborhood to take Mark and Angie to school, and her work hours began before school started. *What to do?* She considered this late Sunday evening when her mind finally grasped the idea that a new week was beginning.

After a moment's hesitation, she did the only thing she could. She called Jake, who was more than willing to pick up Mark and Sarina and drop them off at school. Afterward, they could walk over to the Boys & Girls Club, and Angie would collect them from there.

"How will I lock your house?" Jake asked.

"Oh, geez, another problem," Angie sighed.

"How about leaving your key with the kids? I'll pick them up, lock the house, drop them off at school and then go to a locksmith to have a couple of copies made. I'll leave those and the original with you at The Little Red Barn," Jake suggested.

"Perfect. But pick up four copies, one for you, one for Kate, and a couple of spares. If I need to give the kids one at some time, I have extras. Is that okay?"

"Sure."

While she had Jake on the phone, Angie focused on the next problem—arranging for Mark and Sarina to ride the school bus that stopped at the front gate of Wetlands Acres. Before she had time to worry, Jake offered to pick up the paperwork for their address change and riding the school bus and bring those to her.

Angie sighed. "Jake, you're a godsend."

***

While Angie struggled on the home front, Kate battled the ocean and Steve's injuries. True to Holly's predictions, the storm passed through Oregon headed south. They sailed behind it, experiencing kickback in wind and waves but still able to make decent progress toward their San Francisco destination.

At first, Kate was forced to tie off the helm any time she had to go below to use the head, eat something, or attend to Steve. She didn't like being away from the wheel for any length of time, and once the wind and rain had calmed down, she dragged seat cushions to the floor of the cockpit, brought up blankets and a pillow from below, and took rest breaks there when she couldn't stand at the wheel any longer.

Although Steve had believed he could help sail the sloop, getting him topside was nearly impossible. He was too badly injured to move up the steps by himself, and Kate, although a strong woman, was not able to haul his total weight. After the first day and night, they concluded that they would have to sleep in the cockpit in order for Steve to assist Kate in any way. This meant both of them moving him backwards up the steps, with Kate above pulling and Steve pushing with his one good leg. It was a painful effort, and at one point, Kate feared Steve would pass out. Eventually, they made it and managed to position him on cushions.

They stopped in Brookings, Oregon, and Eureka, California. In both cases, they tied the sloop to a transient dock, slept for six straight hours before eating a meal then sailed south again. These pauses lengthened the trip by nearly one day, but Kate felt that if they had not stopped, they wouldn't have made it at all. Each time they made landfall, Kate was totally exhausted and consumed with Steve's many needs. She just didn't think of calling Angie until they were back at sea and it was too late. She felt bad but had no way to replay the scenario.

Once they had makeshift bedding in the cockpit, and Steve could relieve Kate for breaks, meals, and medical tasks, conditions improved. Steve sat at the helm—in considerable pain but still capable of steering—for two-hour stints while Kate slept. In this manner, she figured she got a few hours of sleep during every twenty-four.

After they left Eureka's Humboldt Bay, Kate felt confident they would make San Francisco, later than planned, yet alive and with an intact sailing craft. As her eyes monitored the seas and the coasts, she thought often of Angie and the kids, but there was nothing she could do about contacting them. Besides, Steve and the *Lavender Loafer* were all consuming.

***

For Angie, the next few days passed both too quickly and too slowly. On Monday, the kids made it to school and the Boys & Girls Club. Then Jake came to the house and helped the cable company activate their account, so computers and televisions would work, the house had WiFi, and that every room had an outlet for an Internet connection.

Jake also took Sarina to Port Angeles for her swim time. Although Jake couldn't coach her like Kate would, she transported her there and back, watched her, and complimented her on her swimming ability. Jake came over to the house just before dark on two evenings and played pitch and catch with Mark, just as Kate would have. The new residents of Wetlands Acres also went to dinner twice at Marianne's and Jake's house, a respite from living without anything to make them comfortable in the house.

Meanwhile, there was no further word from Kate. Angie bit at her nails, something she hadn't done since she was a little girl, and wondered where Kate was and if she and Steve were safe. Her stress built up so much that after dinner, she walked around Friendship Boulevard. She had seen other people walking, mostly with dogs, but some without, and she did as well. Toward the end of the week, she met a mother pushing a stroller with a baby in it and a girl, probably her daughter, about Sarina's age. They talked and made plans for the two girls to play together. The mother, Janie Withers, wasn't currently working because of the infant in the stroller, and she appeared to be a potential resource. Angie heaved a sigh of relief as she continued her walk.

On Friday, she got a call from Holly Sanders, who wondered if they had heard anything from Kate. Angie admitted she had not. After the call, Angie became more anxious and wondered where Kate was. She thought the pilot sounded nice on the phone, older, more Kate's age. She wondered if Holly was a lesbian and whether she might have some interest in Kate. Angie tried not to think like that but her anxiety kept growing.

On Saturday, she took the kids with her into Port Angeles to a furniture store. *She couldn't buy anything, but she could look.* She let each child pick out bedroom furniture, and she looked at furniture for every room, noting numbers, prices, and snapping pictures with her phone. She had made an advance list of the basic things they needed, and it added up to thousands of dollars, making her head swim. Exhausted and frustrated after a couple of hours of looking with no ability to make even one purchase, she took Sarina and Mark out for an ice cream then returned to the house, which, she thought with a sigh, was still barren and hardly felt like a home. *If only Kate would call.* Angie was beginning to worry that something had happened on the ocean. *The boat could have sunk or capsized and they could have drowned. What if Steve had gotten worse? What if? What if?*

On Sunday she looked at television sets at Walmart. After a few minutes, she walked out of the store. They'd just have to survive without any entertainment, except some table games that Jake brought over, saving the day.

Although, as the days passed, Angie was beginning to appreciate the potential of the big house, she felt she would have been less distressed in the apartment until Kate returned home. Maybe they shouldn't have moved yet. Everything they needed was beyond her reach. Life was better and it was worse. Sometimes she wanted to scream. At least the kids were now sleeping in their own rooms, but with little to entertain them, they were growing restless. *Where was Kate?*

***

When her mind became overrun with worry, Angie called Marianne and Jake.

"I'm sure she'll call you soon," Jake reassured her. "She was sailing in rough weather, and when they reached San Francisco, she had to find the marina where the boat was to be docked. Then she had to call 911 for an ambulance to take Steve to the hospital. Next she had to wait for information on his condition and try to locate friends of his—perhaps not an easy task when he's been gone a long time—and get them to provide support for him before she could even think about coming home."

"Yeah," Angie agreed. "I keep going through that in my head, but it's been more than a week, and it just seems that she should have called by now. I could hold on more easily if I knew she was all right."

Marianne was on the line as well. "I'm sure Kate isn't ignoring you on purpose. She went to help Steve out of loyalty. That's a good quality in a person, and that same loyalty will bring her home when her job there is done."

Angie sighed. "I know, I know. I'm being a selfish child. I'm just scared, and I don't know how to make the fears go away until I hear from her."

"Well," suggested Marianne, "if you are terribly upset, maybe you should try calling her. Hearing her voice should calm your nerves. She might be able to give you an estimate of when she will be back, and that would soothe as well."

"Hmmm. But if she's still out at sea and doesn't answer the phone, I'll be worried more."

Jake responded. "You'll have to do what you think best, Angie. Just know that Marianne and I are here for you and will help in any way we can."

"Thanks. Talk to you later."

***

Angie waited one more day, and when she couldn't settle down, she dialed Kate's cell. Dinner was over and the kids were seated at the card table assembling a picture puzzle that she had found in her belongings. As Kate's number rang, Angie paced the living room floor.

Kate answered on the third ring. "Angie! I was just about to call you! We arrived safely, Steve is in the hospital and he's going to have surgery on his leg tomorrow. So far, we managed to avoid infection, and it looks like he's going to be okay. I've been trying to locate some of his old friends—unfortunately several of them have died of AIDS—but I finally found two of them today. Tab and Scott are going to start visiting him at the hospital and will watch out for him until he's well enough to go back to his boat."

Angie had a hard time not interrupting Kate. “When will you be home?”

“As soon as Steve’s surgery is over, and Tab and Scott are on the job, I’ll call for a flight to Seattle and a ride home on that shuttle, what The Rocket?”

Angie could hear noise in the background. Music and voices.

“Where are you?” she asked. “Not at the hospital, I take it.”

“No. While Steve is sleeping, I came down to The Castro to have some dinner.”

“Sounds more like a bar.”

“Well, I am eating in a bar, a lesbian bar. I haven’t been in one for years. I thought I needed a treat after fighting the wind and waves for six days and then dealing with everything here.”

“Are you with someone?”

Kate laughed. “No, Angie, I’m not. I’m just eating a hamburger and having a beer then walking back to my hotel for some much-needed sleep. Is there something wrong? I’m getting a sense that you are upset.”

Angie swallowed. “I’ve just been scared,” she admitted. “It’s been such a long time since I heard from you in Newport. I was afraid you were lost at sea.”

“No, babe,” Kate said. “Thankfully not. When I get home, I’ll tell you all about it and show you some pictures I took.”

“We can’t wait. We’re just sitting here in an almost empty house, and we can’t do anything until you get here.”

“Sorry about that. It was a bad time for this to happen. But I’ll be there soon, and we can start dealing with projects and furniture, okay?”

Angie felt tears of relief stinging her eyes. “I’ve missed you so much. The kids, too.”

“And I’ve missed you, but I had to live in the moment and not think of anything else until we arrived here safely.”

“Well, I love you. See you soon.”

“And I love you. I’ll call with flight information when I have it, okay?”

“Okay. Bye.”

"Bye."

Angie practically slipped to the floor, as her body shook with relief. *Kate was alive and soon to come home.* She hadn't been in touch with just how terribly much she missed Kate and how much she depended on her until she heard her voice again. Now a million different feelings were running through her. She slumped into a captain's chair in the living room and took some deep breaths before she went to tell Mark and Sarina that Kate was all right and would be here soon.

***

Kate sat in the back row of the shuttle van, looking at the scenery as they passed along the I-5 through communities south of Seattle then into Tacoma and across the Tacoma Narrows Bridge. On to forested land, Gig Harbor, through Silverdale, Poulsbo, the Hood Canal Bridge on the 104, and finally merging with the 101 for the rest of the way into Sequim. She realized how little she knew yet about the various peninsulas of the Puget Sound and their communities. Since this was becoming her home, she would really have to explore it.

As she watched, her mind turned inward. She felt a growing excitement along with a touch of anxiety about seeing Angie. After the phone call, she had been berating herself for not having done a better job of keeping in touch. Of course, she had dozens of valid excuses, but when she thought about Angie and the kids, moving without her, sitting in a house with no furniture, with their lives on hold until her return, she felt she could have tried harder. At the time, all she could focus on was Steve, getting him to San Francisco to the hospital and finding someone to take over for her so she could return to Sequim. She was also horribly exhausted from almost no sleep for six days and nights, and her thoughts just hadn't reached beyond staying awake, keeping the boat headed in the right direction, hanging on until the Golden Gate came into view. During that period, Angie, Mark and Sarina were pushed somewhere to the back of her mind and weren't very real. The ocean, the boat, Steve with his occasional groans that reminded her of how much pain he was experiencing, the waves tossing them around and the wind snapping the sails—only those things were real.

Looking back on it, Kate felt that when they docked twice during the trip or in San Francisco when they arrived that, somehow, she could have managed a call. But she hadn't. She now prepared herself for an onslaught of anger and resentment from Angie when she reached Wetlands Acres, and in her own mind she felt she deserved it.

***

It was nearly dark when the shuttle stopped in front of the house, and Kate climbed out and tossed her duffle bag over her shoulder. After giving a tip to the driver, she walked up the path to the front door, wondering if everyone was home. She didn't have a key.

The carriage lights on the garage were lit. A porch light was on. Kate stepped onto the porch and hesitantly raised a hand to knock. *What kind of reception would she receive?*

In a split second, the door was thrown open, and Angie stood before her, her eyes broadcasting feelings that ranged from anger, to fear, to longing, to love.

"Hey," Kate said, a bit awkwardly, "I'm home."

Angie reached out and pulled her roughly into the entryway. "Come here, you big goofball. Welcome home."

Kate stopped her voice with a big, deep and passionate kiss.

***

After Mark and Sarina had enjoyed their part of the reunion and had been sent off to bed, Kate and Angie sat at the card table by the kitchen, draining a bottle of wine between them, and bringing each other up to date. Now that the crisis was over and they were together again, everything was just a bit funny. Kate told her about the trip to San Francisco, and Angie shared details about the move and how they had survived during the week with help from Marianne and Jake.

By the time they were both yawning, Kate asked, "Do you think I could get away with sleeping in your bed tonight?"

Angie grinned. "I think we can make an exception, since you don't have a bed yet."

Laughing, they stood and moved into each other's arms. "I'm totally exhausted," Kate admitted.

"Then I won't put moves on you tonight," Angie grinned. "Having you here is the important thing."

Arm in arm they strolled to the master bedroom, and without ceremony, Kate collapsed onto the bed.

***

Although Saturday dawned gloomy, there was no dismal gray in this household. Angie fixed a big breakfast. Soon after, Jake and Marianne showed up in two vehicles, one of them being Kate's Forester. There were hugs all around and an offer of dinner that evening. Then Jake jumped into Marianne's van to go home.

"I've got to round up my stuff at TC," Kate said to Angie, "and then we'll buy sandwiches and head for Port Angeles to spend tons of money on furniture."

"We'll be here waiting," Angie grinned, giving Kate a big hug.

Kate jumped into the Subaru, waved goodbye and was off. Happy and relieved, Angie watched her go.

***

Shopping in Port Angeles was a grand scale event. Angie had brought her long shopping list, and she suggested to Kate that they help Mark and Sarina first, rather than keep them waiting as the adults went through the rest of the house. A middle-aged salesman with a slight paunch, graying hair, and a nametag that read "Thomas" followed them around yet kept agreeably quiet after Kate explained that they knew what they wanted and would be making some large purchases.

"Girls first," Kate quipped, allowing Sarina to make her choices. Basically, Sarina confirmed what she had selected during their earlier visit to the store. She wanted a room that was all white and a bit fussy. Canopy bed, dresser with mirror, lamp table and white lamp with the figure of a unicorn in its base, a small white desk and chair, a white bookcase, and a wine-colored overstuffed rocker for emphasis. Angie—worrying that Sarina would outgrow this furniture before long—kept waiting for Kate to examine price tags and say it was too much, but she never did. She just complemented Sarina on her good taste.

Mark wanted a bigger desk in mahogany with matching chair, two bookcases, a floor lamp, a reclining chair in rich gold, a lamp table with shelves and lamp for his bed. "You like dark woods, I take it," Kate quipped.

"Yeah, and I'm getting bigger. So, I want grown up things," Mark said with a tilt of his chin.

"Okay," Kate agreed. "You got it. You're the man of the house."

***

When the kids had been outfitted, and the order slips signed for the ever-present Thomas, Kate and Angie strolled into the department that featured living room furniture. "I like leather," Angie explained to Kate, "because it's easier to keep clean and lasts longer."

Kate squeezed her hand. "Whatever you pick, I promise to love it."

Angie sat down on a beige leather sofa and sighed with satisfaction. Kate plopped down beside her and admitted it was comfortable. She nodded at Thomas while pointing to the sofa. He began writing up the item.

"I measured the living room area, and we have space for each of us to have a recliner. What color do you like? Better yet, sit in all of them until you find what you want," Angie suggested while walking to the recliner she had already chosen, again in beige leather to match the sofa.

Kate tried out several recliners, until she found one that fit her long legs. "This is perfect," she said, perusing a stack of color samples. "I'd really like blue, but I don't see any blue. Would green go with everything?"

Angie grinned. “We’ll make it work. Pillows, you know, for accent.”

In a few moments, with Thomas struggling keep up, Angie had pinpointed a coffee table, a side table to match, floor lamps, two tall bookcases, and one long, low one to hold a television set. All were in rich walnut.

In the dining room area of the store, Angie had selected a rectangular, dark wood table with extension, matching six high-backed chairs, and a tall china hutch.

Next, they tackled Kate’s “bonus” room, more complicated because Kate had not looked at furniture in advance. She chose a decent size desk with a pullout keyboard tray, two tall bookcases, a comfortable office chair for the desk, and a dark brown leather sofa that opened out into a queen-sized bed. Angie started to ask a question, and then watched as Mark sat down on the sofa, suddenly realizing that Kate was making her office into a combination workspace and bedroom. *Wise choice*, Angie thought. Kate also selected a tall, slender closet with drawers at the bottom.

The master bedroom came last. Kate encouraged Angie to give herself the best, and she chose lamp tables for the king-sized bed, a mahogany headboard, a matching armoire, another smaller chest, and a bookcase with a side chair to match.

Thomas beamed when he had added up all the sales slips, entered them into the computer and come up with the grand total. Kate signed the credit card receipt with a private grin. *Thomas would undoubtedly be salesman of the month without ever selling a thing. Hopefully, he had a big family to support.*

On the way home, Kate stopped at Costco and picked out two television sets, a bigger one for the living room and a smaller one for the master bedroom. “Now we’ll be in business,” she quipped as she made arrangements for them to be held until she could return alone with the Forester to pick them up. Watching, Angie still found it hard to believe how Kate could pick anything she wanted with no concerns about cost.

After the exhaustion of shopping, they were happy to stop at Marianne’s and Jake’s house for refreshing drinks and dinner. Their hostesses were amused by their tales of the shopping spree, and Kate had a chance to retell the story of her ocean voyage with the injured Steve Gutierrez. The kids were enthralled, and Angie watched Kate with love and admiration. She seemed to have forgiven her for abandoning them on moving day.

***

The "honeymoon" continued into the next few weeks as they settled into the house. Kate stayed at home for the furniture deliveries. Although some items had to be ordered and would take three to four weeks to arrive, most of the furniture was in the house by midweek. Kate saw that everything was placed where needed in Angie's plan.

Life became less stressed. Angie went to work and actually enjoyed her job because she didn't have to worry about where dinner money was coming from. With no rent to pay, she now had plenty of income to stock up at the grocery on anything she might need. She confessed to Carly, "I feel like I'm living in Disneyland!"

Kate had added Angie as a user on one of her credit cards, meaning that Angie could select something for the house and sign for it herself without waiting for Kate. That relieved another residual angst that had been caused by Kate's sudden departure for Oregon.

Kate resumed Sarina's swimming lessons, and their relationship continued to deepen as Sarina's disappointment over Kate's absence gradually faded. The same held true with Mark. He looked forward to his batting, hitting, and catching practices now that Kate was home.

None of them would ever forget Kate's sudden exodus or the disruption of the days while she was gone. Yet settling into the house, returning to familiar routines, living without financial fears, and enjoying her company and good humor all brought peace and stability. Whatever anger Angie had harbored melted in Kate's embrace. With all of them in the same house, intimate moments were easier to come by, and Angie felt both excited and reassured by Kate's presence, touch, and passion.

19

There was a wonderful whirlwind of activity setting up the house, during which Kate felt she was accomplishing something in helping Angie have a better life, while providing all the details that magically turned an empty house into a comfortable home. In addition, Mark and Sarina were quite happy in their rooms once they had furniture, posters on their walls, and a place for their toys.

With Kate spending a lot of time across from him in the other "bonus" room, Mark didn't seem to feel separated from his mom and Sarina as he had at first. Kate had suggested to him that as man of the house he was the first line of defense by the front door. He grinned and swaggered like a grown-up. However, that idea backfired when he awoke with a nightmare and started having trouble getting to sleep.

"What did you say to him?" Angie asked Kate.

Kate flushed. "I was trying to make him feel that he was our protector. I guess he took it too seriously. Now he thinks he has to stay up all night to see that nothing bad happens to us."

"Smart, Kate, really smart!"

"Well, I never dealt with an almost nine-year old before."

"They have big imaginations."

"We could buy him a dog. Then he could sleep because the dog would alert him."

Angie made a fist. "I didn't hear that." She sighed. *She'd have to work with Mark and hopefully get him settled down.*

***

The two children mastered riding the school bus and found other kids in Wetlands Acres who also rode the bus and then became new friends. That made Angie happy. Mark and Sarina's daily routine changed in that on some days they walked to the Boys & Girls Club and remained there until picked up, and on others they rode the bus home and played at their friends' houses until Kate or Angie came home.

***

During the holiday season, family had been especially important to Angie. She and Zack had kept a traditional Christmas focused on Christ, but there were gifts, some parties, dressing up, and good food. This past year had been very depressing. Angie had not been welcomed at anyone's house, and she had celebrated in the apartment with the kids during a very sparse and bleak Christmas.

Now that good luck had come her way, Angie looked forward to the holidays. With help from Kate, she decorated the house indoors and out. She sat with Kate in the evenings and talked about what to give the children for Christmas. What did they need and what were they ready for?

They agreed that cell phones and computers were still a little bit down the road, although Kate pointed out that computers were already being used in the classrooms at their school. Angie was a little nervous about tackling technology. She asked Kate if they could wait a little longer—maybe for their next birthdays.

Kate brought up the word "dog" and Angie flared. "No dog!" she said.

"Some kind of pet? Hamster, goldfish?"

Angie sighed. "I know pets are good for kids, but they haven't asked for a pet yet. Let's wait until they start bringing it up. They're more likely to care for an animal if it's what they want."

Kate acquiesced. "Okay, this year let's stick to things they've already identified. I can buy Mark a major league shirt. I'll try to find out who his favorite player is, probably someone on the Mariners. And Sarina a really cute swimsuit coverup, and maybe some fun things like a snorkel to start her going underwater. I want her water experiences to be fun as well as work and competition."

***

The holidays went off without a hitch. On Thanksgiving and Christmas, they had a big dinner with Marianne and Jake. It seemed to be a hit with everyone. Marianne loved having the children around, and Jake, who also enjoyed the kids, was happy to see Marianne happy. Angie felt surrounded by love again. Kate just sat and looked at everyone and seemed to feel content about everything.

On New Year's Eve there was a party a few doors down the street in Wetlands Acres, and Angie and Kate were invited. They hadn't made plans for the kids, but they decided that since they were nearby, maybe it was okay for them to stay up and watch a movie on TV for the couple of hours Angie and Kate would be gone. Angie popped a big bowl of popcorn and allowed them non-caffeine soft drinks. They put a DVD of a favorite Disney movie on the TV set.

Angie left her cell phone with Mark, with clear instructions of how to reach her via Kate's cell phone, if anything were amiss. Both the kids already knew about 911 and when it was to be used.

The evening passed without any problems, and Angie and Kate were back before midnight. Although a bit drowsy, the kids were still awake, and they all toasted each other at the stroke of midnight. Kate kissed Angie, politely but with a wink and a look toward the bedroom.

There were fireworks somewhere nearby for a few minutes after midnight then things settled down. Angie and Kate tucked Mark and Sarina into bed and headed for the master bedroom, a place Kate still entered only on special occasions. As passionate as they felt toward each other, they downplayed it in front of the kids.

The couple began the New Year—which would be their first full year together—locked in embrace and passionate lovemaking. Angie could not believe how much she loved touching Kate and being touched by her, and Kate was reinforced in her belief that she had met her sexual match. Afterward, they curled up under the comforter, and Kate whispered, "We're perfect together, you know."

"I know," Angie yawned.

They soon drifted off to sleep. Before Kate dozed off, she had a delightful thought. *It was even more perfect now that she quite often shared Angie's bed.*

***

Despite all the great things that had happened during the past few months, Kate began to experience a sense of personal discomfort sometime in the early spring. She had trouble figuring out why. Then she pinpointed the real problem: she was an Aries, and her 40th birthday was coming up soon. That half-life milestone was making her question herself, something she didn't do easily.

On one hand, Kate admitted she was happy with Angie and the kids. She was doing everything she could to make their lives not only livable, but content, and it seemed to be working. They had adjusted to the house. Angie had made her peace with the neighborhood, the school bus, and all the things that were a bit harder than living in town. When Kate realized that a house was a lot more to clean than an apartment, she arranged for a cleaning lady to come once a week. The woman came while Angie was working at The Little Red Barn, and she didn't have to deal with any of it. Angie was just pleased with how nice the house looked. She also was grateful and let Kate know that regularly. Kate grinned when she thought about the wonderful, private ways in which Angie showed her gratitude.

Then Kate had taken charge of scheduling for the kids and made sure they got to all the places they needed to be. Mark was enrolled in Little League, playing right field and developing into a good hitter. Kate worked with him and took him to practices, and Mark was thrilled. Swimming was going well with Sarina, and Kate was pleased with the fact that she was a fine swimmer growing in speed and strength almost daily. The kids often accompanied Kate to the grocery where she taught them about healthy foods and snacks. They brought home supplies for a good dinner which Kate often prepared. Angie would come back from work tired, sometimes a bored tired instead of an exhausted one, but tired nonetheless. A tasty dinner lifted her spirits for a nice evening—and good private time later.

Kate had again reminded Angie that she didn't really have to work, thanks to Kate's trust fund. There was no reason that Angie had to put herself out in such a menial job when there was plenty of money available.

In reply, Angie reminded her, "I need to work. It reinforces some sense of who I am, that I'm contributing, however small, to the good of the family. I've told you that I've always wanted to be a nurse, and I'm just waiting for the right time to apply for training. They have a good program at Peninsula College in Port Angeles, and Olympic Medical Center is always in need of nurses. I could have a real career if I could complete my education. That wasn't possible before, because Zack wouldn't listen to me. Soon it's got to be my time. Right now I would be thirty before I could even start working at my dream job."

"So, apply," Kate encouraged.

Angie's eyes widened. "Really?"

"Yes, really."

Angie hugged and kissed Kate so passionately that Kate was almost ready to yell "uncle." She didn't but, finally, Angie stopped her onslaught and they both laughed.

After that reassuring talk, Angie had spent time after work making phone calls, downloading forms, and filling out applications. She found that she was late for the coming quarter. Since she had been out of school for a decade, she was advised to enroll as a general freshman, take as many basic classes as she could, then move into the nursing program when space became available. At first Angie was deflated, but she soon saw the bright side. "I'll be a better nursing student if I take a few classes and become comfortable with college-level courses. I've read a lot, but I haven't written papers since high school."

Kate encouraged her and a potential relationship crisis was averted.

***

With Angie's main concern sorted out for the time being, Kate considered the down side of her own life balance and her sense of personal dissatisfaction. Well educated, with a decade in a highly competitive job, she had never dreamed of life as a housewife. So, being one—pretty much what she was these days, even if she called herself a "home coordinator"—was not meeting her life goals. And it left large gaps in the day when she had nothing meaningful to do.

Sometimes she could be creative, but trips sightseeing and photographing the natural beauty of the Olympic Peninsula were somewhat limited. Skies were often cloudy if not rainy and just before Christmas they had had an actual snowfall that lasted several days. Although Kate photographed the neighborhood while the snow was fresh, many local roads were closed and she couldn't drive to the places by the Strait or in the mountains that would have made beautiful pictures until after most of the snow had melted. When she couldn't get out or find something creative to do, she felt in a nonspecific way "out of sorts."

By midspring, Kate's distress was building steam. She covered her discomfort around Angie, since it wasn't Angie's fault or her problem, and just tried to work it through on her own in her spare time. She sat at her desk and raised questions: *What do you really want to do with your life? Are you happy here in Sequim? Do you need to take a trip to see some scenery? Do you need a vacation with Angie for some R&R without the kids? Is there, Heaven forbid, something not right in your relationship? What's missing?*

***

When her thinking ran in circles, and she had no answers, she decided to go see Jake, whom she found working, as usual, in on a project in the garage. Jake took a break and suggested that Kate pull up a camp chair and talk.

"I've got an itch I can't seem to scratch," Kate confessed. "I can't even identify the bug that bit me, if you know what I mean."

Jake grinned. "You thought I might understand?"

Kate nodded. "You had to alter your life after Marianne's accident, and in some vague way I've had to alter mine after meeting Angie and falling in love with her. I don't fault that, because all I need to do is think of her, and I have tingles all over. She really has my number."

Jake nodded. “However, good as it is, sex doesn’t a life make.”

Kate shrugged. “Something like that.”

“So, spill the beans, okay?”

Kate told her about her malaise—about caring for the house, the kids, Angie, doing for them and feeling appreciated, yet feeling there was something missing for herself.

“I need to figure out what’s wrong before I do something stupid like run away, thinking it would be better in the city or on an island somewhere. I’ve done that more than once, and it didn’t work in the long run.”

Jake nodded thoughtfully. “Well, all I can tell you from my own perspective is that I would have gone into a deep funk if I didn’t have my woodworking. It’s a project, a hobby—one that I love so much I will fight for it. I’ll see that I have time to do it, even if I have to give up something else. My woodworking defines me, gives me an identity apart from Marianne, Sequim, the Peninsula, and the rest of the world. Marianne understands, and she makes sure that, despite her many needs, there is space in my day to work on my creations.”

Kate sighed. “I wish I knew. When I was a swimmer, making the Olympic team was my dream. I’m too old for that now. I don’t know of anything I’ve done since that I feel that way about. I certainly don’t want to sell advertising again. When I was young I went to college to grow. Now, unless I know what I want to study, it would be useless to take classes.”

“Well,” Jake suggested, “let the idea percolate. Give it a little time, and something will come to you.”

***

Kate drove to the marina, her favorite spot for contemplation. She sprawled for a while on a bench, watching the tide slip lazily onto the beach. Sequim Bay was protected from the Strait by the double-sided spit near TC, and waves inside the bay were normally very gentle. While it was typically spring chilly now, she noticed as she pulled her jacket closer, she remembered last summer when she first arrived in Sequim. She had seen a couple of small sailboats playing with each other one day. On another she had seen a couple of racing shells with crews stroking up and down the bay.

That thought reminded her of how much she loved water. Even if she didn't still swim seriously, Kate loved being around water. She had thrilled to living on the beaches in the South Pacific, and part of what led her to Sequim and kept her here, was the presence of water, just about everywhere—the bays, the Strait, the Sound, and the Ocean. Water on three sides of the Peninsula.

Tucking that thought away for a moment, she let her mind keep on exploring. *She could find a job. Something in sales or marketing? Real estate? Start her own business? Become a professional coach? Would any of that satisfy this inner hunger?*

Kate quickly tossed out the idea of a regular job. If she went to work, Angie would have to pick up some of the things that Kate was doing with and for the kids, and that might mean Angie couldn't work or go to school. Certainly, they didn't need the money for either of them to work. However, although Kate could easily put Angie through college, Angie didn't really want that. She valued her independence. That was one reason she was still driving that old Ford sedan. She wasn't ready to give it up.

No, that plan wasn't very good. There had to be an answer, a win-win answer, not something that worked for Kate but not for Angie, or vice versa. Right now, neither of them was where they wanted to be—yet for Angie, the excitement of all the new things coming her way with the house and their relationship had not worn off. Soon she'd be working seriously toward a nursing career. Kate had to support that. *At the same time, she also had to identify her own dream and follow it as well.*

Climbing back into the Forester, Kate said to herself. "Something involving water. It's got to be about water somehow."

20

To celebrate Kate's fortieth birthday in April, she and Angie left the kids with Marianne and Jake and spent a very private weekend at an oceanfront lodge in the Olympic National Park.

Kate loved the rustic buildings, the natural setting surrounded with evergreens, the sandy beach—and sharing everything with Angie, just Angie. They sat after dinner before a lobby fireplace and toasted with a bottle of champagne—down to the last drop.

"What do you most want for this next year?" Angie whispered in Kate's ear.

Setting aside her inner anguish over personal meaning, Kate kept it light and grinned. "A dog."

Angie heaved a big sigh. "Oh, no, not that again!"

"Yes, a dog, and I'm not giving up on it." Kate gave Angie a determined nod.

"Why, for heaven's sake, Kate, do you want a dog?"

"I've never had one. My parents wouldn't let me. I couldn't have one at college. I didn't think it fair to have one cooped up in an apartment in New York. I didn't stay anywhere long enough in the South Pacific to take care of a dog. Here, everyone has a dog. It's how you meet people. In the neighborhood, on the Discovery Trail, at the marina. Everybody meets and greets with their dogs. I want one for me, and I'll share with the kids."

Angie studied her for a long moment. "You're really serious about this, aren't you?"

Kate nodded. "I am."

"Okay, what kind of a dog do you want?"

"I always see a Collie, Shepherd, or a Lab. Big dog, protective yet loving."

Angie made a face and shivered. "Those all shed. We had big dogs on the farm. Had to keep them outside, because they left fur all over everything."

"Well, I see your point about the shedding. Then something big, protective and loving that doesn't shed?"

Angie suddenly giggled. "How about a labradoodle?"

"A what?"

"A labradoodle. Labrador retriever and poodle mix."

"Never heard of it."

"Maybe it wasn't big in the South Pacific."

"I guess not."

"Well, look it up. If we *have* to have a dog, and a big dog, I might consider one of those."

"Okay, we'll table that topic for the moment as unresolvable without further research. What I want *right now* for my birthday is to jump your bones, my sweet."

Angie kissed her. "That I can happily give you." She stroked Kate's cheek gently.

Kate grinned and motioned toward the stairs. Arm in arm, they climbed the steps to their second-floor room, placed a "Do Not Disturb" sign on the door, dropped their clothing on the floor as they kissed deeply, and moved toward the king-sized bed. In light from the fireplace, they made sweet music together for hours.

Somewhere during the night, Kate thought about how much better her fortieth birthday was than her thirty-ninth. Her world had changed radically for the better. *She had to remember that whenever she was feeling down.*

***

At breakfast in the dining room the next morning—between Mimosas and a plate full of pancakes, ham and scrambled eggs—Kate decided to share her real birthday dream.

"I envy you sometimes," she admitted to Angie. "You know what you want, and even though you've been through rough times, you have known where you were headed. That kept you sane while you struggled. The dream was always there."

Angie nodded. "Yes, the dream has helped me a lot. I see myself as a nurse, and I know I when I get there, I'll be happy."

Kate sighed. "Well, when I was young, I wanted to be an Olympic swimmer, and that dream kept me going, until my mother died. The dream died with her. Following my father's path brought attention from him but it wasn't the same. When he died, I didn't care anymore. I've been wandering ever since, not knowing what I want to do 'when I grow up,' so to speak."

Angie smiled. "You look beautifully grown up to me."

Kate shrugged. "Thanks, but I feel still like a confused adolescent. I need to dedicate myself to something, something for me alone, something that feels important."

A questioning frown crossed Angie's face. "The kids and me aren't enough?"

Kate put a hand on her arm. "You and the kids are very important to me. Central to my happiness. Yet there's something else, something I have to do just for me. The way nursing is important to you, apart from the kids and me. I don't know what my thing is yet. If I did, I'd already be doing it. My big goal for my forty-first year is to work on me, to read and think and exercise and put all of me together and figure out what I want and need to do."

Angie paused a second and then asked, "Do you think you can find it in Sequim?"

Kate smiled at her. "I've not thought of leaving Sequim. There must be something here I can do that will satisfy this inner need. If not, there are ways to accomplish goals without leaving town. Just think of Marianne, working on a job that's based on the East Coast and she never goes out of her home. Lots of people do that. Not to worry, I am not jumping ship. Please believe me."

Angie sighed. "Well, you know me. I'm just scared of being abandoned again."

"I know, and I understand. I just thought it would be better to share my thoughts with you than to keep them a secret."

"You may have to remind me now and then, so I won't worry about losing you."

"Okay, that's off my chest. Now let's enjoy our breakfast before it gets cold, huh?"

Angie laughed. "That's my line. I'm the mommy."

***

While Mark and Sarina were in school that spring, Kate had considerable time on her hands. The house was in good shape. In addition to a house cleaner, she had found a lawn care person for the yard because cutting grass didn't seem very satisfying to her. So, she paid someone else to do it.

After the kids and Angie were gone for most of the day, and the morning dishes cleaned and put away, Kate spread out at her desk and explored the Internet, looking for clues. After five years away from evolving computer technology, she found she had a lot of catching up to do. The language was forever changing, and new technology replaced last year's hot products.

During decent days, as spring brought warmer temperatures and more sun breaks, she drove around. One day she explored in greater depth the Dungeness Refuge where a bluff overlooked the Strait. On one of walking trails, Kate found a bench and sat looking at Canada to the north and Port Angeles to the west. She listened to the waves crashing on the shore below and looked at signs that warned of erosion and commanded visitors to keep safely behind the fences. She even followed the Dungeness Spit for five-and-a-half miles each way at low tide to visit the New Dungeness Lighthouse.

On another day, Kate went to the Railroad Bridge Park and stood on the former railroad trestle that now served as part of the Olympic Discovery Trail. She looked down at the Dungeness River flowing over rocks below. She thought she saw a few salmon in the water. Behind her, women pushed baby buggies, older adults walked dogs, bikers whizzed by, and runners passed her. They all waved in greeting and seemed happily occupied.

Finally, on an unusually sunny day, Kate drove to her favorite spot, the John Wayne Marina, and remained there for hours in contemplation. She began by walking the docks, looking at all the sail and power craft, vessels that brought back memories of the South Pacific and the *Lavender Loafer*. Then she followed the paved paths from one end of the property to the other, impressed with the blossoming beauty. She loved looking at the attractive marina, with more than one hundred craft docked there, mostly sailboats—some rigged for long-distance ocean sailing.

She stopped for lunch in the Soaring Goose, recalling an evening here with Angie, and decided she must bring the whole family, maybe for a birthday. The marina seemed to have everything—including sturdy benches placed along the paths, from the jutting point of land on the north end, which was covered with arching deciduous trees, to the rocky beach on the south end. The public facility was welcoming, with plenty of parking spaces, and while strolling, she met visitors exercising with their dogs. She spoke to a few and kept thinking about the labradoodle that she hoped to find soon.

Especially thoughtful on this day, Kate dropped down on a bench and watched the incoming tide. The water rippled, with sun speckles. She thought of summer coming and imagined sailboats racing around buoys. Maybe some crew shells competing. For a second Kate flashed on the thought of buying a sailboat and sailing the islands, with Angie and the kids. Almost instantly, she dropped that idea. *Not now. Wrong timing. Maybe eventually, when Angie was through with college and Mark and Sarina were older.*

With an inward smile, Kate flashed on the thought that the marina environment seemed to give her the most creative ideas. *But not buying a sailboat. Something bigger, more significant. Sequim*, she mused, *was still a small community, a bit lazy in its ways. That was fine for the retirees who flocked here to visit and live. But for the city to grow, it needed something dynamic, something to make the name Sequim a household word nationwide.* She grinned, sensing that her marketing background was emerging alongside her love of athletics.

Her lifelong involvement with sports played at the edge of her mind. *Something was clicking.* Locally, she had seen trails for biking and hiking, water for boating and crewing, mountains for climbing and skiing. *In fact, Sequim was a potential mecca for many sports.*

Suddenly, it dawned on her. *Why hadn't she thought of this before? Olympic Peninsula, Olympic Mountains, Olympic National Park. The Olympics. What a natural tie-in. Sequim could become a training center for the Olympics!*

Kate pulled out her cell phone and started making notes. This was exciting! This was *her*: *Her love of sports, her experience in marketing, and the beauty and opportunities here in Sequim.*

She practically danced back to her SUV. Kate couldn't wait to tell Marianne and Jake and Angie and the kids. This was something she could devote herself to, and she had the time, energy, and money to do it!

***

Angie was working until midafternoon, and Kate didn't have to pick up the kids until 5. She dropped in on Marianne and Jake. Marianne would just be finishing her East Coast job for the day. Kate couldn't wait to tell them about the ideas that were swirling inside her head.

Settled in the living room, she explained about all the possibilities of Sequim for Olympic level sports. Surprisingly, Marianne laughed and Jake coughed behind her hand when she told them her idea.

Confused, Kate looked at them with a frown. "Something wrong?" she asked.

Marianne waved a hand around. "Oh, no, it's very imaginative. It's just that it'll take the rest of your life to create it, that's all."

Jake looked at her a tad seriously. "I don't want to rain on your parade, but I read about one of those centers in San Diego, out in the desert near the Mexican border. Ran in the red for a long time until they finally turned it over to local government. Little connection with the USOC any longer. What you're talking about is a huge undertaking. You've got local, state and federal agencies to deal with, as well as the USOC. Very expensive, very political, and lots of work."

"You think I shouldn't try to do it?" Kate felt deflated.

"I don't want to say that," Jake explained. "However, do some research, make an outline of what you want to accomplish, and then decide if it's worth the effort—and whether Sequim is ready for something like this."

Marianne nodded. "And while you are at it, think about Angie and two kids who need your devoted energy. If you take on this kind of a project, it will eat at you night and day. Might make some problems for your relationship."

Kate sighed. "I feel like I could do it all, but when I was in marketing, it did seem all consuming. I suppose that's something I need consider."

"What did you sell when you were in marketing?" Jake asked.

"TV ads mostly. Everything from beer to toothpaste to pizzas, medicines to automobiles. I had a lot of successful campaigns, with a team working for me."

"Again," Jake said, "I don't want to dampen your spirits, but do you think TV ads prepare you to create a high-profile athletic training center?"

Kate frowned. "Well, my marketing job involved a lot of research and convincing people that my ideas would sell. I had to identify needs in the marketplace and lots of other things that should be relevant."

"But nothing big enough to take the rest of your life," Marianne observed.

"No, I guess not. Most ad campaigns are limited in scope."

"Well, maybe you should get your feet wet first," Marianne suggested. "You might start out a little smaller. For example, Sequim doesn't have a public swimming pool, as you very well know. You've been driving Sarina to Port Angeles, and she won't have a pool in her back yard this summer, since you moved them to a house. Although nothing can change this year, it might be worth your while to explore this training center dream by creating an Olympic-size pool for the city, maybe over in Carrie Blake Park."

Kate's eyes lit up. "That's a good idea. I like it!"

Jake nodded. "Finding support for that pool will help you realize what you are up against in creating an entire Olympic Training Center. And regardless, Sarina and all the Sequim kids would benefit. In fact, before long, Sarina could ride a bike down from the house, go swimming, and return home on her own."

After a pause, Jake raised an eyebrow. "Pull that off, and you have a stronger position in selling yourself as a developer of a bigger project."

Kate relaxed a bit. "Thanks for not totally shooting me down. I understand your reservations, and although I'm disappointed, I suspect your thoughts are probably right. I could get carried away with something bigger than I am. The pool sounds like a good idea. Experience a bit of local politics and property development, so to speak."

Marianne gave her a thoughtful look. "And in the short run, you might find Angie more supportive if she thinks you're fighting to have a pool built that will benefit her daughter."

"True."

A little less discouraged, Kate jumped into the Forester and buckled up. Time to collect the kids and go help with dinner. She smiled to herself. Maybe she and Angie could work in some "private time" this evening. *That would feel very, very good.*

***

Angie had arrived home from a stressful day at work. Short staffed and with an unusually large number of customers at her counter, she was tired and a bit grouchy. Kate pushed her personal agenda down until later and focused on helping Angie prepare dinner.

When they had finished eating, Kate encouraged Angie to rest while she took Mark out to the back yard to work on pitching and catching.

"Aren't you taking me swimming?" Sarina interrupted.

Kate blanched. "Oh, geez, I got my days mixed up. We go to the pool this evening. You're right. Tomorrow is Mark's game. Okay, I'm caught up."

Angie gave Kate a raised eyebrow and then headed for her bedroom. "You all sort it out. I've got a good romance novel I want to read."

***

Kate settled Mark with her computer. "You are always asking me questions about baseball," she said to him. "While we're gone, I want you to go onto the Internet—I showed you how to do that—and look up the history of baseball. Here's a pad and a pencil. Write down when it began, where, and look up at least three players who were really important to the sport. Name, position, years played, team or teams played for."

"You mean like Joe DiMaggio?"

Kate grinned and ruffled this hair. "Exactly. And when I come home, I want you to tell me all about baseball, okay?"

Mark's eyes sparkled. "Oh, good. This'll be fun."

Sarina came into Kate's office, clad in her swimsuit with a muumuu cover-up. She carried a bag filled with swimming gear.

Kate leaned down and gave Mark a hug as he began moving the mouse around and hitting a few keystrokes. "We'll see you, buddy. Have fun."

***

As she drove along the busy 101, Kate could feel Sarina's eyes on her. "Something on your mind?" she finally asked.

Sarina scrunched up her face. "Are you and Mommy going to get married?"

Kate was taken aback. *Wow!* She shivered. "That's a big grown up topic, my little sweetheart!"

"I know it's your business," Sarina said, "but I wanna know."

"You must have a reason, right?"

"Well, if you get married, you'll stay with us. And if you don't, you might leave. Like go back where you used to be."

"You mean like the South Pacific?"

"Or New York, where you came from."

Kate smiled. *Sarina was really growing up and quickly!*

"Your mom and I care for each other a great deal. We haven't talked about getting married yet. It might happen someday, when we're ready. Does it make a difference if we're married right now?"

"No, I guess not. I just don't want you to leave."

Kate sighed. "Sarina, I'm not planning on going anywhere. I'm very happy with you, Mark and your mom. We're together because we want to be. Marriage doesn't guarantee anything. Your mom was married to your dad, yet when he got upset with her, he left anyway."

Sarina frowned. "I know. I miss him, sometimes."

Kate reached over and touched her cheek fondly. "I'm sure you do. He is your daddy, and no one can ever replace him. Maybe sometime he'll want to see you again, and when you are older, you can go on your own to see him. Maybe he's not gone forever."

Sarina shook her head. "He thinks Mommy's sick and that we're sick, too. I don't understand, but that's what he said before he left."

"Hmmm. It's too bad that he said that. It's not true. Your mommy is just different, and she was born that way, like some people have blond hair and others brown, or blue eyes or brown eyes. Or like Mark is right-handed and you're left-handed. It doesn't mean she's sick or that she loves you any the less."

Sarina looked up at Kate soulfully. "I know Mommy loves us. She does everything she can for us. I'm just glad you came, because it's easier for her now. And you help us a lot, too."

"Thank you, Sarina. I just want all of you to have the best life possible."

***

Kate sat on the bleachers and kept an eye on Sarina doing her laps while she worked on her cell phone. She was researching anything she could find on public swimming pools—history, design, costs, government agencies involved. She was looking generally then specifically checking out Sequim. There wasn't a lot about Sequim, but she did find the name of the city official in charge of city parks.

She looked up to find Sarina hanging onto the side of the pool and looking at her. "Are you watching me?" she asked.

Kate nodded. "Yes, I am."

"Am I stroking right?"

"Yes, you're doing a great job. Just like I showed you."

"Am I getting faster?"

"Yes, you are. You can prove it to yourself." Kate pointed at the clocks on the wall at each end of the pool. "See those big clocks? When you started swimming, it took more than a minute for you to swim a length. Now it's less than a minute. Every few practices, you take another second off your time. When you're at the end, before you take off, especially on backstroke, look up at the clock. When the big hand is right at the top, push off, and when you touch the other end, look up to see where the hand is. That tells how long it took you to do the length."

"Goody. I'm going to watch the clock." Sarina took off swimming to the far end of the pool, and Kate smiled to herself.

***

A few minutes later, as Kate was watching Sarina and alternately researching on her cell phone, a young boy dashed by her and dived into the pool, his hands pushing a paddle board before him.

Kate stood and dropped her phone, some inner sense warning her that Sarina was right in his path.

There was a huge splash, the sound of a collision, and Sarina disappeared from view. Instantly, Kate was in the pool, diving below the surface.

Sarina was at the bottom, inert.

Kate pulled her to the surface, laid her on the side of the pool, and climbed out of the water.

Almost immediately, the boy was at Kate's side. "I'm sorry, I didn't see her," he told her, distraught.

Kate knelt by Sarina, rolled her onto her back and began CPR. She was joined in her efforts almost immediately by the lifeguard, whose station by the diving area rendered him too far away to prevent the accident.

Within a few seconds, Sarina began coughing up water and gasping for breath. Kate talked to her and worked her through the coughing stages and back into full consciousness. Meanwhile, the lifeguard grabbed his cell phone and tapped in 911 for the EMTs.

Sirens sounded quickly. The EMT crew rushed into the pool area and examined Sarina. When she could answer their questions and was able to move arms and legs and stand, they decided she did not need to be transported to the hospital.

One of the EMTs, a sturdily built young woman, commented to Kate, “She’s not bleeding, but she’s going to have a huge bruise and swelling on her forehead and probably a bad headache. If that doesn’t subside tomorrow or she shows any signs of concussion, she should be taken to OMC as a precaution.”

Kate nodded. She was very familiar with concussions. Accidents happened around pools, just as in all sporting venues.

***

Sarina’s workout had abruptly ended. Wrapped in a blanket, she followed Kate out to the SUV.

“My head hurts,” she confessed. “And I don’t feel good.”

“I know, honey. I’ve taken a few knocks on the head in my swimming days, and I have an idea how you’re feeling. We’ll go home, administer some aspirin, then you can go to bed. You’ll be warm and cozy and then sleep. Tomorrow you’ll feel better.”

Still dripping wet in her swimsuit, Kate sat on a towel and shivered all the way back to Sequim.

“Did I do something wrong?”

“No, that little boy wasn’t watching carefully. You couldn’t have seen him while you were swimming backstroke. He needed to check the water more carefully before jumping into the pool. And maybe not running. The lifeguard talked to him. I think the kid was upset, too, and he’ll most likely be more careful in the future.”

***

Angie, as Kate anticipated, was not happy when they arrived home. She looked at Sarina’s bruise and the swelling that was increasing, took her into the bathroom to find an aspirin, and then put her to bed. Kate meanwhile dried off and changed into her clothes.

When Sarina was cared for, Angie returned to Kate. “Where were you when this happened?”

“I was sitting in the stands, front row, watching Sarina swim in the outside lane, right in front of me.”

“You were watching her, and not doing something else, right?”

Kate paled a little. “I was hunting something on my cell phone, occasionally, but I looked at her repeatedly and watched her stroke.”

“But not when this kid jumped into the pool.”

“I didn’t see him. He came out of nowhere, and I’m not sure I could have prevented what happened, no matter whether I was on my phone or not. I was right there, and in the water, pulling her out in a split second. She took a hard knock to the head, but she was out only briefly and she started coughing up water right away. The EMTs thought she was going to be fine but said to watch her tomorrow, in the unlikely chance she has a concussion.”

Angie pulled up to her full height. “A concussion?”

“Not likely but possible.”

“That’s a football injury!”

“It can occur in any sport. Unexpected contact between players—falls, knock downs can happen in any time.”

“Swimming is an individual, not a team sport. They swim in lanes. They shouldn’t have body contact.”

Kate nodded. “I know, but it still happens. Not often, but it does. Around wet surfaces, anything is possible.”

Angie frowned. “I’m going to have to give this swimming thing another thought.” She marched off to her bedroom.

Kate was worried about Angie, and then she saw Mark standing nearby with a notepad, looking subdued. She remembered her assignment to him and, pushing her concern about Angie and Sarina aside, took Mark into her study. “Let’s see what you learned about baseball.”

***

When they went to bed that night, Angie stayed on her side of the bed. She was obviously distressed. She didn't say anything for a long time, yet Kate could feel her tension and sense the thoughts going through her head.

Finally, Angie looked toward Kate and said, "If I decide to let her continue with swimming, you have to promise me that you will watch her all the time. You're her second mother and you're responsible when you're with her and I'm not there. It's not the time to be creatively daydreaming, understood?"

Kate nodded in the dark. "Understood."

Angie turned away without kissing her goodnight which signaled to Kate just how upset she was.

Kate lay there for a long time, reliving the experience, trying to figure out how the boy had gotten by her without her knowing. She came up with no good answers. She also considered that being in a lesbian relationship with kids was different than anything she had ever known. Always, before, it was just two women having sex and good times with each other. On the islands a couple of her partners had had children, but there were others around to care for them. Children had seldom been a presence or an issue for Kate and whomever she was seeing. And in New York she had never spent time with any lesbians who had children. Not to say they weren't there, because she knew they were, but in bars and clubs, she just hadn't happened to hit on any of them for an encounter or a brief relationship.

Sleep took a long time in coming. Kate had to figure out how to be a good supporter of Angie and the kids and still do her own thing. At that moment, she wasn't quite sure how to manage it. Her confidence was a bit shaken by pulling Sarina unconscious from the bottom of the pool.

21

Angie had once mentioned that her mother used to swim in the high school pool. That memory gave Kate an idea. One morning, she'd met a neighbor, John Shafer, while he was out walking his cream-colored Labrador retriever. Shafer was currently serving on the local school district board.

Kate sought him out the next time she saw him stepping off his front porch with the dog in tow. "Male or female?" she asked casually.

John grinned. "Female. Name's Shenandoah, but we call her 'Shen' for short."

"We're thinking of getting a dog. Don't laugh, but maybe a labradoodle."

John didn't even smile. "Good choice. Labs are calm and friendly, and poodles are smart and don't shed. Shen, here, leaves hair all over the house. Constant vacuuming, and even that's not enough. The combination, provided the one you select inherits the best qualities of both breeds, should make a good family dog. Good with kids, and I notice you have a couple."

John started walking with Shen. Kate kept up pace with him. "My partner, Angie, and I have been having a debate over swimming pools. She told me that when her mom was in high school here, there was a pool on the campus, but there isn't one any more. How come?"

John nodded. "I think I can answer that. I'm not the financial person, but our son went through the school system here before he left for college. We asked the same question, because he liked swimming. The high school did have a pool for several years. Apparently, there started to be some maintenance issues. Important and expensive equipment needed to be replaced, the walls developed cracks—I'm sure you can imagine that kind of stuff. And the pool only saw limited activity during the most useful time of the year, the summer, when the school system was largely in recess. For liability reasons, they couldn't turn the facility into a public pool in the summer, so it was decided to repurpose the structure and send our swim team to the local fitness center. Cheaper to have a contract with them, since they have liability insurance and maintenance funds from memberships."

Kate nodded. "I get the picture."

John continued, "As long as there's another available pool nearby, I don't think the school district would want one, even if it were donated."

"That fitness center is now the Y, correct?"

"Yep, that's where the team goes to work out and holds meets."

Kate shook his hand. "Thanks for the info. Our little Sarina loves swimming and I'm checking into all the options for her. At the moment, she's swimming in PA's public pool because there are more lanes available."

John nodded. "For a single swimmer, that's probably true and the best place."

"Thanks, John. See you around."

John waved and continued his walk with Shen as Kate turned back home.

***

She sat at her desk and made notes. There were piles of papers all around.

For example, one pile included research on dogs and where she might find a labradoodle. Talking with John alerted her to the fact that just getting "any" labradoodle might not be the right thing. She had dreamed of bringing home a little puppy, but its habits and personality might not reveal much in the cute stage. A young, yet slightly more mature dog, provided it hadn't been abused, would offer more clear indications of what the adult dog would be like. So, she made a note, in addition to researching online, to connect with all the local animal organizations. Maybe they would luck out.

Then she had piles of notes about swimming pools. She crossed off the high school as a possibility for building a pool in Sequim. Although she would check for sure, it looked more promising to go to the city. There was a nice public park on their side of town—Carrie Blake, Marianne had said—with several acres of open land that didn't appear to be designated for anything. She could envision a nice indoor-outdoor pool there, open to residents year-round. No memberships involved or required—just a place kids could go to swim.

She started thinking about what a pool needed to have—kiddie pool, diving pool, general swimming area, and designated lanes for laps. Picnic area, seating for competition audiences. Of course, her thinking began with her own collegiate experiences and now the flexible PA pool.

Kate was making sketches for a pool design when Angie stuck her head in the door.

"What are you up to, sweetheart?"

Kate looked up and gave her a big smile. "Just daydreaming about swimming pool design."

Angie came over to look at the design and hugged Kate, giving her a kiss on the cheek. Kate felt a shiver of desire in all the right places. *It was time for a date night!*

Angie stood up. "Well, I have to go to the store and pick up sandwiches for dinner. Don't forget it's Little League night. You want to ride with us?"

Kate looked at her design. "No, I'll catch up with you at the field down on Silberhorn."

Angie frowned. "Just don't forget. I'll have your food and Mark is counting on you."

Kate nodded. "I'll be there."

***

After completing a rough design for the pool, Kate mentally replayed her conversation with John Shafer then jumped to the Internet and looked up labradoodles. When she found some cute pictures of puppies, she was tempted to order one from an Oregon breeder. But Angie's voice in her head said, "Don't overdo it, whatever you do. Find one locally, don't waste money on some champion puppy, even if you can afford it."

Kate looked up local breeders, didn't find one, and then went to animal groups. Surely there were some of those. After a brief hunt, she made calls to local no-kill animal welfare organizations that fostered animals.

Sandi James answered the phone at the second group Kate called, Caring for Animals (CFA). Kate told Sandi what she wanted, and Sandi nearly shrieked into the phone. "You must be psychic! We just got a labradoodle in today. We *never* see them here. Everything from peeks to poodles, but rarely a doodle." *Sandi was obviously young and enthusiastic.*

Kate asked, "How come this one, then?"

Sandi laughed. "An older couple—much older couple—wanted a dog. They saw a picture of a labradoodle, learned how it didn't bark, didn't shed, was gentle, and they just had to have it. Went to a breeder who showed them the puppies, cute little things. They didn't fully realize how big and strong the grown dog would be."

Sandi chuckled and continued. "So, they brought home the puppy. It grew and grew and grew. Became too much for them to handle. They loved it and felt sad about giving it up, but when the woman was knocked over and broke her leg, they had to admit the dog was too much for them."

Kate thought a minute. "You have a waiting list for this animal?"

"I don't think so. I can check. Even if I don't, and you want her—it's a girl—we have to prepare her first. Check with the vet on shots and general health then get her properly trained. If she had been to obedience class, that accident might not have happened. At any rate, we won't release her for adoption until she's been thoroughly cleared for health, training, and sociability. I'd say at least a month to six weeks before we can place her, maybe more."

Kate scratched her head. "Is there any chance I could just see her?"

Sandi hesitated. "Well, I shouldn't, but if you really want to, I've got her at my house. I'm not overly busy. You can come over. It's in Sequim."

Kate took the address, jumped into the Forester, and drove to Sandi's house.

Clad in jeans and a sweatshirt, Sandi was gently rounded and had a winning smile. She quickly opened the door for Kate. "Come on in. She's busy chowing down."

Kate followed Sandi into a colorfully decorated kitchen. The dog hovering over its food bowl was large, much larger than in Kate's imagination, ginger brown in color, with four white feet. She looked up. There was white on her chest, her chin, and the top of her head. Perfectly placed and balanced. The dog looked at Kate curiously and padded over to give her a few sniffs. In turn, she accepted a pat on the head by Kate and a stroke down her back.

Sandi watched with approval. "She has most of her size now. She's like a late adolescent. She'll grow out now, like in the chest. She's well marked, don't you think?"

Kate nodded. "She's gorgeous. I've not seen a picture of a labradoodle that looked like this."

Sandi grinned. "I'm sure she was the best of the litter. Four white feet alone would be rare."

"What's her name?"

Sandi rolled her eyes. "They named her Puffball and called her Puffy. Might have fit when she was a little ball of fur. Whoever takes her may change it after they see her in action."

Kate looked at Sandi questioningly.

"Notice she has long legs. She's going to be a strider or a runner, depending on who handles her. Would you be her principal caretaker?"

Kate shrugged. "Well, there's me and my partner, and two kids just about eight and nine, girl and boy."

"She would love the kids. Playtime! Woohoo! She might be a little much for them at first, but they would grow into each other. Good companion for that age group, and she'd be around until they are adults, baring accident or illness, of course."

Kate took a deep breath. "Well, I'm quite impressed. What do I do?"

Sandi took Kate's name, address, and phone number and promised to keep her up to date on Puffball's progress. She also promised to check as to whether anyone had already asked for a labradoodle and let Kate know.

Kate petted the dog again, and said goodbye. On the way home, she found herself humming. Somehow, she felt this dog would be theirs. Never having owned a pet, she knew she had a lot to learn—as did Angie and the kids. But there was this hole in their hearts that Zack had created, and all of them needed unconditional love. Dogs were notorious for doing just that. "But that Puffball name should go," she mused to herself. Maybe the kids could name the dog.

When Kate returned home, she sat down in her office and went back to her projects. She didn't even notice when her tummy began to rumble.

Then her cell phone buzzed. As she located it under a pile of papers, she grimaced. *Oh, boy, she was late to Mark's game!*

"Kate, where are you?" Angie queried. "You said you'd be here."

"Sorry. I'm on my way right now. Five minutes tops, okay?"

***

Kate jumped into the Forester and headed to the ballpark. *Good thing she had done this a few dozen times!*

Leaving the SUV at the first open spot she could find, she trotted to the ballfield and found Angie and Sarina in the home team stand. Kate slid in between them.

Angie gave her a stern look. "Where were you?" she whispered with more than a touch of annoyance. "Mark keeps looking over here for you, which interferes with his play. He'll drop the ball or something and then feel bad about it. You can't do this to him."

Kate shifted uncomfortably. "Sorry. I got caught up and time slipped away."

Angie finally gave her a little smile. "I don't want to sound like the Wicked Witch of the East, but you have to get yourself organized. Dealing with kids is not the same thing as dealing with adults. Know what I mean?"

Kate nodded. "Yes, and I get the picture. I'll try to figure out how to remind myself of everything I've promised to do. I sometimes get carried away with projects. I don't mean any harm, but I can see it's a problem for all of you."

Sarina leaned over. "I'm glad you're here, Kate," she said.

Kate patted her arm. "Thanks, kiddo. I'm glad I'm here, too. How's Mark doing?"

"He got a hit the last inning. He tried to steal second and was put out."

"I'm glad he hit one. Maybe he'll tap another, and I can cheer for him," Kate said.

Mark smiled and waved when he saw Kate in the stand. At his next bat, he swung twice and missed.

Kate shouted to him, "Breathe!"

Mark nodded as he adjusted his cap, took a deep breath, and stood tall while moving back into the batter's box. On the next pitch, he connected with a sharp crack, and the ball sailed high and long. Knowing it was a homer by the sound, the opposing outfielders stood and watched the ball sail out of the park. Mark rounded the bases and was greeted with hugs and high fives by his teammates when he crossed home plate.

A little less effective at fielding, Mark let a couple of balls get by him that shouldn't have. However, the Sequim team still won over Port Angeles. As Mark came running to them, Kate held out her arms for a hug. *She had to work with him more on his fielding technique.*

She held him tight. "Great job, Mark. What a hit!"

Mark grinned. "Thanks. I was afraid you wouldn't be here."

Kate frowned. "I just got busy, and the time passed too fast for me. But, I made it in time to see your homer!"

Mark smiled as they strolled arm in arm off the field.

***

When the kids were tucked in for the night, Angie finished dressing in the bathroom and climbed into the big bed with Kate, who was reading a novel. Angie studied her thoughtfully, until Kate seemed to feel the vibes and put her book down.

"I don't know what to do with you sometimes," Angie finally said. "You can be very sweet and lovable. House or no, I couldn't do this thing we're doing if I didn't love you a lot. But I don't know why you take on things and then drop the ball."

Kate sighed. "I'll try harder. I know what I need to do, and then I get sidetracked."

Angie put her hand gently against Kate's head and pushed a lock of hair back behind her ear.

"It's just hard for me to understand," she said. "Responsibility has always been part of my life."

Kate played with the spine of her book. "I know it's hard to grasp. Your family was so different from mine. I'm sure you all cooperated and took care of each other. I realize that in my head, but it doesn't always sink into my insides because it's so different."

"Help me visualize your world."

"Okay. I grew up outside of Ithaca, NY. That's upstate. We lived near Cornell University, and that's where I went to school. That way my mom could come and watch swimming practices. I didn't get away from home until I moved to New York City to work in advertising.

"We lived on what you would call a ranch or a farm. My father came from money and horse people. So, we had a horse barn, and I started riding when I was quite small. My father would have liked for me to compete in dressage, but I didn't take to it much. I rode horses, gave them treats, and once in a while brushed them down, but we had stable hands that generally took care of them. And I never had a dog, as I told you. There were dogs on the property but they, too, were handled by employees."

Angie nodded. "So, you participated in a sense but never really connected with the animals."

"Right. And as an only child, I was often lonely. I didn't have many kids to play with. I read a lot, did picture puzzles, watched TV, went to meals when called, and did my schoolwork. Well enough to score good grades and admission to Cornell. And I might not have made that except that my dad was a powerful person in Ithaca. If he wanted his daughter to go to school there, it was made to happen. I forgot to mention swimming. We had an outdoor pool at home. In the summer when it was very warm, I was in the pool a lot. My mother had her social activities, some dictated by her marriage, but she did like swimming. In fact, when I was little, she taught me to swim. It was a very special bonding thing between us. It was our time together. I really enjoyed the swimming for itself, but I also tried to be good at it to please her. She really loved watching me."

Angie put an arm on Kate's shoulder. "And you joined the swim team, and she came to see you practice. And you began to dream of the Olympics because she would be proud of you, right?"

Kate sighed. "That was part of it. If I had won a medal, my father would have been proud. My mom just loved every aspect of it and seeing me in the pool and watching every stroke. Medaling would have been less important to her than seeing me participate and being there."

Tears came to Kate's eyes. "It was hard to lose her while I was still in college. It happened so fast, and I couldn't prepare myself. My heart broke, and the swimming just went down the drain. I couldn't do it without seeing her up in the stands."

Angie pulled her into a hug. "Oh, sweetheart, I'm terribly sorry for you. I've lost my family, too, but they are still alive, and I can always hope that maybe someday we'll connect again. But for you there's no hope. She's truly gone, as is your dad. And there are no brothers and sisters to care for you."

Kate nodded and rested her head on Angie's shoulder.

"Our lives have been very different," Angie observed quietly.

They lay there together for a few moments, and then Angie turned out the light. "Well, work calls in the morning. It's time to sleep."

Kate kissed her tenderly.

"I'll try harder to understand," Angie said, "if you'll try harder to be responsible. Okay?"

"Yes, sweetheart. I'll try."

***

Kate asked a multitude of questions around town. She concluded that her first goal was to come up with a proposal—a design for a pool and a location for it—then present it to the city council and hope for approval. She learned enough in the process to realize that, even if she was offering to build the pool and pay for it herself, there were numerous approvals to be won. The whole project could go up in smoke at any step along the way. Environmental impacts. Liability issues. Projected maintenance costs. Neighborhood acceptance.

Her principal argument was that swimming was healthy for all ages and good for kids, especially. Kids didn't have enough activity choices in Sequim—not even a movie theatre, for example—so, if they spent their time on tablets and pads and phones, it was not surprising. And not surprising, too, if they became overweight or involved in drugs. A good pool program with teams and competitions and exercise classes would provide another alternative outlet for youthful energy. And she reminded herself, she intended to make pool use inexpensive, allowing even less fortunate families to afford swimming there.

In the background, she always thought of her Olympic Training Center, but that dream had to start somewhere. Swimming was her forte, so swimming was the right place to begin. She could demonstrate or coach. She would be a hands-on operator of the facility.

Kate spent hours every day working on her project, but she tried to make sure she didn't miss any more promises to Angie or the kids. She kept a list on her desk, prominently displayed, of swim and ball club dates, and family outings scheduled.

She checked that list every morning. "I can't let them down," she would remind herself.

22

Kate was pecking away on her computer when her cell buzzed. She picked it up and stared at the unfamiliar number. *Who in the heck was it?* "Hello?"

"You ready for your dog?"

"Oh, Sandi!" Kate's heart raced. "You mean she's ready, and we can have her?"

"Yep. Everything checked out. You won the lottery. Ha! Puffball is healthy, her shots are current, she's been through obedience training—she's smart and she picked it up immediately. Wants to please and loves her treats. Will do anything you want to her to do. She's affectionate, too. You may have to work to control her enthusiasm with the kids, but she's ready for a home."

Puffball. Kate scratched her head as she arranged to pick up the dog. Not having known if they would get the labradoodle, she hadn't discussed it with Angie or thought about a name. *Maybe it should be a family thing, anyway.*

Later that morning, Kate drove to a Port Angeles shelter where Sandi and the large, ginger-colored dog with four white paws waited for her. Sandi had tons of instructions. Kate tried to listen. Her attention kept going to the dog that sat patiently but attentively, watching everything going on.

"You need a crate big enough for her to sit, lie, stand, and turn around in. That's going to be pretty large, but they'll have it at Petco. Meals of dry kibble or canned food or a combination. Treats. You'll experiment at first until you find what she really likes. Don't change food quickly or she'll have the trots. She's going to need a lot of walking since she's a big energetic dog. Two or three walks a day. Throw balls for her to retrieve. Take her on trails when you can, give her time to sniff, because that's life to her."

Kate's head was spinning. "That's a lot of info. I've never had my own dog."

Sandi grinned. "I think you'll do just fine. But I have a sheet here that covers just about everything. The vet said she's in very good health.

"How do I know what crate to buy? Sounds complicated."

"Petco lets you bring dogs into the store. Take her in and have the staff help you find the right crate, a bed for her to sleep on, and some food and treats. She already has a collar, leash and food samples that are donated to us. She'll quickly tell you what she likes."

Much as she wanted the dog, Kate felt uncertain about taking her out the door.

Sensing as much, Sandi moved away from Kate and then called the dog to her. "Here, Puff. Sit."

The dog immediately turned to face Sandi, approached her, and sat. Sandi produced a treat from her pocket and gave it to Puff. "Good dog."

Sandi pointed to the floor. "Puff, down."

Puff stretched out on the floor, facing Sandi. She was given another treat.

"Puff, stay."

Sandi walked away, but Puff remained in the down position, just watching Sandi.

"Good girl." Sandi returned to Puff with another treat.

Kate was amazed. "Can I try it?"

Sandi grinned. "Sure. Here's the treat bag."

Kate hesitated a second. "Um, Puff, come here. Sit."

Puff waited only a split second and then planted herself in front of Kate, properly in sit position. Kate pulled out a treat and opened her hand to the dog. Puff nosed her palm and took the treat with her tongue.

Kate laughed. "That tickles!"

Sandi's face relaxed into an amused grin.

Kate continued the routine as far as she knew it. The dog responded to each command.

Suddenly Kate asked, "How do I get her home?"

Sandi laughed. "What are you driving?"

"Forester."

"Well, until you have a crate, you can put her in the back seat. Since you have a partner and two kids who will be riding in your vehicle, I would recommend that you put a crate and the dog in your cargo space. The kids will want the dog free to play with it. The dog will want to be in your lap, but she's way too big for that. Or the passenger seat, to be close. Do what you want, but the dog's safety should be primary. You and your family wear seatbelts. If the dog isn't belted in, she could go flying in any accident, and that would be a tragedy for all of you. I hope you'll be a responsible dog owner, for Puff's sake, anyway."

Kate sighed, as she held Puff's leash. "I'm sure you're right. Lots to think about. I guess I really have much to learn."

Sandi shook her free hand. "Good luck. If you have problems or questions, feel free to call. We're here to help."

Kate took the dog out to the Forester, loaded her in the back seat and said, "Stay."

Before Kate could climb into the driver's seat, Puff came through the space between the bucket seats and settled in the passenger seat.

Befuddled, Kate wanted to scream, "Help!"

The dog stared at her then leaned over to lick her hand.

"Okay, you win round one," Kate said. "But I'll figure out how to manage this. I hope."

Puff alternately studied Kate and looked out the front window all the way into Sequim. At Petco, she walked on leash beside Kate and seemed to be at home. A staff member came over. "Hi, Puffball," he said. He studied Kate. "Something happen to the Johnsons?" he asked.

"Oh, the dog became too much for them, so they gave her to CFA. I'm just adopting her today. I have to buy a crate, a bed, and some food and treats."

Andy, according to his nametag, grinned. "That'll be easy. She's a good dog. What do you eat, Puff?"

The dog pranced ahead of Kate and the grocery cart, up an aisle, and stood in front of a brand of dog food. Kate looked perplexed.

"That's her food. She likes chicken the best," Andy offered.

Within minutes, the cart was filled with a big bag of chicken kibble, a case of canned chicken dog food, a package of rawhide treats, a flat, comfortable day bed for her to lie on, a crate that seemed huge to Kate, and food and water bowls. The crate came folded down, to be assembled at home. Kate also had picked up a training manual and a "how to care for your dog" book.

Several hundred dollars later, Kate left Petco with Puff and all her trappings.

***

Once they arrived back home, Kate let Puff sniff around the house while she assembled the dog crate and figured out where to put it. She finally resigned herself to the reality that it could be moved later. *Angie would have something to say about it.*

Puffball sniffed at the back door, leading Kate to think that maybe a dog or another animal had lived in this house. Kate opened the back door and let Puff out. The dog bounded into the fenced yard and began sniffing everywhere. Finally, she squatted briefly and then jumped up onto the patio deck and headed back into the house.

"Dog door," Kate muttered to herself. *Something else to put on a list.*

Kate spent the rest of the afternoon giving commands, petting, being licked repeatedly, and generally getting to know Puff. She put down food and water in the kitchen and listened to Puff slurping. *More chores to do, keeping things clean.*

Kate was torn between fascination with the dog and the realization that she hadn't a clue, really, how to care for her. It would be hit and miss, trial and error, until she learned. And Angie might be a bit touchy about all of this since a dog was not her idea and she had shown a lot of resistance to Kate's plan. The kids, she was sure, would love Puffball. Kate was fond of her already, even the goofy name that was beginning to grow on her.

***

Just before 5 p.m., a car rolled up into the driveway. Puff stood up from where she was stretched out on the dog bed near

Kate's desk. She looked at the door and then back at Kate, as if deciding what to do.

The front door opened. Suddenly, Angie and the kids were confronted by a large, curly haired, barking dog that they had never before seen.

"What the—?" Angie gasped.

Kate ran to the rescue. "This is Puff, our new dog."

Mark and Sarina immediately were all over Puff, and the dog was all over them. Barking, laughing and cuddling ensued. Meanwhile, Angie stood glaring at Kate.

"Sorry to take you by surprise." Kate looked uncomfortable. "Although I knew about her a month ago, there was a list. She had to be cleared, and I had no idea if we would even get her. This morning they called and said she was ours and to come pick her up. I've been working with her all day."

Angie huffed her way into the kitchen and dumped her groceries on the counter. She observed, not happily, the water and food bowl on the floor.

Kate followed her. "She's a labradoodle, no shedding."

"Well, that's a relief!" Angie's tone was sarcastic.

"She's been trained. She's a year old, and the Petco staff knows all the things she likes. I picked up everything."

Mark ran into the kitchen. "We need a toy for her, to throw!"

Kate sighed. "I forgot about toys. Darn!"

"Dog toys can wait. We need to fix dinner." Angie banged a few pans onto the stove.

***

The meal was pandemonium. Eventually, they all were fed, including Puff, who had stood by the table sniffing everything touched by her humans. She was curious, and her big brown eyes followed every move they made.

"Why do you call her Puff?" Sarina asked.

Kate smiled. "Because she was named Puffball by her original owners. They were elderly, and she grew too big for them. She answers to Puff, which is easier."

Sarina looked thoughtful. "Well, I don't know, but if that's her name, I think we should keep it."

Mark agreed, and Kate sighed with relief. *One less issue to worry about, now that she had gotten used to Puffball.*

***

After dinner, Angie went to Kate in the living room. "Look, I need a break from this. I'm going to Walmart to pick up some things I need. I promise to bring home a ball and a couple of toys for HER. Meanwhile, I want you to get things under control. Teach them some commands to give her to settle her down. Otherwise, we can't live with this."

With misgivings, Kate watched Angie leave. Then she sat on the floor with Mark and Sarina and played with Puff. As they all became more familiar with each other, the noise level noticeably dropped. Kate told the kids about the commands and handed each of them some treats. One by one, they gave commands to Puff, and very willingly, she responded to them. They rewarded her, laughing when her nose and tongue tickled their palms as she vacuumed up the treats.

By the time Angie returned, Kate and the kids were seated on the sofa, with Puff at their feet. The television was on, and there was relative quiet in the house.

Angie breathed a sigh of relief, handed Kate the dog toys, and headed for her room.

Shortly, the kids got ready for bed, and Kate led Puff to her crate. She was happy that the previous owners had used a crate for the dog, because Puff entered it without complaint. Kate gave her a treat and told her to have a good night. Turning out the lights in the living room, she went back to the master suite where Angie was in bed reading.

"I'm really sorry to have dumped Puff on you without warning. It was either take her or let her go to someone else."

Angie nodded, both weary and resigned. "I know. I also know how much you wanted a dog. I can understand how you didn't want to talk about it in case it didn't happen. And I can even see how happy the kids are. It was probably a good idea. It's just a lot for me."

Kate gave her a hug. "I know, sweetheart."

Angie looked into Kate's eyes. "We've made so many changes in such a short period of time. I can't handle another challenge. Please be patient with me. Just know that Puff is your problem. I don't want to hear about any issues. Take care of her and teach the kids to care for her. Or else she goes."

Kate sighed. "Okay, I get it. I have a lot to figure out, and the kids do, too. Somehow, we'll take care of her, I promise."

When Kate climbed into bed a few minutes later, Angie seemed less stressed. She smiled playfully. "Now I don't want to become jealous of a dog. You'll take care of her, but you won't forget about me, right?"

Kate grinned and stroked Angie's cheek. "I could never forget about you."

She kissed Angie, at first lightly and then more deeply, and Angie responded. The covers were tossed off and Kate began to explore tenderly. All the confusions and frustrations of the day disappeared in a round of passionate lovemaking.

23

For the next few weeks, peace reigned. The kids were delighted with Puffball and played with her regularly. They brushed her, taught her tricks, and went along with Kate on dog walks.

Angie admitted that having them playing with a dog was better than their spending hours in front of a television set. They were learning to care for a living creature and to feel love for it. That was a good thing. And getting exercise at the same time.

Meanwhile, Angie was enrolled in the spring quarter at Peninsula College, taking those first preparatory classes to enter the nursing program. She was busier, if that was possible, and Kate took on more kitchen responsibilities. Sarina and Mark wanted to help as well, and the three of them tried new recipes and managed to have a meal on the table every evening, always juggling around swim sessions, baseball practice, and dog care.

At night, Kate and Angie fell into the big king-sized bed exhausted. However, they always talked for a few minutes, reviewing the day, exchanging kisses, and sometimes even having enough energy left to make love.

After one of those intimate sessions, Angie whispered to Kate. "I don't always understand you, and I don't always know what to do with you, but I am glad you stopped in at The Little Red Barn that day and noticed me. Our world is complicated, and it's only going to become worse, but I *do* love you, and I'm glad you're here sharing all of this with me."

Kate kissed her gently. "Me, too."

***

Kate's office began to overflow with books, mail and maps, drawings and designs. She was glad that she was now sharing Angie's bed because there was no room left in her office to sleep—the convertible sofa was covered in project materials. Kate was handling a multitude of things at once. She was gathering data and history on swimming pools. She was exploring the surrounding county, because a pool, if she managed to build one, might be located inside or outside the city limits. More people lived outside the city than in. The city's actual footprint was relatively small. Finding enough land for a swim building and adequate parking might be a challenge, especially if she limited her choices to the city proper, especially Carrie Blake Park.

Not having given up on her dream of an Olympic Training Center, Kate was also reading up on similar centers, learning where they were located, studying their history, and cataloguing which sports were covered by other centers. These training centers brought up questions about other governmental agencies, state and federal, and the US Olympics governing body. Kate knew almost nothing about government. She spent hours online and with her head buried in books, trying to quickly gather the information that would make her sound less like a rank amateur.

***

One afternoon, toward the end of the school year—meaning that baseball playoffs were beginning—Kate was engaged in research, when the front door opened and Angie peeped in to her office. "Hi," she said with a grin, "you look very busy."

Kate nodded. "No matter how much I learn, there's always more."

Angie called back as she walked toward the kitchen. "It's still raining out. I'll start dinner, something in the oven, and then I'll pick up the kids at the club."

There was a moment of silence. "Kate, where's the dog?"

Kate looked up, not having noticed that Puff was no longer lying on her usual spot by Kate's desk.

"I don't know. Maybe out in the back yard."

Angie opened the back door and called Puff. There was quiet for a moment, and then another call. Angie disappeared outside.

Kate began to feel uncomfortable. *Something was amiss.*

Angie returned and stared at Kate. "She's not in the yard. A gate is open. Looks like she took off."

Kate jumped up—her heart thumping in her chest—grabbed her jacket, and headed out the front door. Because of the rain, she drove the Forester and circled the neighborhood, looking for the dog. No sign of Puff anywhere. Kate then went out on the main road and entered all of the surrounding neighborhoods, leaning out the window and calling for Puff. No dog responded. The rain became heavier.

Finally, resigned, Kate returned to the house. Angie's car was gone, and Kate realized she was picking up the kids. What could she tell them? Puff was indeed seriously missing.

Kate phoned the police, the county sheriff, every dog rescue group she could find on the Internet and then sat there staring at the wall. *What had happened? How did Puff get out? Had she left the gate open?* She couldn't remember even being near the backyard gate anytime in the last day or so. Did one of the kids open the gate to do something and then forget to close it? Losing Puff would be tragic for the family. She just had to be somewhere, and hopefully she was safe. Her collar had all the information required to return her, and she was chipped. Maybe someone would find her and call.

Angie returned with the kids. Everyone sat down to dinner, but no one had an appetite. Angie told them to eat, but the efforts were half-hearted. They all stared at each other. "I don't think I opened the gate," Mark said sadly.

"I don't think I did either," Sarina said.

"Well, she got out somehow." Angie sighed.

Kate looked at them all. "Could she have flipped the latch on her own?"

Angie shrugged.

"She's a big dog. She's smart and has a lot of curiosity. Maybe we didn't let her out. Maybe she opened the gate by herself."

None of them cared about doing anything. The TV was on, but no one watched it. Angie told them to do their homework, but they didn't care. Baseball practice was scheduled for that evening but in the pouring rain had been called off.

***

About 8 p.m. the phone rang and Kate picked up the cell. An older man was on the line. "Are you missing a dog?"

Kate held the phone tightly. "Yes, did you find one? Ours is called Puff for Puffball."

"Well, yes. She was wandering down the alley behind our house. All sopping wet. No collar on her. I have a dog myself, so I took this one to my vet, just down the street. This poodle, or something like a poodle, had a chip in its ear. We contacted the people identified by the chip, and they said they didn't have the dog any longer. They had turned it over to an animal group. We called them, and it's taken a long time to get a call back. But they knew the dog and said that she was taken by Kate Brighton at this phone number."

Kate sighed. "That's me."

Kate took the address, and the whole family climbed into the Forester to drive into downtown Sequim. At the given address, they knocked on the front door and heard a dog barking inside. Clearly Puffball's bark. Everyone grinned in relief, because they had their dog back.

They thanked the gentleman and offered a reward, but he was just happy to return their dog in one piece. Okay, if still very wet.

***

That evening, after Puffball had been given an emergency bath and dried with every hairdryer in the house, she went to bed with Mark, and Kate and Angie fell into the big bed, both exhausted.

"We were lucky this time," Angie said quietly to Kate.

"I know. The kids would have been devastated if something had happened to her."

"Well, although I don't want to have a big scene over it, this is what I meant about you taking care and being responsible. That's a big, strong, young, intelligent, and inquisitive animal. Give her an inch and she'll take the proverbial mile."

"I can see that."

"You're going to have to pay more attention. She got very far away. She lost her collar somehow but thank goodness she was chipped or we might never have found her. You're here more than anyone. You need to watch what she's doing. Had you noticed sooner, she might not have escaped the neighborhood and you might have found her right away."

"Actually," Kate admitted, "I've already decided to change the latches on the gates. They need to be something she can't undo by herself. I think the fence is tall enough to keep her in, but the latches aren't very sophisticated. I'll have them replaced right away."

Angie yawned. "Well, let's say a prayer of thanksgiving and go to sleep."

Kate gave her a kiss. "Okay, sweetheart."

"And I don't mind that she's sleeping with Mark."

"She'll never return to the crate, you know."

"I know." Sigh.

24

Puff lay at Kate's feet, chewing mightily on a large rawhide stick.

Kate was surrounded by papers for another research project, but she had her latest version of a schedule posted on the wall in front of her—noting all the swimming times, the practices for baseball, Angie's work hours, Puff's daily walks, and everything else that Kate could think of that had to be monitored.

Kate's mind drifted from the pamphlet she was reading. The thought had just occurred to her that they needed a family vacation. Summer was on the horizon. Angie would soon be in finals and then summer classes at Peninsula College, preparing to begin nursing school in the fall quarter. She'd also be working, just shorter shifts.

Somewhere, before all of those things hit, they needed an escape, even if it was just a brief weekend. Opening her laptop, Kate found Ocean Shores on the west coast of the Peninsula. It offered something different, with a broad beach, horseback riding, a little boat trip through canals, and some other things to see in the area, including the historic town of Aberdeen, and Westport, with a lighthouse where they could climb to the top of the tower. Angie would like it, as would the kids.

Kate sighed. She needed to pull this off to convince Angie that she was putting family first. Sometimes, she understood, it was difficult for a family person like Angie to deal with someone as independent as Kate whose natural curiosity and deep pockets would always involve her in an adventure of some kind—activities that could take her away, in time or in spirit, from home. It was an issue they would always have, one that hopefully would not destroy their relationship. Kate didn't know how to be any other way. At the same time, she accepted the need to focus, especially on the kids, who required undivided attention and lots of it.

***

With a warm sun beating down and a cooling ocean breeze behind their backs, Kate and Angie led two children, two horses, two ponies, and one labradoodle away from the stable and onto the wide, sandy Ocean Shores beach. Once in the sand, Kate called the parade to a halt. She began her teaching stint, looking out at two excited young faces.

"Here, Mark, put your left foot in this stirrup," she instructed, "and hold onto my belt with your left hand."

Awkwardly, but with intense concentration, Mark did as instructed.

"Now move your left hand up to that hump, the pommel, at the front of the saddle, okay, and push yourself up, swinging your right leg over the saddle then holding onto the pommel with both hands. Slip your right food into the stirrup."

Mark wobbled yet managed to push himself up and swing his foot over. Once he was firmly in the saddle, with feet planted in the stirrups, a big grin crossed his face.

"Good boy," Kate said with a nod. "We'll make you a champion rider really quick."

Angie, smiling broadly, moved closer to keep a hand on Mark's paint pony, Magee, while Kate helped Sarina through the same process of mounting her pony, the golden Ginger.

When they were both seated on their ponies, deliriously happy and laughing at each other, Kate grinned at Angie. Angie mounted her horse, while Kate controlled the excited Puff. When Angie was up, Kate passed Puff's leash to her, then Kate climbed astride her own horse.

Puff had at first been a little sensitive around the four animals, creatures much larger than she. She soon settled down and sniffed them curiously. Meanwhile, the horses stood still, snorted, and flicked their tails, while seeming untroubled by the labradoodle.

Kate told Mark and Sarina where to put their hands on the saddle and demonstrated the way to hold the reins. She showed them how to start and stop their ponies and how to turn. The gentle animals were accustomed to carrying inexperienced humans on their backs and responded casually yet promptly to the commands.

When Kate had everyone headed the same direction, they moved at a walk rather easily down the beach.

"This is bumpy," Sarina called out and giggled.

"Yeah, a walk is bumpy. We'll have you really riding soon, and then it'll be much smoother."

After a few moments at a walk, Kate brought the horses and ponies to a halt. "I want to take a few pictures on my phone," she said to Angie. "Why don't you take over the training?"

Angie nodded and gave Kate a wink. She moved her mare around the ponies and demonstrated how to rein in the horse and how to use heels to prompt the horse to start and even go faster. She encouraged them to go easy with the heels.

It became clear that Puff was staying close to their group, so Kate briefly dismounted and unclipped the dog from her leash. "You stay with us, now," she instructed. Puff barked once and seemed to nod her head. "Don't wander off."

The first lesson lasted an hour. By the end of it, Sarina and Mark wanted to run their ponies full out. Kate shook her head. "You're more tired than you realize. It's time to quit for the day but we can come back tomorrow. Maybe then we can do a run with our mounts."

Sarina offered a mock frown then laughed. They turned the animals back toward the stable, with Puff following behind. Although the labradoodle made a few quick trips down to the surf and sniffed here and there, she quickly caught up with her pack.

For a summer day, the beach was amazingly quiet, something Kate treasured and hadn't expected to see.

Within an hour of their riding lesson, the kids were complaining about sore muscles. The resort had a swimming pool and a hot tub, and Kate encouraged them to soak in the hot tub then play in the pool for a while.

Kate and Angie hung out in the hot tub. "I adore you when you're like this," Angie whispered to Kate.

Kate smiled. "I love times like this, too. We'll have to do it more often. That's one thing we share, a history and knowledge of horses, and we can give Mark and Sarina a chance to love them, too."

Angie nodded. "They know the history of Zack's and my families being involved on the prairie with farming and horses, but they've mostly lived in town. Barns, hay, and horses haven't been real for them. I'm appreciating the chance to enjoy it again for myself—and especially for them."

She added, "I love seeing you on a horse. You're quite confident."

Kate grinned. "You, too." She pulled Angie's ponytail below the waterline and swiped her hand against Angie's thigh.

"Careful," Angie laughed. "This isn't the place for me to ravish you."

Kate winked at her.

***

Mark and Sarina stayed awake long enough to consume a steak dinner at a local eatery, but they were totally exhausted and soon went to bed. Kate had rented a condo large enough for each child to have a private room.

Kate and Angie went into the master suite and turned their television on with the volume up a bit. Experience told Angie that hearing the TV down the hallway was soothing to her children, and it covered any lovemaking noises not appropriate for their ears.

Angie pulled up the sheets in the king-sized bed and slipped out of her nightgown, tossing it to the floor. She snuggled up to Kate, who had seemed to be ready for sleep and was curled up.

"I'm tired out," Kate whispered. "I don't think I can make love tonight."

Angie put her hand under Kate's nightshirt and teasingly pinched a breast. "You're not getting away with that. I've got you and you are going to make love with me."

Kate turned over, a big grin on her face. "You go, girl. I'm ready and waiting."

"You're such a tease." Angie tugged on Kate's shirt and tossed it away. She climbed on top of Kate and began kissing every inch of skin she could find. Kate shivered with delight and smiled broadly. "God, woman, what you do to me!"

Sometime later, after their lovemaking, Kate fell back on the bed with a groan and a deep sigh. "I didn't know I had it in me."

"It's the horses," Angie whispered. They do all the foreplay. All you have to do is let it happen."

They lay in each other's arms, both about to nod off. Kate planted a soft kiss on Angie's lips and said, "I love you, beautiful."

Angie nodded. "I love you, too. Never more than now."

***

Kate required several cups of coffee to awaken fully the next day. When Angie teased her, she replied, "You know I'm an old woman, past forty. Be patient with me!"

"Ha," Angie quipped. "You're not going to slip out of your promises that easily."

After warm showers and a hot breakfast, the foursome returned to the stables for the anticipated second ride. Thankfully, the same mounts were available. Kate had reserved them but one never knew. The kids were still a little tired, but as soon as they saw the ponies, they brightened. Any unease they'd shown the day before disappeared. Sarina and Mark both petted their ponies and helped saddle them before climbing up with very little hesitation or stumbling.

Back on the beach, they rehearsed again, handling the reins, starting a pony up and pulling back on the reins to slow and stop the animal.

When all were mounted, Puff was allowed to follow them untethered. Kate had brought treats to reinforce the dog's behavior. The doodle always knew Kate had treats in her pocket. Given that incentive, she wasn't about to wander off.

After a brief walk, Kate urged her horse to a trot, and almost without a touch on the rains or heels, the other three mounts followed. Sarina and Mark both laughed and giggled as they bounced around on their ponies.

Seeing that they were successfully hanging on, Kate instructed them to hold their knees tightly against their ponies, and she moved for a run. All four mounts went forward together.

At a run, the ride was much gentler on butts, hips, thighs, and knees. Everything smoothed out.

After a moderate run, Kate reined in her horse and called the others to pull back on their reins. All the animals came to a walk then a stop.

"Everybody okay?" It was a needless question because the look on their faces spoke of glorious wonder.

In a few minutes, they did another brief run at the end of which Sarina commented that she was getting tired. Mark was thrilled and wanted more.

Angie and Sarina both dismounted and turned back to the stable. They walked in the sand, their rides and Puff behind them, all moving at a gentle pace.

"Did you like it?" Angie asked.

"Yes," Sarina replied. "I like it. I love my pony." She patted Ginger's velvet nose. "But riding is rough on me. I like the speed and the wind in my hair, but I think I like swimming better. It's softer."

Trying not to be disappointed, Angie said, "It's okay, Sarina. I'm glad you're honest about it, and if swimming's really your thing, we'll always see that you can do it."

Sarina looked up at her, a question on her face. "I wouldn't mind riding now and then. I know there are trails at home, and I bet you'd like to ride them."

Angie smiled. "Well, sometime we will." *Sarina was a good and thoughtful child, wanting to please.*

Mark had wanted to keep going. Kate took him on several runs, his riding skills improving each time. He was quick and sure. *A born athlete*, Kate thought to herself.

After the mounts had been returned to the stable, with both children stroking their ponies and saying a wistful goodbye, the foursome took a drive to enjoy the other attractions of the area. By dinnertime, the kids were totally worn out. Kate rounded up a pizza. Before long, the kids were in bed asleep.

Kate and Angie sat for a while in the living room and watched TV.

"This, for me, is what family life is all about," Angie said quietly, putting her hand on Kate's thigh.

Kate's eyes brimmed. "Me, too. I never had this. I did things with my mother, like the riding and swimming, but my father was almost always away, and always busy. Even a dinner with all of us was rare. The holidays were forced, so this is something really new to me. I'm not sure I know how to take it."

"Just relax and enjoy it. It could become a habit."

25

When Angie drove up to the house after her classes at Peninsula College, carrying a stack of books for a paper she needed to write that evening, it was instantly clear to her that Kate wasn't around. The blue Forester was not sitting askew in the driveway, as Kate often left it when she was thinking about something else and absentmindedly parked it.

Struggling to keep her books balanced, Angie used her key to open the front door—hoping, anyway, that the kids would be there, the dog bounding up to say hello, and Kate, despite the absence of the SUV, working on something in her office.

However, her suspicions were correct. No kids, no dog, no Kate, no sounds. *Now what?*

Angie peeped into Kate's lair and noted that her laptop was not on her desk, her briefcase was missing, and one glance in the freestanding closet revealed there was no duffle bag. Angie always laughed at the duffle bag, which didn't conform to the big-league lifestyle that Kate was currently pursuing. Angie sighed. *No duffle, no Kate. Where in the world was she? And everyone else?*

The only one who might know was Jake. Angie grabbed her cell phone.

"Hi, Angie," Jake responded on the first ring. "I've been waiting for your call. Not to worry, Puff and the kids are over here."

Angie steamed. "That's fine, but where's Kate? She was supposed to keep the kids busy this evening while I write a term paper. My whole grade is hanging on it."

"Kate's gone to Washington, D.C., to see some important people on the USOC. She got a call this morning, and I drove her to SeaTac, because she had to be there today, no options."

"But—" Angie stammered in frustration.

Jake broke in gently. "I'm sure you are a bit upset, probably concerned, and that you have a paper to write. Come over here for a bowl of stew—I've got a wonderful one cooking on the stove—and we'll talk about it. The kids have their tent set up in the living room. They'll stay here tonight, and I'll drop them off at school in the morning. Puff is here and can remain here until Kate gets back—I'll pick her up at the airport, probably early tomorrow morning."

Angie sighed. "Okay, I'll be right there."

Grumbling to herself, she tossed her books back into the car and drove over to Jake's and Marianne's house. During the trip she mumbled over all the things that annoyed her about Kate and how much in the toilet her life was at this particular moment.

Angie's annoyance nearly disappeared when she saw the kids and their tent in the living room. Mark and Sarina were playing some kind of wild-west story, with Native Americans, their children, and various animals. Mark had a feather stuck over his ear, and Puff was wearing a cardboard construction on her head that only Sarina could have designed. Angie couldn't help but smother a laugh or two.

Shortly, Marianne called "Beep, beep," as she wheeled herself out of her office and joined the others at the dining room table. Jake had a fresh loaf of sliced sourdough bread to pass around with a mound of butter and steaming bowls of rich meat and veggie stew.

"You are the champion of delicious one-bowl meals," Angie commented to Jake with a laugh. She was consumed with eating for several minutes, and her pique waned, temporarily at least, in the face of good food that was particularly delightful after a long day of classes and labs.

Sarina and Mark finished their food quickly. They were offered a cookie for dessert, which they accepted gleefully, then asked to be excused to go back to their game.

When they were gone, Angie realized that she was watching them wistfully. *They were growing up so quickly and were much less dependent and more flexible than they had been even a few months ago.*

Jake studied her for a moment then spoke. "Angie, I know you're uncomfortable with Kate being gone. And without warning. But before she confirmed the trip, she called me to see if I could take over for her for the day. She checked with me before she agreed to attend the meeting late this evening. She barely made it to the airport for her flight, and crossing the country takes several hours. DC is also in a three-hour later time zone. She's probably meeting an important political figure for a rushed dinner and an overnight flight home."

Angie selected another piece of bread, buttered it, took a bite and chewed on it while she thought. Then she released a deep sigh. "I know Kate doesn't mean it, I know she has dreams, too, and these are wonderful things she wants to accomplish. But she promised to support me while I finish school. When she takes off like this, I feel nervous and insecure and wonder if I'm going to be able to complete my degree. It means a lot to me to become an educated adult who will be able to support my children, no matter what. I want to make my own mark in the world."

Marianne took a drink of ice tea and nodded. "We know you do. Your goals are very realistic and something you can accomplish. And as a nurse, you will be a gift to the world. Capable nurses are really special, and you're strong, smart, and caring. You will make a very good nurse."

Angie blushed. "Really? Maybe I don't see that in myself."

"You've moved heaven and earth for your children, despite all the wrongs done to you. You'll take that same character into nursing, that same determination and helpfulness."

Angie's eyebrows shot up. "I've never thought of it that way. It just always seemed right for me to do that. I was just being practical."

"Once you're through the program, you'll see how well you fit," Marianne observed.

Angie sighed. "Well, that's a ways down the road. For now I have to be able to do my work."

Marianne studied Angie for a moment, gently and thoughtfully. "You are what, twenty-six, twenty-seven?"

"Twenty-seven, now."

"And you're clear on what you want to do and be. You've chosen a skill that can be learned locally. You not only have a dream, but the tools are here and potential employment is right here too. When you're trained, you'll have choices about whether to stay in Sequim or go somewhere else."

Angie nodded.

"Well, for a moment, think about Kate. She is now forty and still doesn't know what she wants to do. She's been here, there, and everywhere, and nothing has stuck with her. Now, because of her feelings for you, she wants to remain in Sequim, hopefully to find herself at last. It's really time. I know she's made promises and it's important for both of you and your relationship that she keep them—just give her a little room once in a while for a slip. She hasn't your history, which made you strong even if it was painful. Instead she was spoiled as a child and at the same time denied affection and personal confidence. When things become tough or confusing for her, or she feels sad, she moves on."

Angie nodded. "That's what scares me."

"She loves you very much. And she wants to succeed at something, to impress you and make you proud. She's lost in some ways. She doesn't know what a real achievement is, or when money is good or in the way. You and your children are providing her with an education in living in the real world. Sequim, not Manhattan, or Upstate New York, or even the beautiful, remote islands of the South Pacific. Someplace interesting and creative yet down to earth—she's never had that. Give her a little time to sort it out."

Angie stood, leaned over and gave Marianne a big hug. "We'd never make it without you and Jake. We'd be fighting and quitting and making a big mess of it all around."

Marianne returned her hug. "I'm glad we can be of help. And it's been good for us, too. I always wanted children but couldn't have them. This is such a treat for me to have two little ones playing on the living room floor. They'll grow up before long, but I'll have these memories. As long as they're safe, don't worry too much about Kate and her comings and goings."

Angie looked at her watch. "Speaking of which—"

Marianne nodded. "You run along to do your studying. The house will be quiet for you tonight. Puff will sleep by the kids on the floor, I'm sure. If Kate calls for a ride back from SeaTac, Jake will get up quietly and drive there whether tonight or early morning. She'll bring Kate here to sleep on the couch. You won't be disturbed."

Angie shuddered. “Marianne. Jake. You are both so wonderful. However, I do have to go.”

“That’s fine,” Jake called out. “We’ve got your back. Just go write your paper.”

***

When they heard Angie’s car start, Marianne turned to Jake. “How long is nursing school?”

Jake shrugged. “Two, maybe three years, why?”

Marianne looked at the kids inside the tent and listened to their play. “Well, it’s going to be interesting around here.”

“You bet, babe. You up for it?”

“I’d better be, hadn’t I?”

***

Jake pulled up to the curb at SeaTac arrivals terminal just as Kate came running through the exit door. She unlocked the passenger side for Kate to toss her duffle over the seat and climb in.

“Thanks for coming. I’m dead tired and can’t wait to be home and jump into the sack.”

Jake cleared her throat as she pulled out into traffic. She was dead tired, too, having driven nearly three hours in traffic to SeaTac, returning, and having done it again for the second time in twenty-four hours. And it wasn’t even daylight yet.

Kate started to push herself down in the seat, as if to take a nap. Noticing, Jake raised an eyebrow and asked, “Did you accomplish what you set out to do?”

“Me? Oh, yeah.” She sat up and warmed to the subject despite her proclaimed exhaustion. “It was really great. I went to dinner with these people from the Olympics. I have their names written down but off the top of my head I don’t remember them. Some were government types and some from the USOC. I learned a lot from them.”

There was a moment of silence, and Jake pushed. “Well, what kind of things?”

"Oh, okay, I know now that there are several locations that would like to have training centers. And there are some that were but it didn't pay off and were taken over by cities and other municipalities. It was suggested that I visit that one near San Diego to see what happened there and what they learned from it."

"So, more travel, huh?"

"Yeah, sure. They were clear that there are no guarantees, just because you want it."

Jake nodded. Kate's summary was not too specific yet suggestive.

Kate glanced over at Jake. "How are the kids? Everything okay?"

"Oh, the kids are fine. They've put the tent in our living room and are camping there. They were asleep with Puff curled up beside them when I left. But, Kate, in all honesty, Angie is pretty upset. She came home from school and found you gone. There was no message and she had no idea where you were or where the kids or the dog were. Thankfully, she started with us."

Kate sighed. "I got the call in the morning and they said to come pronto. I just grabbed my stuff and called you. I didn't think about putting out a message for her."

Jake mulled her words for a moment. "Well, if you're going to be doing this again, and it sounds like you will, you'd better think a little more about the impact of your comings and goings on Angie, the kids, and even the dog. Angie's under a lot of stress with school, and she needs to be able to count on you."

Kate bristled slightly. "I know that, and I really try. But, I'm following my dream, too, just like she is. Understanding goes both ways."

Jake nodded. "I realize that this is your dream. It's a dream that will take a lifetime to accomplish. You aren't going to build this center overnight, that's for sure. Meanwhile, Angie's been out of school for a decade. If she doesn't make the grade in these classes and finish the program quickly, she might not be successful in becoming a nurse. She really can't wait, and while your dream is important, you could slow the pace a little until she gets out of school and settles into a job."

Kate became defensive and sat up in her seat. “Well, she doesn't have to work at the coffeehouse. That would make it easier for her.”

Jake nodded. “Yes, I know, Kate. However, her not working wouldn’t change anything about the suddenness of some of your actions, your unpredictable behavior. And you know she works to feel independent, not to be beholden to you for every dime in her life.”

“Well, I have plenty. There is no need for her to work.”

“Financial need is not the same as emotional need, and you know it.”

“Ah, shoot, we’ve been over this and over this.”

Jake was silent for a moment, just keeping her eyes on the dark road as they were leaving the Seattle area, crossing the Tacoma Narrows Bridge and entering the Kitsap Peninsula. Traffic on the 16 was light, pre-dawn and pre-rush hour.

“Kate,” Jake finally said, “I’ve enjoyed your company this past year. I really like you, and I think you are smart and funny. You also have a naiveté about you that doesn’t seem to fit for an intelligent woman. You have an easy expectation for people to be there for you in one way or another, and you sometimes don’t even say thank-you for it. I’m not sure where this lack of life awareness comes from—maybe your childhood, with too many things, experiences, and paid help but not enough personal caring from your parents?”

Kate suddenly sniffled. “Could be. I was raised more by maids and nannies and barn staff than I was by my parents. I was treated like royalty by them, but that isn’t the same as loving affection from a mother or father.”

Jake studied her thoughtfully. “And relationships after you left home? In New York? Or the South Pacific?”

“My relationships in New York were never more than dalliances. One-night stands or maybe a few weeks. Professional women, others who didn’t have time to invest, just wanted fun or stress relief in bed. In some of the islands, well, it was different. A totally different society, larger family units, with add-on aunts, grannies, sisters, cousins. I was with single women, some real lesbians, some straight or even married with children. Yet, somehow, there was a fluidity about sexual pleasure. And if there were kids, someone else would take care of them. If things got too heavy, I moved on to another island. So, while I may be forty, this is my first real attempt at a relationship. And my fantasies didn't include kids."

Jake nodded. "You have money to buy childcare so you can romance Angie the right and fun way, don't you?"

"Angie doesn't want the kids farmed out. She allows them to come to your place because she knows you and feels comfortable, but she wants consistency in care for them."

"Given your own upbringing, I suspect you understand that, right?"

"Yes, I do. And that makes it hard to insist that we send them away somewhere or that we go away to have a night together without 'Mama, I have a toothache,' or something else like that."

Jake studied the coming dawn in her rear window. "Well," she finally said, "I'm not a shrink, and I've never raised kids. I have no idea all the things you're dealing with. Aside from that, I think you and Angie are at risk. You both have too much on your plates simultaneously to be really able to support one another. And you don't have time for romance on a regular basis—that'll kill a relationship sooner than anything else. It's obvious that you're attracted to each other. And I feel that you are both in love, and you have something of beauty to build. But if you don't work on it, steadily, you'll lose it."

Kate uttered a deep sigh. "I hate to admit that I'm afraid you're right."

"Well, my suggestion to you, after you have a few hours sleep, is that you figure out something to do this weekend with Angie. Eventually, you're going to need a regular sitter, but if it's just this weekend, Marianne and I can take the kids for an overnight again. Go with Angie out to the lodge at Lake Crescent, sit in the moonlight on the beach, make love in a room at the Lodge. If she can free up more than just an evening and night, take her on the ferry into Seattle, have dinner at a really good restaurant, see a movie, and end up in a hotel and make love and have room service for breakfast. Show her how much she means to you. I think she's losing sight of that."

Kate put a hand on Jake's arm. "Thanks, Jake, I needed that. It's hard to hear, yet it's true. I've been rattlebrained and running from one thing to another. Although the kids are an ongoing problem, it's not their fault. However, their very existence prevents me from doing what a lover instinctively wants to do. Angie is very protective of them, and sometimes I'm confused and just accept her rules because I don't know what else to do. You've given me a few ideas to think about. Thanks."

26

They stood on the lower auto deck of the Bainbridge Ferry and watched a rising moon create sparkling diamonds across the water. Kate's arm rested around Angie's shoulders, and Angie's head leaned against Kate with her arm circling Kate's waist.

Angie smiled to herself. This was what she had needed with Kate from the very beginning, and it just hadn't happened. Well, maybe they hadn't *made* it happen, and it was both of their faults, not just Kate's. She realized that.

"I love you so terribly much when we're being good to each other like this," Angie confessed.

Kate grinned. "I'm glad, because I love you, too."

They kissed deeply, oblivious to the other drivers returning to their vehicles as the ferry approached the Seattle docks. Finally breaking apart while still holding hands, they grabbed their suitcases and scurried up the flight of steps to the main deck where they joined the other walk-on passengers.

"Now what do we do?" Angie asked as they moved through the crowds toward Alaskan Way, where cabs and other vehicles awaited.

"Well, we're going to Uber to the hotel," Kate said.

"Uber? How do you know how to Uber?"

"Research, sweetheart. I asked how to get around Seattle without a car. The answer came back, Uber, and I downloaded the app."

She opened her smart phone and tapped a button that opened the application. With a couple of clicks, she had her driver. Angie watched and noticed that Kate's picture was provided to the driver and vice versa. There was even a photo of the car picking them up.

At street level, it took only a moment to connect. Their driver smilingly opened the rear door for the couple to climb in to a shiny new Toyota Corolla.

Angie gave Kate a little pinch. "This is cool."

Kate grinned. "Glad you like it."

Their driver was Sergio. He confirmed their destination, the Westin, a popular twin-tower high-rise. Kate nodded and

Sergio smiled. "Okay, here we go." Angie's eyes popped wide open when she heard the name of the hotel.

Kate leaned into Angie. "Do you want to stay at the hotel right away, or are you up to doing some sightseeing tonight?"

"Hmmm. Do you have something in mind?"

Kate nodded. "It can wait until tomorrow."

"No, don't wait. I want to make some fun memories with you. We have all night to make those 'other' memories." She laughed and Kate joined in.

When they pulled up to the Westin, Kate asked Sergio if he could go around the block or something to allow them time enough to check in and leave their luggage in their room, then pick them up at the front door.

"Your time, your money. I'll be glad to do that for you. You look like honeymooners, if you don't mind me saying so."

Kate grinned. "You are just about right on the money."

Kate and Angie quickly entered the hotel, grateful that there wasn't a line at the front desk. With room key cards in hand, they took the high-speed elevator to the thirty-fifth floor and found their number, 3515.

Once inside, Angie oohed and aahed. Her reaction amused Kate, who as a child had stayed in any number of fancy hotel rooms. For Angie, this was a first. Her heart pounded. "You don't have to do anything else to impress me. This is amazing." She looked inside the elegant bathroom, fingered the linens on the giant bed, and glanced out the window at the nighttime sky. "Okay. I know we're coming back here later, so this is enough for now. Let's just hop into that Uber and do this other exciting thing you have mapped out."

Sergio waited at the curb, and they climbed into his silver Toyota.

"The waterfront, please, the Big Wheel," Kate told him.

Sergio nodded. "It's a clear night tonight. You'll enjoy the ride."

Angie kissed Kate on the cheek. "Zack and I did this once with the kids, but riding it with you will be a fantastic new experience."

Kate smiled gently. "Just remember, I've not spent any time in Seattle. Everything here is new to me."

Sergio dropped them in front of the waterfront compound where the Big Wheel was located. The huge circular structure was lit up for the night and Angie's heart skipped a few beats. She squeezed Kate's hand.

Kate bought their tickets and they waited in line for the ride. There were several tourists ahead of them, including couples that appeared to be, like them, having a date night out.

Angie whispered excitedly, "Friday night, that's why there are lots of people here."

Kate nodded. "I don't mind the wait."

Under a three-quarter moon in a clear night sky, Angie pointed out downtown buildings they could see all lit up. "When we climb on the wheel, we'll see even more."

Finally, they stepped into their gondola, which was fully enclosed for safety and air conditioned. A young man and woman sat down across from them. Kate nodded to them and the young man nodded back. His girlfriend, Kate assumed, glanced back and forth at Kate and Angie and then squeezed her partner's hand. He squeezed back. After that there was no direct or indirect reference to the fact that the heterosexuals were sitting across from a lesbian couple.

The rotation of the wheel began, and after a few stops for new passengers to enter and others to leave the gondolas, the wheel went around a full circle. As they climbed to the top, Angie was enthralled. "It's so different at night!" she gushed.

Kate smiled, while gripping her hand. "It's very beautiful."

They looked at the brightly lit Space Needle that appeared between buildings to the north as the Wheel followed its own circular path. Angie also pointed out the lighted ballparks for the Mariners and Seahawks to the south.

She noticed how Kate's eyes gleamed in reflected lights. That and the strength of Kate's hold on her hand told Angie that Kate was having a very good time.

***

Back in the hotel, Kate ordered a bottle of champagne from room service. Glasses in hand, they retired to the king-sized bed with lights turned low and music on the television.

After loving glances and a few sips of champagne from clinked glasses, Angie quietly commented, "I hope this outing is as good for you as it is for me."

Kate wiggled her nose. "Fantastic. I don't know how I've been here more than a year and not seen Seattle—especially not with you." She leaned over and gave Angie a deep kiss.

"Maybe our priorities have been screwed."

"Maybe."

Angie leaned back against her pile of soft pure-white pillows. "I love it when you're like this, really *with* me. I can feel *us* in the air, and sometimes I lose sight of that."

Kate sighed. "Well, I'm sure I'm much to blame. You've had nine years to become used to being a parent as well as a partner, and I've had one. I've not spent time around kids and having to put them into every equation."

Angie frowned. "Do you resent my children?"

Kate took her hand, the one not holding a glass of champagne. "Sometimes, but not really. I just need to learn how to create "us" time, rather than having it naturally available to me. I love Mark and Sarina. They're adorable, really nice kids, because they've had good parenting. I just don't always know what to do with them, or for them. The swimming and the baseball gave me an opening. I know that life is much more complicated than that, and their needs are more complex. I'm trying, though it isn't always easy."

Angie ran a finger up Kate's arm. "Do you think we can make it, with such different backgrounds and life experiences?"

"That tickles and I love it." Kate nodded and then looked deeply into Angie's eyes. "I hope there can always be an *us*. I'm trying to give it my all."

"Me, too. How about we work on the physical part of that *us*?"

Angie set down her glass of champagne and turned out the bedside light. She scooted close to Kate and began kissing her. In return, Kate put her glass down and began undoing

Angie's long braid, after which she uttered a very satisfied sigh. Then her lamp went out.

With a hunger they hadn't been able to express for weeks, they dumped clothes and bedding and reached for skin and lips and touched everything that needed touching. As the excitement grew, they both began trembling almost simultaneously, and body heat rose as arms held on tight while both of them convulsed in climax.

Shivering and sighing, Angie fell back on the bed. "OMG! I've never felt anything like that before. You're such a marvelous lover!"

Kate grinned. "When it's right, it's as easy as falling off a log."

Angie pulled Kate close. "I'm exhausted, but very happy. Thank you, thank you!"

"You are welcome, my love. And there's more where that came from."

"Could we sleep a little first?"

Kate laughed. "Of course. I won't jump your bones again until you've had at least an hour of sleep."

"Just an hour? Aren't you going to sleep, too?"

"Probably, maybe. I'll just lie here and dream of making love with you. Perhaps I'll fall asleep."

***

When Angie awoke, dreamily recalling the last evening, Kate was up and dressed in a robe.

"Breakfast is on its way," she said, leaning over to give Angie a kiss.

"Already?"

"It's 10 a.m."

"What?"

Kate giggled. "I gave you a little more than an hour of sleep. Now the sun is up, and we have a day to enjoy."

"Oh?" Angie tried to shake the sleep out of her head.

"Why don't you jump in the shower while I wait for breakfast to arrive? I've already had my turn. I suggest you put on casual clothes with a jacket. We're going to take a cruise."

"Huh?"

"The locks. Have you ever done that?"

"No. I've not been a *real* Seattle tourist, ever."

"I guess we're kind of at the same place, for once."

***

Javier, the graying, wavy-haired Hispanic man who brought up breakfast on a rolling tray, put everything on a small table by the big windows that looked out toward the waterfront. When he was done, he looked at Kate for approval, and she nodded, reaching out to give him a tip.

"Thank you, ma'am, and have a nice breakfast." Javier nodded with a slight bow and left the room, closing the door behind him.

Angie emerged from the shower, dressed casually—Kate thought deliciously—her braid back in place but still a little damp.

Kate pulled out a chair for her. Angie blushed and sat down. "I'm not used to such service," she admitted shyly.

"I love spoiling you," Kate admitted with a mischievous grin.

Angie looked at all the food—eggs, biscuits, ham, fresh fruit, condiments, hot tea and coffee, ice water, beautiful silverware. She picked up a heavy silver spoon, "Not Betty Crocker, for sure."

"Betty who?"

"Betty Crocker, of the cookbooks? My mother bought silverware, one piece at a time, with coupons from Betty Crocker products."

"I would have thought your mother would have made everything from scratch."

"She could, had been taught to, yet with a farm, church all day Sundays, kids, the animals, she also learned to take a few shortcuts. She saved time on baking to allow more for the main dishes. Her meatloaf was to die for."

Kate let out a huge laugh. "I don't think meatloaf ever appeared on our table."

Angie frowned. "Are you making fun of me?"

Kate put a hand on her arm. “No, I’m just meaning that we missed out on a lot of interesting, I’m sure good, things that other people take for granted.”

“Well, one day I’ll make my mother’s meatloaf for you, and you can decide for yourself.”

***

Uber dropped them off at the waterfront pier where Kate showed her prepaid reservation for the Ballard Locks tour. They were directed to a large passenger ferry and boarded it. The boat was nearly filled with tourists by the time they left the dock.

First, they viewed the Seattle skyline—with details broadcast via an onboard loud speaker—passed the cruise ship docks and marinas then curved around the north shore and back to the locks. After their boat entered the locks, the gates closed, and the water was raised to the level of Lake Union. Then gates at the other end opened for them. After the ferry left the locks, it cruised through the lake channel, where looking at houseboats reminded Angie of the movie *Sleepless in Seattle*.

Their trip ended at the Maritime Museum, and they explored the gift shop. Kate bought Angie a gold necklace with a lighthouse attached, and Angie picked out nautical gifts for Sarina and Mark—a sailor doll for Sarina and for Mark a tall ship to be assembled. “What should I pick for you?” Angie asked.

“You are my gift,” Kate responded. “Spending time with you and seeing you happy, having fun, and without worry are the only gifts I need.”

“I’ll find something,” Angie declared and began checking out every item in the store. She finally settled on a ballcap in royal blue with the museum name on it. “You wear caps, I know. I’ve seen you in them. You love boats, and the color blue, so this seems like you.”

Kate grinned. “I couldn’t have chosen better myself. I love it, and I’ll wear it always.” She slipped the cap on and posed. Getting the message, Angie pulled out her cell phone and snapped a picture.

“Cute!” she said, showing the photo to Kate.

"Well, I'm not as photogenic as you but, all things considered, I'll admit it isn't bad."

***

A bus waited outside to take them back to the wharf downtown. Before they could board, Kate asked, "Are you hungry?"

Angie shrugged. "I could be. Why?"

"Well, there's a famous restaurant here on Lake Union. Anchor and Chain. I read about it. Really good seafood. We could hike from here, have lunch, and then Uber back downtown, if you like."

Angie frowned. "But the bus is already paid for." She caught herself and laughed. "I guess money isn't the issue, is it?"

"No, ma'am. I only care about giving you pleasure."

"If we walk around to the restaurant, I *will* be hungry by the time we're there."

***

After enjoying elegant service, looking out at the lake, and consuming a plate of seafood delights, Angie and Kate went by Uber back to the Westin to drop off their souvenirs. Then they returned to the waterfront.

Kate asked, "Have you ever been to the Seattle Aquarium?"

Angie shook her head. "Never."

"Okay. Do you mind if we go?"

Grinning ear to ear, Angie replied. "I'd love to."

Kate bought two tickets and they entered the large building that filled one dock. While waltzing through exhibits of various sea creatures from octopuses to sea otters, they kidded, teased, and joked and snapped photos of all the colorful sea life.

"I feel just like a kid, only I didn't do this as a kid," Angie observed.

"Me, neither."

"You mean we actually have something else in common?"

"Could be."

When they had enough of the crowds and staring through glass at water world inhabitants, they spent a few minutes in the gift shop and bought each other a memento of their first visit to an aquarium. They also remembered to pick up stuffed animals for Sarina and Mark.

Back out on the sidewalk, Kate asked. "What would you like to do next?"

"What do you suggest?"

"Well, we could do the Space Needle. Or we could go to a movie, if you've done enough walking for one day, and save the Space Needle for another time."

Angie thought a moment. "I vote movie. What's playing?"

Kate checked movie schedules on her cell. She found a romantic comedy starting in less than an hour. Angie agreed to that choice, saying it would be perfect.

"We have to sit in the back, where we can, you know—"

"I know." Kate grinned from ear to ear and squeezed Angie's hand.

They walked briskly together uphill until they reached Seattle's theatre and movie district.

"Let me buy the tickets," Angie offered. "This is something I can afford."

Kate shrugged but winked at her. Kate didn't need to be treated yet she enjoyed it nevertheless, and she knew it made Angie feel good.

Once inside the theatre, they bought soft drinks, skipped the popcorn. In the auditorium, they managed to find seats in a back corner where they held hands and made out with each other. Kate could see Angie's eyes sparkle in light reflected from the movie screen. The electricity between them was palpable.

***

Two hours later, with hands linked, they stood outside the movie theatre. "That was fun. Now what would you like?" Kate asked.

Angie looked up at the sky. The sun was creeping toward the Olympic Mountains. It would soon be evening.

She looked at Kate. “You know what? I’ve changed my mind. This would be a perfect time to go to the Space Needle to watch the sunset from the observation deck. How about it?”

“Uber, walk, or what?”

“It would be a long walk, but we’re not far from the monorail. Let’s take that.”

Kate didn’t know anything about a monorail, but she walked hand in hand with Angie through crowded streets and between tall buildings until they found the entrance to Westlake Center and the third floor Seattle Center Monorail ticket booth. Then they waited, with a number of other tourists, for the next departure for the two-mile ride.

***

Angie and Kate stared up at the Space Needle then entered the elevator to be whisked up to the observation platform where, hand in hand, they walked around the outdoor area. Angie pointed out more Seattle sights to Kate. This view was totally different: the city high-rises around them, the harbor, the Big Wheel, and the Olympics across the bay. The sun was indeed setting behind the mountains as they stared to the west and snapped photos with each other.

As they prepared to take the elevator down, Kate asked, “Would you like to have dinner here?”

Angie looked thoughtful. “Well, I would love to have lunch or dinner here with you sometime, but we had such a big meal earlier that I don’t think I want much more to eat. A burger or tacos or something? Are you disappointed?”

Kate shook her head. “We could pick up something on the way to the hotel, or order from room service.”

“Ah, room service. I would never think of that, but it’s a great idea.” She winked at Kate.

“Okay, the Westin it is.” Kate ordered an Uber ride from the Space Needle to the hotel. With supreme efficiency, the car awaited them when they emerged from the elevator. “We didn’t pick out any souvenirs,” Angie mused.

"Next time. There will be a next time, I assure you."

***

After returning to their hotel room, they both admitted feeling exhausted from all they had done. "Satisfied but tired," they agreed.

Kate ordered sandwiches from room service and turned on the TV while they waited. Angie freshened up and slipped into her pajamas and a silky multi-colored robe.

After the food came, Kate excused herself to change as well. When she returned, Angie was sitting by the window, fingering her sandwich and looking out at the nighttime lights.

"Oh," Kate gasped, "You should have gone ahead and eaten. You look like you're are really hungry."

Angie smiled. "I'm fine. I wanted to wait for you."

They downed their meal while the television played a classic movie. "Should have been *Casablanca*," Kate said with a grin when she glanced at the TV screen.

"Are we star-crossed lovers?" Angie asked.

"I hope not. But that's probably the most romantic movie ever made."

"You don't know a lot about romance, do you?"

Kate shook her head. "My parents were anything but romantic, I'm afraid. I learned little from them. Nothing that would help me survive beyond one-night stands in Manhattan."

Angie smiled. "Zack was romantic, in a small-town sort of way, until he put a wedding ring on my finger. Once he had me, and I was pregnant with Mark, I think he started wandering. I can't prove it, and you'd think if he were two-timing me in Sequim, I would eventually hear about it. Essentially, I became the one who was just there, while he went off and did whatever he wanted, with precious little communication about it. When he finally found the perfect woman, he dumped all over me about not being responsive.

"Dating him taught me how to be romantic, what to do for fun and how to spend private time together, but I didn't know until much later that I was failing in the love-making department.

Although I tried to please him, it was never meant to be, or to last."

"Well, you were a lesbian. It would never have worked, eventually."

"I suppose not, but it sure tore up my life and my sense of security. If I can't be number one in my own relationship, I don't want to be in a relationship. I'd rather be alone than not be important to my partner."

Kate put a hand on Angie's arm. "I love you, Angie, and although I don't always know how to show it, I do want to please you and make you feel wanted, needed, and secure in my love."

Angie smiled. "I feel it right now, so you are capable of being perfect for me. I think we just need more *us* time. It's hard when we didn't meet before I had children and issues from a failed marriage."

"I have issues, too. We just have to work them out."

Despite their busy day, once they were in bed, Angie and Kate gave in to new waves of desire. Another session of intense lovemaking followed, after which Angie exclaimed, "I thought it was great last night—this was even better."

"Maybe I'm getting the hang of it," Kate quipped.

***

The next morning, they faced reality. After allowing a casual start with breakfast in bed, they then showered and gathered their things. Check out came too soon. The Bainbridge ferry followed, after which they collected the SUV at the ferry terminal and drove back to Sequim.

On the trip home, they both were alternately happy and thoughtful. Angie had studies to keep her busy for the rest of the day. Kate would have to manage the kids after picking them up at Marianne's and Jake's house and hearing how they passed the weekend. Despite the wonderful, passionate outing, Kate recognized that she had to work harder juggling her own ambitions and at the same time serving as backup to Angie in childcare. *And keeping romance in their relationship.*

Focus, focus, she reminded herself.

27

After passing midterms with good grades, Angie felt a wave of relief and began to believe that becoming a registered nurse could really happen. Her insecurities about her limited educational background receded as she demonstrated an ability to learn and grow.

Meanwhile, Kate reminded herself to make sure that things were taken care of for the family, before she settled in to do her daily research.

While walking Puff in the neighborhood each morning, she encountered other dog walkers and asked each of them if they knew anyone who might be available to look after Mark, Sarina, and Puff sometimes in the evenings and occasionally on a weekend. Usually the answer was "Sorry," but Kate kept asking and finally obtained the name of Louise Wallman, a new renter who had moved in quietly, worked part-time, and had a little girl.

Late one afternoon when she was outdoors with Puff on leash, Kate introduced herself to this new neighbor. Louise was pleasant and responded positively to the dog, a good start. Kate met her daughter, Lisa, a shy, slender blonde a bit younger than Sarina. At first, Lisa was hesitant with Puff because the labradoodle was large, but Puff soon won her over with a friendly attitude and playful antics.

After a few outdoor encounters, Louise invited Kate and Puff into her house. It seemed small, a bit dark and cluttered, but Kate tried not to judge. Offered a glass of ice tea, Kate sat down on a well-worn sofa and told Louise a little more about herself, Angie, and the kids. She could tell by Louise's questions that she understood Kate and Angie were a couple yet didn't seem bothered by that fact.

Louise shared that she worked from 9 to 1 in a downtown insurance office in order to be here in the afternoons when Lisa came home from school. There apparently was a divorce in the background, and Louise was receiving support payments. "Not enough," she admitted wryly, "but we get by."

Before leaving, Kate asked Louise if she and Lisa would like to join their family for dinner sometime soon, and Louise seemed to brighten at the idea. Kate said she'd call with details.

***

Kate anticipated that Angie would not want a babysitter if there were any way around it. The next step was having Louise and Lisa over for dinner. Hopefully, once Angie had met them, she would come on board for a childcare plan. Strategically, Kate told Angie that Louise was new in the neighborhood and didn't know anyone, adding that she was divorced and had a little girl. Being naturally helpful toward anyone in trouble, Angie readily agreed to invite the new neighbors to share a meal. She picked an evening the following week when her own homework would be the lightest.

Louise accepted readily and at the appointed time showed up at their front door with her daughter in tow. Sarina immediately latched on to Lisa and pulled her into her bedroom. Mark looked a little crestfallen, and Kate beckoned to him. She found something he could do in the kitchen that would make him feel useful and important.

Dinner featured the long-promised meatloaf, and Kate admitted it was tasty. Angie added a fresh salad, baked potatoes, and a scoop of ice cream for dessert. During the meal, there was a lot of talking and sharing. Reactions seemed to be positive all around—Kate was particularly watching to see how Angie reacted to Louise.

At one point, as they sat over coffee, and all the kids were settled in the living room playing a game, Angie asked, "As a single parent, how do you manage some time for yourself, for a date, or just to get out of the house for fun?"

A waved of sadness crossed Louise's face. "I haven't had much time yet. Of course, we just moved here, and I don't know many people. Kate is the first person to make any effort to know me, as far as the neighborhood goes."

"Get a dog," Kate quipped, "and you'll soon know everybody."

"Oh, I love your Puffball, but not right now. Later, maybe."

"Money?" Angie asked flatly.

"Partly, yes, and Lisa is a bit insecure. I don't want to leave her anywhere that makes her uncomfortable or add an animal to the mix, nice as that might be for her eventually."

Angie nodded. "Well, meanwhile, it looks like Lisa is doing well here. If Kate doesn't mind, there is no reason she couldn't come over to play sometimes, and Puff is always here and willing to be in on the fun."

Louise looked relieved. "That would be very nice."

Before their new neighbor had left, the suggestion was made lightly that, assuming the kids continued to enjoy each other's company, maybe they could trade now and then to give the parents a break. Louise appeared open to the idea, and since Angie had mentioned it, Kate kept her mouth shut.

The unofficial arrangement worked better than Angie would have thought and Kate could have dreamed. The kids got along famously. Louise had skills with children, as well as in the kitchen, and proved very flexible. Best of all, Angie and Kate both liked her, which was very important. And Louise cared not a wit that they were lesbians or that Lisa was being "exposed" to a lesbian household. Kate sighed with relief. *How could they be so lucky?*

***

When Kate and Angie wanted an evening out, and studying wasn't too intense, Louise came down to the house, fixed and shared dinner with the kids. Then she helped them do a jigsaw puzzle on the dining room table, played Mexican Train with dominoes, or picked out a movie for the TV. When it was time for bed, Lisa curled up with Sarina in her bed. Louise read a novel in the living room, with Puff curled up at her feet or sharing the sofa with her. Louise was an inveterate reader and appreciated the time while waiting for Angie and Kate to come home. A change of clothes was left for Lisa so that Louise could pick her up the following morning and drop her off at school before going to work. Kate offered her money, which she accepted gratefully.

"This is marvelous," Angie quipped after a few evenings were managed perfectly. Kate just smiled, fingers privately crossed.

"Glad you like it," she finally said.

***

Eventually, a weekend came up, and Louise was equally willing to stay at the house for an extended period. She slept in the master bedroom with Puffball curled up beside her—when the doodle wasn't in Mark's room—and later admitted that when the kids had each other, she had less pressure from Lisa for constant attention. Watching three in some ways seemed less work for her than one. She was happy to take it on, at least occasionally.

With Louise in charge at home, Kate and Angie left early Saturday morning to catch a ferry to Seattle. After leaving their luggage at the Westin, they revisited the Space Needle for lunch at the revolving restaurant just below the observation deck. Afterward, they "monorailed" downtown and visited Pike Place Market, a top tourist attraction with enough venders to consume an entire afternoon. Arms loaded with souvenirs, they took Uber to the hotel to rest. That turned into a session of making love followed by a light dinner ordered from room service.

The weekend's big event was an evening performance of a Broadway musical, a revival of *The Sound of Music*. They left the theatre laughing and singing and returned to the hotel to flop into bed.

"I'm really glad we had another weekend like this," Angie admitted. "It means the first one wasn't a fluke, and I love you all the more."

"I'm glad you do, because it would kill me if you didn't," Kate said with a big grin. She reached over for a tender kiss and that started the lovemaking all over again. Neither of them could get enough touching and kissing, the excitement they created, and the climaxes that followed. Late in the night, they finally fell asleep.

On the ferry home, they stood on the outside deck and allowed the wind to blow through their hair. Angie looked at Kate. "I want this romancing to go on forever. Sometimes I'm still scared that you'll want something new or different and leave me, or leave us, I should say."

Kate pulled her into a close embrace. "I can't imagine anything in the world that would change what I feel for you, or anyplace else in the world that I would want to be."

"Sequim is big enough for you?"

"As long as you're in it."

***

A little voice inside Angie's head periodically asked "but what if—" and she tried to ignore it. *Life was just too good to question her good fortune.* Finals were around the corner, and she couldn't worry about anything except studying and making good grades. Her personal future depended on that.

When the time came, she handed Kate a sheet with her exam schedule on it and reminded her that she would be dependent on her for most of the child care, shopping, dog walking, etc., for her period of study the week before and then during the several days of finals. "Please, whatever you do, try not to schedule something important on your project during these days. Afterward, I'll be in vacation time and can help out a lot and free you up to do your own thing. But, I really am going to need your full attention for the days on the calendar. Okay?"

Kate nodded and gave her a kiss. "Sure, honey, I'll take care of it. Not to worry. If there's something I can't do, I'll arrange for Louise. She'll help, too. You know that."

Angie frowned. "I can't be worrying about home. Nothing gets forgotten, nothing drops through the cracks because you forgot. This is very important."

Kate smiled. "I get it, Angie. No worries. Okay?"

***

Angie was headed out the door, anxiety written across her face. "Today is biology. I think I can ace it," she had said as they finished breakfast. "But tomorrow is A&P. There is so much detail, so many terms and names, I just don't know about that one. I'm sure I'll be up most of the night studying."

Kate smiled. "I know you're scared, but you have a fine, detail-oriented mind. You'll do great, I know it."

After Kate kissed her goodbye and gave her a hug, Angie was gone.

Kate went into her office, settled down at her desk, and gave Puff a few strokes under the chin. The dog, always at her feet, moaned with contentment.

Kate laughed. "You're a funny dog. You fit in here very well. And I love you, even if you *are* a bit weird."

***

Her desk was littered with information packets from swimming pool construction companies. Kate decided to go through them, examining features and pricing out the costs of each choice. She knew what she wanted in a pool yet, even with her seemingly unlimited resources, she also knew that she had to be practical. In the long run, she wanted to fund more than just a swimming pool.

As she immersed herself in construction details, her cell phone buzzed. Pulling the phone from her pocket, she looked at the number—someone in Washington, D.C., she could tell by the area code. She took the call.

"This is Kate, right? Josh Winston, here. How are you?"

Kate sat up straight. Despite his relaxed familiarity with her, she knew exactly who he was. "Yes, Senator. I'm fine. All is well out here in sunny Sequim. What's up?"

"Well, I had dinner last evening with some folks from a USOC support group. One of them, Rick Garcia, is flying out this morning to San Diego to meet with the Chula Vista training center staff to ferret out additional details about what worked and what didn't while the USOC was in charge of that facility. I mentioned my conversations with you, and Rick said if you could get yourself down there this evening, he could spend some time with you, provide for you the information you've been seeking. I don't know if you can pull it off, but if you can, he'll be at the Hotel America downtown tonight and can meet with you there. He'll be flying out early in the morning, which means it has to be this evening, if it's to happen at all. And less of a trip for you than flying all the way back to D.C."

"Yes, you're right. I'll see what I can do," Kate responded, her heart pumping fast, and her hands writing down names and phone numbers as quickly as the senator could give them to her."

When she hung up, Kate opened her laptop and punched up Southwest Airlines, looking for the first early afternoon flight that she could possibly make—if she left for the airport in the next few minutes. Once she had pinpointed a flight, she ordered her ticket for today and the return the next morning, printed her boarding passes, and closed her computer. Opening her closet, she pulled out a decent outfit to wear this evening and a change of clothes for tomorrow, plus her notepad and proposals, some pens and her Dopp bag. Everything went into the travel-worn duffle. *One of these days she would replace that bag, but not today!*

Her brain jumped from thought to thought. *She'd have to drive like a bat out of hell to arrive at SeaTac in time. The Hood Canal Bridge better be open! And she'd better have enough gas. She should start keeping the tank filled. Never knew when there would be an emergency.*

Looking at her watch, Kate knew she needed to go. "Puff, you're going to be alone today. Can you handle it?"

Puff turned her head sideways and studied the duffle. She licked Kate's hand and barked once.

"I guess that's a yes." Kate leaned down and hugged her. "Take care of everyone for me. I'll be back tomorrow. I love you, girl!"

***

Kate grabbed her keys and was out the door in a flash. When the engine of the SUV turned over, she saw there was enough gas. It was a go. Since it was mid-morning, the traffic shouldn't be bad. She raced through the housing development, headed for the highway, and while doing that, punched in

Louise's phone number. The phone rang several times and then a voice said. "Sorry to have missed you. Lisa and I will be out of town for the next few days. Leave your name and number and I'll get back to you when we return. Thanks!"

Shit! This couldn't be happening!

Now Kate tapped in Marianne's phone number. It rang and rang, and an answering machine picked up. "Sorry we are not available. Please leave a message."

Upset and anxious, Kate left a message, "Please call my cell as soon as possible," and then tossed the phone down in the passenger seat while swearing for the next couple of miles.

They just had to be home. Maybe Jake was running an errand and Marianne was working. She looked at her watch. *Yeah, Marianne would be working. Her break should come up soon.*

Kate drove and cursed and worried.

Finally, on the Kitsap Peninsula side of the Hood Canal Bridge, her phone rang.

"Hey, Kate, you sound stressed. What's up?" Marianne coughed into the phone, and Kate noticed that her voice sounded funny. *Oh, no, she couldn't be sick. Not today.*

"I'm on my way to the airport for an important meeting this evening in San Diego. The babysitter is out of town. I didn't know she was leaving. Now I don't have anyone to watch Puff and the kids tonight. Angie has a big final tomorrow."

Marianne was silent for a moment. "Kate, I don't know what to say. Jake is sick in bed with a cold, and I'm coming down with it. This is not a place for two healthy children. If they become sick and give it to Angie, it could ruin her finals. Can't you put this trip off?"

"No, Senator Winston just called and had already made the arrangements. He said it had to be tonight. The person I need to see flies back to DC in the morning. I got the last seat on a flight at 2:00 out of SeaTac to San Diego and I'm on the way now."

"If there is no other way, I guess I'll take the van and pick up the kids at the Boys & Girls Club at 5 p.m. I'll feed them something and put them in front of the TV. Oh, and I'll go collect the dog. You still use that garage code to get in the house?"

"Yeah, 4522."

"When does Angie get home?"

"She didn't say exactly. She's studying at the college library until early evening, then coming home for a late dinner and spending the rest of the evening working in her room."

"Did you tell Angie what's up?"

"She's in an exam. I don't know how to reach her."

"You know she's not going to be happy about this. You'd better at least send her a text."

Kate swallowed. "Okay, I will."

"Just in case, when I pick up the kids and go to your house for the dog and some food for her, I'll write out a note for Angie that she will find whenever she gets home."

"Thanks."

"You are going to owe me big time for this. If everybody gets sick, you may owe all of us more than that, especially Angie!"

"Yeah. I got to go. A cop just passed by going the other way. I shouldn't be driving and talking. Thanks. Later."

***

Kate arrived at SeaTac at the last minute, parked her car in a storage lot, ran to the terminal dragging her duffle and just managed to pass through security. Sans food or water, she arrived at the gate barely in time to trot down the jetway and board the aircraft. She wouldn't have been quite that late if she hadn't been stopped by a State Patrolman and given a ticket for using her cell phone while driving. Caught red handed, Kate knew better than to complain.

28

Exhausted but relieved that she had passed biology, Angie pulled into the driveway just before 6 p.m. She was famished and hoped Kate had something ready for dinner. She needed comfort food in order to keep on studying this evening and had little extra energy to fix anything.

Entering the house through the garage, Angie noted that Kate's Forester wasn't there. She then observed that there were no lights or TV on, and Puff didn't run to meet her. The house was quiet. Her heart skipped a beat. *Oh, no. What now?*

She checked the living room and the kids' rooms and then looked into Kate's office. *Damn! All the telltale signs that Kate was gone. Again. Computer, cell phone missing. Good clothes gone from the closet. No duffle there. A flight number written on a pad on her desk. San Diego?*

Grinding her teeth and trying to keep control, Angie grabbed her cell to call Louise. The kids and Puff were probably down there, although Louise usually came up to their house. Instead of an answer, Angie listened to the unwelcomed message that Louise was out of town.

Where were they? She punched in Marianne's number. Marianne answered and sounded as if she had a bad cough. "Yes, Puff and the kids are here. However, don't come. Jake's sick in bed with a cold, and I'm coming down with it. That other sitter was gone, and Kate called here. I picked up Mark and Sarina and got Puff from the house. Kate was supposed to text you, and I left you a message, but maybe you haven't found it yet. It's on the kitchen table."

"Did you tell Kate you were sick?"

"Yes, and I told her you'd be unhappy if the kids got sick and then brought it home to you while you're taking finals. I really don't know if she had another choice."

Angie grumbled. "Marianne, you *know* Kate had another choice. She didn't have to go, wherever it is she off to."

"Well, that pool and the Olympic thing are important to her, and she could only see this man tonight in San Diego."

Angie sighed, tears starting to form at the edge of her eyes. "I guess we're not very important."

"I understand what you're feeling. I don't think she means harm, but it comes out that way sometimes."

Angie swallowed and pulled herself up. "Okay, if the kids are all right, I've got to study for anatomy and physiology tonight. I'm scared to death of this test, and I don't have the energy to deal with Kate. I have to survive finals, no ifs, ands, or buts."

Marianne coughed. "Look, if the kids wake up feeling punk in the morning, I won't bring them home or take them to school. Jake's a little better today. She'll be able to keep them entertained or filled up with cold medicine if they're getting sick. We'll get through it, but I don't want you catching this bug."

"Marianne, you're a sweetheart. If Kate shows up there tomorrow without calling first, don't let her in the door. If she gets exposed to what you've got, then send her to a motel, so she can be sick there and not here. Serves her right. She can come home when my finals are over. By that time everyone should be recovering."

"Don't let this wrinkle bother you, honey," Marianne said before hanging up. "Your classes are too important to let her impulsiveness ruin everything for you."

"Thanks, Marianne."

Angie hung up and heaved a big sigh. *Westways Pizza would deliver—she'd just order her favorite pizza, which would last her a couple of days.* She put the teakettle on the stove and headed for the shower. As she walked to her bedroom, she scrolled through messages on her phone and found Kate's text from that afternoon. She just shook her head.

***

Kate arrived at the house early the following afternoon. Angie's car wasn't in the driveway. Kate assumed she was at the college taking an exam or studying in the library.

Tired from the whirlwind trip to San Diego, which had been productive or at least informative, Kate pulled her duffle out of the car along with a sack full of souvenirs and entered the house through the front door. All was quiet. She guessed the kids were with Marianne and Jake. She felt bad that they might be sick, and she worried, now that she thought about it, that the kids would bring home something and they *all* would get sick.

She dialed Marianne's house. Jake answered.

"Hi, Kate. Well, you're safely home. Glad you called. Don't come over here. We're all sick. You don't want it. You don't want Angie to get it. You still have that key to the unit at TC?"

Kate thought a minute. "Might. I'll have to look around."

"Well, if it doesn't turn up, call me and I'll put a key in an envelope under the porch mat. Come and get it, stock up on groceries for the rest of the week, and go out there. Angie was really upset about your leaving. I'm sure that doesn't surprise you. I think she's managed to get herself back on track to study for her finals, but she's staying away from here, and you should, too. After her exams are done on Friday, then we can sort it out. Do yourself a favor and don't stir anything up right now."

Kate sighed. "I don't like it but I get the picture. Okay, if I don't find the key, I'll stop by to get another one and won't do anything more than wave through the window and take off. I won't unpack. That'll make it easy. Thanks, Jake."

"You're welcome. I'm glad I'm on the mend, myself, or we'd have a real mess here."

"You sure you can handle it?"

"Sure, Kate. Just don't you pick up this bug. It's nasty."

***

Kate dropped the souvenirs onto the sofa in her office and pulled a couple of promising novels from the bookshelf, along with pool research papers, her cell phone and computer. She would also take the duffle and one change of clothing. Then she searched for the TC key which turned up in a drawer of her desk. *One less problem to solve.*

She drove dispiritedly to the grocery and stocked up on items she might need for breakfast for a few days plus a fat chicken sandwich at the deli. After gassing up the SUV, she worked her way out the winding road to TC. At first she couldn't remember the gate access code. After a moment of feeling stupid, she finally recalled the numbers and was able to open the gate.

While driving down the street to the unit, she encountered Sid with her dog. Kate sighed. A wave wouldn't do it. She opened the driver's side window.

"Hey," Sid called out, "you back again? Something go wrong?"

Kate grimaced inwardly. "No, I just came back from a trip to California and found that the kids are sick with something. They don't want me at home, so I'm hanging out here until Angie finishes her finals at Peninsula College. Maybe a couple of days. Everything okay with you?"

"Oh, sure. Just putting in my steps with Fluffy. Got 6,500 today. Few more to go. Well, see you around. There's a party tomorrow evening in the clubhouse if you want to come."

"Thanks. I'll remember that."

"6:30, dessert, a movie, you know."

"Okay. See you." *Why did she always run into Sid?* Kate shook her head. *Well, the fact that Sid lived three doors down the same street and had a dog to walk might have something to do with it.*

***

Kate set her belongings on the sofa. The RV was stuffy and she opened several windows to clear the air. With the afternoon sun, it would soon warm up. Eventually, she'd have to run the A/C, but at least there would be fresh air to breathe.

When her groceries were put away, Kate turned on the TV only to realize that with no one living here, the cable service had been turned off. She had electricity for lights, heat and A/C and that was it. *And if she didn't remember to turn on the water heater, she could expect a cold shower in the morning.*

Okay, so be it. She'd do some thinking, take notes for the pool project, and read. Maybe tomorrow she'd go to that party, if nothing else turned up.

For a moment, she thought about calling Angie. Then she stopped. Angie was upset, she knew, and she had more exams coming up. Talking would more than likely make things worse and that would affect her ability to study. Better to just leave things be, as Marianne had suggested.

So, dropping her phone on the coffee table, Kate pulled out the novel *Texas Two-Step* by Jackie Ennis that had been a Christmas present from Angie. Kate examined the book, wondering why Angie had chosen it for her.

Stretched out on the sofa with a Diet Coke, she opened the novel. After a few pages of muttering sarcastic potshots, Kate gradually became involved with the story. She noted that a main character was an only child, and that caused her interest to spike. The blurb on the cover had said the two women were "star-crossed lovers." *Had Angie noticed that when she picked out the book?*

The story was set in Amarillo, Texas. One character was a farm girl from a large family, and the other—the only child person—was assistant manager at a local feed-supply store. Kate laughed. *Where did they come up with these ideas?*

After a while, Kate put down the novel and retrieved her sandwich from the refrigerator. Her stomach was grumbling, even though she didn't feel very hungry.

With the Coke and her sandwich on a plate, Kate returned to the novel. She had some ideas about the story but wanted to see how close she was to the author's intent.

Farm girl Judy was social, friendly and greeted everyone when she came into town on errands. The only child, Alex, was a bit reclusive and didn't say much beyond what was needed to deal with customers. *A female Gary Cooper*, Kate thought to herself with amusement.

Of course, the two characters were gradually drawn to each other, especially when they discovered they both liked horseback riding. One particular palomino mare in the farm family's corral appealed to both of them and drew out Alex.

When Judy finally asked Alex why she was so quiet and aloof, Alex said, "Well, my mama died when I was about ten. I guess I just never got over losing her."

Despite Kate's initial skepticism—*these romance novels are so light and predictable*—when the "mama's" death was mentioned, tears came to her eyes. She wiped them away, feeling a bit surprised, and continued reading.

A few chapters later, she put the novel down, because those words, "never got over it," kept playing back in her head. Her own mother had died two decades ago. At the time, Kate had been devastated and cried a lot, but that was long ago and *so* much had happened since then that she didn't understand why those words touched her now. *Especially in a silly lesbian romance novel.*

Kate stood up and went for a walk, risking another encounter with Sid, or someone just like her, another lonely single woman with a dog or two. *Maybe there was something in their pasts that they had never quite gotten over.*

When the walk didn't change her sad and bitter mood, Kate decided to go to bed, even though it wasn't even dark. She had been up late the night before and had risen early to catch her flight home. *Not much sleep, and that might be making her weepy. By morning she should feel better.*

***

Kate woke up several times during the night, plagued with strange and unexpected dreams. Her mother's tragic death, her memorial service, Kate's lethargy in the swimming pool, her father dying suddenly without a chance for her to say goodbye. Kate woke up one time remembering a dream in which she was walking alone in Antarctic cold, no one around and only white sheets of snow and ice on the horizon.

Just before dawn, she got up and fixed herself a cup of tea then returned to the novel. She read for nearly two hours, wiping tears from her eyes every few minutes, and then, feeling exhausted, dropped off to sleep again.

Her watch read 10:03 when Kate finally hauled herself out of bed for good. A warm shower helped, but she experienced a strong sense of depression and isolation. She didn't dare go home or to Marianne's and Jake's house. She couldn't set off an argument with Angie and she couldn't pick up the cold from the kids—shouldn't even be around them for at least another few days.

Even though her San Diego trip had been enlightening, she couldn't connect emotionally with that right now. Nothing seemed important.

A morning walk around TC lifted her spirits a little then she drove into downtown Sequim to pass time and pick up something for dinner. It was strange to feel so alone in what had gradually emerged as her home. Deciding not to stop at The Little Red Barn, Kate crossed to the west side of town and bought a latte at Starbucks. The hot drink was good but it didn't taste like the coffees Angie whipped up for her at TLRB. That fact alone made her feel very sad.

Angie, she considered, was probably taking another final today. Kate didn't remember which one was up, and she faulted herself for not paying enough attention to Angie's schedule to know which challenge she was facing that day. Angie could have used the encouragement, Kate was sure.

She finished her drink then ordered a croissant for tomorrow's breakfast. After tossing the package in the SUV, she strolled to Home Depot and paced through the aisles, trying to think of projects that needed doing at home. She hadn't been much involved with the house either, after the first excitement of moving in. *Angie wanted the bathrooms and kitchen updated. They never even discussed it.* Next Kate went to Michael's and paced those aisles, picking out a couple of stuffed figures for the kids—something sweet and cuddly. Oh, the dog. She had forgotten about Puffball. She left Michael's and hiked back to Petco to select some big dog treats for the labradoodle.

Coming out of Petco, Kate for a moment couldn't remember where the Forester was then realized she had left it at Starbucks. She sighed. *She was a basket case, for sure.*

A few blocks down and across the street at Safeway, Kate ordered a custom sandwich for dinner and bought a case of water. She didn't feel like cooking, and another sandwich would have to do.

On her way back to TC, Kate strolled through Carrie Blake Park and looked at the open plot of land where she hoped to put a community swimming pool. It was easy for her to imagine kids playing in the water, swimming classes in progress, and a city swim team working out. If she could ever pull it off, it would be great for the town.

With a deep sigh, Kate climbed into the SUV and headed back to East Sequim Bay Road. As she drove through the RV park gate, she remembered the party that night. Oh, shoot, she wasn't feeling very social. Her sandwich would be it. And that book. *She would finish it tonight, even if she went through a whole box of Kleenex. Somehow that novel related to her life, and she needed to figure out why it touched her so very much.*

***

Angie paced the living room. She missed the kids. Jake said they were getting better but maybe should be left until the weekend, or when Angie's finals were done, at least. She had two more days to go. She had thanked Jake and asked her to tell Marianne how much she appreciated them making it possible for her to complete this quarter. She dreaded even the idea of having to do make-up exams had she gotten sick. *Or taking classes over, or whatever else would have been involved.*

And when she came home, she missed seeing Kate seated at her computer, her project designs scattered all over the floor, along with all her books, manuscripts, and folders. Kate always thought everything was possible, and maybe with money it was. *Yet there was more to Kate, a side she didn't show.* Angie figured it had something to do with her family, her privileged yet lonely childhood. It was easy to sympathize with that since she had virtually lost her own family as well. That thought made her tear up.

"You can't get all gloomy," she told herself aloud. "You have two more exams to take. You can't fail yourself now." *All this emotional stuff with Kate—and the worry about how it was going to turn out—had to be pushed aside for now.*

Angie pulled out her textbook for Nursing Practices and sat down to study.

29

Angie arrived, anxious to give Mark and Sarina big hugs and to feel their loving warmth surround her. Marianne had told her they must have had some three-day virus, because everyone was snapping back after a couple of nights. What was lingering didn't seem to be serious enough to be a common cold that always lasted a couple of weeks.

After Angie was satisfied that Mark and Sarina would definitely survive, she felt ready to deal with Kate and their issues. As per plan with Marianne, Jake took the kids and Puffball and left the house in her truck. "The Railroad Bridge Park," Jake announced as she went out the door.

Marianne settled herself with a cup of coffee, and Angie found a spot on the sofa. "As I told you on the phone," Marianne reminded her, "I'm no marriage counselor. However, you both seem to need help looking at this ongoing conflict. If we can't figure out something here, then I recommend seeing a therapist. Otherwise, what could have grown into a deeply committed relationship may turn into a failed romance—and everybody will be hurt, especially two innocent children."

Angie sighed. "Thank you, Marianne. I haven't known what to say to Kate. I was very upset when I came home and found she was gone, yet again, when I specifically asked her not to leave and she promised she would be taking care of things."

There was a knock at the front door. Marianne put up a hand. "I think that's her." She called out, "Come on in, Kate."

Kate opened the door hesitantly and looked around, assessing the room. There was a grim and haunted look about her face. She crossed to Marianne and handed her a bottle of wine. "This is for you and Jake, for helping with Sarina and Mark—and us, too."

Marianne smiled as she accepted the wine. "That's one of my favorites. Jake and I will enjoy sharing it."

Kate nodded wordlessly.

"Have a seat," Marianne motioned as she put the bottle down beside her chair. "Or, if you like, the Keurig is hot in the kitchen. You can get yourself a cup of coffee."

Kate heaved a sigh and seemed a little lost. She chose a recliner across from Angie. "I'm okay, I've had three cups already this morning. That's probably as much as my bladder can stand." She smiled awkwardly, trying to make a joke.

Marianne nodded "Okay, then. I'm going to try to help you talk with each other about these issues you both seem to have and which are leading to ongoing, repetitive distress. If you can't get beyond this impasse, then you may need to dissolve the relationship—or figure out how to live together without reacting to these triggers."

Angie stared at Kate. Kate frowned uncomfortably and looked at the floor.

"First, I'd like to set the stage by looking at what brought you together in the first place. Angie, what did you see in Kate that made you open yourself to her and subject your children to her presence in your life?"

Despite herself, Angie blushed. "When she came into the coffee bar, I was sure she was a lesbian. That made me curious. When I watched her, I thought she was cute, really, really cute, and unlike anyone I'd ever seen before. I figured she was a bit older than me, but her casual look, dress, attitude—all of that was very appealing. The more I saw her, she became more significant, almost bigger than life to me. Sarina kind of captured the feeling when she called her Esther Williams. That tall, outdoorsy, tanned, muscular yet graceful look was very sexy. She also was intriguing because she wasn't anyone I'd ever seen around Sequim."

"Your first interest in her was mostly physical, sexual?"

"Yes, and no. Some of it was attraction. I wanted to touch her. But it was more than that. She came from this bigger world. By comparison mine seemed small. The only strong card I had was the 'mother card,' because she didn't have children. In that arena, I had more experience than she did, and I felt that I knew how to care for kids. Otherwise, it was easy to feel overwhelmed. I admired her and wanted to spend time with her."

"There is also your marriage, right?"

"Well, yes, I guess there is that. I was a devoted wife for nearly a decade, and I guess Kate hasn't had that experience, either. I did have an advantage in building and maintaining a relationship."

Kate was taking all this in with downcast eyes, and Marianne turned to her.

"What attracted you to Angie when you first met her?"

Kate cleared her throat. "Well, I was walking into town from the marina. It looked pretty ordinary to me. There are really neat things and lots of beauty here, but at first glance, they don't stand out. The storefronts aren't big and fancy like businesses in New York City, and they aren't exotic like in the South Pacific. I didn't have any expectations of being thrilled here, and I was wondering why you, Marianne, had moved here. I went into this coffee bar, and I saw this woman. She didn't look like my first impression of Sequim, the name of which I could hardly pronounce. I noticed the curve of her hips that swayed as she walked, and that long braid down her back. Her sparkling eyes that penetrated. I was definitely attracted to her and surprised that someone that gorgeous was hanging out in this small town. Then I found out she was divorced, had two kids, and no money. I was really surprised, even shocked, by her story, and since I was in a position to help, I wanted to do that. I respected what she was doing on her own, but it was hard, and I didn't think it needed to be that hard."

"So, you were physically attracted and you also wanted to help her."

"Yeah, that's where it started. It became a lot more as time went on."

Marianne coughed a bit and took a sip of coffee. "So, Angie, as you knew Kate longer, did your attraction for her increase or change?"

Angie glanced at Kate and then said, "I've never known such good sex from anyone. That doesn't mean I have all that much experience, but Kate is great in bed, and I can't imagine anything sexual that could be any better than what we do together. She also began doing supportive things for me, and I loved her for her consideration and caring. She planned fun things with the kids, and I appreciated that. It felt like we could go on growing this way forever. However, there were some issues."

Marianne held up a hand. "Hold that thought. Let's catch Kate up first." She looked at Kate kindly. "And how did your feelings for Angie change over time?"

Kate smiled. "She's great in bed. She may not have all the experience, but she has all the moves. I know from reading books and magazine articles that good sex is important for a relationship to last. And she's a great and loving person. But she doesn't trust much, and sometimes I don't know what to do with that."

Marianne sighed. "Now we get down to issues." She looked back at Angie. "Let's start with the first conflict that you felt with Kate."

Angie studied Kate a moment. "Well, you have to understand that I live in a concrete world. It's real, it has limitations and consequences. When I was a kid, I got to ride horses, because we had them on the farm. After riding a horse, I had to cool it down, take off the saddle, wipe it down, give it fresh water, offer it treats, and see that its feed bucket was full before I could go back into the house. From what Kate's told me, she rode horses, too—that's one thing we have in common from our very different lives. However, when she got off a horse, stable hands took over. Her relationship to horses was limited to the fun side and not to the work. She went off and did something else, and that was different from my experience. Maybe, if you have money, you don't have the same consequences as when you don't have money and everything falls to you to fix or do without."

Kate was watching Angie and seemed deeply in thought. She squirmed a little in her seat.

"How did this difference play out in your relationship?"

"She would do nice things for me and for the kids and then drop the ball. She'd forget to come to Mark's ball game. She'd take Sarina swimming and then work on her phone, while some kid jumped into the water and ran straight into Sarina. Sarina survived it, although it should never have happened if Kate had been paying attention. I think Kate's more imaginative and cerebral than practical and concrete. In my mind, to be a good parent or a good partner, you have to be both."

Marianne looked at Kate. "What do you feel about what she's saying?"

"I don't like hearing it—some of it for the umpteenth time—however, I can understand it. She has a point, I think."

"Anything you want to add?"

"No. I know she's been upset, and I just want to get it all out in the open."

"Okay, Angie, I'm going back to you. Kate says you are not trusting. How do those words strike you?"

For a second there was a flash of anger in her eyes as Angie stared at Kate. Then she took a deep breath. "She's right that I don't trust easily. Kate knows the history. My husband rejected me totally and completely, and my children as well, because of something he figured out and I didn't even consciously know. Then my parents, my brothers, and my grandparents shunned me. Zack's parents avoided me except for the children. Through no real fault of my own, I ended up totally alone with Mark and Sarina to raise without support. Kate and I share this, being abandoned and alone. Her parents both died, which is very sad, and I feel for her about it. However, they didn't intend to die. My family had choices and decided against me. About that I am royally pissed. And definitely mistrusting. I don't want to be abandoned again by anyone—or be in a position where I can be.

"So, when I ask Kate if she intends to stay in Sequim with us, and she gives me some indirect answer like 'well, if I should leave someday, you'll have the house and be better off,' it sets off warning bells. That certainly isn't a life commitment, and it doesn't make me trust her more, but rather less. And I'm scared to take anything more from her than I already have because if one day she takes off, the hurt is going to be greater. I love her yet I'm afraid of what I already feel and afraid of getting even closer."

Kate slid down in her chair and wiped a tear from her eye.

"What's going on, Kate?" Marianne asked.

"I'm not sure. Angie gave me a novel to read, and it had a scene about losing your parents, and I got all teary over it and then I couldn't sleep that night. My mother died twenty years ago, and my father died six years ago. That's long enough that I shouldn't still be grieving over them. I don't know what it's all about."

"Sounds like you need to figure it out," Marianne said gently. "If Angie is right and you have a problem with commitment, you won't be able to resolve that until you deal with this emotional tie to your late parents. Your being able to commit may be the clue to her being able to trust—they *do* go hand in hand."

Marianne looked at Angie and Kate. "Is there anything else that needs to be said, while we are here and focused?"

Angie shook her head. Kate buried her face in her hands then waved Marianne off, suggesting that she had nothing else to add.

Marianne smiled at them gently. "Well, I think we've made some progress." They nodded, both seeming very solemn. "However, we haven't gotten to the specific reason we are sitting here—the event that set Angie off and brought all the anger and frustration to the surface. Angie, do you feel up to talking about this?"

Angie sighed. "Yes, I think so." She looked directly at Kate.

"I don't ever want you to think that I'm not grateful for everything you've done for us from the very beginning. You've always been helpful and supportive of me and the kids, even though I know raising children wasn't in your life plan. However, for all the good you've done, you've also made life difficult by letting us down at the worst times. When we *most* needed you, you weren't there. And you *could* have been. The first time was when we were moving into the house and you left suddenly for Oregon because of the guy in the boat. I tried to understand, but it was hard, being left with a house with no furniture, no moving plan, no money to buy things we needed, and just having to wait. You set things in motion for a better life and then suddenly disappeared.

"Then recently, when I had a big term paper to write, and you knew it, you took off for Washington, D.C., on a moment's notice and left me holding the bag. Then we came to finals, and you did it again, off to San Diego, putting a demand on Marianne and Jake that wasn't fair. Surely these things could have been done at a better time and with planned support for us. Not crises."

Kate slid down in her chair. "I thought I had it covered. I thought you would be okay."

"Well, I wasn't. We weren't. Marianne and Jake weren't. They were sick and yet you expected them to carry the ball for you. And then you want me to trust you. How can I?"

Kate was going through Kleenexes by the pile. "I guess not."

Marianne put out a hand to her. "This is not jump-all-over-Kate," she said, "although it may feel like it. But if these issues aren't expressed, you'll never get beyond them."

Kate nodded.

"What I hear," Marianne summarized, "is that things are out of balance."

Angie nodded. "I think Kate cares about me, but I don't think she feels that my plans and needs are as important as hers. Much as I love her, I don't think that I can match up. She has too much and I have too little, and I'm not sure how to change that, or if it's even possible."

Marianne thought for a moment. "What would equalize things for you?"

"Right now all I can see is that she has this big plan to bring an Olympic Training Center to Sequim. And it's more important than anything else. Since I've lived here all my life, I see kids who don't have enough to eat, a library that is grossly inadequate, schools that need to be rebuilt or modernized, teens that need places to go after school and on weekends, a town that doesn't even have a movie theatre or a bookstore. Sequim's not a bad place and has many good things, but it also has real needs. And to me, an Olympic Training Center isn't one of them. The swimming pool part, I get. The kids, especially the ones that can't afford a private club membership, could use it. I just wish that Kate could stay focused on that for the next two or three years. The pool is real and it's local, so most of her work would be here instead of everywhere else.

"What I don't want is a run-around. A big house in the hills with a live-in nanny and a chauffeur to take the kids everywhere so that Kate won't have to be personally responsible. I need Kate, not paid servants." Angie's face was red, and her anger quite apparent.

***

Jake peeped in the front door. She had Sarina and Mark. "Is the coast clear?" she whispered.

Marianne laughed and suppressed a cough. "Well, for the moment. I think we could use a breather."

Angie jumped up. "I need to take the kids home and settle everything down. It's been a rough week, one we wouldn't have survived without your help."

Marianne nodded and let Angie disengage.

***

Kate remained seated, deep in thought, while Angie gathered her things and the kids' belongings and took them out the door—after hugs for Aunties Marianne and Jake.

Marianne patted Kate on the knee as she passed in her wheelchair. "Wait a minute. There is something else I'd like to discuss with you."

Kate nodded.

When all the goodbyes had been said, and the house was quiet, Marianne wheeled herself back to Kate. "I don't know if you can work this out on your own. You may need to see a therapist."

Kate sighed and nodded again.

"I hate to add to your burdens, but there is something that might be helpful to you. I knew your mother pretty well. You remember all those times we sat by the pool while you were in practices or swim meets?"

"Yes." Kate allowed a smile to flit across her face.

"When you were a student, I knew her better than I did you. In our conversations, I picked up how much your mother and father had their own lives and how seldom their paths crossed. She had her charities, her women's groups and friends, and he had his business trips, associates and conferences. It seemed as if you all were rarely in one place, and I wondered if their marriage had been one of convenience. From the warmth I felt from her, I thought maybe she was a lesbian, even if an unconscious one. It's just a thought, but something for you to consider. When someone is caught up in an emotional attachment to the past, to losses, to parents who have passed, sometimes it's because of something unsatisfied. We're missing what we *didn't* receive rather than mourning what we no longer have.

"It would be a lot easier in many ways for you to let this romance die, return to New York, find yourself a beautiful lesbian woman—and I know there are many of them there—with credentials, a profession, no children or other trappings, someone who could have fun with you, be with you, travel with you, give you right now what Angie may not be able to give until she finishes school and maybe even until her children are grown and on their own. Being patient and waiting for years for what you could have right now may be very difficult for you.

"If you decide to stay and fight for this relationship, consider that maybe you have needs you aren't fully aware of—not just a lover, but a sense of family, or a closeness that you have never had and may not know how to create."

Marianne sighed. "As I said, I'm not a counselor. I've just known you since you were a late teen. Having wanted children myself, I feel empathy for you having them and not knowing how to deal with them. They need a lot, consume a lot, and you have to be willing. Angie comes with baggage that you have to help carry."

Kate looked at Marianne through tear-filled eyes. "And I have my own baggage, too."

30

Kate sat on her favorite bench at the marina and stared out at the rippling water. The day was sunny, with a slight breeze that carried a hint of cool. Angie and the kids were off on a shopping trip for school clothes, and Kate had begged off. She came here to think as she had been doing regularly since the big confrontation that Marianne had monitored.

Kate had never been one to spend time analyzing herself. She followed her feelings and intuitions, sometimes impulsively, as when she quit swimming and when she left her job in New York. When she had felt she needed to go away, she went. And when she tired of lazing in the South Pacific, she decided to return to the US and did.

Angie's complaints and Marianne's comments hit her hard. She did bounce back, because she always had, or it seemed she had. Yet the words, along with that novel Angie had given her, began nagging at her, and she starting seriously thinking, remembering, and exploring within her own mind. The biggest questions that now plagued her—and had never really touched her before—were why, *really*, underneath it all, had she given up swimming when her mother died of cancer, and why had she walked away from her career when her father suffered a fatal heart attack?

Going over that history repeatedly in her mind, and adding in what Marianne had suggested, Kate began to wonder just how much love there had been in her family. *Maybe her parents—perfect on the outside—were putting on a front for a marriage that had not worked. Maybe they were not suited to one another. Maybe Marianne was right that her mother might have been a lesbian, even unconsciously. It would explain a lot if it were true. Maybe it wasn't significant by itself one way or the other, because it couldn't be changed. What was important was the impact it had had, and was still having, on Kate. Was she insecure in her mother's love, even though her mother had been attentive? Did she try so hard at swimming to make her mother love her? Her swimming wasn't to please her father, because it wasn't his thing.*

When Kate's mother was gone, Kate had no one to turn to except her father. She switched her focus to business which won his approval. When she earned awards, he was proud and toasted her success. *She best could attract his attention by being good at something* he *appreciated.*

The death of a second parent left her with a void, *no one to perform for*. So, she didn't. She lay around on beaches, made love to beautiful tropical women, sailed oceans and bays of the Southern Hemisphere. *And didn't think about a thing*. She didn't need money. There was nothing to push her to find answers. She just drifted.

"Now," she said aloud, "I have a home, friends, a beautiful partner who would marry me, I think anyway, in a heartbeat, two lovely children who want me to be there for them, and I still don't know for sure what I need for myself that would make sense of everything."

Why did she want the Olympic Training Center? Who was she trying to impress now? Her late mother, who was in heaven or in spirit somewhere in the great beyond? Her father, also long departed, would have appreciated her business acumen if she pulled off such a feat, provided he were still here? But why try to please two people long gone? Was she now trying to please politicians and members of the USOC? Maybe she was just being a bit crazy. And missing the whole point?

In the last few days Kate had gone around town looking at Angie's world, trying to see Sequim as she did. She also was attempting to come to grips with issues. If she was going to stay in the relationship, she would have to pay more attention to potential consequences of her acts or non-acts. Angie, the kids, the house, the cars. Everything needed maintenance. While Kate could easily put out the money to buy things, she assumed someone else would care for them as they had in her childhood. Her head was always in the clouds somewhere, dreaming up big projects. *Avoiding the truth?*

Kate visited the library and saw how small and crowded it was, inside and in the parking lot. A real, concrete need not met, a problem that would take imagination, money, and political savvy to solve. She went to the food bank and watched people coming and going, picking up cartons of food and thought about how they didn't have enough money even to eat. In addition, she checked in with the school system's main kitchen and asked how many meals they prepared for students whose families couldn't pay. She was amazed by the numbers! Kate had thought that Angie's situation was unique, or at least unusual. *Perhaps not.* Beautiful and popular Sequim also had its down side, a side Kate hadn't noticed but of which Angie was well aware.

One staff member told her, "This is not a down-trodden community in any sense of the word. Sequim has lots of wealth. We also have a couple hundred school kids who are homeless and sleeping in automobiles and who knows where else."

Kate had returned to her car, uttering a deep sigh. Sequim had real needs, some of them desperate, and they certainly didn't include an Olympic Training Center.

***

Everyone was home. Kate could hear Puffball barking somewhere, which meant the labradoodle was playing with one or both of the kids.

She found Angie in the bedroom, sewing buttons on a shirt for Mark.

"Hi, Angie, shopping go well?"

Angie gave her a warm smile and a wink. "Yeah. I think I have them outfitted for another semester of school. They are both growing quickly. I'm beginning to think that Mark is going to be tall."

"How tall is Zack?"

"Six, two."

"Could be then. But you're aren't short, either."

"Five, seven. Isn't that average? At least it doesn't match your five, nine."

Kate laughed. "Is that our problem, that I'm two inches taller than you?"

Angie frowned for a second and then grinned. "I guess that shouldn't be a deal breaker, should it?"

"I don't think so." Kate leaned down and kissed Angie on the cheek and then walked over to the window and glanced out at the back yard. The kids were throwing a ball for Puff, who was happily returning it to them.

"Angie, whenever we can arrange it, I'd like to have time with you, to talk, maybe a dinner out, maybe an evening together to do something?"

"If you want to do it this weekend, perhaps we could send the kids down to Louise's on Saturday for play time and a sleep over. If Louise is willing, of course."

"That would be fine. Want me to call her?"

"Yes, please."

"Okay, I'll do it."

"Thank you, Kate."

***

Late Saturday afternoon, Kate left Sarina and Mark, accompanied by Puffball, at Louise's house. Lisa seemed excited to see them, and Puffball was ecstatic at a new adventure. She sniffed everything in sight, and they all laughed at her antics.

"Thanks, Louise. And turnabout is fair play. We'll do this for you, very soon."

Louise winked at Kate. "You go have a good time."

Kate drove Angie to the atmospheric dockside restaurant at the marina, where they enjoyed cocktails and ordered a big-enough-for-two seafood dinner plate with crème brulee for dessert.

When they first sat down, they were quiet, occupying themselves with the surroundings, enjoying the seafood fragrances, and looking at sailboats entering the marina.

Finally, Angie focused directly on Kate. "What are we celebrating?"

"I guess I'll put a name on it after we have our discussion."

"Okay, let's discuss."

Kate blushed slightly. "I've been doing a lot of thinking about what was said at Marianne's and Jake's house. I think I do have a lot of personal issues that I had never admitted to myself, and I've spent a lot of time thinking about that. It actually started with that novel you gave me, which made me cry. I was really surprised by the way it touched me. I figured that there must be a reason, some sort of personal connection. Our meeting with Marianne added more to consider.

"I think what I've done and not done with my life reveal that I've been still mourning the loss of my parents. I haven't really moved on. I don't see myself as a lazy person, but obviously, my conflicts have left me acting like one. The Olympic Training Center idea gave me something to dream about. It fit me in a way, since I am a marketing specialist, and much of creating a center and running it is an aspect of marketing. But to spend my life doing that—and it would take my whole life, most likely—would be an alliance with my father's wishes. It would also make my mother proud.

"Once I recognized that reality, my dedication to the idea started to fade. The next question is what do I really want for *me*?"

Angie gently put a hand on Kate's arm.

"First, I want to allow myself to grow up. I'm past forty. I think it's time I became an adult instead of an impulsive child. I want to think as much about others as amusing myself. That's a big goal for me. Others in that goal include you, Mark, and Sarina, oh, and Puffball. I want to be there for Jake and Marianne, too. They've done so much for me, for us, as well. I think Jake needs more breaks from her constant care and worry over Marianne, and I want to find a way to help her, and them. I had promised Jake to go hiking, and I have a couple of times. Now I think I need to make a real commitment to plan at least once a month to take a day-long outing with her."

Angie smiled. "You *have* been doing some deep thinking. I'm really glad. You've been almost bigger than life—like Esther Williams, as Sarina said—and I have a hard time standing up to you. I thought I could in the beginning, but you're bigger and taller and older and wealthier, and there is nothing you want that you can't have or obtain. It's hard sometimes standing my ground. Most of the time you aren't a real problem, but when you *are*, you're a *big* one."

Kate shrugged and heaved a sigh. "Well, as to your nursing degree and my plans—"

Angie broke in. "That's part of what I meant. I'm from a small town, and you are from the world. I barely got through high school, and you have a fancy college degree. You've had a career; I've had a job. I need something more for me, and the only work that makes sense is nursing. I want to help people."

Kate cocked her head. "Doctors help people. You could become a doctor."

"No, I'm being real for *me*. I'm not sure you understand life on my personal scale. I want more patient contact. Nurses do real work in the unit and in patients' rooms. Even that contact is fading in current medical practice, but before it's gone, I want to do it. When I finish school, I'll have a degree after my name. I'll be somebody. After all I've been through, that's important to me."

"You already *are* somebody."

"All right, I'll *feel* like I'm somebody."

"Okay, I understand, but just remember that you *are* somebody right now. Somebody who cares, who puts others before yourself. If I needed anything, if I were sick, you'd be right there seeing that I got the best care in the world—just like you do for the kids. I've thought about that, and it seems like a natural thing for you. You'll be a good nurse."

Angie frowned. "But I won't reach that goal unless you keep focused on us, instead of your projects, until I'm done with training. By then, Mark and Sarina will be more independent, and we'll be able to leave them at home alone once in a while for short periods. There will be more freedom for us individually and together as they mature—and as I complete school."

Kate ran a finger down Angie's pert nose. "That's what I've been thinking. I'm going to work it out so that nothing gets in your way until after graduation, and maybe not even then."

She gave Angie a gentle smile and then continued, "I *am* going to work on the city swimming pool. I think it can be done. There's a lot of red tape of course with various government agencies, but since I'm donating the facility and they don't have to raise taxes for it or hold a bond issue, I think eventually I'll push my project through the hoops and have it built in Carrie Blake Park. It'll be my gift to the children of Sequim, and I'll make sure that any child who wants to use the pool will be able to do so. When the pool is built, and up and running, we'll see what happens next."

"That'll be wonderful when you pull it off. I know you will."

"It'll probably take me as long to build the pool as it'll take you to finish college, maybe longer. I do hope I can do it, because then I'll have accomplished something useful, and because someday I want you to marry me. I won't ask you until you earn your degree and I successfully prove that I can be a responsible partner. And second mother, I guess. While I never planned for kids, I certainly love the two that came along when you entered my life."

Angie held up her wine glass. "Here's to my becoming bigger than just a little girl from Sequim and you becoming less like a movie star and more like the woman I want to love until the day I die."

Kate clinked glasses with her. "I'm all for that."

"Let's go home and consummate the contract."

***

The house was quiet, as they wanted it to be. Kate put some soft romantic music on the stereo and turned the lights down low. They danced shoeless on the living room floor, pulling each other closer, and then kissing and rubbing noses.

"Let's go to bed," Angie suggested coyly.

"I thought you'd never ask," Kate grinned.

Still moving to the music, they drifted toward the master bedroom. Clothes fell to the floor, sheets and covers were thrown back, and holding each other tightly, they sank down onto the bed—doing the one thing for which they already had shown equal skill, the one and very significant part of their relationship that already was working perfectly.

"I love you!"

"Me, too. Kiss me."

EPILOGUE

Kate completed her swimming pool and felt great pride in her achievement. This wasn't a head game like marketing, designed to push people into buying things that might or might not be worth the money or even needed. This was something made of concrete, steel, paint, roofing, windows, and water, the real deal—and quite useful.

A year-round pool totally enclosed during the winter months—but with panels that could slide back and open up one side to the outdoors and a picnic area during the summer—Kate's pool was for the people. Especially the children. With her deep pockets, Kate came up with a payment schedule that allowed anyone and everyone to swim.

At first, she enjoyed the accomplishment and loved the local press—stories and photos—about the pool and her as the builder/sponsor. Then for a few moments, Kate felt a letdown and wished to move on to another, bigger project.

That angst didn't last because running the pool gradually became totally her responsibility—something Kate hadn't considered when building it. As with many facilities, there were problems, and things weren't always fixed right unless she did the job herself or supervised personally. Swimming instructors Kate hired didn't measure up to her own standards, and she soon took over practices and handled competitions herself. Kate found she had an unexpected skill with small children, beginners in the pool. She could have them swimming safely in much less time than other teachers, and thus these junior swimmers became her own pet project.

Kate was excited to have Sarina around the pool on an almost daily basis. The little mermaid remained a happy and dedicated athlete. Kate noticed that she was building muscles while growing taller, broader in the shoulders, and slender. *Yes, a swimmer in the making.* Kate wouldn't have missed a moment of Sarina's increasing speed and skill—this, she realized, was as much of an Olympic Training Center as she really needed.

Mark, shooting up in height like a string bean, still played ball, kept improving in his catching, running, and hitting.

No matter what went on at the pool, Kate made sure that she never again missed one of his games.

***

As her life with Kate settled into a more-predictable pattern, Angie's grades improved from very good to excellent. She graduated from Peninsula College with high marks, passed the state nursing exams, and was quickly hired at Olympic Medical Center as a short-stay surgical floor nurse. Her shifts were a little wacky at first, as Kate and Angie had expected they would be, but they both felt that in time her schedule would straighten itself out. Angie said goodbye, finally, to her job and the staff at The Little Red Barn.

Kate had agonized over Angie's aging Ford but had learned not to push Angie into a change she wasn't ready to make. One day the old sedan failed on Angie's way to work in Port Angeles. Kate had to rush to pick her up and deliver her to Olympic Medical Center in time for her shift. Kate finally spoke up and suggested that something needed to be done about the car, Angie's choice, of course.

When Angie's shift ended, Kate asked, "What is your pleasure? Have you had time to think about it?"

"Yes, I want a red, sporty Civic. Good mileage, not expensive, and perfect for me."

So, at long last, the old Ford went to the junkyard where it belonged, and Angie drove home in a bright red Honda that was just feisty enough to suit her personality.

***

Marianne's and Jake's graduation present was a long hoped-for invitation to attend the lesbian women's lunch group. Angie thought the gift was perfect; Kate laughed and said, "You mean we finally have it together enough to pass inspection?"

Marianne smiled. "Your words, not mine."

The potluck luncheon was held in the meeting room at TC. The four friends rode there in Marianne's van. Thirty women showed up for the potluck. During the two-hour gathering, Angie and Kate had an opportunity to speak directly with several of the women, and they were introduced to others.

Among those attending was the pilot, Holly Sanders, and her partner, Susan Foxworth. Kate loved catching up with Holly and introducing her and Susan to Angie. After a moment, Angie realized that Susan was a veterinarian at the animal clinic they used for Puffball. "That's wonderful," Angie enthused. "I would never have guessed."

Moments later, Holly pulled Kate aside. "I've always been curious," she asked with an amused grin, "what happened to Steve?"

Kate smiled. "He's fine. I hear from him once in a while. The accident at sea was a wake-up call for him to make some changes. He bucked up from his fear of AIDS and has returned to San Francisco to stay. He sails for fun now, but he's not living on the boat anymore. He even has a new friend, and it sounds like it might be serious. Thanks for asking. I don't talk about him much because, well, you're the only one here who has ever met him."

Holly nodded. "To use a cliché, all's well that end's well. Guess that's true for Steve, as well as some other folks I know." She winked.

***

During their ride home, Angie was gushing with excitement. "I can't believe all the doctors, nurses, psychologists, social workers, in one small group! I could have listened to them all day! I feel less alone knowing that they all live right around here in Sequim, Port Angeles, TC, and even Port Townsend!"

"I could see the delight in your face," Marianne commented with a warm smile. "How about you, Kate?"

Kate grinned. "It was marvelous. A few knew my name right off from the swimming pool project. Others knew about the pool but didn't know who was behind it. It's nice to be recognized and thanked. And it's great to be in a room surrounded by intelligent lesbians."

Jake spoke up. "You both looked like you were having fun. I'm sure you'll be put on the mailing list and invited again in the future."

***

A few days later, Kate, Angie, Sarina, and Mark had dinner with Marianne and Jake. Jake had whipped up a special meal with something for everyone. The adults toasted with wine, the kids with fruit juice.

Before dessert was served, Kate went down on bended knee and asked Angie to marry her. Everyone cried tears of joy.

***

Angie wanted a small wedding with only close friends attending. None of her family would be there. That fact gave her moments of sadness but she wasn't going to let it ruin her life.

With some managing on Kate's part, they secured after-hours use of The Little Red Barn, where their story had begun. A local justice of the peace officiated. Marianne and Jake served as Angie's attendants, Mark was best man, and Sarina the flower girl. Louise brought Lisa, and a few women from the lunch group and from TC came, including Sid, who managed to leave Fluffy at home. Puffball, who also did not attend, was given special treats later. The coffeehouse staff, paid handsomely of course, remained on duty during the ceremony and served the guests at the following reception.

Kate and Angie had written their own ceremony in which they promised as partners to love, respect, and cherish each other throughout all the days of their lives. By the time they spoke those words, Kate was sure she could keep them, and Angie trusted that Kate actually would.

After the brides kissed each other, they and their guests celebrated with wine for the adults, lemonade for the kids, and freshly-made Little Red Barn sandwiches: turkey, cheddar, and cranberry on sourdough bread with cool ranch dressing, and blueberry scones for dessert. *Wedding cake? Who needed it?*

ACKNOWLEDGMENTS

Sequim is a real community on Washington's Olympic Peninsula. I have lived here since 2010—after spending most of my life in cities like Indianapolis, Oakland, New Orleans, Phoenix, and San Diego—and I love the natural beauty of a largely rural environment and close proximity to both large bodies of water and beautiful mountains. Because I am at home here, I have for some time thought about setting a novel in this special environment as a way of sharing with others my love of Sequim and the Olympic Peninsula.

Being a fiction writer, I have taken many liberties with this environment to be able to tell my love story without causing offense. You will find real places, some businesses, and some real issues, but you will also find fictional settings, people, and projects. None of the characters or locations reflect or are intended to reflect negatively on any real person, place or organization known by me in Sequim.

Thanks to those who have helped the story come to life in print: my partner, Connie Jenkins, for allowing me the time to work; Morgayne Love, Ruth Messing, Sharon Hampton, Connie Jenkins, Kyra Humphrey, and Teri Johnson for reading drafts and making comments; Ronni Sanlo for final editing, arranging for cover design by Barbara Gottlieb, and bringing my fourth novel to completion.

Life is about love. Nothing else, despite all appearances, is really important. Whom we love, and how we love, are less significant than *that* we love.

ABOUT THE AUTHOR

Dorothy Rice Bennett grew up in the Midwest. She began filling spiral notebooks with fanciful stories that she shared with her school classmates when she was ten years old. Her heroines were women of action—they flew Navy jets, competed in hydroplane boat races, drove Indy cars, and raced horses as jockeys. In short, Dorothy was way ahead of her time, and little could she dream that women would someday do these very things.

Dorothy earned a bachelor's degree from Mills College, a master's degree from the University of California, Davis, and a Ph.D. from Tulane University, all in the field of theatre. She also holds a master's degree in counseling from Arizona State University.

As an adult, Dorothy still loved writing, yet her busy careers in mental health and in journalism, as well as parenting an adopted daughter, commanded her time and energy. Eventually, in retirement she pushed other tasks aside and began putting words on paper. *NORTH COAST: A Contemporary Love Story* was her first published novel in 2015. *GIRLS ON THE RUN* followed in 2016 and *THE ARTEMIS ADVENTURE* in 2017.

Dorothy lives on the Olympic Peninsula of Washington State with her partner and two toy poodles.

Dorothy Rice Bennett may be found on Facebook and Twitter and reached via email at *dorothyricebennett@yahoo.com* or at *www.dorothyricebennett.com*.

WHAT AMAZON CUSTOMERS ARE SAYING ABOUT DOROTHY RICE BENNETT NOVELS

NORTH COAST: A Contemporary Love Story

5 Stars!

"Finally, a great love story that evolves. Not just a roll in the hay, but a learning experience for both partners. The writing was excellent. I enjoyed this book immensely. I couldn't put it down…."

"I really enjoyed this book...Finished it in less than a day. It's not the typical "lesbian romance"—It's even better! I'll look forward to more good reads from this author…."

"I appreciated a lesbian romance novel that was set on the North Coast, that dealt with older women in community, and that addressed some of the long-term effects of internalized homophobia…."

"Undeniably, the book is a good love story. The reader is engaged in women who experience processes of loving others and the intricacies of developing an intimate lasting relationship. A wonderful read for those who have relationships come and go, yet still desire fulfillment…."

"This is one of those books you cannot put down! It is quite well written with engaging, distinct characters and a strong story. Great job on your first novel, Dorothy…."

"Dorothy Rice Bennett describes her characters with rigorous emotional honesty, which allows the reader to easily relate to the characters' strengths and flaws. This book is a wonderful tribute to the importance of genuine relationships and the hope we hold that even after life-shattering events, the gift of friendship can bring a new light and warmth to our lives…."

GIRLS ON THE RUN

5 Stars!

"Dorothy Rice Bennett has published another lesbian romance novel that appeals not just to lesbians, but to anybody who has ever struggled with the question of who they are or who they are supposed to be. Girls on the Run follows two protagonists through a natural and sweet progression of new love…."

"Interesting, kept my attention all the way through. Sweet love story that brought me to tears several times…."

"Girls on the Run was a captivating novel of friendship, love and the evolution of family dynamics. I enjoyed the book and have passed it on to my daughter to read!..."

"This is my first time reading a novel from Dorothy Rice Bennett and I can say that it will not be my last. Dorothy did a wonderful job of crafting a complex story of two young ladies and detailing their development from being on the run across the United States to the life that they eventually setup for themselves in San Francisco..."

"Great book keep my interest all the way though. The characters were wonderful, I really felt I knew them. I think all kinds of people would enjoy this book…."

"There is something in it for everyone to relate to and not once did I think the characters were too young for me (76) to relate to. A few scenes brought tears, more brought smiles. A great, easy read and not one to be missed…."

THE ARTEMIS ADVENTURE

5 Stars!

“If you've ever dreamed of a brighter future, questioned your sexuality, or struggled with your purpose in life, Kiki Rodriquez is likely to become your kindred spirit in this delightful story. Dorothy Rice Bennett has proven herself a wonderful story-teller in this, her third novel. Kiki … is a steady and consistent character that endures real-life situations and contemplates them with a keen awareness. I’m sure all readers will find themselves rooting for her—as I did—every step of the way!”

“From the title of the book to its romantic conclusion I thoroughly enjoyed and highly recommend The Artemis Adventure. . . a journey of self-discovery for the protagonist, Kiki Rodriguez. Kiki was open to every experience and that curiosity served her well.”

“What a truly delightful story and a joy to read. I could not put it down! The main character was so well developed… a creative, courageous young woman and so clearly aware of what changes she wanted to make in life, and when she went for it, it was like the universe was there to support her in some of the most unlikely ways. Truly a story of courage, creativity, community and a strange and wonderful kind of faith.”

“I usually don’t read books such as this one, much prefer historical fiction. However, after attending a reading by the author, I bought the book, and then couldn’t put it down. Following the main character Kiki’s adventures was very real and I am sure many readers can relate to her challenges.”

“I have now read three of her books and consider her one of my favorites. The characters she creates are honest and real. What a sweet take on Kiki’s first experience with her partner. I will be looking forward to her next book.”

CPSIA information can be obtained
at www.ICGtesting.com
Printed in the USA
FSHW020955270720
72498FS

9 781088 706886